THE AFGHAN
CAMPAIGN

DOUBLEDAY
New York
London Toronto
Sydney Auckland

THE AFGHAN
CAMPAIGN

STEVEN
PRESSFIELD

For Ruthie

HISTORICAL NOTE

Alexander's Afghan campaign began in the summer of 330 B.C., when his army entered Artacoana (modern Herat), and continued until spring 327, when he departed Bactra (near contemporary Mazur-i-Sharif) and crossed the Hindu Kush into India.

The campaign was the lengthiest of Alexander's career and the most difficult he ever fought. His adversaries were not main-force armies, but free tribesmen of what is today Afghanistan and Turkmenistan, and horse warriors who inhabited the steppes and mountains that would become Uzbekistan and Tajikistan. Measures of barbarity were employed by both sides, unprecedented in prior campaigns, and the boundaries of warfare were stretched. Despite numerous victories, Alexander did not subdue the region until well into the third year, when he concluded an alliance with the warlord Oxyartes by taking to wife Oxyartes' daughter Roxane.

The stubbornness of the opposition may be gauged from the fact that when Alexander moved on to India in 327, he left in Afghanistan no fewer than ten thousand infantry and 3500 cavalry—fully a fifth of his army—to keep the country from reverting to insurgency.

For a glossary of slang used in this book, see page 353.

"Do you believe that so many nations accustomed to the name and rule of another, united with us neither by religion, nor customs, nor community of language, have been subdued in the same battle in which they were overcome? It is by your arms alone that they are restrained, not by their dispositions, and those who fear us when we are present, in our absence will be enemies. We are dealing with savage beasts, which lapse of time only can tame, when they are caught and caged, because their own nature cannot tame them. . . . Accordingly, we must either give up what we have taken, or we must seize what we do not yet hold."

—Alexander, addressing his troops
on the approach to Afghanistan
IN QUINTUS CURTIUS, *History of Alexander*

PROLOGUE

A Wedding in Asia

THE WAR IS OVER. Or it will be by sundown tonight, when Alexander takes to wife the Afghan princess Roxane.

Across the Plain of Sorrows, so named for the multitude of its burial grounds, the camps of the Macedonians sprawl flank-by-flank alongside those of the enemy. There must be half a thousand of the latter, those bivouacs the Afghans call *tafiran* ("circles"), each housing between fifty and five hundred men. Every tribe and clan from Artacoana to the Jaxartes has trekked in for the celebration, along with vendors and whores in thousands, tailors, seamstresses, acrobats, musicians, fortune-tellers. The whole Mack expeditionary force is here, including foreign units, horse and foot. Every captain and corporal parades in his finery, eager for the festivities. Except me and my mates Flag, Boxer, and Little Red. We've still got work to do.

Give Alexander credit. By marrying the Afghan princess, he turns his most formidable foe, the warlord Oxyartes, into his father-in-law. No other stunt could have produced victory in this war—or that state of affairs that can plausibly be passed off as victory.

So we shall have peace. I doubt that any cessation of hostilities has been longed for more ardently than this. A campaign that was supposed to take three months has dragged on with unbroken terror and brutality for almost three years. Those of us who came out from home as boys have become first men and then something closer to beasts or devils. The Afghans have suffered worse. Two hundred thousand dead, that's the figure you hear. I believe it. Hardly a village remains in this country that our troops haven't leveled, or a city that we haven't taken apart stone by stone.

So this wedding is much looked forward to. The deal between Alexander and Oxyartes is this: The warlord gives away his daughter and accepts our king as his sovereign. In return, Alexander anoints him First Kinsman and his own Royal Companion. This makes Oxyartes premier among all Bactrian barons and the biggest fish east of the Euphrates. Then we Macedonians pack up and leave. I don't know who's happier—us to get out or the Afghans to see us go.

I'm getting married tonight myself. Fourteen hundred Macks will be linking with Afghan girls in one collective ceremony. My bride's name is Shinar. It's a long story; I'll tell it as we go along.

My mate Flag dismounts now outside the tent as I finish arming. He's about forty and the hardest knot I know. He has taught me everything. I would march into hell at his side.

He enters dressed in formal military kit, for the wedding. I indicate his cloak. "You'll be roasting in that thing."

Flag tugs back one wing. Beneath his left arm, a *xiphos* sword is strapped to his ribs. He's got an Afghan long-knife lashed along one thigh and throwing-daggers inside both boots. He carries two more weapons in plain view, a ceremonial sword on a baldric and a nine-foot half-pike. These are for show. To give Baz (the name we Macedonians apply to any Afghan) something to fix his eyes on.

Boxer and Little Red have reined outside. In a few moments we'll make our way across the plain to the camp of the Aletai Pactyans. There, I will meet the brother of my bride and pay him off, an indemnity of honor, so he won't murder me and his sister. The price is four years' wages and my best horse.

Such is Afghanistan. Only out here do you have to bribe a brother not to slaughter his own sister. Her crime: being with me.

Of course I suspect treachery. That's what the weapons are for. In a way I'm hoping for it. Otherwise, our own Mack code of *philoxenia* ("love for the stranger") forbids me to take the life of one of the family I marry into. I'm an idiot for still buying it, but there it is.

Atop the citadel, the crier calls. Two hours past noon. The Persian day starts at sundown. That's when the wedding will take place. Lesser ceremonies have been going on all day. Late afternoon will be the military tattoo. The whole Mack army and all the Afghan clans and tribes will pass in review before Alexander, Roxane, and the dignitaries. The big wedding, the royal one, will take place in Chorienes' palace atop the fortress of Bal Teghrib, "Stone Mountain." The mass ceremony, the one where Shinar and I will get tied, takes place outdoors in the new stadium at the foot of the hill. When the weddings are over, the celebrations begin.

"All right," says Flag. "Let's go over this one more time."

Flag is by far our senior. His rank is Flag Sergeant. He has a personal name but I've never heard anyone use it. We just call him by his rank.

He rehearses us in blocking moves. What's critical is that Shinar's brother and his two cousins not escape. They can't be allowed to break away or survive with wounds. Our blows must be fatal. These three are Shinar's last male kin. No others stand under the obligation of *nangwali,* the Afghan code of honor, to see that "justice" is done. Brother and cousins slain, we can buy our way out of the crime. Money will patch it up. But these three must go down.

I am grateful to my comrades. This is serious peril that they undergo for my sake. I'd do the same for them, and they know it. They'll be embarrassed if I express gratitude overtly. When it's over, if we're all alive, I'll get each of them a woman or a horse.

"All I can say," says Little Red as we finish our preparations, "is this is a hell of a way to warm up for a wedding."

As my mates and I cinch up, my bride appears in the portal. She will bathe now and, assisted by her bridesmaids, perform the *karahal*, the Pactyan purification rite. No male may witness this. She meets my eye. "When will you go, Matthias?"

"Now."

A groom brings my horse. My mates have already mounted.

The Afghan farewell is *tel badir*, "With God's care." Shinar signs this to me. I sign back. Flag's heels tap his pony. "Now or never."

We're off. To perform, if we must, one final murder; then get the hell out of this country.

BOOK
ONE

A Common Soldier

1.

I am the third and last son of my family to come out to Afghanistan. My older brothers went out as cavalrymen. I signed with the infantry.

The distinction between horse and foot is not so great in Afghanistan as it was in Alexander's earlier campaigns in Asia Minor, Mesopotamia, and Persia. Out east, an infantryman is expected to leap onto the back of any creature that will bear his weight—horse, mule, ass, or *yaboo* (the Afghan pony)—and ride to the site of action, there to dismount and fight, or even fight from the beast's back if necessary. Likewise horse troopers, even the King's Companions, think nothing of hitting the ground and slugging it out on foot alongside the dirt-eaters.

My father was killed in Afghanistan, or more precisely he expired of sepsis in a military hospital in Susia, in the province of Areia, which lies on the western border of the country. My father was not a mounted warrior or a foot soldier but a combat engineer of the siege train—what the troops call a "bucket man" because miners and sappers dig their trenches and raise their earthworks with wicker baskets. His name was the same as mine, Matthias.

My father fought at the Granicus River, at Tyre, Gaza, and at Issus. He was an authentic hero. My brothers are too. Once, when I was sixteen, my father sent home an army warrant worth a quarter talent of gold. We bought a second farm with it, with two barns and a year-round creek, and had enough left over to fence the place in stone.

It was my father's keenest wish that I, the youngest brother, not come out to war. My mother, further, was violently opposed to any step that would take me away from the land. "You may call it your misfortune, Matthias," she declared, "to have been whelped last of the litter. But, like it or not, you are my bulwark and the bulwark of this farm. Your father is gone. We shall never see your brothers again. Lust for glory will be their finish; they will leave great names and nothing more."

My mother feared that I, gone overseas, would tread into the snare of some foreign wench and, taking her to wife, never return to Macedon.

I was eighteen, however, and as mad for glory as every other overheated young blood in a kingdom whose twenty-five-year-old sovereign, Alexander son of Philip, had in only four years sacked earth's mightiest empire and turned our homeland delirious with conquest, fame, and treasure.

In the Macedonian army, enlistments are measured not by years but by cycles, or "bumps." A bump is eighteen months. Minimum enlistment is two bumps, one to be trained and one to serve, but a man must commit for a third cycle, a total of four and a half years, if and when he is called overseas. It worked this way: A recruit entered service with a regiment of the Occupation Army. This was the force left behind by Alexander to hold down Greece and the tribal north. All these contingents were territorial; you had to come from the district or you couldn't get in. As Alexander's needs in Asia necessitated, he sent home for replacements. Sometimes entire regiments were called up; other times individuals, either those in specific military specialties such as intelligence or siege engineering, or simply infantrymen with seniority whose lucky number came up.

All this was moot for a youth of my district, Apollonia. Apollonia has no infantry regiment. The region is cavalry country. The most famous squadron of Alexander's Companions, the *ile* of Socrates Sathon, comes from Apollonia. This squadron, in which both my brothers served, led the charge at the battle of the Granicus River; it fought at Alexander's right hand in the great victories of Issus and Gaugamela. It has more hero statues at Dium than any other squadron, including the Royal. My best friend Lucas and I, and every other war-crazed youth in the territory, had trained year-round since before we could walk, on fire for the day we would enter the trials and with heaven's aid become, like Apollonia's heroes before us, King's Companions.

We were too late, Lucas and I. By the time our hour came, Alexander's army had pushed so deep into Asia and had assimilated troops from so many vanquished nations that our king no longer sent home for Companion cavalry, except to replace men killed, wounded, or retired. The horse troops he employed now were all hired squadrons—Persians mostly, with Syrians, Lydians, Cappadocians, and riders of other kingdoms of the conquered East. No Mack could join these, even if he could get overseas, which he couldn't, or could speak the barbarian tongue, which he wouldn't.

There was only one way for Lucas and me to get out to Asia. As hired infantry. As mercenaries.

At that time, scores of private contractors—called *pilophoroi* for the felt caps they wore—traveled the cities of Greece and Asia Minor, signing up troops. It was a business. Candidates paid a fee, called a "pony" because it was so steep a man could buy a fine colt with it. The felt-caps got them in.

Turning eighteen, Lucas and I trekked three days to the port of Methone, the hiring depot for mercenary infantry. The taverns were crawling with grizzled professionals—Arcadians and Syracusans, Cretans and Rhodians, even officers of the Achaeans and Spartans. They all knew each other from prior hitches; they had mates and commanders who could get them aboard. Lucas and I were the youngest by years. We knew nobody. No *pilophoros* would touch us, no matter how convincingly we lied about our age or our service histories (of which we had none).

We stayed ten days, with our payoff cash dwindling rapidly, trying to talk or buy our way in anywhere. At the last hour we went seeking the recruiting general himself. Of course we couldn't get near him. A Line Sergeant from Pella kicked us out. "Wait a minute," he said, hearing our accents. "Are you boys from Apollonia?"

He wanted to know if we could ride.

We were centaurs!

The sergeant drew up our papers on the spot and wouldn't take any money either. He put us down as Mounted Infantry. That was what Alexander needed most. Lucas and I could not believe our luck. We asked what outfit we'd be with and when we'd get our horses.

"No outfits," the sergeant said. "And no horses neither." He had put us on the rolls because we were Macedonians, amid all these foreigners. "No overseas captain ever turned down a lad from home."

We thanked him with all our hearts. He brushed it off. "Don't worry about what outfit you ship out with, or if you never see an hour of drill. Out east," he said, "the king'll draft you wherever he needs you."

2.

Our force of replacements landed at Tripolis in Syria on the sixteenth of Daesius, early summer, in the sixth year of Alexander's reign, the fourth since the expeditionary force had crossed out of Europe into Asia. The king and his army were then a thousand miles east, on their way from Persepolis, Persia's capital, to Ecbatana in Media, the summer palace of her kings. The Persian Empire had fallen; Alexander now pursued its fugitive king. Our lord's pack train, reports said, was seven thousand camels and ten thousand pairs of asses, all laden with gold.

Our detachment of replacements was sixty-one hundred in forty-seven ships. The harbor at Tripolis couldn't hold that many, and, as the vessels had neither berths nor provisions to lie-to overnight in the roads, a conference was held of the captains, who were just merchant skippers hired for pay, at which it was decided that our ferry (which is what it was) and about ten others would be rowed to shallow water, where we scuffs were told to grab our kit, hop over the side, and swim for it. Which we did. It was a grand lark, except that I ruined a fine pair of boots in the saltwater, growing too weary to hold them over my head. This is how I landed in Asia, soaked as a drowned cat, and barefoot.

Replacements are not an army. Our mob had been formed not into regiments but into "S.C.'s," shipboard contingents, and did not, when we landed, even have our arms. The cavalry didn't have its horses. The animals were following in other transports. There was a tent city waiting, and an escort of six hundred Syrian mercenaries, and fourteen hundred hired infantry of Lycia, with Macedonian officers, who were to take us up to Marathus and from there by way of Larissa to Thapsacus, where we would cross the Euphrates into Mesopotamian Syria and Kurdistan. The march to catch up with Alexander would take between three and four months.

As always in a new camp, the troops plunged at once into their favored pastimes—touring the site looking up friends, and poaching every item of kit they could lay hands on. You couldn't set down a heel of bread without somebody snatching it, and a decent hat or a pair of road-slappers were sure goners. A man hung his purse next to his testicles and, after shaking hands with a stranger, checked to make sure both sacks were still where he had left them.

In Alexander's fighting army, every trooper knew the mark he was to stand on. But here, a thousand miles to the rear, the show was all orphan stew. You ate when the cooks opened the tents and bunked where you could find a patch of dirt wide enough to hold your bones. You kept with your mates to keep the scroungers from picking you blind. My bunch was Lucas; Terres, called "Rags" for his dandy's love of clothes; and Peithon, undersized, called "Flea." We were all from Apollonia, all eighteen, and had known each other all our lives.

Lucas was our leader. He was a born operator and set out to keep our heads above the general ruck. We were supposed to get paid on landing at Tripolis (it'd been a month, marshaling and crossing), but if there was any shine with this mob, I never saw it. In fact we had to pay, ourselves. The slugs at the cook-tent wanted cash to get in. You had to pay to take a crap.

"We've got to find ourselves a bull," pronounced Lucas. Meaning someone with rank to attach ourselves to.

We found him in a Color Sergeant named Tolmides. Tollo for short. He was a stubby fellow with great mustaches and a boar's-tusk cap, a mate of Lucas's father, and in charge here of a company of Lycian infantry. Lucas spotted him in the latrine line. "Hey, Tollo! Where's a scuff take a free shit around here?"

Tollo came over, laughing. "By Hades' balls, you little off-scourings got all growed up, did you?" His rank was no joke though. He was a big onion. He got us out of camp. We chowed down with his Lycians out on the plain.

What, we asked, were the chances of getting paid?

About the same as crapping ivory.

When do we get assigned to regiments?

When you pay off the officers escorting you.

What about kit?

We would not be issued arms till Thapsacus or later, Tollo told us, and when we did we'd have to cough up for those too. "Don't worry, the quartermaster'll put it against your roll." Meaning our pay records. We'd tick it down out of time served.

Lucas looked glum. "They didn't tell us this back home."

"If they did, you wouldn't have come out," said Tollo. And he laughed.

We glued ourselves to him. He and his Mack comrades had served as scouts in Forward Operations, running reconnaissance for

Alexander in Areia and Afghanistan. They had been sent back to train us replacements on the march. They got double pay for this, and double that for escort duty.

"Don't take to gloom, little brothers." Tollo pointed east, into the Asiatic night. "Men drop like flies out there, from heat, sickness, or they just run queer." And he tapped his skull. "You'll make grade fast if you show strong stuff. Keep your sheet clean and do what you're told. You'll work fine."

There were six other Macks in Tollo's cadre, including Stephanos of Aegae, the celebrated war poet. He was a decorated hero and a genuine celebrity. Stephanos was thirty-five; he should have been a captain or at least a full lieutenant, but he stayed a Line Sergeant. He liked it that way. Here is one of the poems that had made him famous back home and a favorite, even, of the women.

A SOLDIER'S PACK

Experience has taught the soldier how to
pack his pannier, with the stuff he needs most
near the top, where he can get at it. In the outer pockets
he stows his onions and garlic, sealed tight so they don't
stink up the weather kit and half-fleece on the other side.
At the bottom, deep inside, he stashes those items that must
at all costs be protected, against dust, against being
dropped, against the elements. There, in the doeskin
you gave me, I keep your letters, my darling wife.

The youngest of these Mack cadre was past thirty; several were fifty and more. They were the roughest planks we had ever seen. We were scared to death of them. Any one, by himself, could have manhandled the pack of us. We found ourselves running errands for them and shouldering their kit, without anyone ordering us, just so they wouldn't bite our heads off. Lucas and I were slouching back into camp with firewood one night when we were called over by one of them, a Flag Sergeant whose real name no one dared ask and whom the troopers called simply "Flag," the customary title of address for one of his rank.

"You two, learn something."

We dropped our brush and scurried to him like schoolboys. Flag summoned one of his Lycians and had the fellow face about. He thrust the shaft of his half-pike (the shorter version of the *sarissa* used then in Asia) into my fist.

"Kill him," he commanded.

I turned bright plum. Could he be serious?

"How do you finish a man who's running from you?"

I didn't know.

Flag tugged the Lycian around. "What if he turns about and faces you?"

I didn't know.

"Take his place."

"What?"

Suddenly I found myself in the Lycian's spot. "Run," Flag commanded. Before I could take one step, I found myself facedown in the dirt with the wind hammered out of me. I didn't even know where Flag had hit me. I felt the butt of his half-pike upend me in one instant, then smash my skull in the next. I couldn't move or breathe; I was helpless.

"Like this." I could hear him instruct Lucas. "Sideways, so the blade doesn't jam between the ribs." And he stabbed me. Not a pin-prick, but in so far I could feel the edge scrape the bone. I howled in pain.

Flag yanked me to my feet. Lucas's face was white. "If the

enemy faces you, lance him here. One push. Pull it straight out so it doesn't jam."

Then, to me: "When you hit a man, how hard do you do it?"

Before I could speak, Flag had swatted Lucas across the chest with the shaft of his half-pike. I have never heard such a blow. My mate crashed as if dead.

"Do that to the Afghan," Flag said. "Before he does it to you."

3.

The Macedonian infantry phalanx is based on a file of sixteen. Sixteen men, one behind the other. Two files is a section. This is commanded by a Line Sergeant. Four files is a platoon, led by a lieutenant and a Flag Sergeant. A square is four platoons, sixteen-by-sixteen, 256 men. A brigade is six squares, 1,536. There are six brigades in Alexander's army. In depth of sixteen, the phalanx's front is above six hundred yards.

The enlisted commander of each platoon is a Flag Sergeant, so named for the pennant he mounts on the peak of his two-handed pike, his *sarissa*. His post is up front. Second in rank to him is a Lance Sergeant, or file-closer. He is called a "back." He takes the rear. In many ways his job is more important than the Flag's (also called a "First" or a "Top") because his will drives the file forward, and any man who thinks of dropping back has to face him.

Third in rank in each file is the ninth man, a Sergeant or Lance

Corporal. Why the ninth? Because when the command is given to "double front," the file of sixteen divides into two half-files of eight, called litters, and the rear eight hastens up alongside the front eight. The ninth man becomes the first in the new file. By this evolution, the brigade has gone from roughly a hundred-man front, sixteen deep, to a two-hundred-man front, eight deep. Across the entire phalanx the front has expanded from six hundred to twelve hundred yards.

This configuration is how the Occupation Army trained at home, and how Alexander's expeditionary force fought in the first three years of the Persian war, in its great conventional battles at the Granicus River, Issus, and Gaugamela.

In Afghanistan, we are now told, things will not be so simple. The place is all mountain and desert. You can't use the phalanx there. The foe will not face it in pitched battle. Why should he? We would annihilate him if he did.

In the training at home with the eighteen-foot *sarissa*, a file had to be perfectly aligned front-to-back. Otherwise the formation would be tripping over its own feet. This was called advancing "on the axis." The warrior virtue of being "on the axis" meant being sharp, obedient, never deviating. A good soldier was on the axis in everything he did.

Out east, we begin to see, there is no axis. The eighteen-foot *sarissa* has become the nine-foot half-pike; the phalanx exists on the parade ground only. Only two precepts remain: one, sacrifice everything in the cause of the main effort, and, two, never leave another Mack behind.

"Warfare out east," our poet-sergeant Stephanos instructs us, "is of three types. In the plains, cavalry action. Against strongholds, siege warfare. In the mountains, mobile infantry."

The fourth type of action was against villages. Our instructors didn't tell us about that.

4.

Our force of replacements is supposed to march out from Tripolis
three days after we land, but we wind up stuck there for twenty-two
more. Waiting for the cavalry's horses and our own arms. This is no
joke, as our bunch still hasn't been paid (no one has), and what little shine we have left is not enough to live on. We wind up stealing
like Spartans. Everyone does. The escort troops will not let us into
the city, so we scrounge, scavenge, pilfer, trade, and wager. Somehow it works. I wind up with most of my kit refurbished—and a decent pair of boots to replace the ones ruined in the sea. And Lucas
and I connect with a pair of Companion cavalrymen rotating home
to Apollonia, who know both my brothers and have news of them.

Elias has been wounded but is well; he is in hospital now at
Phrada in southern Afghanistan. Philip (Elias is nine years older
than I, Philip fourteen) has been promoted to Major. He is in India

now, as an envoy with Forward Operations, negotiating alliances with the native potentates in advance of Alexander's army's push over the Hindu Kush into the Punjab. Such place names sound impossibly romantic to me. My brothers! What illustrious fellows! How will I live up to their achievements? Will I even recognize them when I see them?

The Companion cavalry, in which both my brothers serve, is the elite arm of Alexander's fighting corps. To be accepted into a squadron is to be made for life. A man becomes in fact the king's companion. He may dine with him, carouse with him, address him as "Alexander" (though, it is true, few dare.) The phalanx brigades share the name Companions (*petzhetairoi*, "Foot Companions"). But it's not the same thing, as the king is a cavalryman and his closest mates are horsemen too.

In theory, each squadron of Companions is composed only of riders from its home district—Apollonia, Bottiaea, Torone, Methone, Olynthus, Amphipolis, and Anthemos being the squadrons taken by Alexander to Asia. (There are eight other squadrons, from other parts of Macedonia, but these remained home to garrison Greece and the tribal north.) But in practice, outstanding riders come from all over the kingdom seeking a berth. I have known men to marry or get themselves adopted into a local family, just to have a shot in the tryouts.

The trials take place over four days. The first two are compulsory exercises; the third is cross-country; the fourth is combat. A rider must show up with a string of seven horses. He is required to use no fewer than four during the ring work (to show he is not cheating by riding a smart animal), and one of those four must serve as his mount in either the steeplechase or the fighting tests. A good cavalry mount takes ten years to train and costs as much as a small farm. Only a rich man's son can try, unless he is sponsored, as my brothers were, by another rich man, or if he has a father who has been decorated by the king.

Both my brothers were grooms as lads and rode as jockeys in the hippodrome. I cannot tell you how many nights they came home with cracked skulls and busted shins. Nothing could stop them. In the trials at Apollonia, when Elias was only ten, he slipped into the paddock while the horses were being saddled and leapt aboard not one but two champions, placing a foot on each bare back while clasping the reins of one horse in his left hand and the other in his right; he not only rode off at top speed without so much as a watch-my-kit, but jumped the horses over both walls, in and out, all the while standing on the horses' backs as if he were nailed to them. The thrashing he received as punishment nearly carried him off, but it was worth it; he had made his name. He and Philip, five years older, could touch down off a horse's back at the all-out and spring back aboard, yoked only by a wrist through the animal's mane; they could "wrap around" (swing under a horse's belly and back up the other side). It was nothing to either of them to dice a pear with the long lance one-handed at the stretching run, and their knowledge of veterinary medicine and what we call horsemastership (everything inside the barn) was the equal of any physician in the kingdom. Yet both failed to qualify, not once but four times—that's how many superlative riders the realm held—before finally getting sent out in the expedition's second year with four thousand reinforcements under Amyntas Andromenes. They crossed by sea to Gaza in Palestine and joined the king's army in Egypt.

Our own belated contingent moves out from Tripolis, now, on the twenty-third day. The season is high summer. Every surface of armor must have a woven cover; otherwise the sun will turn it into a skillet. At home we have trained to march thirty miles a day with full kit and rations. Trekking now across Syria, fifteen miles feels like forty, and twenty like a hundred. The sun squats on our shoulders; we breathe dust instead of air. Our tongues are lolling like dogs' on the tramp to Marathus.

I fall in beside Flag. He can see I'm suffering. "The Afghan," he says, "will make fifty miles a day afoot and a hundred on horseback. He doesn't drink and he doesn't eat. Hack off his head and he'll take two more swipes at you before he goes down."

Reveille is three hours before dawn; march-out beats the sun by two. Lead elements of the column are in camp by midafternoon, with the stragglers and baggage train catching up by dark. An hour before noon a halt is called and the asses and mules are off-loaded; the beasts can go six to eight hours, but they have to get the weight off for two, otherwise they break down. No such luck for us. We get twenty minutes, then pack 'em up! At one stop on the third day, Lucas moves off to make water. Flag looks on, disapproving. "You shouldn't have a drop in you." If you can still draw piss, he says, you're not trekking hard enough.

We have our weapons now. When we make camp early, we train. Cordon operations. Block and search. We have never heard of such things. High-lining. Sweep by flying columns. These are all new to us.

On treks over great distances, the day's march is planned to take us from one inhabited area to another—a city or town that has been tasked to supply bread and fodder, or at least provide a market for the army. Now on selected days, for training, the column begins bypassing these. We chop from nowhere to nowhere, throw up a "hasty camp," a circular ditch-and-berm, spiked with palisade stakes. No wheat-bread in these. We dine on "mooch"—barley gruel, whipped up out of our meal bags, which every man packs (holding ten days' grain ration) and seasoned with whatever cresses we can scrounge and the odd pullet or goose liberated from a barn-yard. Breakfast is wine, olive oil, and "hurry bread" (groats soaked overnight and half-baked on flat stones from the watch fire or directly over the flame on "paddles," the iron flat-plates of the cata-pults). The feed we all dread is "scratch," millet porridge, but even this is preferable to "cicada's lunch," meaning no grub at all. Tollo and Stephanos build in one starve-day in seven, to lean out our guts and get us used to what's coming.

Flag has adopted me, after his fashion, or I should say I have fastened onto him like a barnacle. At Marathus an incident occurs. We have gotten paid finally. To celebrate, my mates and I hunt up a local shop for a barbering; when we get back to camp, we can't find our purse. Lucas keeps this with him at all times; it holds our pooled stash. Now it's gone. This is serious. No pay is coming until next month, and we can't stand another siege of starvation. I go to Flag, tell him the last place we'd had our wallet is at the barber's.

"Show me," he says.

He enlists Tollo and a Mack corporal called Little Red. The barber's dwelling and shop are the same, a mud-brick hut with a shade canopy out front and a cooking kitchen on the side. It's suppertime; the wife won't open the gate. She's a snippy bitch and dishes out a smart dose of sauce.

Flag kicks the slats in. The shops in town all lie in the market district, a choleric rat-run called the Terik, "pigeon." In moments every stall-keeper in the lane has collected, all gibbering in their tongue and ordering us to screw off. The barber's shack is thick with urchins and grandfolks, with three or four brothers or cousins, young men, all armed and on their feet in a state of outrage. Flag is packing his hook, a wicked weapon used for unhorsing cavalry, with a short-sword on a shoulder sling; Tollo and Red wear their blades; Lucas and I do too but, God help us, we have no intention of using them. Flag makes straight for the barber. By signs and pidgin, he lets him know we want our money.

Get out! the fellow shouts back. Leave my home! I have taken nothing!

Flag seizes him by the gullet and jams him against the wall. Tollo and Little Red begin overturning furniture, what few sticks there are; they bowl over the cooking kettle, kicking the flat loaves across the floor. By now half the street is pressing tight about us, all bawling in indignation, and all proclaiming innocence. Lucas and I are certain we have made a mistake. We must've lost the money somewhere else! Leave these poor people alone!

The barber's face has gone purple. He is gagging and calling on the gods to witness his blamelessness.

"Flag! They're innocent! Let's go!"

Flag ignores me, dumps the barber, and snatches up a small boy who is clinging in terror to the old man's breeches.

"Whose brat is this?"

The haircutter makes no reply. No one does. But clearly the child is his.

Flag turns to Tollo. "Cut his foot off."

Tollo and Little Red spreadeagle the boy. The child is screaming blue murder. Tollo unsheathes his edge. The mob begins brandishing their own daggers. Lucas and I beg Flag to stop. Flag looks to the barber. "Where's the money?" No response. To the mother. Nothing. He signs to Tollo. Up goes the sword.

At the last instant a girl-child wails, indicating a corner of the dirt floor. Her mother wallops her across the face. Chaos redoubles. Flag probes where the girl has pointed. Up comes our wallet.

Outside on the street, Lucas and I can't stop shaking.

"Liars and thieves," Tollo is muttering. "Every one of 'em."

We try to give Flag part of our recovered cash. He won't take it.

"Mark one thing," he says, directing our attention back to the barber's hut. "If Little Sis hadn't squealed, Mom and Pop would've let us take their son's foot."

He is right.

"And would you have taken it?"

Flag doesn't answer. "They'll beat the hell out of that little girl now. Thrash her within an inch of her life."

Three days later we're humping up the pass out of the Reghez Valley. I have a sixty-pound pannier across my back and a counterpack, half that again, in front; the rope straps are gouging my shoulders raw. Flag falls into step alongside. "You're thinking again, aren't you?"

And he smiles and treks on.

To watch Flag march is like watching water flow. His skull is the color of parchment; the sun might as well be beating on stone. He can feel my gaze tracking him. "You're wondering what a soldier is, aren't you?"

I tell him I am.

He indicates a laden beast, mounting the track before us.

"We're mules, lad. Mules that kill."

5.

It takes our column of replacements 127 days out of Tripolis to catch up, at last, with the trailing elements of Alexander's army. We have trekked 1,696 miles, according to the army surveyors (who measure the roads down to the half-hand's-breadth), crossing all of Syria and most of Mesopotamia, Media, Mardia, Hyrcania, and no small portions of Parthia and Areia. I have gone through three pairs of road-beaters and my march-pay twice over. My kit is rags. I arrive at the front—if such a term can be used for a war that is prosecuted across a theater 1,000 miles broad and 900 deep—already three months in debt. So does everyone else.

When you march long distances in column, you pass the time by landmarks. Say you come over a rise into a desert valley, a pan twenty or fifty miles across. You'll set your object as the hills on the far side and march to that, marking your progress as you approach. That will be your day. Or you'll pick out intermediate landmarks, little hills, washes, dry riverbeds—wadis or nullahs, as they call them out east.

You can see weather for miles, crossing Media and Hyrcania. Squalls play across the pans at midday. Rain falls on one section of the column but not another. You'll see precipitation sheet from the bellies of the clouds, never to reach the ground but burning away high in the heat of the air. Great shadows play across the plains, making the earth dark in one spot, bright in another, in shifting patterns as the clouds transit the sky. Thunderheads collect over the mountains; you get downpours late in the day.

Alexander's commanders will not stand for a body of men straggling in one long column; it's unsightly and unmilitary; you can't fight from such a formation. So when terrain permits, the troops are fanned out ten or fifteen columns across. This is good because when you reach camp, the whole body can catch up in an hour instead of four. The column packs up everything at night, so it's ready to go in the dark before dawn. Cavalry other than reconnaissance ride their horses sparingly on the march; they tramp on foot alongside, to conserve the animals' strength. Grooms lead a remount in each hand. Horses are never permitted to herd on their own, even at rivers where they water. Otherwise they'll revert to equine hierarchies and be worthless as cavalry.

Crossing Media, we see game in abundance. Gazelle and wild asses; the column spots them from miles, trailing their dust in the clear air. Hunting parties are organized like military operations: Divisions send mounted companies to envelop the game, circling as widely as twenty miles sometimes to cut off the herds' flight, drive them into rope pens if they have time to rig them, or simply run them to exhaustion on the open plain. Riders return with meat for the army's pots. This is great sport; everyone wants to go. It breaks the monotony.

An army passing through a territory attracts commerce and curiosity of every kind. Actors have come out from Ephesus and Smyrna; we have dancers and acrobats, harpers and reciters, poets, rhapsodes; even sophists offering lectures, which to my astonishment are actually attended. I took in a fascinating one on solid geometry in the middle of a thunderstorm on the High Line in Armenia. Between camps the caravan traders, or just natives loading up asses with anything they can sell, trek alongside the column, peddling dates and sheep, pistachio beer, eggs, meat, cheese. What do the lads crave most? Fresh onions. Back home onions go to flavor a stew. Out here you eat 'em raw. They taste sweet as apples. A man'll give half a day's pay for a good onion. They keep your teeth from falling out.

I have a fiancée at home. Her name is Danae. On the march I write letters to her in my head. I talk about money, not love. When we get married, Danae and I will need the equivalent of six years' pay to make an offer on a farm, since neither of us wish to be beholden to our families. I will volunteer for Forward Operations, first chance I get. Double pay. I cannot tell Danae this. She will worry.

There are many things a fellow cannot tell his sweetheart. Women for one. An army travels accompanied by a second army of whores and trollops, not to mention the camp wives, who constitute a more permanent auxiliary, and when these melt away in "wolf country," enemy territory, their numbers are made up by locals. We have heard much about the Asiatic's sequestration of his women, and no doubt this is true in normal times. But when an army as laden with plunder as Alexander's passes through, even the most hawkeyed patriarch can't keep watch over his daughters forever. The maids dog the column, seeking novelty, freedom, romance, and even the lamest scuff can gin them down to nothing for a quick roll-me-over. The girls'll even stay to mend kit and do the laundry. Half the young cooches are blinkered—with child, that is—made so by our fellows passing through with Alexander months before. This doesn't stop us from stropping them. Not me of course, or Lucas. We hold true to our girls back home, much to the amusement of our comrades.

Tollo is the primary fig-hound. He's sluicing the natives two at a time. "One on each hip," he says, "just to keep warm." Tollo's Color Sergeant pay, counting bonuses, is four drachmas a day (four times my packet). You can buy a house for that here, or hire half a village to do any labor you want.

The army has its own language. "Steam" is soldiers' slang for women. Dish. Fig. Cooch. Hank or bert (from the native *tallabert*, "mother") for an Afghan. The locals have their slang for us too. Mack. Scuff. *Bullah* (from their word for "stupid"). Sex is qum-qum. The enemy himself our lads call "Baz," the most common name for an Afghan male—as in, "Baz is out there tonight."

Women are of two types in Areia and Afghanistan. Those beneath the protection of fathers and brothers are called *tir bazal*, "the jewel." If you so much as glance at them, their people will slit your throat. The other type has lost the protection of the clan. Maybe their male kin have been killed in feuds or war, or the females have committed some transgression and been cast out. These are the girls we Macks take up with. They're not tramps though. They have dignity. You have to marry them.

Marriage here is not like back home. One of my littermates, Philotas, met a girl in a village west of Susia. By night they were married. No ceremony; you just declare it and that's it. My mates make fun of me because I take wedlock seriously. That's how I feel. I can't accept these riteless, walk-away hitch-ups. They seem wrong to me.

We get mail on the column. The post from home catches up every ten days; the troops even get letters from the army out east. This from my mother:

> *You need not write me chatty notes, dear, nor do I care*
> *to learn the progress of the latest campaign. Just let me*
> *know you are well. Stay alive, my child, and come home*
> *to me.*

A letter comes from my brother Elias, ahead with Alexander's corps in Afghanistan. It has no toll-seal. Mail from the fighting army travels free.

All letters report the same news:

Darius is dead.

The king of Persia has fallen, slain by his own generals as they flee before Alexander. In our column of replacements, we are cast down to hear this. The war will soon be over. We'll pack home as broke as we started.

Elias sounds in fine fettle.

> *Matthias, you hound! How are you? Have you snagged*
> *your first Asiatic cooch? Welcome to the fighting army,*
> *you poor scuff!*

He is well, my brother says, except for a wound he downplays. He is in hospital now, as I said, at Phrada near the Great Salt Desert; that's how he has time to write.

> *The Persian war is drawing down, little brother. The*
> *enemy's big augers all seek terms. It's a capital show,*
> *these grandees coming in. They send their lieutenants*

> *first, under a flag, or their sons if they have them. Their*
> *mules are loaded with loot—"for Iskander." That's*
> *Persian for Alexander. We take them in like wayward*
> *kittens. Our orders are to treat them as if they were sugar*
> *and we must carry them home on our tongues.*

Great generals and governors of the Persians, nobles who have fought our fellows across all Asia—Artabazus, Phrataphernes, Nabarzanes, Autophradates, as well as the slayers of Darius: Satibarzanes and his cohort Barsaentes—have bent the knee and been received with clemency by Alexander. Who else can run the empire for him? Even the mercenaries Glaucus and Patron, commanders of Darius's crack heavy infantry, have come in with their commands and made their peace. They now form a unit of Alexander's army.

Only one enemy remains wild. The Persian general Bessus, with 8,000 Afghan cavalry and access to 30,000 more—Scythian raiders from beyond the Jaxartes. He is calling himself Darius's successor and raising an army to fight on.

> *Don't worry, little brother. His own generals can read the*
> *wind. They'll bring in his hat—with his head in it—soon*
> *enough.*

In Areia, nearing the frontier of Afghanistan, we get our first chance outside of training to unsheathe our arms. Tollo and Flag are assigned, with half our company of mercenaries, to provide security for a train of supplies to be delivered to a village two days off the military highway. Lucas and I go along. Halfway out, in wild ravine country, a detachment of tribal riders shows itself on a ridge ahead. Tollo, Flag, and the mercs take off after them, leaving us rawbones with a few muleteers and natives to guard the train. Sure enough, as soon as our mates drop from sight, a party of thirty more bandits materializes. We are twelve, only four of us armed. The brigands are the most savage-looking villains we have ever seen. They have no fear of us whatever. They ride straight up to our goods and start helping themselves. We try to brass it out, shouting threats and brandishing our weapons. The foe brandishes back, with a good deal more credibility. Our natives have hotfooted it up the hill, clear of bowshot. Pretty soon we're up there too. Lucas wants to attack; he says we'll be court-martialed for cowardice if we don't. "Are you crazy?" declares Rags. "These sand-trotters'll murder us all."

The bandits take everything. We feel like fools. Tollo and Flag return; without a word they mount a pursuit. When the raiders see our mob coming, they dump the loot and flee. We recover it all. "Don't lose a wink over this," Tollo reassures us afterward. "You did right. It was my fault for leaving you."

But we are chastened. We have seen our wits go blank with terror and felt our limbs turn to stone from fear.

On the march, the army lays over every five days to rest the stock. At home these would be off-days, spent in recreation or refurbishing of kit. Not in Alexander's army. Out east, we train.

We learn defense against cavalry. We learn hollow squares and moving screens; we learn how to feign a rush and how to recover. We even get to ride a little. For every primary mount, the grooms lead two remounts. These strings are the property of individual cavalrymen; in conventional warfare, the troopers would never let you near one. Not in this theater. Out here there's no such thing as a led horse. We are recruited, those on the books as Mounted Infantry. In the event of action, should our primary cavalry be drawn off, we will form an auxiliary of remounts to shield the column.

On we trek. We practice cordon operations; encirclement of villages. Our companies rehearse on dummy sites across Armenia and Mesopotamian Syria, then on the real thing in the Kurdish mountains east of the Tigris. The force surrounds a farm hamlet in the dark, to be in assault position at first light. The job is carried out in strict silence. Its purpose is to let no villager escape. The formation for assault is open order,

POINT   POINT

WING   WING   WING

BACK   BACK

in three ranks. The same configuration is employed in pursuit of the foe. Its principle is the inverted swallowtail,

WING   WING

BACK

in which an individual of the foe is passed through the points, attacked by the wings, and finished off by the backs.

When the cordon rings the village, an avenue of escape is always left. Cavalry and missile troops conceal themselves on the flanks of this getaway lane. This is how we are taught to take prisoners, running them down as they flee (the highest-ranking are always first out), instead of attempting to selectively take captives in the confusion of the assault.

We spend more time now practicing killing blows. It's unsettling. Can we do the same to a living man?

Will we freeze in the crucial moment?

We are keenly aware that we are boys, not men like Flag and Tollo. We do nothing like they do. We don't talk like them or stand like them; we can't even piss like them. They inhabit a sphere that is magnitudes above us. We ape them. We study them as if we were children. They remain beyond us.

The column has passed through Susia now. My father's bones lie here in the military cemetery. We are given no time to stop. The Afghan kingdoms lie only a few marches ahead. For days our force has been tracked by "clouds" and "ghosts," army slang for the ragged, *yaboo*-mounted tribesmen who, our guides tell us, are not Afghans but Areians and Parthians, peoples we have supposedly conquered. Lucas eyes them dubiously. "They don't look very conquered to me."

Our column advances under arms at all times now, with cavalry on both wings. One thing I have not anticipated, coming out to the army, is the prodigious consumption of liquor. The boozing is breathtaking. Veterans drink themselves blind every night. They collapse like the dead. You have to kick them awake each morning, and even that doesn't work sometimes. The column packs out in a cacophony of hacking, spewing, hawking, puking; the men are blind as ticks for the first five miles. The foe attacking at dawn would make mince of us.

It'll get worse, Flag says, after the first action. He advises Lucas and me to start drinking now; get our bellies used to it. "At the front, you can't do without it." "Pank" and "jack" are army slang for the fiery cheap bozzle that knocks a man out like a blow to the

temple. Such spirits are not wine cut with water, as gentlemen im-
bibe at dinner to enliven the conversation, but hard liquor guzzled
neat. Distillers arise from the column who know how to cook up the
stuff from rice and barley, rye, beets, pistachios, date palms; they
make a brew from millet and sesame, vile as rancid curd, but with
such a kick that fellows stand in line for it, and flag colonels exempt
the brewmasters from duty, sending them off with cavalry escorts
even, to steam up their mash, which the army cannot function
without. Hogsheads of rye and wheat beer, so thick with lees that
you have to suck it up through a reed, are trucked to depots along
the column of march. One stretch of four days in Areia, the column
ran out of souse; mates were getting in knife fights just from nerves.
The commanders had to send out armed parties to scrounge up
some form of spirits, such stuff even as peels paint off ships' planks,
just to keep the men from murdering each other.

Why do soldiers drink? To keep from thinking, says Flag. If you
think, you start to fear.

The primary narcotic in Afghanistan is *naswar,* or "nazz"—a
dark resinous gum made from poppy opiates. You roll it into a ball
and stick it under your lip. It turns your gums black. The drug comes
in two types, black and brown. Brown is cheaper; it still has the
seeds in. The troops call it "birdseed." Black is a pure paste. The
joke is you can tell an officer from an enlisted man by whether he
uses "black" or "bird." Myself, I will not touch such stuff. But many
cannot stand up for count without it. Other drugs are *hosheesh,*
kanna, and *bhang,* opium. You burn the first and third in a pipe and
crush the second between your teeth. All three are cheap as turnips
and as easy to come by. Alexander has outlawed the use of all but
wine. But even he cannot curb this traffic.

Every night, drink carries off one or two men. Their sergeants
have to write the widow letters. Stephanos supplements his pay by

composing fictional demises for these reports. You cannot tell a wife that her husband has fried his wits on black nazz and split his skull plunging into a ditch.

Afghan ghosts continue to track the column. Our pace picks up; we close in on Alexander. Messengers arrive who have been with him only six days before.

When will we see action?

Flag answers: "When we least expect it."

6.

The column reaches Artacoana, principal city of Areia, on the 127th day out of Tripolis. Hell itself could not be uglier than the lower town, along the dry river, but the upper city, the Citadel, is surprisingly smart and civilized. Women are permitted on the streets, though bundled from sole to crown. You can hear them giggling behind their veils. Parks are everywhere. Tamarisk groves provide shade, their branches weeping a kind of sugary stuff the locals call *amassa*. You can eat it all day and your belly's as empty as when you started. Cloudbursts drench the town late in the afternoon, draining through the soil in moments, leaving it as parched and sterile as it was before. Persians, installed by Alexander, administer the city. Alexander himself has pushed on north and east with the army, pursuing the pretender Bessus. Our king will invade Afghanistan from the north before winter closes the passes.

Artacoana is famous for its shoe factories. The whole south side smells like a tannery. You can get extraordinary boots, bags, and saddles for next to nothing. Lucas and I get fitted for ankle-toppers the first morning; the bootmaker promises the finished pairs for late the next day. To our joy, he delivers. As the cobbler fits us, a commotion erupts in the lane. Boys and women race past in alarm. On their heels appear two Mack dispatch riders, pounding hard for the upper city. A soldier's instinct, sensing trouble, is to rally to his unit. We come out into the street, Lucas and I, in time to see, straggling in from the desert, a ragged column of Macedonian infantry. That they have no cavalry escort means something terrible has happened.

We find Flag and Tollo on the track back to camp. Stephanos is with them. A massacre has occurred, we are told, two days south of the city. Rebels led by the traitor Satibarzanes and his cavalry commander Spitamenes (called for his cunning "the Desert Wolf") have ambushed a company of 90 Macks, including 60 Companions, and 120 mercenaries, slaughtering all except the party we saw straggling in from the desert. Two pursuit columns will be mounted to avenge this. Lucas and I are drafted into the second.

The first party takes off at once. They are the chase column. It's their job to pick up the foe's trail and track him. Our chore in the second column is to load up and follow, bringing armor, rations, and the heavy kit. It is something to watch Flag and Tollo, and particularly Stephanos, rack the gear and rig it. God help the foe when these men catch up with him.

Our pursuit column is a quarter-brigade, about four hundred, half Macks and half Achaeans. Its commander is Amyntas Aeropus, called Bullock. The company has never trained or fought together. We have not even drilled. Tollo splits our sixty-four in half, with Flag commanding one section, Stephanos the other. Lucas and I are under the poet. Every man is mounted (my mate and I on asses) and leads one laden mule. We tag the first column's trail till dusk. Fallback riders meet us and guide us on in the dark. My new boots still haven't been stitched closed. I stuff my played-out road-beaters into a pannier and ride barefoot.

We overhaul the chase column two hours before dawn. Time for a feed and a couple hours' rest. Both elements press on all next day. The country south of Artacoana is desert valleys; one range of hills succeeds another. Toward nightfall of the second day scout riders come galloping in. Captains are called to assemble. The column is split into three—one blocking force circling southeast, a second assault force southwest (that's us), the third to set up a base camp with covering positions and follow when summoned.

We set off on foot into the dark. No one tells Lucas or me anything. No orders are issued and we are too embarrassed to ask. I have nothing but my worn-out clompers; my soles by now are a chewed-up mess.

The last scout trots back an hour before dawn. Finally Tollo calls our sections together. We assemble in a draw beneath a basalt ridge; the moon is just setting. We can make out a desert river, a hundred feet across and an inch deep, shining like a ribbon out beyond the ridge's shoulder. Apparently it twines past a village that is out of sight around the hill. The enemy has taken refuge in the village. His horses have been spotted. He does not know we are here.

Tollo sketches the village in the dirt. It will be a cordon operation. The columns will ring the site and go in at first light.

I am thinking: Can I do this? Can I stand up to the foe face-to-face? What will I do when he bolts, in rage or terror, straight at me?

"Prisoners?" asks one of the sergeants I don't know.

Tollo regards him. "What do you think?"

The caucus breaks up. Still no one has given Lucas and me a word. Here comes Stephanos.

"You'll take the women."

He indicates a Mack corporal called Barrel. We are to stick with him. In a second Stephanos is gone, arming. Barrel is about forty, with one milky eye and arms like iron bands. Six others form up with him, four Macks and two Achaeans. They are stowing their spears and gathering ropes, which they work skillfully and swiftly into nooses. No one gives us orders or shows us what to do. The others keep their swords, so we keep ours.

Lucas catches up to Barrel as we start out.

"What do we do with the women?"

The corporal stops.

"Well," he says, "you ain't gonna propose to 'em."

7.

The cordon force comes down the hill in great skimming strides, crossing the ground like the shadow of the moon. I have never seen men move so swiftly or so silently.

Afghan villages are laid out in circles like forts. A mud-brick wall rings all. Our men vault this in scores, like water over the lip of a dam. Lucas and I scramble behind, trying to keep Barrel in sight. Our job is not to kill anyone; we are too green to be entrusted with such responsibility. Just corral the women and children and hold them to be sold later as slaves. We top the wall at a dead run. Two dogs sprawl with their throats slashed; our fellows' work to silence these sentries. Inside are more walls. The place is a hive of kitchen gardens and sheepfolds. We stumble over goats and into wicker cotes for pullets and geese.

Cries have started now, our men's and the enemies'. Hounds bawl everywhere. You get into an Afghan house through the court.

These are wattle and thatch. Our men set the roofs on fire as they burst through. Our mob races into the south quarter of the town. Barrel is shouting, pointing to a row of hovels against the fort wall.

"Take them as they come out!"

Matrons and urchins pour from the blazing huts. Barrel and others herd them into the sheep pens along the wall. In moments our squad has a dozen, all wailing in terror, with more flooding in.

I turn back toward the village. Horses fill every lane. The foe is bolting, barefoot, half naked. Our fellows lance them with the half-pike or tear them from their ponies' backs with grapnel hooks. It is simultaneously extraordinary and appalling to see how efficiently our Macks work this. They slaughter an entire male household with barely a sound, so swiftly that the wives and infants are cast into dumbstruck shock. It is the kill of wolves or lions, the cold kill of predation. It is work.

Our squad holds the women and children. At our feet bleats a carpet of goats and kids, pressing themselves against the wattle walls of the pen in such terror that the whole thing bows and threatens to topple. I still have no idea what we're supposed to do. I peer across the pen to Barrel. Suddenly one of the dames pulls something from beneath her garment and thrusts it into his belly.

Barrel does not move, simply looks down with an expression of bland startlement, then lifts his eyes to the face of the matron, who stands motionless before him with a look of equal astonishment. She has stabbed him.

Barrel has his sword in his right hand. Absent all haste, he seizes the dame with his left hand by the fabric of her headdress and, in one short punch, drives the iron butt of his weapon into the center of her forehead. I turn to Lucas. We can hear the woman's skull split all the way across the pen.

At once every Mack and Achaean turns in slaughter upon his captives. In moments, twenty women have become carcasses. Blood spills in quantities as if as many great wine jars had been tipped over at once. There is no struggle, for so swiftly and lethally do the Macedonians perform their labor that the victims have been stripped of life before they can even cry out. By no means is the act impelled by bloodlust, nor is satisfaction taken from it. On the contrary, the Macks evince exasperation, because this lot of females could have been sold for good money.

I am paralyzed with horror. It is one thing to recount such a holocaust from the secure remove of memory and another to behold it before one's eyes. An Afghan woman clings to my knees, crying out in supplication. Two children bury their faces in her dress.

"Dice her!" a man's voice bellows at me. It is one of the Macks I don't know. Knuckles is his name. Lucas has moved beside me. "Obey, Matthias!" I turn to him as if in a dream. What shall I do? I am certainly not going to harm this poor, desperate mother.

A blow spins me round. Knuckles again. "Are you trying to kill me?" he roars. I have no idea what he's talking about. He wallops me, an elbow to the jaw. As I reel I see him turn his blade upon the matron while her babes shrill in terror.

Lucas hauls me clear. We are outside the pens now. Mack cavalry is everywhere. You can see the foe by dozens, mounted, streaming away across the hills. Our fellows go after them.

I bolt through the streets. I am on my own now, striding between baked-brick hovels. Somehow I have lost my weapon. Macks in twos and threes dash past, trapping Afghans in dead ends and cutting them down. The foe—those butchers, that is, who have massacred our comrades in the desert—have all fled. What's left is the village, the native yeomen who have given them sanctuary. I stalk through the chaos of downed walls and overturned carts. I understand that I have committed a capital felony by hesitating in the sheep pens. If one wench has a weapon, they all do. Immediate action must be taken. A soldier who cannot be counted on by his mates is more dangerous than an enemy. I grasp this. I keep running. In a lane I see Amyntas the sapper lance an Afghan low in the back. He is aiming between the shoulder blades, but as the man clambers up a wall, trying to escape, Amyntas's nine-footer plunges into the meat of his buttocks, through the bowl of his hip, and out his belly. The man screams and falls back; Amyntas's shaft snaps as the impaled Afghan's weight twists it over. The poor fellow's entrails spill from the ghastly gash opened by this plunge; they catch on the ladder beneath him, which is not a proper ladder but just a debarked tree with half-branches extending as steps. The man struggles to collect his guts, stuffing them back inside himself, all the while crying in horror. I turn and run. In the street more scenes of slaughter present themselves. I am trying to flee from the sight of them, in fear that their apparition will drive me mad. At the same time I know my mates will notice if I flee, so I seek to make my flight appear purposeful. That I am alone and apart from my unit is a whipping offense; that I have lost my weapon means death. And I have no blood on me. This is even worse. It gives me away. Everyone else is slathered with the stuff. I think frantically: Where can I get some blood to smear on myself?

A fist seizes me from behind. Tollo. He has found me out. Without a word he drives me out of the lane and into a dirt courtyard. Half a dozen Macks fill the space. Tollo propels me through the low entry of a hut, into a cramped dark room. I crack my skull so hard on the lintel it nearly knocks me cold. Tollo shoves me toward something in the center of the room. A man. A striking-looking Afghan, probably fifty, held by two Macks I don't recognize. The captive's teeth have been knocked out; his mouth is a mass of blood.

He's on his knees. Tollo seizes my right hand and shoves the hilt of a gut-cutter, the short Spartan-type sword, into it.

No need to issue an order. What I must do is clear.

I cannot.

"Air him out!" Tollo bawls at me. How? I have no idea what type of blow to strike. The Afghan's eyes fasten onto mine. He says something in his tongue that I can't understand. I feel Tollo's blade touch my neck. The old man repeats his curse, shouting now.

I thrust my blade into his gut. But I have not struck hard enough; the man squirms sideways with a cry; I feel my edge glance off the cage of his ribs and squirt free. I have not even drawn blood. Tollo cuffs me hard, appending a sheaf of obscenities. I can hear men laughing behind me. I feel a burning shame. The two Macks who hold the old man wrest him back before me. He is spitting into my face now, screaming that same oath. I seize my hilt with both hands and drive the blade, uppercutting, into his belly. But now I have pushed too far. The swordpoint has run clear through him and shot out the far side. It is jammed between the ribs of his back. The blade is stuck. I can't get it out. I hear the two Macks behind me, convulsed with hysterics. Tollo pummels me again. I set my heel on the old man's chest and haul the sword clear. His guts open, but he loses not a jot of animation. He continues to spit and curse me.

I raise the weapon and plunge it, aiming for the big artery of the foe's thigh, but somehow I cut not him but myself. A gash opens on my right leg, from which blood sheets in quantities unimaginable. I am beside myself with shame, mortification, fear, rage, and grief. Now even Tollo is laughing. Somehow a dog has got into the room. It sets up a dreadful racket. The Afghan keeps spitting on me. A form moves into my vision above me and on my left. I feel, more than see, a fist seize the old man by the hair; the form delivers one powerful backhand slash, then a second and third. The captive's head comes off. Marrow gushes from the cervical spine, painting the killer's feet.

It is Flag. He drops the head; it plops onto the floor with the sound of a squashed melon. The Macks release the headless body. It pitches forward onto me, sheeting blood from the void of its neck. I puke up everything I have eaten for the last three days.

Outside, I am aware of the sorry spectacle I present. Unlike my veteran countrymen, whose spear hands and smock fronts are lacquered like skilled workmen of the slaughterhouse, I am soaked from thigh to heel with alien blood and with my own, and with vomit, piss, and dirt. Lucas stanches my wound. I recognize the Mack colonel Bullock as he passes with several officers, eyeing me with bemusement and contempt.

"What's this then?" he inquires.

Tollo emerges from the hut. "The New Corps."

Bullock shakes his head. "God help us."

8.

I am too ashamed to take chow that night. Tollo has to order me. I strip my clothes but can't wash them. "Burn 'em," says Flag.

Our outfit is on the trot two hours before dawn, Lucas and I mounted on *yaboos*, with our pack-asses with the trailers following on. Chase-riders of our outfit have kept up all night with those Afghans who got away. They guide us by stations. The enemy's numbers are about fifty, half horseback and half on foot; we are above two hundred, all mounted, leaving aside those wounded and others left behind to hold the village and to raze three more settlements down-valley.

We ride four days. The word for that country is *tora balan*, "black stones." Waterless badlands creased by serried basalt ridges. It's like riding down the streets of a city. You proceed by canyons pinched between ridges, whose courses may be blind or dry or both.

Ten times a day we backtrack out of dead ends. Our party has Afghan guides, but they're worthless except to find water and forage, and the only reason they do this is so they themselves don't starve. Our mounts wear down after the second day. The pursuit looks more like a death march. At night we collapse like corpses.

I haven't slept since the village. When I close my eyes I hear women screaming and see the old man pitch headless into my lap.

I have resolved to murder no innocents. I can tell this to no one, not even Lucas. I try but he will not hear it.

"Did you kill anyone in the village?" I ask as we settle the first night, apart from the others, into our bedrolls. He did not. I ask what he will do.

"What do you mean?"

"Next time. What will you do?"

My friend kicks his groundcloth open.

"What will I do? I'll tell you what I'll do. Exactly what *you'll* do. I'll do what they tell me to. I'll do what Flag and Tollo tell me to!"

He hears the anger in his voice and looks away, ashamed.

"Don't bring this up anymore, Matthias. I don't want to hear it. Whatever you're thinking, keep it to yourself!"

And he pulls his ground cover over him and turns his back.

I am thinking that we are like criminals. When a new man is initiated into the confederacy of murderers, his seniors make him commit the same crime they have. Now he is as guilty as they. He cannot turn on them. He is one of them.

I tell this to Flag. "You're still thinking," he says.

The sixth noon we top a rise and there they are—a ragged column of shoeless, dismounted fugitives. About two dozen, tracking single-file along the base of a black stone ridge. Afghans look different from Macks at a distance. A column of ours would bristle with spearshafts and lanceheads. The Afghan fights with bow and sling, and with three knives—small, medium, and large—which he carries along with his mooch in a belt-sash called a *gitwa*.

The Afghans get away. When we rush them, they climb like goats, slinging boulders down behind them and setting off slides, which start out as pea-rollers and build into avalanches by the time they drive us onto our bellies in the scree. A rock the size of an army kettle screams past my ear, hurtling like a sling bullet. Horses can't climb that shingle; we have to chase on foot. We don't come within a hundred feet of the foe. He tops the crest and turns into smoke.

We chase him two more days, on foot now, leading our exhausted ponies. Our guides have vanished. We're lost. Everything turns now on finding water; if we spot a trickle at noon, we don't dare chase too far, for fear of finding no more and not making it back by night. Making camp beside a mudhole the sixth evening, Flag sends me and all the other rookies searching for a spring. I'm by myself, tramping down a dry canyon. I come round a corner. Ten feet away, an Afghan squats in the dust, taking a shit.

My first impulse is to apologize. It occurs to me, with ridiculous blandness, that this is the enemy. He's staring at me, as frozen with astonishment as I am. I want to shout for my mates. Nothing comes. Terror has stricken me mute.

The Afghan is on his feet now. He's about thirty, with black eyes set in a beard as dense as a curry brush. I'm paralyzed. I think: Maybe I can scare him. I lunge two steps, thrusting my half-pike. Fear fills his eyes. He gulps one breath and hurls himself at me. Before I can think, he has catapulted past my spearpoint; he seizes the shaft in both fists. He pulls. I pull. We're having a tug-of-war.

The fellow is shouting now. It occurs to me that he must have been standing sentry. There's probably an Afghan camp a hundred feet round the corner.

Now I'm screaming. Flag! Tollo! The Afghan releases my spear-shaft and flings himself on me. He seems to have forgotten he has weapons. His fingers claw at my eye sockets, his teeth sink into my shoulder. We tumble together in the dust, which is fine as powder and hot as ashes in the sun. I am not frightened now. I am embarrassed. The idea that I will die in this ludicrous manner propels me to prodigies. I lurch free. Both hands are empty. I feel naked and blind with rage at my own stupidity. The Afghan has found his dagger. I grab a rock the size of a boot. The man thrusts at me; I feel his blade tangle in my cloak as I smash the stone with all my strength into his face. I can hear his teeth shatter. He reels and falls. I drop on him with my full weight, breastbone to breastbone.

I beat his brains out with the stone. It takes no time. I feel the skull crack and the hot soup gush over my fingers. Voices cry above me. Three men of the Afghans sprint into view just as Tollo, Rags, and two mercs whose names I don't know race up from behind me.

Fear, men say, is the most primal emotion. I don't believe it. Shame is. My feeling as Tollo bolts past after the foe is one of joy and relief, that my senior sergeant has seen me take down my man, however clumsily, and profound release that my humiliation from the village has been at least partly effaced.

More of our fellows pound past. I join the pack. Flag and Lucas sprint ahead. I experience elation, not so much to have slain a man as to have survived him trying to slay me. I race down the canyon. In a shaft of sunlight squats the Afghan camp. Our fellows fall on the foe like wolves. I plunge into the melee. I want frantically to kill again, as quickly as possible and as many of the enemy as I can, not out of lust for blood, but because I can feel the return of my own terror, looming moments away like a wave. I must perform some act of valor before it crashes over me. I dash past a hollow in the canyon wall; two mercs have pinned a lone Afghan but hang back at full shafts'-length, poking at him with their lanceheads. My appearance tips the tide. Three-on-one, we spit the poor fellow like a fish on a spear. He thrashes, impaled, struggling to twist free of our shafts buried in his guts. "Kill him!" all three of us are shouting preposterously. We drive the man back against the canyon wall till we can feel our spearheads, through his belly, scraping stone. His eyes are so human! He is a man, not an animal. The sight of his agony wrenches my heart. A thrust from the first merc finishes him; he drops, dead weight. My mates dance over him, a jig less of triumph than of release from fear. I shout something and haul my comrades into the pursuit. To my astonishment they follow me.

The day ends with a horse chase, in which Stephanos and six of our mercs run down the last fugitives. They bring back four prisoners. Our kill is seventeen. We suffer one dead (the lead merc who bolted past me alongside Tollo) and three wounded, one of them my mate Boxer, breaking his ankle in a fall. Night descends. Our fellows make prizes of the dead men's weapons. They wolf a meal of the enemy's mooch and toast their backs around blazes of his firewood. Two Afghans have fallen by my hand this day. Later, I will see their faces in my dreams. Later, remorse will torment me. Later, but now. Now I am happy. I feel pride as I abrade my forearms with Afghan dust, chafing off the blood of men who would have killed me and my comrades if they could. Sleep finds me guiltless and unrepentant. I have never been happier in my life.

.

9.

The distance our column has covered in six nights chasing the foe, it takes nearly twice as long to traverse returning; we are so exhausted and so is our stock. We have to link up with our other patrols. We can't track as the hawk flies but have to detour from village to village to fill our bellies.

One of the chores of a rookie is to forage for food. In our litter, it's Lucas and me who draw this duty. Bring back dinner! Get us something to eat! The practice of "living off the land" is indispensable, we see, to a young trooper's education. It teaches him how to rough up civilians, intimidate farmers and housedames. The youth learns how to tear up a floor, rip open a roof, how to shake people down. It trains him to take nothing at face value, not the weeping grandmother, the pleading wife, the starving urchin. They're all lying. They've all got mooch.

On the ninth noon returning to Artacoana, a messenger gallops up, mounted on the most spectacular piece of horseflesh I have ever seen. He is a full captain of Alexander's Companions, bringing orders from the king himself. Three Afghan guides accompany him, perched on plug *yaboos* that look like hounds alongside the captain's thoroughbred. But these ponies can fly. While the captain confers with Tollo and Stephanos, our mob grills the scrubs.

Alexander is here, they tell us. At Artacoana. Informed by fast couriers of Satibarzanes' and Spitamenes' insurrection, the king has broken off his eastward advance. He has turned about, leaving the heavy corps with his general Craterus, while he with the cavalry and light troops has crossed 180 miles of desert in three days. The rebel horse has shown its heels at his approach. Alexander has cornered the foot troops, thirteen thousand, atop a natural fortress called the Mother's Breast. If the insurgents will accept him as sovereign, Alexander has pledged, all may return in peace to their homes. The foe has sent back a gutted dog. It means go to hell.

Our own orders, delivered by the Companion captain, are not to return to Artacoana but to make all speed to the site of the original massacre, secure the place, and protect the corpses of our countrymen from further desecration. We are to remain on-site until Alexander himself can conclude his business with the foe and arrive to tender proper honors to the fallen. Two of the Afghans on *yaboos* will guide us.

The site, when we reach it three dusks later, is in a narrow throat between granite crags. An understrength company of Arcadian mercenaries mans a perimeter. They are ecstatic to see us, as our numbers will hold at bay the droves of Afghan dames who have already picked the gorge clean of plunder and still loiter on the high-lines, awaiting the chance to dash in and make off with the odd buckle or lancehead, whose bronze and iron are worth fortunes in this desert, not to mention their value as trophies.

The Arcadians tell us what happened to our countrymen. Those who survived the initial ambush were beaten and stripped naked; the enemy staked them out on the earth, spread-eagled on their backs, and drove long knives into their thighs, ripping gashes to the bone. They disemboweled our fellows, put out their eyes, and hacked off their genitals. Then they painted them with terebinth oil—turpentine—and set them on fire. All this while they were still alive.

It is the women and children, we learn from the Afghan guides, who have committed these atrocities upon our countrymen. This, they tell us, is the custom of the country. Captives are turned over to the clan females for their pleasure. The tribes do this not only to us but to each other.

The Arcadians have collected the bodies of our comrades in the center of the camp. This is so the Afghan women can't skulk in after dark and plunder them further. The corpses are wrapped, and we newcomers make no attempt to peek under.

After dark our female besiegers begin to keen. A bloodcurdling ululation commences on one flank of the gorge, answered by an equally mane-blanching chorus from the other. Soon the whole pass is wailing in some ungodly primordial cacophony.

"Is that jackals or people?" Flea asks.

Lucas glances to me. "Jackals would sound more human."

The evening is warm but we're all shivering. In camp it is custom for rookies only to stand sentry; this night the vets take their turn too.

Sometime in the third watch an Afghan vixen is slain by two of Bullock's grooms; she has crawled in, past the guard, all the way to the picketed horses, one of which she is in the act of hamstringing, just a pebble's toss from the commander's tent. Next morning, I and several others are detailed to remove the bodies of our countrymen to an even more secure site in the camp. We grab the first wrapped form to lift it; it plunges free of its shroud, in sections, at our feet. The man has been beheaded and cut off at the knees.

10.

Our column returns to Artacoana to find the lower city abandoned and the upper city reduced to rubble. In our absence the natives have risen and been crushed. East in the hills, the siege of the Mother's Breast is over. Alexander and his elite corps have already started south, into Drangiana, in pursuit of the rebel Barsaentes and the cavalry commander, Spitamenes.

It is Spitamenes' men, we learn, whom our pursuit party has been chasing. The original massacre was his work. By his orders our luckless countrymen were betrayed; at his command were they turned over for mutilation.

He is clever, too, this villain. While our chase companies have spent themselves on his false trail into the desert, he himself has doubled back with his main force. He has led Artacoana into revolt.

Where is he now? Fled again.

I have never seen a city devastated. The lane where our bootmaker's shop had stood is now stone and ash. The tannery district lies in ruins; kites and packs of wild dogs colonize the neighborhoods of the wealthy. Only the parks survive unscathed. Tent camps fill them; maids carrying water in earthen jugs shuttle back and forth to the river.

Our column of replacements still hasn't linked with Alexander. We catch up instead with the heavy divisions under Craterus, which have returned to Artacoana, trailing Alexander. The siege train is just now loading out to move south; it is their artillery that has taken the city down. We inspect their handiwork. Half the city walls have been battered to powder; the timber mantlets remain, shielding the trenches from which our engineers and bucket-men have excavated their undermines. A dozen great stone-throwers, quarter-milers, lie burned and broken, the result apparently of sallies in force by the foe. The entire pine summit of the Mother's Breast has been scorched to cinder.

Our outfit is given ten days to rest and refit. We are permitted to go up to the citadel and take a look. You can see where lanes have been barricaded by the foe with wagons and wicker hurdles. All are ash now. The successive ramparts, which are not stone but only mud-brick, lie beaten apart like children's castles. Seared skeletons of the enemy litter rooms as black as the insides of smithies; your tread crunches over brittle bones.

We trek out, sightseers, to the Mother's Breast. This is a spectacularly defensible outcrop, stronger than the city itself. Dense woods stud its flanks. Bluffs front the west. A dry course marks the eastern slope, which is less precipitous; two bridges span this. We can see where Alexander had these escape routes cut to trap the enemy, and where he massed his own troops along the cliffs. He waited for the wind to come round out of the west, then ordered his sappers to light off the dense, desiccated pines. He left an avenue of egress on the eastern flank, where the ground funneled the foe in flight into a rocky defile; he stationed his javelin men on the high ground close in and his cavalry on the flanks farther down. Their orders were to let no man escape. When the city fell the next day, our fellows put to the sword all males of military age and sold into slavery every woman and child.

Craterus has orders, now, to pay out the wider region for its complicity in the revolt. Our outfit is integrated into his corps. We will serve as blocking forces. Eleven villages line the valley. Our companies' task is to cut off avenues of escape. Craterus's men will take care of the villages.

I have never seen warriors as terrifying as these. They are of a whole order beyond Flag, Tollo, and Stephanos. They make no show of their prowess. This is work to them. These are veterans who learned their trade in the Balkan Wars under King Philip; they were old hands when Alexander was a child. Their arms broke Athens and Thebes and humbled mighty Sparta. Persia and her empire have fallen before them. The victories of the Granicus, Issus, and Gaugamela stand as their trophies; it is they who sacked Tyre and Gaza, captured Babylon and Susa and Persepolis.

These Afghan villages are scrap meat to them. They cordon two in a morning and scorch them to ashes by noon. The foe falls before them like wheat. It does the enemy no good to hide in garner or grain crib; Craterus's men drag him forth and gut him where he stands. Village elders confront them in indignation, cursing the invaders in a tongue they can't understand and care nothing for. The Macks drive them to their knees and butcher them like hogs. It is farmer's work. Slaughter.

Lucas and I look on in horror from our posts on the perimeter. Most appalling is the outcry of the women, rounded up for the slavers' train. The dames howl like animals; nothing can make them stop. Prayers to heaven ascend amid swirling dust and columns of black smoke. We herd the fugitives like cattle. Those that get away, we leave for wolves and crows. Mute urchins gape with eyes dark as death, while black-cawled crones lift palms to the Almighty to call down damnation upon us.

The operation takes eleven days. When we return to Arta-coana, the engineers have laid out a new city. The metropolis, to be called Alexandria-in-Areia, is a model of our young king's shrewd-ness and of his reckoning of the weakness and cupidity of the foe.

All Afghans look alike to us scuffs; we can't tell one from another. But Alexander calculates more cannily. He sees this coun-try as a devil's barnyard of contending clans and *khels*, who have warred with each other for centuries. The tribes of southern Areia have long coveted this valley, which has been held, beneath Persian sway, by their hated northern rivals. Why not let the new kickers have a crack at it? Why should we Macks spend blood and treasure to suppress the aboriginals? Let their foes do it for us.

Alexander puts out the call, not only for masons, carpenters, and teamsters, to whom he promises work at wages unheard-of in these kingdoms, but for settlers and pioneers as well. To these he pledges land and pasturage, rights of way, warrants of exclusivity for trade and commerce. The southern tribes flood in, delirious at the prospect of lording it over their northern adversaries. Within days the construction site is overrun with every able-bodied tribesman in the region and half the respectable women, who serve as cooks and tailors, laundresses, nurses, vendors, seamstresses (a vital function, sewing tents and pack covers, ground rolls, straps, and panniers). Dispossessed females flock here too, *peshnarwan*, "those left be-hind," to perform such services as their more fortunate sisters will not.

Our king's scheme works. What had been, days before, the site of a grisly valley-wide massacre has become a burgeoning boom-town. New arrivals have displaced the old, all owing their good fortune to Alexander. Jobs are plentiful. Pay and hopes are high. By art as much as by might, our king has brought the country to its knees.

Those elements of the army not employed in providing security for the construction, which means us (Craterus's brigades having marched south to overhaul Alexander and the elite elements), are kept busy on night raids, mopping up the last of the resistance. We strike downvalley, the same villages Craterus's men devastated before, where Afghan sons who have taken to the hills return after dark to visit their wives and mothers, to have wounds tended, and to get food or news. We kick down their gates and drag them into the dark. Orders have been issued not to put captives to the sword in front of their women. Better to haul them off into the desert, leaving their ends unknown; this produces a more abiding terror because of the natives' belief in djinns and demons. The scent of blood draws wolves, who scavenge the corpses. The packs learn to follow us. Their yellow eyes glitter in the torchlight. They cannot be driven off, even when pelted with stones.

It is Lucas who hates this work the most. His eyes have gone dark and hollow. "Are we more civilized than the foe?" he demands one night as we young men sprawl exhausted beside some trail, trekking back from the evening's labor. "By what definition of virtue do we call ourselves soldiers and the enemy savages?"

Boxer warns Lucas to keep it down. Officers might hear and think he takes the Afghans' side.

"Fuck the Afghans," Lucas says. "I don't care an iron spit for these murderous cowards. I'm talking about *us*. You and me, Boxer—and Matthias and Rags and every other young scuff thrown into this hell. What's happening to *us*?"

The fact is clear, though no rookie other than Lucas owns the bowels to give it voice, that we have entered a crucible of the soul, of war's horror, and that it will change us. It has changed us already. Where will it end? Who will we be then? Myself, I feel its weight nightlong inside my skull, as spectacles of slaughter re-present themselves with such ghastliness that I dare not even shut my eyes.

"Part of me is dying," says Lucas. "Something evil grows in its place. I don't know what it is, but I fear and hate it. I fear and hate myself."

Lucas calls us all on our jockeying within formation. He has seen us edge away from the fore line, where the butchery takes place. He's right. The gruesomeness of war has hit us hard. Many can't sleep. Others have withdrawn into silence and self-isolation. "We're all thinking the same thing," Lucas says. " 'What have I gotten myself into? Can I endure it? Will it drive me mad?' I see it on all our faces; we're running schemes in our heads: 'How can I get out? What act will it take to get me sent home?' "

"Not all of us," says Boxer. Rags and Flea back him up.

"What about you, Matthias? How can you endure this?"

"My father and brothers," I respond with truth, though I have not even thought about it before this moment. All three are warriors and heroes. I would sooner die than prove unworthy of them. Shame at my failure in the first village (and other acts of reluctance and irresolution since then) has made me, if anything, even harder on myself—to banish doubt, to be a soldier, to reject all such arguments as my friend voices now. "We can't let ourselves think that way. This is war, Lucas!"

"Yes," my friend answers. "But what kind of war?"

BOOK
TWO

A New Kind of War

11.

Alexander enters from the wing and mounts to the stage with a single athletic bound. A sigh expels from the company. There he is!

Twenty-six days' trek has taken us to Phrada, southern Afghanistan. On our right, the column skirts the Dasht-i-Margo, the Desert of Death. To the left ascend the foothills of the Paropamisus ("that over which the eagle cannot fly") and, beyond, the shoulders of the Hindu Kush. We can see the peaks a hundred miles off, already mantled with snow. Here, on the military highway, the grit underfoot is blistering. The night crawls with adders and scorpions.

It is autumn. The Wind of a Hundred and Twenty Days has begun. For four days in Phrada, our companies—those Macks who will be integrated into the regular corps—are assembled at dawn to be addressed by our king. For four days Alexander doesn't show. We stand down each time, to hunker wretchedly in the furnace-blast of the gale.

What makes Afghanistan so miserable is there's no shelter. The wind howls out of the mountains with not a twig to break its rush. Terrain is spectacular, but its beauty, if you can call it that, is stern and unforgiving. No trees intercept the rain, which descends, when it does, in volumes unimaginable. In the hot season you bind covers round every surface of metal exposed to the sun. To touch them unprotected blisters you to the bone. Now comes the wind.

To trek in such a gale is like marching in a tunnel. The universe contracts to the cylinder between your muffled eyes and the rucksack of the man in front of you. Where are we? As usual, nobody tells us. On a downgrade somewhere east of Lake Seistan, a colorful-looking fellow overhauls the column, driving a two-mule wagon. "Halloo, the highway!" he bawls, trying to use his downhill momentum to work through the jam. We are jostled onto the shoulder. The tourist is a chronicler, one of the cohort of freeloading correspondents who have attached themselves to Alexander's party, pledging to record for posterity all exploits of the expedition. Soldiers love and hate these half-obol Homers, whom they perceive as spectating from safety upon that stage where they, the troops, bleed real blood. Still they are here with us, these ink-mice, eating the same dust and shaking the same serpents out of their boots. Besides, they know the news.

"Hey, wax-scratcher!" Tollo hails the fellow. "What's the story!"

The chronicler brightens, hearing our sergeant's brogue. "Are you Macks?" The column is all Achaeans and Lycians. "What are you doing back here?"

"You tell us, you're the one in the know."

"Where are you from?"

This is the question all correspondents ask soldiers. It makes suckers of us, as it must every other mob of witless scuffs. We shout

out our hometowns, as if we believe our new crony will record them in his dispatches and make us famous.

The correspondent's name is Costas. He has the dandy's look of an actor or musician; the kind of good-looking, glib fellow who has never plowed a row in his life. Like many of his colleagues, he affects a soldierly aspect; he wears a military cloak and a desert cap with a floppy brim. "Why don't you write a book about *us?*" Rags calls to him. "We're the real army."

"I would," the chronicler laughs. "But who'd read it?"

The column pushes south to Phrada. Finally, on the fifth dawn, our king's standard appears. Royal pages and knights of the Life Guard shuttle us again into a stockade in the lee of a scarp, a site that had been a ring for horse auctions. The gale relents. Alexander enters.

It is as if the sun has been lowered in on a rope. All gloom is dispelled; the daylight, which had been flat and featureless, turns golden bright. I have not expected our lord to be so handsome. He wears a plain cavalry cloak with no insignia of rank or kingship. He is taller than I had expected. I think: This must have been what it was like to behold Perseus or Bellerophon, or Achilles himself. Citations erupt and will not cease despite the king's extended arms and his calls for silence. He grins. He looks impossibly young. His athletic bearing augments the impression of boyishness, and his clean-shaven good looks enlarge the sense of youth and vigor.

"Gentlemen!" We read his lips, though no sound can be heard above the clamor. "My friends, please . . ."

When the uproar abates, Alexander welcomes us, informing us that we are no longer replacements. We are soldiers of the expeditionary force. We shall commence drawing combat pay from the date of our arrival at Artacoana, and all expenses of the out-march will be reimbursed. We will be assigned to regiments. I witness for the first time that faculty of the king's, which has been so much remarked upon, that is, his knowledge of men's names and faces. He scans the foremost ranks, greeting fellows by name and patronymic and remarking with an easy jest upon older brothers or fathers who have served with the corps from its inception and exhorting them, the newcomers, to live up to their elders' fame. "Believe me, brothers, there is still plenty of glory to be won—and plenty of loot!"

The hall erupts again. Alexander speaks briefly of the current campaign and lays out his design for the operations to come. The fight, he says, will soon be over. All that remains is the pursuit of an enemy who is already on the run and the killing or capturing of commanders who are already beaten. We will be out of here by fall, he pledges, and on to India, whose riches and plunder will dwarf even the vast treasure of Persia. "That said," Alexander adds, "no foe, however primitive, should be taken lightly, and we shall not commit that error here."

At once his expression becomes grave. He strides to the prow of the platform, which had been the auctioneer's stand, and steps out onto its cornice, as if to get as close as possible to his neophyte troopers.

"My friends, brief as your sojourn in the Afghan kingdoms has been, you cannot have failed to notice that we are fighting, here, a different kind of war. You may feel, some of you, that this is not what you signed up for. These are not the fields of glory of which you dreamed. Understand: The actions we take in this campaign are as legitimate as those enacted in any other. This is not conventional warfare. It is unconventional. And we must fight it in an unconventional way.

"Here the foe will not meet us in pitched battle, as other armies we have dueled in the past, save under conditions of his own choosing. His word to us is worthless. He routinely violates truces; he betrays the peace. When we defeat him, he will not accept our dominion. He comes back again and again. He hates us with a passion whose depth is exceeded only by his patience and his capacity for suffering. His boys and old men, even his women, fight us as combatants. They do not do this openly, however, but instead present themselves as innocents, even as victims, seeking our aid. When we show compassion, they strike with stealth. You have all seen what they do to us when they take us alive.

"Please note, my friends, that I have made good and generous offers to the native peoples. I intend them no harm. I would make them our allies and friends. I abhor this kind of fighting. If an alternative existed, I would seize it at once. But the foe will not have it. We have seen his methods. We have no choice but to adapt to them."

The king speaks of will—our own and the enemy's. The foe, he declares, has no chance of overcoming us in the field. But if he can sap our resolution by his doggedness, his relentlessness; if he can appall us by his acts of barbarity, he can, if not defeat us, then prevent us from defeating him. Our will must master the enemy's. Our resolve must outlast his.

"The types of operations we are now compelled to wage; methods of pursuit, of capture and interrogation; the treatment of so-called noncombatants; all actions we take in this theater—these are war too. And you are the warriors who must perform these acts. That said, I am not insensitive to the fact that numbers of you have fathers and brothers who have sought and found glory in an entirely different kind of war, and that you may not have the stomach for this sterner, less illustrious type. It is not my object to compel you. Nor will I force a voice vote here on the spot, for I know that, with the influence of your comrades upon you, many will cry out with enthusiasm for any course I suggest, and this will intimidate others and carry them, like one of these swift Afghan rivers, along a course they do not in their hearts wish to follow.

"Therefore let this assembly conclude. Let the evening and the morrow pass. Take time, each of you, to consult his own heart, to confer with his mates. Decide what you want to do. Do you, then, speak in private with your sergeants and warrant officers. If you believe you cannot participate in this war, either the corps will find other ways to use you, in supply, support, or garrison service, or, if you so desire, you may join one of the columns returning home, with no hard feelings and full pay for time in service, including the trek to Macedon. Full pay and bonuses for those who remain."

At this, the assembly explodes. Alexander again calls for silence.

"But if you elect to remain, my friends, know what I demand of you: that you commit yourselves wholeheartedly to this undertaking. No grumbling. No holding back. Fight alongside your officers and comrades; fight alongside your king. Know that it is my object to bring into subjection all lands formerly held by the throne of Persia. That means India. It means Afghanistan. Make no mistake, this country is vital to our cause. It constitutes the gateway to the Punjab, the indispensable highway between West and East; it must be subdued before we can move on.

"More important perhaps, the Bactrian plain has been for centuries the invasion route for Scythian nomads. These barbarians have ravaged this country again and again, sweeping down out of the Wild Lands to the north and fleeing back into them. Along this frontier, two hundred years ago, Cyrus the Great erected a wall of forts to keep out these savages. Here he himself fell, cut down by the horse tribesmen we call Massagetae. He failed. We shall not. We will pursue the barbarian into his sanctuaries and strike such terror that he will beg for peace. This country must be secured. That is what you are here to do, and that is what we shall do. When the job is done, we will cross the Hindu Kush into India, where I hope to find and to deliver into your hands not only wealth beyond even that which we now possess, but a more honorable form of enemy and a nobler kind of war.

"But before India comes Afghanistan.

"That's it, my friends. Get some meat in your bellies. Find a place to rest your bones. I know the trials of this theater are not what you expected. But you are proud sons of a celebrated nation. As your fathers and brothers have overcome every force of man or nature, so shall you, never fear. Rest today. Tomorrow you will join your regiments."

12.

We are assigned—Lucas and me and our mates Rags and Flea—to the regiment of Foot Companions under Coenus and the Persian lord Artabazus, or, more precisely, to this and its "flying column." We fall in for reconfiguration the next day. Alexander has already moved on; his fast units have made away south for the Helmand Valley and what will become the city of Kandahar.

Coenus's *taxis* is number two in the army, behind only Alexander's elite brigades. The phalanx regiments stand in a hierarchy of precedence and prestige. In conventional order of battle, the senior brigade would hold the post of honor on the extreme right of the line, abutting the Royal Guards and Alexander's Companion cavalry. In this new war, honor post means being handed the toughest and most hazardous operations, against the sternest elements of the foe.

This is not good news. For us rookies it's worse. Mired in rank sixteen, Lucas and I are condemned to eat dirt all day in column, stagger into camp hours after dark, when all hot chow is gone and every dry bedding spot preempted. As "new onions," we are slaves to every trooper senior in rank (which means the entire regiment) and obliged to mend his kit, scrounge for his forage and firewood, and stand his watch as well as our own. Worse, we are sick. Lucas ails with piles and diarrhea. I've got worms, and the soles of my feet are ribbons. To top off our misery, we have lost Flag, Tollo, and Stephanos, who have been reassigned to their original units. What can we do? In desperation, we approach our new Color Sergeant, whom the men call Thatch for the dense gray brush atop his crown, and, advertising ourselves as superior riders from cavalry-renowned Apollonia, request transfer to the unit's mounted scouts.

"So you're horsemen, are you?" our new chief inquires.

We're centaurs!

"Outstanding," says he—and assigns us as muleteers with the baggage.

Now we are truly screwed. As wranglers, we must rise three hours before dawn to rig and pack out the train, trek in the column's bung all day, then toil till midnight putting up the mules and asses. The Wind of a Hundred Twenty Days has, by our count, ninety-one still to go. Despair would finish us, except for the miracle awaiting in Kandahar.

My brother.

Elias finds me in the city. Or to be exact, Stephanos finds him. Together they track me and Lucas down in the bazaar.

What joy to see him! Elias beams. "Can this be our own Little Philosopher?" He holds me at arm's length, admiring my growth (I was fifteen the last time he saw me), then wraps me in a bone-crushing clinch. My brother weeps. I do too. "I never expected," he says, "to see you alive."

"Nor I you."

My brother is a celebrity. Two Silver Lions and one Gold stud his scarlet cloak of Companion cavalry; his belt of snakeskin holds so many "spits"—iron rivets, one for each enemy slain—it seems made of metal. His mount (his seventh, he reports, since leaving Macedon) is a gorgeous chestnut mare called Meli, "Honey," with a white blaze and four white stockings. He has two more in his string, geldings even handsomer, and a gorgeous Afghan mistress to boot; I will meet her tonight, when we celebrate. Elias, it seems, has only one more day in the city. Then he and his company—he is a warrant officer of Forward Operations—must head north up the valley of the Arghandab River, into the mountains, seeking alliances and pledges of supplies from the local *maliks*.

"Then the army *is* going over?" asks Lucas, confirming rumors we've been hearing for days.

Alexander's aim, Elias bears out, is to cross the Hindu Kush before snow closes the passes. He will invade Afghanistan from the south—not the north, as previously planned—and attack Bessus and Spitamenes on the Bactrian plain. "Get yourself a fleece wrapper and stout snow boots. The lowest pass, they say, is two miles high."

Elias leaves us in the market. Our chore that day, assigned by Thatch, is to hire sixteen new mules. "Get me beasts that can carry a load," our chief has instructed Lucas and me that morning.

"Yes, Color Sergeant."

"And, lads . . ."

We turn back.

"Pick some that look tasty. In case we need to eat 'em."

The column, as configured now, employs thirty thousand horses and mules. But all have been hired out of Phrada and villages along the western track. Their owners won't let us take them over the mountains, fearing to lose them to the cold or to bandits, and they won't go up with them themselves. So the corps' forward scouts put out the word for more. The region responds. On the littoral before the village of Gram Tal, the livestock market sprawls for miles. Tents and *bichees*—three-sided flies, stitched of goatskin—stretch in avenues like a city. Every mule, camel, and *yaboo* for a hundred miles has been collected, with their owners putting them out to rent.

What, you ask, is the difference between a horse and a mule? A mule is easier to catch. This is no small thing when packing out in the dark. Mules are better-tempered than horses. They form attachments; you can picket the leader and leave the others free. Mules' front legs are longer than horses'; they don't balk at downhills, and their bones don't break as easily. Mules are less prone to panic. A horse mired in a snowdrift will burst its heart thrashing to get free; a mule has the sense to stand still and wait for help. Mules are more headstrong, though. A horse is loyal; if you fall and break a leg, a good mount will stick with you. A mule will give you that look that says, "Sorry, mate"—and make away at the hot trot.

If you wonder what makes Alexander's army superior to all rivals, among other things, it is this: No one ever tells you anything. You have to figure everything out for yourself. This promotes initiative. In other armies, scuffs like Lucas and me would be paralyzed to take action absent superiors' orders. In Alexander's corps, a sergeant is as ready to seize responsibility as a captain, and a private as a sergeant.

Alas, this self-initiative works against us now, as every other rear-ranker of the baggage train, dispatched on the same errand as we, either pulls rank or plain chucks us out of the public way. We are novices; the vets eat us alive. Worse, a column of twelve thousand rested troops, including all four phalanx brigades from

Ecbatana, have here caught up with the army. They need mules too. They swamp the marketplace. Lucas and I are supposed to return to camp with sixteen animals. By day's end our string numbers eight of the scruffiest plugs in Asia; we have no idea where to scrounge up the second eight. The region has been picked clean. To add to our troubles, we've had to lay out double to an Afghan stock-trader named Ashnagur, whom we call Ash, who is reaming us royally. Lucas and I have barely enough cash for two more mules. How will we get eight? Ash takes pity on us, invites us into his *bichee*, which he shares with a clan of at least twenty, for a feed of chicken and rice, with curds and plates of chupatties, flat bread, delivered by his wife or one of his daughters, we can't tell which, as all we glimpse are her hands as she passes the meal through the half-open flap. We dine on carpets on the packed-dirt floor.

"Mules can be expensive," Ash observes.

We tell him we are learning this.

"Women are cheaper."

We don't understand.

Our host mimes the hefting of a cargo pack. "Three women can carry as much as one mule and eat only half. And at night in camp," he grins, "you can get a leg over."

We find our way to my brother's quarters two hours before midnight. Elias and two other Companions have rented a house in Gram Tal, the town that will become the city of Kandahar.

The place is packed when we enter and booming with timbrel and kithara. Tapers light the hall. We can't find Elias. On campaign there is no such thing as an *andron*, a room for men only. Here wives and lovers dine at their men's shoulders. We run into Costas, the young correspondent we met on the track from Phrada. He becomes our guide. Four separate banquets pack the apartments; our countrymen are so blind and so affable, it takes us a quarter of an hour to work through to the rear chamber, where my brother and his mates host their salon.

The room is low and broad and laid out Afghan-style, no couches or chairs, everyone on carpets on the floor. Macks in various stages of inebriation litter the chamber, some passed out in corners, others sprawled against walls. The main body surrounds a low table, animated with conversation. Elias hails us. We are crunched in beside him and his lady. Costas carries a bumper of wine, which he contributes to the *krater*, to round applause. The troopers are all from F.O., Forward Operations; every man swanks the black-and-tan scarf that marks him as Reconnaissance.

My brother bawls introductions. At his back stands an Afghan *shikari*. The word means "mountain wolf." These are guides, ferocious-looking specimens who accompany all forward cavalry. I have never seen one up close. The man is between fifty and sixty, lean as a reed, with great black mustaches that he keeps rigid with paraffin. His trousers are baggy *khurgans* bloused into lambskin boots, with vest, jacket, and *pettu*, the long woolen wrap that serves as greatcoat, wind shelter, and sleeping roll. He carries the standard three Afghan knives, tucked into a crimson sash round his waist, and packs as well two javelins of cornel wood with blades of iron. Elias makes no introductions; to do so apparently would violate proper form. I know from his letters that Elias's familiarity with the northern tribes is extensive. He has fought Bactrian and Sogdian cavalry in the Babylonian and Persian campaigns, and, serving after victory as a courier to them and later an envoy, has brought in numbers for hire in special units under Alexander. Elias owns acquaintance with the two great barons, Spitamenes and Oxyartes, who ride with the pretender Bessus now on the Bactrian side of the mountains. He says nothing of this throughout the evening, nor do I observe him exchange a single word with his guide, though the man remains at his shoulder—standing, never taking a seat—all night.

I beg Elias to pull strings and get me and Lucas included in his company; we will serve even as grooms. With a laugh my brother dismisses this, citing several transparent pretexts. Clearly he is protecting me. Forward Operations is dangerous. "Drink up," he shouts. "We'll talk later."

I am astonished at the quantities of spirits my brother pours down. In Macedon, Elias was always the most moderate of topers. Now he is tight as a clam. They all are. Liquor is hard, distilled from rye and barley, fiery enough to gag a horse. I try to keep up but the room starts spinning. My brother sees and grins with delight. Sozzled as he is, he has lost no sense. When he rises to pour a libation, not a drop spills.

As the evening's revels unspool, I get a chance to study him. His hair falls in curls to his shoulders, copper shot through with gray, concealing a scar that can only be from the blow of a saber, descending from beneath his left ear, half of which has been sheared off, traversing his jaw all the way to his chin. Two fingers are missing on his left hand. His right arm is frozen at a permanent angle; when he reaches to the bowl, he has to use his shoulder or he can't make the stretch. Twice he excuses himself to relieve his bladder. Both times he can rise only with the aid of his mistress, not from intoxication, I reckon, but because the sinews of his back refuse to unseize. He notes me watching and laughs. "You disapprove my bibulations, little brother! But tomorrow at dawn, while you groan in bed with your eyes nailed shut, I'll be in the saddle, ready for anything."

I believe him. His kit is threadbare, his skin burnt to leather by the sun. He is a warrior. His mates too. None wear beards. Like

Alexander, the Companions of Forward Operations all favor the clean-shaven look.

Elias's mistress occupies the square of carpet next to mine, but, as with his guide, my brother demurs at introducing her. She is lovely, a Pactyan from the country around Ghazni, though I will not learn this till later. That she and the other wives and ladies are included in the all-male sanctuary of the drinking party is a breach of decorum unthinkable in Macedon and worthy of murder here in the East. No one notices or cares. In lulls in the revels, Elias's bride teaches me phrases in Dari. Her Greek is studded with soldiers' profanities, which she offers with a charming ingenuousness. I am falling a little in love with her myself. I cannot get her to tell me how she met my brother or under what circumstances they came to be joined. She volunteers news of our elder brother Philip, though. He has returned safely from India. He rides now with an elite detachment of mountain rangers; they are already over the Hindu Kush and into northern Afghanistan, behind enemy lines, seeking tribal alliances for Alexander. Their packhorses' bundles are freighted with gold.

Past midnight Costas the chronicler gets into a shoutdown with two of Elias's comrades. They clash over the recent plot against the king. At Phrada, Alexander has brought his commander of Companion cavalry—Philotas, son of Parmenio—before the army on charges of treason. The corps has convicted the man and put him to death. Philotas's father Parmenio, seventy years old and the army's senior general since Philip's day, has been executed as well, at Alexander's orders, though no evidence links him to his son's crime. Many in the army have voiced outrage at this. Alexander, further, has taken action against some twenty other officers who had bonds to the family of Parmenio, executing some, dismissing or imprisoning others. My brother's mates defend these acts. Such is the law of kings since before Agamemnon, declares a captain named Demetrius. "If a man plots against the throne, not only must he pay with his own life but with those of every male of his family, including infants. Otherwise, those spared will seek revenge, if not immediately, then later. Never is such action more imperative than now, with the army at war, in an enemy land."

With a smile, Costas applauds the captain's sentiments. "My friend, you cite the war between ourselves and the Afghans. That's not the campaign Alexander is waging. His war is *within the army*, between the Old Corps and the New."

The Companions will not hear Alexander's name impeached, even in jest. "Do you dare," says the captain, "call the king conspirator?"

"I remark only," replies the correspondent, "on the convenience of these convictions."

Have you not noticed, says Costas, that half the army is now foreign? The corps, which at campaign's start had been virtually all-Macedonian, has become more alien than native, more mercenary than free, more Persian and Median, Syrian, Armenian, Lydian, Cappadocian than European. "Look around you, brothers. Two-thirds of our cavalry were fighting *against us* a year ago. To whom are these foreigners loyal? That man, only, to whose clemency they owe their lives, and upon whose favor their hopes and fortunes depend."

"What is your point, friend?"

"My point, brave captain, is that this war, which all of us believed had finished half a year ago, is about to become a second war, whose end no man can see. Do you imagine that your regiments will mop up Afghanistan and be home before Frost Festival? Never! Our king fashions for himself a new army, with which he will fight here and eastward forever. Overthrowing the Persian Empire is the least of his conquests. He has vanquished *you*, and you don't even know it!"

"Do not condescend to us, thou obituarist."

It is my brother who speaks. The room turns toward him. "You have told us to look around. We say the same to you." Elias's gesture takes in the soused and sprawling company. "Here are men, damn your bones, at whose shoulders stands Death, yet who will ride out with tomorrow's dawn to face Him. What do we care where our king leads us, or against whom? He is our lord!"

At this the chamber explodes.

"His right arm has vanquished our enemies! His might has lifted us from obscurity to renown! By his will, the wide world is given into our hands! What are we without him? Where would we be, serving another?"

The hall booms with citation after citation.

"Do you know Xenophon's *Cyropaedia*?" my brother demands of the correspondent.

With you, we are not afraid, even in the enemy's land.
Without you, we are afraid, even to go home.

We part, Elias and I, beneath the stars. Tomorrow will take him away into the mountains. He clasps me in a farewell embrace. "Don't you want to know," I ask, "about Mother and Eleni?" Our younger sister.

Yes, yes, of course.

But as I tell him, I see his attention wander. The *shikari* boosts my brother's consort into the saddle. She waits. I break off.

Elias meets my eyes with an expression at once caring and stern. "Don't waste your time thinking of home, Matthias. It can't help and can only hurt."

13.

The army sets off into the Hindu Kush on a brilliant autumn morning. Ash, the Afghan muleteer, has indeed supplied the women we need to make up for the beasts we couldn't hire. Good bearers, he swears. Strong. No trouble.

I have been in Afghanistan too long.

The plan sounds good.

I like it.

Kandahar City, from which the army departs, has risen entirely new. We have built the place ourselves over twenty days, at Alexander's orders, erecting walls and palisades, laying out streets, and excavating defensive ditches. It's a tent city now, but soon settlers and immigrants will make it a real one. A garrison has been put in place, constituted of Greek mercs, disabled vets, and Macks who either wish to stay for their own reasons or whose health renders them no longer fit for service. The new city will command the river and road junctions of the lower Arghandab Valley and hold them open for trade, communication, and supply for the corps.

The city's official name is Alexandria-in-Arachosia. The natives already call it Iskandahar, "Alexander's City," after *Iskander*, the Persian version of our king's name.

Iskandahar is full of women, mostly young and all starving. They are *peshnarwan*, outcasts, dispossessed by war.

The greenbelt of southern Afghanistan is a torment of fleas and horseflies, hornets, blow-bugs, and lice. The track into the mountains winds along irrigation canals, from whose sloughs insects ascend in hissing, steaming clouds. They swarm into your mouth and eyes. They colonize your ass. Horses and mules suffer horribly. You march in full kit, legs plastered with mud (which the bugs bore through anyway) and a mesh cowl over your skull. The trail works along the Arghandab for about fifty miles, climbing steadily, before it commences the all-out ascent into the peaks. At a village called Omir Zadt, "Schoolmaster's Nose," the straight path turns to switchbacks. The column strings out over miles. Camps at night hang off the mountainside. Rain descends one minute, hail and snow the next, then all three mixed. Mules bawl all night. They smell winter coming; they want to turn back for the barn, not climb into thinner and more frigid air.

Our section, as I said, has hired female porters—eleven in all, to go with our eight mules—and two more that Ash miraculously discovers when he learns I have half a *daric* left. Nor is our outfit the only one to make use of this expedient. Every brigade has at least two hundred, all dressed in trousers with vest and *pettu*, and the rag footgear the Afghans call *pashin*.

The reason contractors take women instead of mules into the mountains is if a woman breaks down or dies, the loss is less. A mule is a serious investment. Still, one would be a liar to say his glance does not roam over these lean, dark-eyed maids. One of them, whose real name is Shinar, has been nicknamed "Biscuits" by the Macks because she makes no shame to lift her *pettu* and squat by the roadside. She is between the age of my sister and my sweetheart, about seventeen, and the only one, except a long-limbed lass named Ghilla, with the light of intelligence in her eyes. She is slender but strong. I watch her carry a sack of sesame that weighs half as much as she does. She never speaks. The fourth night I approach Ash; I want him to ask her how she has come to this life as a porter. Ash reproves me. "Such questions must never be put."

I am made to understand that the young woman's case is unexceptional. All these girls' villages have been burned, Ash declares; all their fathers and brothers driven off or slain.

"By Macks?"

"*Narik ta?*" What difference does it make?

The old man's attitude toward his charges is that they are lucky to be alive. In his eyes, he is their savior. He fills their bellies, gives them work. Who else would do this? Their own gods and ancestors have abandoned them, for crimes committed in this life or another. I ask Ash how he knows this. He elevates his palms to heaven. "If God had not wished it this way, He would not have made it so."

Ash treats the women like mules. He directs their exertions not by verbal commands, but by "gee" and "haw," driving them with the lash and halting them by blows and cuffs.

You have never seen a mule laden until you've seen an Afghan do it. The poor beasts are so overloaded they can barely totter. For women it's worse. The females are provided neither pack frames nor straps but simply handed a sack or crate and pointed up the trail. If they falter, they are beaten; if they fall out, their loads are divided among the others and they themselves left for dead.

The girl called Biscuits is the first to talk back. I chance to witness this, at a site where the trail crosses a torrent. She draws up and addresses Ash. The old villain could not have reacted with greater surprise if a mule itself had broken into speech. He seizes his *chatta*, a double rope with knots twisted into its ends. I have never witnessed such a beating. I stride to stop it. Our sergeant Thatch catches me.

"The girl's his property; you insult his honor if you break in."

"To hell with his honor!"

The old man continues to savage the girl. Thatch clamps me hard. By the gods, I cannot endure this. Ash marks my state and lays on a few extra stripes, just to show who rules this caravan. Then he stops. The maid lies motionless. Not one of her sisters makes a move to help her, nor am I permitted to bring her aid.

When the column packs out half an hour later, the girl lies in the same place. Clearly she is dead. But a few miles up the trail, I see her again. Her sisters have divvied her load and hauled it for her. She struggles along, mute as a beast.

The column has entered the mountains now. At night the women sleep in a huddle, wrapped in nothing but their threadbare *pettus*. One midnight Thatch makes an incursion into their camp, declaring his globes so swollen he will mount a woman or an ass, whichever he can get behind first. "Ough, the smell!" And he scurries back to finish his business on his own.

Up we trek. In other armies, soldiers have servants. In Alexander's a man shoulders his own kit; pack animals are used only to bear ropes and tents, road-building tools, spare weapons and armor, and their own fodder. One mule in three hauls nothing but hay and grain, with nosebags tied on top and snapping like pennants in the gale. How the night howls at this elevation! The broader the valley, the more bearable the wind; in the gorges it really whistles. At times the trail is overarched, literally carved from the mountainside. Crouch or you'll crack your skull. The gale blasts uphill in the morning and downhill at night, except in storms, when it comes from everywhere.

I'll give Ash this: He is right about the women. They are tough. Tougher than we are. Soles bound only in rags, they tread surefootedly across scree falls and ice dumps, uncomplaining as mules. Lucas ogles several as we trek. "I've been on this trail too long, Matthias. Some of these girls are starting to look good to me."

The industry of Afghanistan is banditry. Every vale is home to a different clan, and each extracts a toll from the traveler. It is Alexander's policy to subdue all wild tribes along any route he traverses. This means sending troops up to high-line the ridges, that is, seizing the high ground to protect a route of march. Lucas and I volunteer. Anything to break the monotony.

We take to the high country like cats to a creamery. There are skirmishes every day. The foe are ragged tribesmen mostly, armed not with bows (the wind blows the hell out of arrows at this altitude) but with slings, with which they can launch a stone the size of a child's fist a quarter mile downhill. If one of these drills you above the eyeline, you won't have to worry about next payday. We chase these bandits. They retreat from fort to rockpile fort, launching curses and skull-busters, then show their heels when we close within range. Their sons, nimble as goats, serve as lookouts.

We camp above the clouds now. Terrain is all snowfields. In the bare patches, alpine meadows show carpets of broom and heather. Days blaze with sun-dazzle; nights are ungodly cold. It takes forever to heat a bowl of broth. Boiling an egg is impossible. Breath comes hard. A dash of two hundred feet leaves us heaving. Astonishingly, the bugs are still with us.

On the fifth dawn we run into Flag, Tollo, and Stephanos. Every high-line party is supposed to return to the column for rest after five days. Bung that! We're not about to get unyoked from our mentors again. We like it up here. No one gives us orders and, if we can keep from getting brained by the enemy's hand-catapults, the chances of getting minced are remote.

Among the peaks even Ash becomes a good fellow. We come upon abandoned camps of the foe. Nothing could be more primitive. Ash points out signs of different clans, boundaries over which the *khels* would never trespass in normal times. Now, invaded by great Alexander, the tribes are one.

I ask about Spitamenes. Ash knows him, or knew his father. The old man was a hero who fell in glory fighting Alexander's squadrons, defending the Persian Gates. The son Spitamenes was not raised to be a soldier, says Ash. He was sickly as a youth, and bookish. His schooling was as an astronomer and Zoroastrian scholar.

"Well, he's made up ground fast," says Flag. He tells Ash of the atrocities performed upon our men under orders from the Desert Wolf. Ash shrugs. Flag regards him. "You'd drink our blood too, wouldn't you, you treacherous old sheep-stealer?"

"With relish," says Ash, laughing.

He predicts that Spitamenes will be the stubbornest foe Alexander has faced. "For this young man is bolder even than your king, and his gift for war is from God. See how already he has dragged your army across half this country, yet you stand no closer to him than you did when you began."

Spitamenes has escaped across the mountains, Ash declares; we won't catch up with him till spring. He will fight us like a wolf in the darkness. "Where you turn, he will be elsewhere. When you tire, he will strike."

Spitamenes will wear us down, Ash predicts, and use our own aggressiveness and impatience against us. "In the end, your own men will beg to get out of this country. And your king will take any peace he can find."

Glare is ferocious at this altitude. Instructed by our *shikaris*, we fashion "pinpointers" of leather and wood and bind them across our eyes. Otherwise we'll go peak-blind. The light burns through anyway. It blazes through the walls of the goatskin tent or a doubled woolen blanket; we swipe horsehair from the torsion catapults to make blinders that we wrap atop our pinpointers. If you squint you can see. The vistas are spectacular. "How high do you reckon we are?" I ask Flag atop one ridgeline. He indicates a peak two hundred feet below. "Back home that would be Olympus."

I believe him.

An odd pair have become cronies up here: Ash and Stephanos. Muleteer and poet can be glimpsed, nattering away at all hours. We break camp one dawn; Stephanos splashes our backsides with water—"Godspeed" in Pactyan.

The old man tutors the poet in Afghan proverbs.

God is timid, like a mouse in a hollow wall.

Meaning, says Ash, that one must approach the divinity in silence and with humility. Stephanos admires this. I am repelled.

"What does God say," I ask the miscreant, "about beating the hell out of a woman?"

"Why don't you ask Him?" replies Ash.

"I'm asking you."

"Perhaps, Matthias," Stephanos says, "you and I might profit, in an alien land, by suspension of judgment."

Though blind, God sees; though deaf, He hears.

What the hell does that mean?

Pray to God on an empty stomach.

I'm disgusted. What religion do these blackguards follow anyway, that lets them mutilate our men while they're still alive? What lice-ridden deity do they pray to, who immures them in ignorance and squalor?

"Each precept of wisdom you gain," says Ash, "bears you farther from God."

Ash tells us his religion has no name, though Stephanos has pieced together, from this villain and other sources, that the Afghans are descended from the sons of Afghana, son of Saul, son of Jeremiah, who was Solomon of Israel's commander and who built the temple at Jerusalem. Nebuchadnezzar bore the multitude off into captivity at Babylon, where they flourished and intermarried with their Assyrian masters, and later with Persians and Medes. The tribes finally settled in the desert of Ghor, around Artacoana, calling themselves the Bani-Afghan or Bani-Israel. They believed in one God, creator of the universe. This fit well with the Persian faith of Zoroaster (himself born in Bactra, northern Afghanistan), whose God of Light, Ahura Mazda, was not far off from the Jehovah of the Jews.

In any event, says Stephanos, the congregations hit it off. A fresh race came into being, interbred with Medes and Tapurians, Daans, Scythians, and Gandhari, but all, in their minds, were Afghans, all following a version of the same Afghan God.

This stuff rings like a tub of humbug to me. Ash's religion, as best I can divine, amounts to tribal superstition, no better than our highlanders at home, who worship luck, tombs, and ancestors. I ask Stephanos what his religion is.

"Mine?" he laughs. "I worship poetry!"

I would give a month's wages to hear him expound upon this subject, but he ducks my queries, continuing with the evening feed. I learn one thing: Stephanos is not his real name. The word means "laurel"; he took it for himself, he acknowledges, from a crown he won once at Delphi.

"Then what's your real name?"

"I can't remember."

"What name did you enlist under?"

"I forget."

He advises me to change my name too.

"Take a war-name, Matthias. It solves a lot of problems."

Fires at this altitude are made of heather and furze. You rip the stringy stems from the turf; they start hard and give off so little heat you can stick your hand right in them. But they're all we've got to toast our mooch.

I ask Stephanos how he can be a poet and a soldier. Aren't the vocations in conflict, if not irreconcilable?

Again he evades the question, returning to the subject of war-names. "Consider our friend Flag here. Did you know he was a *mathematicos* in his earlier life?"

A teacher of music and geometry?

"He will not confirm this, Matthias," Stephanos continues, "but I have seen him take up a hand-harp and produce melodies sweet as nectar."

I ask, "Where do you come from, Flag?"

"I can't remember."

"Oh, come on!"

"It's slipped my mind."

Ash perches beside me on his sheepskin. *"Narik ta?"* he says. What difference does it make? (Literally, "So, then?")

Stephanos approves with a laugh. "Do you grasp, Matthias, the depth and subtlety of the Afghan religion?"

"I do not."

"When our friend Ash asks, 'What difference does it make?'— he is not speaking from despair or hopelessness, as you or I might, employing the same phrase. Rather he propounds a pure philosophical query: What difference *does* it make?"

"All the difference in the world!" I reply. "This is no religion. It offers no hope; it negates free will, action, enterprise. It's the antithesis of everything this army stands for, for what does Alexander's achievement mean if not the power of a single man's will?"

"And what achievement is that?"

"Look around you!"

At this, the litter breaks up.

"So then," Stephanos asks me, "is conquest *your* religion?"

"Action is. And virtue. As you and Flag and our king embody it."

"Do we now?"

The veterans snort into their muffled fleeces. It's getting too cold to keep up this colloquium.

"You know," Stephanos says, "I've taken to you from the start, Matthias. Shall I tell you why?"

"Because," says Flag, "he never shuts up."

"Because he asks questions."

"That's his problem."

"And one day he might get answers."

Chattering teeth compel the symposium to a close. Stephanos rises, to make his rounds of the sentry posts.

"You ask, my friend, how I can be a soldier and a poet? I answer: How can one be a soldier and *not* a poet?"

We sleep that night beside a pocket lake. Waking, a mountain ram and his ewes eye us from a cleft above. When we rattle stones around them, the flock scampers up the face as nimbly as you or I would mount a flight of stairs.

That day we make contact with the enemy. It becomes a real fight. In it Lucas kills his first man. The fellow hurls a great stone, then rushes upon him with dagger and sword. Lucas impales him on his half-pike. The enemy takes minutes to die. Lucas squats at the fellow's shoulder, too stricken to offer aid, bawling like a child.

14.

On the ninth day, we rotate back to column. A parcel is waiting for me—small and heavy—delivered, I am told, by a courier from Headquarters Expeditionary Force. The litter presses round. I undo the tie.

To my astonishment, the packet holds six golden *darics*—half a year's pay. Next to the coins nestles a Bronze Lion, the decoration awarded to soldiers wounded in battle. My name is on it. "This must be a mistake."

Flag reads the citation. The medal is for the night in the cordoned village, when I failed so ingloriously in the hovel with the old Afghan. Only the actions ascribed to me by headquarters are outrageous fiction, painting me a hero.

"Well, I can't keep this," I say.

"Why not? You were wounded in action."

"I stabbed myself!"

"What difference does that make?"

The squad howls. Flag and Tollo stifle laughter. Clearly it is they who put me in for this counterfeit commendation. Tollo divides the gold, setting one *daric* in my fist and distributing the rest to the litter.

"One month's pay belongs to you, my boy, and the rest to your mates. That's only fair. As for the Bronze Lion, the time will come, believe me, when you'll earn one for real, and the army, rump-stuffed as it is, won't stand you up for a gob of spit."

And he pins the medallion to my cloak.

"Take it now, while you've got it."

I USE THE *daric* to buy freedom for the girl Biscuits. We are back on the trail when Ash again puts the whip to her. I will not bear this a second time. I haul him off, declaring to him (an argument I have rehearsed in my head) that he has no right to render his property unserviceable to the army, which has contracted for it in good faith, and that if he disables the maid by his mistreatment of her, I will see that he loses his hire-pay.

"Then, damn the army," says Ash. "It must buy this property."

"It will, you wretched villain!"

I pay him the whole *daric*. Of course, the army won't make it good. In the end I am disciplined for exceeding my authority—ludicrous, as the only elements I outrank are mules and slaves—and endure several perfunctory stripes, delivered by Lucas in his capacity as second-from-the-bottom in the litter, much to Ash's gratification. "Now," says he, "you own a mouth to feed. May it eat you out of house and home."

I cut Biscuits loose on the trail, stuffing her kit with *kishar*, dried goat meat, and lentils; Ash chips in a swift kick to get her started back down the mountain. I watch her booger off and congratulate myself on a deed well turned.

Ten minutes later she's back in line, packing her same sack of sesame. No threat I can offer will make her wing away.

It turns out to be not so simple, purchasing a woman's liberty. Strictly speaking, Biscuits is not a slave; she belongs to no one, not Ash, not even herself. In the Afghan lexicon of *tor*—matters concerning the honor of women—every female must be *az hakak*, "in the guardianship of" a male—her father before she's married; then husband; finally brother, uncle, even son if her spouse dies or is killed. The tail of the shirt is I'm now that guardian. "You are her husband," Ash giggles. "She is your wife."

My predicament becomes a source of amusement to Flag and Tollo, who warn that I have violated the Afghan code of *nangwali*. If the girl's male kin show up, I'll have to kill them or they'll kill me. My mates regard this as great sport.

"What you must understand, Meckie" (this is what Ash calls all of us, his version of Mack, for Macedonian), "is that a woman like this"—and he elevates both palms as if warding off a curse—"is *nawarzal*, unclean, and *affir*, unacceptable."

"Then let her work on for pay."

"I am but a poor man."

"You are a pirate."

What can I do? I leave Biscuits with Ash and let him continue collecting her pay from the army. I can't get him to give her even a tenth. Such an arrangement would set, he declares, "an unwholesome precedent."

Through the course of this clash I come to appreciate the old gaffer. He begins sharing his table with me, or I should say his rock by the side of the trail. I am not so insensitive as to be unaware of the compliment.

One night I write a letter to my fiancée. Ash looks on. "You tell her everything, Meckie?"

"Everything she needs to know."

And he cackles gaily.

15.

The army winters at Bagram, a garrison town built centuries past by Cyrus the Great, in the temperate high valley at the foot of the central massif. Two rivers, the Kophen (or Kabul) and the Panjshir, water a broad, peak-rimmed plain.

The place is paradise for the moment. It possesses abundant cantonments for the army, dry fodder for the animals, and flat ground to train on. The northern passes, we are told, lie already under twenty feet of snow. The accumulation will reach sixty by midwinter. Not even Alexander can figure a way across into Bactria. As Ash predicted, we will not get at Bessus and Spitamenes till spring.

Mule and camel trains continue to work up from Kandahar, bringing armor, weapons, grain, and horses for the coming assault. My brother Elias's woman has come up with one of the columns. Her name is Daria. Her beauty makes her something of a celebrity, at least among the Macks. The Afghans abhor her—and every other native daughter who has taken up with the invader. She and Elias take apartments in the old section of Kapisa, a pleasant lane under winter mulberry trees and wild plums. They establish a salon. I am able to place Biscuits in her service. A weight off my mind.

The army trains and begins construction of another garrison town. This one will be called Alexandria-under-the-Caucasus.

We see the king all the time now. Every day he makes the rounds of the regiments in training, accompanied by only a couple of couriers and a page or two as bodyguards. He dismounts and instructs the men personally. The troops adore him.

We live in sixteen-man tents with packed-straw floors. The women do the cooking and the service work. Even Lucas has a girl now, the long-legged Ghilla. I am the last of our litter to hold myself apart, though, I confess, I have taken on occasion to visiting the day-raters. Am I faithless to my betrothed? I am drinking more than I used to. You have to, for the cold and the boredom.

Ash has stayed on. The army pays for foddering his stock. He will cross the mountains with us in the spring. The women, he has dismissed. Why feed them, he says, when they can find work in the new town or else catch on as "chickens," the lowest rung of camp wives.

To my wonder, I have become quite close to the old villain. He has mates everywhere. As rookies, Lucas and I are assigned every drudge detail; we never finish before dark. We wind up taking chow more with the Afghans attached to the army than with our own Macks. In normal times, Ash explains, his tribe, the Dadicai, would be feuding fiercely with at least two or three others. Now, under invasion, they are all the best of mates—Pactyans, including the Apyratai and Hygenni; Thyraoi and Thamanai; Maioni, Sattagyadai, a hundred others. I ask Ash how he can accept employment from Alexander if he hates us so much. "In the end we will drive you out, Meckie."

And he laughs and passes me another *chupattie*.

Lucas is still suffering terribly over his killing of the foe on the high line. He experiences shame at his inability to finish the fellow off and feels blameworthy, at the same time, that he did not aid him to save his life. The Afghan's eyes haunt Lucas's sleep, reproving. Worse, he confesses, is the visceral memory, which will not leave him, of planting his spear in another man's guts. I try to make him feel less alone, reckoning his anguish from my own gloryless experience of murder: the sense of horrible pleasure in the instant, succeeded at once by an excruciating remorse, disgust, and chagrin, with yourself and the whole human race, and the sense that you are changed forever, and far, far for the worst. But nothing I can say helps; I'm his peer, as callow as he is. He needs to hear it from someone senior, someone who knows. It is Tollo, of all people, who eases Lucas's woe.

"Piercing the melon, that's the toughest."

He means killing a man with a thrust through the belly, also known as "spilling the groceries." We're at work one day on the new city, breaking midday for a feed. "Every buck trooper balks at it. They wave their pike in both hands, like housemaids batting at a rat with a broom. To bury your blade in a living man's guts—that takes courage. And the feeling never leaves you."

This is helping Lucas. Tollo sees it.

"The disciplined trooper," Tollo says, "strikes with both feet planted, eyes on the foe, shoulders square. Trust your weapon and stand fast. You did it right on the high line, Lucas. I saw you. I was proud of you."

My friend flushes. Tollo grins.

"Think you're a soldier now?" And he cuffs Lucas affectionately. "But you're no longer a boy!"

We drill and continue construction of the garrison town. I have never been in training in a force commanded by Alexander. We get more days off than any corps I have heard of. No curfew, no bed check. The whole army knocks off every day from noon till two hours after. Wine is plentiful and cheap. Troopers are exempted from duty to take part in hunts (in fact, training is often replaced by hunting) and are given time off to train at the gymnasiums, which are the first structures the engineers erect, even before chapels and mess halls. Women are permitted throughout the camp, unlike the Old Corps under Philip and Alexander's original expeditionary force; they may sleep in cantonments with their officer lovers (and in the tents of us scuffs) and may accompany the column in the field. Such are the perquisites of serving in a corps commanded by Alexander. Now to the hard part.

All units in training are in formation under arms at two hours before dawn. No day's trek is shorter than thirty miles and many are above forty. The pace eats twenty miles before noon, nor are these one-day jaunts, but five and often ten. No mooch but what you carry; run out and you starve. God help the man who develops blisters or worms. In training at home, the sergeants drove you. Here it is the men themselves. Alexander issues no orders. He simply acts. He treks beside the men, on foot, with weapons and armor, and no buck in the army can keep up with him. He trains in all weathers, day and night. An officer who distinguishes himself shall dine in the king's tent, at the shoulders of great Craterus and Hephaestion. Corporal punishment does not exist in Alexander's army. Our lord brings us to heel by threat of exclusion from the corps and from his own favor, alongside which fate death itself has no meaning. One disapproving glance from Alexander will plummet the stock of the most decorated vet, while a smile or a word of praise elevates the meanest to renown.

The men are in love with Alexander. This is no overstatement. The troops are aware of his movements, moment by moment, as pack dogs are of the stud wolf. The corps gravitates to his apparition and feeds upon sight of him, as the lover on that of his darling. If any mishap should befall him, the army senses it, even at a remove of miles, and reacts with alarm and distress, which are not allayed until they see their lord again and satisfy themselves that he is whole.

The corps will endure anything for its commander. The most tedious drills are borne without an oath or a grumble. Exercises for which no purpose can be discerned are enacted with a will. At orders from headquarters, we strike camp, stripping the five-mile site to bare dirt. Fresh orders arrive: We unpack and set it up all over again. Building the city, the troops chop frozen sod all day, booze and fornicate all night. They are lean as leopards and as eager for action.

The king has half a hundred Forward Operations units at work in the mountains. My brother Elias and his comrades form one of them. These are elite outfits, composed entirely of Companions, the tallest and handsomest, mounted on the most spectacular stock. Their job is to negotiate with the tribes. They carry gifts of honor—golden cups, Damascene swords—and are authorized to speak and deal in Alexander's name. They have guides of the Panjshiri, Salangai, and Khawak Pactyans, the tribesmen who inhabit the high valleys and passes that the army must take in spring. Will the clans resist our passage? Their numbers are said to be between 125,000 and 175,000, including the *khels* and sub-*khels* of valleys and side-valleys. No invader, including Cyrus the Great, has ever made them yield.

Our training is clearly to take on these trotters. Every battalion has its high-line artillery, to take possession of the commanding heights, and its companies of missile troops. We train in snow boots and fleece bundlers. Engineers and pioneers keep the track out of Kapisa clear, all the way to the head of the Panjshir.

We see the foe constantly. Hundreds winter here, with their families, in the Kabul Valley. Thousands more have descended to milder elevations roundabout. Their sword shops line the lanes in Bagram City. All are mounted and all are armed to the teeth.

Many find employment with the army. We have several in our unofficial mess. I come to know two, Kakuk and Hazar, brothers, about my age. The first word they teach me, indicating themselves, is *tashar*, meaning wild young bucks. Both are fine fellows, handsome as lions, the former with blond hair, the latter of black, both with great bushy beards of which they are vainer than gamecocks. They care nothing for pay and routinely spree a month's wages in an evening. They consort with us for the novelty and the adventure. Their kit is the felt Bactrian cap with earflaps, heavy woolen trousers bloused into lambskin boots, vest, waistcoat, and *pettu*. The sashes round their waists are tribal colors; in them they tuck their lunch, medicine, and their three iron-edged man-killers—short, medium, and long. They are curious as cats. They cannot hear enough about my home country. Each custom I relate sends them spooling into gales of hilarity. More genial companions could not be imagined, though it is plain they will carve our livers, or their fellow Afghans', over the most trivial matter of honor, and that, when the army marches out in spring, violating the integrity of their territory, they will hurl themselves upon us with all the violence they possess. The pride of the Panjshiris, I learn, is their great valley, which is to them home and heaven. Will Alexander serve up the toll to march through under *badraga*, official escort? Cyrus did. Or will our king attempt to force his passage? He has never bowed yet to extortion. As with Ash, the brothers, Kakuk and Hazar, see no contradiction between working for Alexander and looking forward to eviscerating him.

It is impossible to dislike these fellows. I find myself envying their proud, free life. Labor is unknown to them. Their ponies graze on sweet grass in summer, dry fodder when the passes close. Their wives and sisters weave their garments, prepare their *dal* and *ghee*. Families shelter in stone houses, ownership of which they recite back twenty generations, whose only removable parts are the wooden doors and roofs (in case of evacuation due to feuds). Every kin-group holds two residences, summer and winter. If a rival clan raids, the *khels* drive them out through superior local knowledge. Should an alien power enter in force, as Cyrus in the past or Alexander now, the tribes withdraw to loftier fastnesses, sending to wider spheres of kinsmen until they assemble the necessary numbers; then they strike.

Nangwali is the Afghan warrior code. Its tenets are *nang*, honor; *badal*, revenge; and *melmastia*, hospitality. *Tor*, "black," covers all matters concerning the virtue of women. An affront to a sister or wife's honor can be made *spin*, "white," by no means short of death. Blood feuds, the brothers tell me, start over *zar*, *zan*, and *zamin*: money, women, and land.

In cases of *badal*, vengeance is taken by father or son. In *tor*, it's the husband, except in the case of unmarried women; then all males of the family may not rest until justice has been exacted. The code of *nangwali* forbids theft, rape, adultery, and false witness; it prosecutes cowardice, abandonment of parents or children, and usury. The code prescribes rites for births and death, armistices, reparations, prayer, almsgiving, and all other passages of life. Poverty is no crime. Reverence for elders is the cardinal virtue, succeeded by patience, humility, silence, and obedience. Statues for hygiene are strict, the brothers swear, though if any were adhered to within my vision, I must have missed it. The view of life is that of a noble resignation to fate. God determines all, the Afghan believes. One can do nothing except be a man and bear up.

As for my guardianship of the girl Biscuits, this will bring trouble, my friends declare. The maid has at least one living brother, a captain of horse serving now with Spitamenes. Kakuk and Hazar know the man, champion of a rival tribe. If I come upon him I must strike without hesitation. In matters of *tor,* blood is everything. A dead man can always be paid for.

One morning I wake to find Kakuk and Hazar gone. Every other Panjshiri in camp has skipped too. Spring approaches. The buds are on the mulberries. Scouts report tribesmen in the hundreds slipping back into the high valleys, by routes known only to themselves. I quiz Flag for the latest. "The passes," he says, "are still under twenty feet of snow. Nothing without wings is getting over for at least another month."

But Ash tells a different tale. The contractors of the pack train are balking, he reports. They won't take their stock up into the Panjshir, not if the clans are given time to get home and become organized into armies.

That night Alexander calls another pack-up. We strike tents and load up the train, as we have done in a dozen previous drills.

This time it's no exercise. Two hours before dawn, lead elements of the army are on the march, with the king at the fore, up the track into the Panjshir.

16.

Kabul's elevation is seven thousand feet. By the second day the column is at nine. The summit, at the Khawak Pass, will be twelve thousand. The date is Artemisius 6. Early. Very early.

The sun burns hot this high, so strong in fact the first day that we strip our winter cloaks and trek bathed in sweat. The string is one mule per man; half the beasts bear nothing but fodder, each man's pannier is the better part mooch. Even cavalry mounts are loaded; they carry their own snow boots, blankets, and wrappers. The army packs no heavy baggage and few dependents. These will follow at a safer time. The women porters trek with us. Alexander has doubled their wages; the overage will be paid to them, not their handlers. Biscuits hikes with me, Ghilla with Lucas.

The column marches in four sections. The vanguard breaks the trail. These are army engineers. Their division leads three thousands camels, laden with timber posts and beams, cables, ropes, planking, and fittings; they will fabricate bridges to span the torrents and gorges in spate. The van drives sheep and oxen as well, not only to drag timbers for the construction but to beat down the trail—and to be slaughtered for meat. To protect the fore elements, the engineers have archers, slingers, and javelineers, mercenary cavalry of Lydia, Armenia, and Media, with hired Afghans of the west, mountain troops who hate the Panjshiri, and our own Mack pioneers. The latter are miscreants of the army, stripped of the privilege of bearing arms, and handed axes and mattocks instead. The poor scuffs are clearing tracks through twenty- and thirty-foot-high drifts. Alexander and the elite units come next, the *agema* of the Companions, the Royal Guardsmen, battalions of Perdiccas's and Craterus's crack brigades, with Agrianian javelineers, Cretan archers, and other specialized mountain companies, including combat engineers with stone-throwers and bolt-hurlers. These divisions will take the foe in strength, here in the Panjshir if the tribesmen contest our passage, and on the plains of Bactria beyond, when the king overhauls Bessus's and Spitamenes' cavalry. Next the central phalanx brigades, including ours, Hephaestion's and Ptolemy's, and the nondetached battalions of Perdiccas and Craterus; then the heavy sections; then the light brigades of Erygius, Attalus, Gorgias, Meleager, and Polyperchon, along with mercenary and Iranian cavalry. The baggage, such as there is, comes between them and the rear guard, composed of other foreign contingents and native light troops. The total is nearly fifty thousand.

Up we go. Winter has broken with a vengeance; spring torrents thunder down the gorges, the color of mud. The summit is supposed to take thirteen days. The track runs straight through the Panjshir. Seventy miles. Scores of tributary valleys branch from this central axis. Each donates its plunging cataract, glacier-spawned, and each descends with deafening fury. No non-Panjshiri has ever been back in these fastnesses.

"When we reach the summit," Rags relays the army bucket-wash, "we'll be at twelve thousand feet. The Khawak Pass starts here. Forty-seven miles long."

The first storm strikes on the third day. Hail first, then snow, then hail again. Stones the size of sling bullets make us break out shields and helmets, beneath which we hunker, on our knees against any outcrop we can find, while the mules and horses bunch in mute misery till the drubbing ceases. The trail has gone to ice. Every rope and line is encased in the stuff; the slopes glisten, sheer and treacherous. A frigid wind whips in the wake of the storm. We are drenched, every one, and shivering like colts. "Up, lads! Keep moving!"

The column has entered the Panjshir proper. The valley is beautiful, far broader than I had imagined, and not, despite its elevation, particularly "mountainous." Great terraces are carved, our guides tell us, beneath the snow; in fall the natives harvest rice, barley, cucumbers, lentils, and broad beans from hillsides that now dazzle blindingly. Whole orchards hide beneath the snowpack— mulberries and pears, pistachios, wild plums, and more apricots, we are told, than can be loaded onto mules and driven to market.

We make camp early in the middle of a second storm. We can't spread fodder for the animals; hail and sleet drench it instantly. We feed them using nosebags, themselves frozen, lashed to frozen halters. There's no wood, so no fires. Chow is cold *kishar*, goat meat, and curds gone to ice. I choke down a frost-ball onion. "Day three," grins Flag. "Only ten more to the summit."

We bonze in a huddle, women too, using the tethered beasts as windbreaks. Twice in the night we hear attacks resound at a distance up the column. We're too wretched even to budge. I'm squeezed between Biscuits and Lucas when I feel a rhythmic thrusting somewhere south of my soles. "Tollo, you swine!" Laughter follows.

"Just trying to keep from freezing, mate."

No one sleeps that night or the next. Each soul prays for sunrise, which comes late because the peaks block the sun's warmth till midmorning. By noon men have stripped naked, despite the cold, except for their boots. We trek, spreading our sodden gear atop the pack rigs, letting the gale whip it dry.

"You're not really wet," pronounces Tollo, "till the crease of your ass is soaked."

"It's soaked!"

"Then may the gods bless you."

Stephanos cheers the men by predicting victory in Bactria. We'll catch Bessus and Spitamenes, he swears, with their bollocks in the breeze. Why? "Because they're men of intelligence. It's beyond their imagination to believe that anyone in their right salt-sucking mind would cross these mountains at this season."

Day five. We trek, two miles high now. Storms strike morning and evening, dumping snow and hail, then dispelling to vapor, followed by fierce sun. Now comes the melt. The whole mountain weeps. A thousand rills and runnels come flushing from the rock, racing together into tributary torrents, then plunging as cataracts to the river below. The stone has been splintered over millennia; it's all scree and shingle, poised to slide. Step wrong and you're in the books, as soldiers say. It's the same all the way to Khawak, so we hear, only up there it gets worse. At that elevation, nearing three miles high, rivers become glaciers, rimmed by slatey, unstable moraines, the only avenues of passage. The ice fields themselves are untrekkable, wide as half a mile, crazed with fissures, cracks, and crevasses, and upshot with great jumbled towers of ice.

The fifth noon the male porters revolt. About a hundred serve our division; they dump their loads and refuse to climb farther. They want more pay. Stephanos is our section commander. What can he do, massacre them? He capitulates, paying out of his own purse (the porters refuse army chits).

All night hail and snow pound the camp; in the morning it takes hours to shake the rebels out of their dens. Now the muleteers revolt too. Ash is one of their leaders. They are not warriors! They did not sign up for such an ordeal!

Ash wants his mules back. They all do. Stephanos and the other officers spend half the morning negotiating. The column is breaking apart. Forward elements push on without us. Gaps open. Behind us, other revolts must be in progress because no section is pressing us from the rear. By noon Stephanos succeeds in quelling the insurrection. The sun has returned; optimism rekindles. But within an hour purple clouds descend, temperature plummets, deluges of sleet and hail thunder down. The gale is so fierce a man can't advance a pace into it; even the mules spill and tumble on the treacherous underfoot. We make camp three hours before dark, simply because it's impossible to go on.

I search for Ash. He has vanished. So have the other muleteers. They have abandoned their stock, their livelihood, preferring to take their chances, alone and afoot, on the trail back down.

Darkness descends. Our bones rattle with the cold. The women endure it, uncomplaining. At night Biscuits sleeps barefoot, with her foot-wraps round her chest to dry, burying her soles for warmth against another girl's belly, for whom, beneath her own *pettu*, she performs the same favor. She has me protect my hands under the tucks of her arms. We learn to site our sleeping hole out of the narrow gorges, where gales howl. It's better in the wide parts of the trail, or in the lee of an outcrop if you can find one before your mates do. Nights are unbearable, no matter what you do.

"Only eight more wake-ups," says Flag.

Dawn: Stephanos has the Macks fall in under arms. We roust the male porters from their snowholes. Before they can issue the next ultimatum, Stephanos publishes his own: Get out! Hell take you—and your loads. At spearpoint, we drive the mob back down the trail. They want food. Indeed, answers Stephanos, I'm sure you do. We want our fleeces and shelters, they cry. "Come and take them," replies Stephanos, quoting Leonidas.

The porters yield. Stephanos harangues them. Press on to the Khawak! Downhill from there! Bonuses for all in Bactria!

We make a good day, and another after that. Where is the summit? We have lost touch with the column in front and behind. Our *shikaris* are useless; they don't know the mountain. Each storm buries the trail deeper. Sun is worse. Its heat spawns avalanches. None have threatened our section yet. But their great falls, plunging ahead, wipe out the trail. It takes hours to break a new one and when we emerge on the far side, only prayer reassures us we have not lost our way.

The seventh day, fodder runs out for the mules and horses. We ourselves have been on half rations since the fourth dawn. My belly echoes like a hollow tank. Each step has become agony. "Tollo," I say, laboring beside him. "Should we be getting worried?"

"Put your faith," he says, "in the benevolent gods."

"I thought you didn't believe in the gods."

"I don't."

We hear no more talk of mutiny. Porters trek tight beside us. We will live or die together.

This is the way peril overhauls you. One hand's-breadth at a time. Suddenly you're in it. I glance to Lucas. Even in his pinpointers, bundled like a bear, I read his apprehension. The issue is no longer war. It has become survival.

Night seven: Two rangers stagger into camp, sent back from the section before us to guide us on. A village! Just three miles ahead! The natives' bunkers, beneath the snow, hold food and fodder. We survive another interminable siege of darkness, succored by hope.

All next day the section treks in a stiff gale. This is good; it means we're near the summit. Around noon we spot fresh graves. Our own countrymen, from the sections ahead. With shame we welcome the sight. It means we're still on the trail. Mountain sickness adds to our woes. No one can eat; you can't keep anything down. We are weak and disoriented. The simplest chore becomes monumental. You recall, say, a chunk of jerked meat in your kit. Now try and get it. To wring one mitt off your fist takes the count of fifty. By then you've forgotten what you took it off for. Two fellows put up their pinpointers and forget to tug them down; they go snow-blind. They must be roped and led.

We put our heads down and march. Each man recedes into his own cylinder of pain. You see your own feet and hear the crunch of your tread. Where are our guides? The rangers told us that men have been posted along the trail to wait for us and steer us in. Lucas works up beside me as we trek. "Something's wrong." He indicates the sun. "We're heading northeast."

"Where should we be heading?"

"I don't know. But not there."

The trail twines in so many directions, turning up switchbacks and across shoulders and ridgelines. Who can tell anything?

Traversing such a wilderness, you find yourself naming landmarks. A knife-edge crest: "The Clothesline." "Two Towers." "The

Ice House." Where is the village? Can there really be mooch ahead? Will we have a fire?

Postnoon. We trek a ridge of slate and shingle. A glacial moraine, gouged by the great frozen river that has cut this basin. Glare is fierce; gaps open in the column again and again. The event becomes normal, prompting no alarm. We're blind anyway.

Suddenly a commotion ahead. The village? A line of our countrymen churns past us in the opposite direction.

Wrong way, brothers.

We've lost the trail.

Gone up the wrong valley.

"Brilliant work, mates!"

"What genius is in charge of this bung-fuck?"

Men and animals beat past us, heading back down the way we came. I grab Lucas. "This is serious."

No one has panicked yet. But we feel chaos coming. We turn back down the track. The column becomes even more dislocated, as some litters countermarch, cutting into the line hastening back down the moraine. Bad luck never arrives in isolation. Now: a fresh storm. The heavens go purple; gales howl; the cold hits us like a wall of ice.

Men are shoving and heaving. Troops push past in mounting terror. The mules and horses have caught fright too. "Halt in place!" Stephanos bawls, striding the length of the column. "Brothers, get ahold of yourselves!" He calls mates by name, summoning them to order. It works. March integrity is restored.

The women are the strongest. Not one dumps her load or makes a move to bolt. Biscuits and Ghilla stay tight to me and Lucas. "Ka'neesha?" I shout into the gale. Are you all right? They nod, muffled from sole to crown. The column starts again. Three hours till darkness. No orders have been passed, but every man understands: We must regain the trail and find the village. No one will survive a night in this storm.

Down we go. Past the Ice House. Past the Two Towers.

Now the Clothesline. An exposed backbone crest, five hundred paces end to end. A plume of snow blasts laterally, driven by the gale. We must trek in the lee, meaning blind in the blow-off. "Rope up! No exceptions!"

The column traverses the spine by steps cut from the ice during our earlier crossing. Use your half-pike. Plunge it, butt-spike-first, into the slope; give it the count of two to set; then haul yourself forward. Two steps, then plant again and belay your mate behind you. Everyone together. Amazingly, we make it.

"The trail!"

Joy flashes the length of the column. Our guides cry from ahead. Shelter! Shelter by nightfall! In jubilation we pound each other's bundled shoulders and backs. Head count! The column forms up to start again.

"Where's Tollo?"

It's Flag, checking the roster.

"I saw him," Little Red points back, "just before we crossed."

"Where is he now?"

No one knows.

Flag works back along the column. Pulling off mufflers and pinpointers. Examining every face.

"Was he roped? Who saw him rope up?"

The column has gotten off the pitch now. Out of the gale. A face of the mountain protects us. We feel almost warm.

Behind us the Clothesline howls in the open.

Flag comes back. He hasn't found Tollo. "Go on!" he commands, driving us forward in the direction of the village.

"What about you, Flag?"

"Get moving!"

Lucas and I hold up. We can see Flag and Red go at each other. We can't hear much. Red points down the ice face.

". . . if Tollo's down there, he's bought his ticket!"

Flag turns away. We can see him hauling rope and a hatchet from the pack of a mule. Red rejoins the column, moving on. The mass shuffles forward, toward the village. Lucas and I look at each other.

"I'll stay," he says.

I look in his eyes. He's worse off than me. He'll freeze in an hour.

"No." I'm an idiot. "You go on."

A push gets Lucas started.

"Save me something warm."

17.

Flag and I find Tollo five hundred feet down, alive and delirious.

He doesn't know who we are. His pinpointers are gone. He's blind. He orders us back up the face.

I want to go. I would. But it's not so simple. Five hundred feet have taken Flag and me two hours. The face is steep as a ladder and slick as frozen snot. My boots are rags, frostbound as boards; their soles glisten with ice.

Darkness has fallen. Cold-sickness has taken Flag. Frozen vomit plasters his breast; his speech is slurred; he can no longer close either hand.

We cling to a shelf no wider than the sole of a shoe. Tollo sprawls thirty feet below. Upside down, hung up on an outcrop by a rope caught round his ankle. His other leg, from the knee down, is turned around backward.

"Who is it? Is that you, Matthias?"

I'm going to have to go down to him. The distance seems like nothing in the recounting. In summer a child could scamper it with ease. But now, in the dark and the plunging cold, with our own exhaustion and our icebound boots, the pitch seems distant as the moon. I would leave Tollo. I'm ready to start back up the face. Then I see Flag, with his frost-benumbed mitts, readying to start down. I curse him in language that would get me strung up under tamer circumstances.

I can't let him go down.

It has to be me.

I make it somehow, belayed by the line Flag lowers from the ledge.

Tollo doesn't know me. Even when I shout in his ear. His leg is turned around completely. When I touch it, it's hard as a block of stone.

"My cap," he says. "Can you see my cap?"

He has lost his boar's-tusk skullcap. It must have fallen off, he says. There it is. He points it out to me. About ten feet down, across the ice. "Can you get it for me?" he asks in a voice so faint I have to put my ear right next to the ice-hole which is his beard, and even then I can barely hear him. He is like a child. My heart is wrung. At the same time I hate him. I hate him for falling. The selfish bastard will kill me. My life will end on this face and all he wants is his salt-sucking cap.

"Let it go, Tollo."

"My cap." He says he has to have it.

"What for?"

He coughs something I can't understand.

What? I shout at him.

"In hell," he says. It will be disrespectful to appear without a cap. Sure, why not? Why shouldn't I die for his bung-fucked cap?

I get it. I plant it on his skull, beneath his fleece hood. I press my mouth to his ear: "Let's get the fuck out of here."

We rope Tollo under the arms, Flag and I. The back of his cloak is solid ice; it makes a sledge. If we climb, pitch to pitch, we can haul Tollo up behind us. One stage at a time. We start up. One traverse. Two. Except now Flag is failing too. He can't talk. I fear for his extremities. I can still feel my own. I'm all right. Youth. Youth is everything.

". . . the crest . . ." Flag manages to croak. He means we must regain the trail.

"Why? So we can die there instead of here?"

I have entered a state of rage so towering, words cannot give it expression. "Tollo!" I shout down. "How about pulling your weight? Use your arms, damn you!"

"Shut up," barks Flag.

"Why didn't he rope himself? We're gonna top off because of this ass-wit."

"Shut up."

I keep babbling. I know I'm cracking but I can't stop. A part of me has entered delirium and I know it, but another part remains surprisingly lucid. I figure I have half an hour before I lose all sensation in my hands and feet. Beyond that, what? An hour till I'm frozen head to foot. What is particularly galling about going into the books this way is that within twenty days there'll be flowers on this slope. It will be spring. In a month, Panjshiris will be grazing sheep here. They'll strip our corpses and jig over our bones—ours and however many other hundreds of our compatriots will have gone briskets-down before the column gets over these mountains.

"Wake up!"

I gape at Flag like a man surfacing from a nightmare. He bawls into my ear: "Got to make the trail!"

I can't tell whether he's lost his mind or I have. What's waiting for us at the trail? Nothing. The column has moved on. We'll never be able to track them in the dark, and certainly not sledging Tollo. Our only hope is if the section following us has come up. But they'd be crazy to do that. Cross the Clothesline in this cold and dark? Never. They've scratched out a camp somewhere below.

"Right," I shout back. Make the trail. Good plan.

The way we climb is with the butts of our half-pikes. Plunge the spike into the ice, pull your weight up by the shaft. Knee first, then foot; when you know it's solid, seat the rope over your shoulder, the one that's hauling Tollo; then push up with that leg.

At places the slope isn't bad. We can chop steps into the ice. Have we climbed a hundred feet or a thousand? I know I'm hallucinating. It seems like I can hear Biscuits' voice. In Greek. Pretty good Greek too. She has waited for us. The column is gone but she's still there, at the trail. That's a good hallucination. I appreciate it. It's like one of those dreams you have, where you say, By heaven, that is imaginative! I glance over to Flag, wondering if he's seeing the same mirage I am. Apparently not. He just keeps climbing. By Zeus's iron balls, he's got guts. What a soldier! I'm proud to step off for hell beside him.

"Hey! Flag!" I'm going to tell him I love him; I don't care how unmilitary it is.

"Shut up!"

I want to tell him about Biscuits. Where did she learn Greek so well? Must have been from Macks who had her before we came on the scene. She's above us, shouting down. Something about a rope. "Grab it! Pull yourselves up!" I am really impressed with her Greek.

Flag struggles to catch the rope. This is strange. How can he be after the rope that's in *my* mirage?

Now I've got the rope. Somehow we've reached the trail.

Crawling. Facedown. Rolling over the lip, propelled by our knees. Stand? I can't. Biscuits and Flag haul up the rope that I seem to remember is attached to Tollo. It occurs to me that this might not be delirium.

"Hey!"

Biscuits kneels over me. I'm on my face on the ice; she rolls me over.

Hey!

What?

She grabs me by the hair and shakes me so hard the roots almost come out.

"Hey!" she shouts into my ear. "Are you stupid?"

18.

What saves our lives are Tollo's fleece and military cloak. With these we roof the shallow kennel that Biscuits has chopped out of the ice. I am struggling, she tells me later, to drag Tollo in with us. It takes Flag pummeling me with both elbows (he can no longer feel his hands) before I understand our Color Sergeant is dead.

"He was croaked at the bottom," Flag declares.

I'm furious. Why didn't Flag tell me? He has made us break our backs. But I am in awe of him too. My God, what a soldier! What a friend.

"Strip the corpse!" Biscuits shouts over the wind. Without Tollo's kit, the three of us cannot survive the night.

Never! I cry. And leave him naked?

The absurdity hits me. Flag too. We start laughing. We can't stop.

It takes ten minutes to beat Tollo's garments apart from his frozen flesh. Flag and I remain convulsed. Flag takes the boar's-tusk cap. This prompts another round of hilarity. Tears freeze round our eyes; ice mats our beards.

Poor Tollo lies naked. Blue with frost. Slippery. We have to moor him like a dinghy, to a half-pike planted in the ice, to keep him from plunging again over the side. We are ashamed of our hysteria but we can't stop.

We endure the endless night in our ice-hole, Biscuits and I, with Flag between us. His feet ride against my belly; she clamps his hands under her arms. In the morning, we are rescued by advance elements of the column coming up from behind. They prize us from our tomb, rigid as the dead. Incredibly, the day turns warm. By noon, when we reunite with Knuckles and Little Red, sent back in search of us by Stephanos, the sun blazes so fiercely that we have to strip our cloaks. We tie them atop the oxhide sledge on which we haul Tollo's corpse.

The descent to the plains takes nine more days. It is on this stretch, the northern (sunless) flanks of the Hindu Kush, that the army's suffering approaches its apogee. We transit the Khawak Pass for six days. It seems we will never get out. Twenty-two miles to the summit, twenty-four more to the Foothill Trail. Flag has vowed to pack Tollo all the way down to the plains; he will not see his mate interred in some icebound den, to be dishonored in spring by wolves or Afghans. But we have no strength to haul his weight. Scores of others labor like we do, sledging the corpses of comrades lost to the cold. In the end we plant Tollo beneath a rock cairn with thirty others. Big rocks, that predators and barbarians can't shoulder aside.

Each day starts in deep shadow. The sun is up but the peaks block it. Bellies are empty; legs feel like lead. The column packs out. By noon, heaven's heat is assaulting the peaks above. Now come the avalanches. It is spring. The high melt loosens the snow-mass clinging to the face. Again and again slides bury the trail. It takes forever to dig through. The first day in the pass we make three miles. The third, less than one. The native *tiris,* underground bunkers where the locals hide their winter stores, cannot be located, even by our guides paid fortunes. The worst is that so much of what we have jettisoned in our extremity is food. Nothing left. We gnaw wax and wood; we eat our spare shoes. The army has trained, in Kabul, to too much leanness; there's no grease on our bones. And so many are ill equipped in clothing and footgear. Beside the trail, men lie down and do not get up, close their eyes and never open them again.

With hunger, column discipline breaks down. The infuriating hurry-up-and-stop rhythm, common to any line of men strung out one behind the other, becomes lethal as snowslides break the column into sections cut off from one another. Whoever has even a patch of food finds himself under siege from mates starving. A jar of honey goes for six months' wages. Sesame oil to rub ourselves down against the cold (olive oil is all gone) fetches an empress's ransom. This was Biscuits' cargo, but she has dumped it on the Clothesline to help haul Tollo. The order comes to slaughter the pack animals, one per company. No wood to make a fire; we gag the meat down raw.

On the sixth day Alexander appears. Incredibly, our king has trekked back, miles from the column's head, accompanied by Hephaestion and some pages of his suite. Yes, the troops have cursed his name. Watching comrades perish, no few have condemned our lord for his recklessness to dare this wilderness so early in the season. Now at sight of him, they are struck through with shame. Here before us, in his plain cavalryman's cloak, stands our sovereign, who could be dining in the warmth of the lowlands by now but has chosen instead to come back to us and bear our sufferings at our side. He does not ride. He walks. He has no food. None for us, none for himself. When the column halts for camp, our lord digs roots of silphium from beneath the snow with the blade of his own pike and on this fodder for goats makes his supper. Seeing a man down, Alexander lifts him with his own hands. Troops at the column's head, he tells us, will in three days' time be plucking pears from orchards on Bactria's sun-warmed plains. Take heart, mates! Bear up! The sufferings we endure now, bitter as they may be, will be made good in the currency of comrades' lives spared when we descend in the enemy's rear, where he does not expect us and has prepared no defenses.

The foe will fly, Alexander pledges, struck through with terror by our appearance in strength from these cruel passes, which feat was believed impossible at this season until we did it.

BOOK
THREE

The Bactrian Plain

19.

The Bactrian plain, to which the army descends now with joy, is an oasis of green and plenty. The men's spirits revive at the sight of orchards of pear and plum, and terraced fields of rice and barley. The Bactrians are civilized; they have towns, not villages. In other words, something to lose. Forty places surrender in eleven days. The corps strides in warm sun, on good roads, into Afghanistan's breadbasket.

Alexander's gamble has paid off. Bessus and Spitamenes flee north, to put the Oxus River between themselves and their Macedonian pursuers. Signs of the enemy's hasty decampment are everywhere. The foe has attempted to scorch the country, but the local planters (whose property Bessus and Spitamenes would send up in smoke) have by mighty exertions rescued their goods. They double- and triple-charge us, but we don't care; we're so happy to be warm and alive.

At Drapsaca, army engineers erect a vast tent hospital to treat the thousands of cases of frostbite and exposure. The army's kit is rags; half the corps treks barefoot. Our animals are skin and bones. Still Alexander and the elite brigades make ready to push on. Stephanos calls our mob together. We are free, he says, to enter the hospital. "But if you do, you can kiss your career good-bye. Alexander pursues the enemy now, and he'll remember the name of every man who marches with him."

Flag has two black fingers and one gone toe. He chops them off himself with a maul and a sawyer's wedge. Hundreds do likewise throughout the corps, or have mates do it for them. Men would sooner die than enter the medics' tent.

The army crosses the Stone Desert in an ordeal of heat and thirst. Three hundred more perish, and seven hundred horses. Alexander reaches the Oxus two days behind the foe. The river is twelve hundred yards wide. Bessus and Spitamenes have crossed, burning their boats behind them. The Mack army pitches camp and starts building bridges and rafts.

Our women are still with us. The ordeals of mountain and desert have transformed them. They have earned our respect and their own. They fear now only the halt, when the corps may decide it no longer needs them. Biscuits paints my sore-pocked soles with vinegar and binds them with moleskin. Ghilla sets bones. Another girl, Jenin, sets up as the outfit's source for nazz and pank. The women have become indispensable. Even Flag defends them.

Our sergeant has changed, too, since the mountains. Tollo's death has hit him hard. Grief makes Flag more human. I hear him use the word "son," addressing Lucas. At Drapsaca, he is awarded a Silver Lion, his fourth. The citation comes with half a talent of silver. Flag pays for the burial of the four women lost in the mountains and arranges a clean abortion, in-hospital by an army doctor, for a fifth. He refits all our kit. What's left he sends home to Tollo's kin.

I have come to know this man whom, before, I regarded more with awe and fear than respect. I see the whole of him now. He is a soldier in the noblest sense of the word. Tough, selfless, long-suffering. "Here, this is for you." He tugs me aside at the town of Taloqan, setting Tollo's boar's-tusk cap in my fist.

I can't wear it.

I don't deserve it.

But at Flag's insistence I tuck it inside my pack. "Ghosts are good luck," he says. He calls our half section together. The second litter will have a new Number One: me.

Can he be joking?

"You're promoted to Corporal, Matthias. Congratulations."

From that day, I attend all command briefings. It feels ridiculous. I can't make myself give orders to Rags or Knuckles or Lucas. "Learn how," Flag commands. He includes me now in his private thoughts and deliberations. Every noise he gets from up the chain, he shares with me. I can walk up to Stephanos now and address him as if he were a friend. Indeed, he becomes short with me if I don't.

Flag passes Tollo's boots and cloak to Biscuits, with ten drachmas (a year's wages for a porter) from our fallen comrade's purse. She has earned it. "What gift," he inquires of her in the squad's name, "would you like from us?" Name it, our fellows agree, and we will grant it if we can.

"I would like you all," she declares, "to stop calling me Biscuits."

20.

The European cannot appreciate the wretchedness of station of a lone female in the East. Such a creature is lower than a dog, for the animal at least has a worthy use to guard the camp. An unprotected woman isn't fit, in the eyes of her Afghan countrymen, even to be raped and murdered. They would sooner stone her. She is an outcast, abandoned by God and her ancestors. Evil fortune attaches to her, and the clansman fears nothing so much as bad luck.

Despite ourselves, we become our women's guardians. The army's provisions, which would have been loaded onto the backs of mules, go instead onto our females'. They are overjoyed to take them.

So it is Biscuits no longer. Shinar from now on. A pretty name. It means "sanctuary" in Dari.

"In villages of Ghor where we come from," says Ghilla, "there is always a small stone house, sometimes only a pile of rocks with a roof, built in the hills above the town. This place belongs to all.

Anyone may take shelter there, even the criminal, and no one may take him away against his wishes. This sanctuary is called *shinar*."

You wonder, I suppose, what happens at night between me and Shinar. Exactly what you think happens. Does this mean I am faithless to my betrothed? The army has a saying:

Who sheds his blood for King and Corps
shall dine for free o'er alien shore.

It means the niceties of home don't count out here. This is war. Might as well ask a man to fight without liquor or opium as to endure this life without women.

I did not feel this way coming out. I would stay true to Danae, I thought. I would be the first ever.

The Oxus, as I said, is twelve hundred yards wide. While army engineers rig pontoon bridges and the corps prepares rafts and *bhoosa* bags (tent skins stuffed with straw and sewn watertight) for the crossing, our company is sent with a number of others to search the villages up and down the bank. Our orders are to bring back anything that floats and anything the army can ride or eat. The women stay behind, to do the work of camp and to labor in the manufacture of rope for cable.

I stand watch with Lucas the first night downvalley. "What's it like," I ask him, "between you and Ghilla?"

He asks what I mean.

"You know. In bed."

My friend considers this. "Good," he says.

This is embarrassing. I stop.

"What?" Lucas asks. "What's on your mind?"

I hesitate. "Is there affection between you and Ghilla? I mean do you talk . . . or laugh?"

Of course, says Lucas. He's not sure what I'm getting at. I'm not either. "With Shinar," I say, "there's not a word. Nothing. Not before, during, or after. It's like it's not even me she's sluicing. I could be anybody."

"You mean she's cold?"

"No, the opposite. She wears me out. But the whole sense of the thing is . . ."

"What?"

". . . of shame. She hates herself afterward. But the next night she's back, as hungry as ever." I meet Lucas's eyes. "I just wanted to know if all Afghan women are like that."

Flag approaches, checking the sentries. I clam up. I can only talk to Lucas about this kind of stuff.

Our column advances downvalley. The country along the Oxus is completely different from that around Bactra. There, in the central plains, stand cities you could call jewels. Here, it's all mud-and-wattle. Raider country. The men are all warriors; every eminence is a fort. If you're a boy, you clear out at dawn with your goats, heading into the camel thorn. Girls squat and weave. Lunch is *khisma*, walnuts and parched mulberries. The cheese of the country is *naffa*, salty as brine and solid as stone. It keeps five years. Men are long gone when we enter a village. When we question the old women, they cup hands to their ears.

"Everyone's deaf in this country," observes Knuckles.

"Deaf and stupid," says Little Red.

We have a guide with the Hebrew name Elihu; he keeps the Passover but follows Zoroaster. An interesting fellow, he is fluent in Farsi, Dari, and Greek. He has lived at Halicarnassus and made a pilgrimage up the Nile. I ask him his opinion: How soon will this war be over?

"Never," says he with a laugh.

We trek atop a sandstone promontory. You can see fifty miles. "In just this country"—Elihu indicates the barren pan—"rule seven warlords. Each is a petty king, backed by his own army. These men are laws unto themselves. They dispense justice, enforce truces, preside at tribal councils; they defend widows and orphans, shelter the aged and infirm. In battle they lead from the front. They hate each other but hate you Macedonians more."

Elihu draws a map in the dirt. "Belasaris, Miamenes, and Petenes lord it between the Oxus and Bactra City. Oxyartes rules south and east. Spitamenes' and Dataphernes' base was in the west, between Artacoana and the Bamian Pass, but now they have come north and allied with chiefs beyond the frontier. Chorienes, Catanes, Melpanor, Histanes; these are chiefs north and east into Sogdiana. Beneath these ride hundreds, thousands, of subcaptains and commanders. This is not counting the Daans, Sacae, and Massagetae north of the Jaxartes. Their numbers are tens of thousands and they are more ungovernable even than these Afghans."

From Elihu I learn the tribal law of A'shaara, which regulates the conduct of women. "A'shaara means 'covenant.' It is that which binds the individual to the family, the tribe, and the ancestors. Most important are the ancestors. When they turn their backs on you, God turns his back too."

I tell him about Shinar and the burden of shame she seems to bear. He affirms this. "You should have killed her," he says, "instead of protecting her."

The crime I have committed, Elihu explains, is called in Dari al satwa. The Hebrews have a term for it, too—tol davi. It means to bring shame upon someone by performing an act of responsibility that they have failed to perform themselves.

"If a stranger stops at my father's gate," Elihu says, "and my father has no food to offer, this is unfortunate but no crime. If our neighbor, however, then provides a meal to the stranger, he has committed *al satwa* against my father. Do you understand, Matthias? The neighbor has shamed my father before the stranger. This is a terrible transgression in our country. The crime is even worse in your case, for you have rescued a sister when her brother should have done so. You have shamed him mortally, do you see?"

"Well, where the hell was *he*," I ask, "when Shinar needed him? I wouldn't have had to do anything if he had been there to look out for her!"

"Exactly."

"He should be grateful to me! Haven't I defended his sister? Haven't I saved her life? By the gods, my dearest wish is only to return her safely to him!"

No, says Elihu. "You have shamed this woman's kin by doing for her *what they should have done themselves*—and for that, they can never forgive you. As for her, she is the vehicle of this shame. The ancestors have witnessed. This is what she experiences now, being with you. And if you evoke feeling in her, her shame is double."

"In other words," I say, "to an Afghan it would be preferable that Ash the muleteer continue to beat and abuse Shinar, even kill her, than that I should help her."

"Indeed."

"Or that Tollo or some other scuff should rape and outrage her. That would be better too."

"Precisely," says Elihu.

All I can do is shake my head.

"And I will tell you something else," says our guide. "Every act of kindness you perform toward this woman will only drive her deeper into shame. In her eyes, you must understand, she is unworthy. She has broken the covenant of *A'shaara*. For this," says Elihu, "God has turned his back on her."

"Well, what kind of a god is that?"

"I am not a priest, Matthias."

"It is no god at all. It's a devil."

Elihu turns palms skyward—the same gesture Ash employs, which is equivalent to a Macedonian shrug. "This is the devil's country," he says. "And you are fighting the devil's war."

Another of our column's assignments is to take prisoners. Rabbit-hunting, the soldiers call it. We are to snatch any male we can lay hands on, the higher-ranking the better, and deliver him alive and unhurt to Alexander's officers.

We cordon villages, roust grandmothers and wives. Where is your son? Give us your husband! It is forlorn duty. When you collar a man, he plays deaf and dumb, or enacts outraged innocence. You know he's with the enemy; they all are. But what can you do?

Our company holds to good capture-discipline, because of Stephanos, who will not permit brutality. But many other litters play rough. It is not our business to stop them. In their view, we're the ones who are derelict. But the pulverization of the powerless is sickening to watch—and of course it makes the Afghans hate us more—particularly when it is performed in front of the captive's wife, mother, and children.

"Do you ever think of your own mother?" Lucas asks me one afternoon, when we have shaken down three hamlets since morning.

"All the time. And my sister. And Danae."

We rough up another village that evening, tear open another string of underground ricks. Here are three families' stores of rice and lentils. We seize them. The mothers clutch at us, wailing that they will starve. Flag scribbles "C.C.'s," certificates of compensation. The housedames stare in incomprehension.

"Present this to the quartermaster. The officers will pay you when they come through."

Elihu translates. The matrons blink, unhearing. "Pay you twice what your stuff is worth."

The old women don't get it.

"They're all deaf and stupid."

21.

Our litter returns from the rabbit-hunt to find four-fifths of the army across the Oxus. The camp blazes with excitement. The war may soon be over! Spitamenes and Oxyartes have sent messengers to Alexander. They have taken the pretender Bessus into custody. They will turn him over to Macedonian justice if our king will give them peace. Of course he will. The treaty may be signed in days.

A further bonus awaits us: horses.

In our absence downvalley, Alexander has discharged with honor three cavalry squadrons of Thessaly, 660 men. He is sending them home richer than princes. Their mounts go up for sale. We're all too broke to buy one, of course. The army steps in; it will pick up the tariff. The price is one bump: eighteen months' extension of enlistment. "Take it or leave it," says Stephanos. He takes it and so do we. We cross the Oxus as mounted infantry.

Our orders, now, are to scour the region for riding stock to replace that lost in the mountains and the Stone Desert. Alexander wants seven thousand mounts and remounts, fit to ride, by fall. By then Afghanistan will be incorporated into the empire. The army will recross the Hindu Kush, this time for India, before the first snows.

I love my horse. She's a Nisaean mare—milk-colored, with a brand on her right quarter in the shape of a panther. Her name is Chione, "Snow." She cost three silver talents when her original rider acquired her in Media. I got her for half. A steal. She's nine years old and boasts more wounds than Alexander. Her conformation is only ordinary, though she has a strong neck, long legs, and a deep, powerful chest. She has quirks. She likes to be fed from a manger; she won't touch hay, even oats, spread on the earth. She is spooked by anything white. She nips. She butts. She will not be hobbled. She is terrified of bees. She loves pears and will eat mulberries till she makes herself sick.

She is also a first-rate cavalry mount. Hare-quick from a standing start, she will hold a line like a carpenter's rule and not balk at any trench, wall, or obstacle. She can gallop boot to boot without skippering—seeking to outpace her wing mounts—and in the wedge she turns like a swallow in a flock. I do not train her; she trains me. She is the finest horse I have ever owned and I love her as dearly as my own mother.

As mounted infantry, we receive the same allowance for feed and care, called a "stunt," as regular cavalrymen. We use this to hire grooms, namely our women. Ghilla stays with Lucas; Shinar keeps with me. Our stunt of a drachma a day covers expenses with ease, and the best part is, in steppe country where our mounts can graze, we get to stick the overage into our purse.

And we're making a killing in the horse trade.

The tribesmen know the war is almost over. Every bandit wants to unload his ponies. In half a month our outfit acquires more stock than we can herd and more new friends than we can play host to. Returning from the prairie east of Maracanda, we escort 310 horses and nearly as many men—Bactrians, Sogdians, even a few wild Daans and Massagetae—all eager to sign up for pay with Alexander. Spirits are high. We have all become the best of mates.

One night an incident occurs.

A brave of the Sogdians takes a fancy to Shinar. He offers a fine colt for her. Clearly he expects me to comply. The hour approaches midnight; the settlement is our Macedonian camp, within which several score of these wildhearts have congregated, all cockeyed on *khoumiss*—fermented mare's milk—and randy as stallions. The situation calls for no small delicacy. To offend the fellow (who is backed by a number of his equally assholed mates) could precipitate a fracas, even a bloodbath.

I explain to the Sogdian, with respect, that Shinar is my wife.

This elicits gales of hilarity. In the Afghans' eyes, the girl is clearly outcasted. The buck intends, it is plain, to pass her round to his mates like a banquet favor.

"What fault do you find with my colt?" he asks, meaning the price he offers.

"None. It is a fine animal."

He turns palms up, as if to say, Then let's make a deal.

"The woman," I repeat, "is my wife."

The brave now believes I am toying with him. I disrespect him. I have affronted his pride.

Flag appears and defuses the moment. He buys the colt for three times its worth. The buck and his cronies, satisfied, take their party elsewhere.

Except now Shinar is furious. She stalks off in outrage. How have I offended her? I have no idea. Ghilla goes after her. Even she can't bring her back.

At dawn when the column moves out, Shinar is missing. Someone has found her hair, hacked off and thrown on the ground. What this means, I can't begin to guess.

Over the next two nights, Ghilla seeks to enlighten me. That the Afghan buck sought to degrade Shinar as a whore was insult enough, reminding her as it did of the terrible vulnerability of her station. But that I would claim her as my wife, when she was not (and, more critically, when her Afghan countrymen *knew* she was not), is insult on top of insult.

I don't get it. Didn't I defend her? Wasn't I ready to shed blood on her account?

Ghilla sighs. "Can you be so blind as to how she feels about you?"

"Oh please. Don't tell me that."

"When you say she is your wife, when she is not and can never be, you rub her nose in her bitter fate."

Next day Shinar is back. She resumes her duties as my groom, but will not speak to me or meet my gaze. She won't tell me why she chopped off her hair. Fine. I am in a theater of war three thousand miles from home. This is drama enough. I refuse to participate in any additional theatrics.

Two days later our column reaches Adana, first in the string of Seven Forts. Alexander has been here some days past; the place has surrendered and been welcomed into the fold. Alexander himself has pressed on to the Jaxartes, ultimate outpost of the empire of Persia.

Here our king will halt.

Here, at this frontier, Alexander will mark the limit of his northern advance.

A Mack garrison holds Adana. The six other Fort Cities, we learn, have fallen without a shout. Our mates garrison them too. The news is all good. Now that Bessus has been arrested, his Daan,

Sacae, and Massagetae allies have made off to their native steppe north of the Jaxartes; his Bactrians and Sogdians have scattered to their villages. The warlords have agreed to peace. Alexander has presented Spitamenes and Oxyartes with prize Nisaean chargers and has sent back to Bactra City for more gifts of honor. He will convene a congress on the Jaxartes. There, in a ceremony, he will make the Afghan barons his kinsmen and incorporate into the army at top pay whichever of their sons and princes wish to enroll themselves in the ongoing adventure. The warlords themselves, if they desire, will ride with Alexander's Companions when the army advances to India.

Our company reaches the Jaxartes two days later. New stock pens have been erected outside Alexander's camp. Quartermasters log in our 310 ponies (other companies have brought in over 4,000, with another 3,000, we hear, at the Seven Forts). Ten days more and the corps will have made good all its losses in pack and riding stock.

Our share is a slick fortune. The litter is flush. I pay off my debts, with enough left over to refurbish my kit and even address some of Snow's infirmities. The lads rally for a bust-up along the river. The whores' camp has caught up with the army; we have flute-girls for those without women, and enough pank and nazz to get properly varnished.

I collect a bouquet of lupines to make peace with Shinar. She won't have it. She stalks away, down to the river.

Oh hell.

"Am I a beast to you?" She confronts me when I follow her. "I have heard your soldier's saying, 'Who sheds his blood for King and Corps . . .' Do you think I don't know what this means?"

I tell her she hasn't heard *me* say it.

"It means," she says, "that we are animals to you. What you do in this foreign land means nothing. Ghilla is nothing to Lucas, and I am nothing to you."

"Is that why you cut your hair off?"

"Yes."

"And why you ran away?"

"Yes."

Would you have preferred it, I ask, if I gave you to that young buck to be passed around to his cronies?

She accuses me of twisting everything.

"Should I have left you with Ash? Should I have trekked on, leaving you beaten by the side of the trail?"

"I am not your wife!"

"What does that mean? Are you relieved or angry?" I catch her by both shoulders. "Shinar. Shinar . . ."

"You should respect me. I have saved your life!"

Respect? I remind her it was I who bought her freedom.

"I don't want freedom! What can I do with freedom?"

I don't get it. "What do you want from me?"

"Nothing. I want nothing from you."

She starts throwing her kit together. I have watched other Macks in a hundred dust-ups with Afghan women. Now I'm the idiot. I can't believe it.

"Where are you going?"

"What do you care?"

Again I marvel at her Greek. "Where did you learn to speak so well?"

"From you."

Exasperation overcomes me. I order her back to camp. She confronts me with arms folded. "Can't you understand, Matthias? I have lost everything. I have nothing but you."

And she breaks down. I take her in my arms. For once she doesn't fight me.

"Shinar," I tell her, "when I first saw you in the mountains, I was struck to the heart by your beauty. Your eyes, your skin. The way the wind blew your hair across your face . . ."

I am no lover. I'm no good at this stuff. All I can do is tell her what she makes me feel. It seems to help. Little by little she relents. I make her promise not to run away again.

"Were you unhappy when I was gone?" she asks.

"Yes. I had no one to fight with."

We climb the hill back to camp with our arms around each other. Nights get cold fast in that country; her woman's warmth feels good at my side. Already I am looking forward to evening's end.

But when we reach the bonfire, instead of a blow-out in full blaze, we find Rags and Little Red kicking sand onto dead ashes. Horses are being saddled for action, arms and armor are being trundled up.

"Red, what's happened?"

Flag appears on horseback, leading my mare. He's in armor, with his half-pike in his fist and my kit and weapons across my animal's back.

"Our dear friend Spitamenes," he says. "He couldn't let us finish our party."

The Wolf, Flag reports, has struck again with treachery. Crossing the Jaxartes by night with four thousand, he has attacked and overrun all Seven Forts. He has massacred our garrisons. The whole country has gone up in flames.

Flag slings me my gear.

The war, it appears, is not over. It has just begun.

145

BOOK
FOUR

The Desert Wolf

22.

Every man in the Jaxartes camp is ordered to pack seven days' rations. Advance units are dispatched in darkness to the nearest of the Seven Forts. Their orders are to cordon the sites, permitting no man of the foe to escape to bring warning to the others. Additional divisions are sent at first light to ring the farthermost forts. Alexander sends for the siege train. This and the other heavy baggage still have not reached the Jaxartes. Miraculously the column has escaped Spitamenes' marauders; otherwise it would have been massacred too. Two squadrons of fast cavalry are dispatched to locate these troops and turn them toward the Seven Forts. Rams, bolt catapults, and stone-throwers are never transported assembled. They're too heavy. Only the iron fittings are conveyed, with the shafts and ratchet wheels of the windlasses, and the torsion bands made of human hair. Wooden members of the artillery are cut and fabricated on-site of local timber. It is a marvel how quickly the engineers can trim up the pieces and get the engines assembled and ready to fire. These will raze the walls of the Seven Forts. All except the largest, Cyropolis, are of mud-brick. They will crack like candy.

Word is passed as the army marshals to move out from the Jaxartes camp: For the first time Alexander permits the troops to take women and children captives under their own hand and sell them for their own profit.

The king addresses our brigade alongside the stock pens as the sky begins to lighten. A drizzle has got up, making the troops, whose hair and clothing are matted with dust from the night's packing-out, look like men made of mud. Horses stand hobbled, nosebags on; mules bawl as their stockmen wrangle them into trains.

"My friends, no few of you have comrades and friends in the garrisons of the Seven Forts. Give up all hope of finding them alive. The Desert Wolf has no reason to restrain his own savagery or that of his troops. Now answer me, brothers, and speak the truth. Can you govern your hearts in the attack? Can you fight as soldiers and not as wild beasts? If you can't, say so now and I will leave you here. Make no mistake, I intend that no man of the enemy shall escape our vengeance. But we will do this as an army, not as a rabble. Can you control yourselves? Can I count on you?"

Adana falls in a morning. Alexander does not direct affairs from afar. He goes up a ladder with the first assault. Inside the city, even lads and old men are put to the sword. By midday the troops have crossed the six miles to the second fort, Gaza, already ringed by Polyperchon's brigade. Our company under Flag and Stephanos is dismounted; we leave the horses on the cordon and go in to take the place by storm.

Inside the gates the fighting is house-to-house. The defenders punch passageways through the party walls; as our fellows clear one room, the foe skips to the next, loosing a cascade of bricks and rubble behind him. If we press too close, he darts round and strikes from the rear. He has learned to shoot through windows and to sling arrows and darts from heights.

You clear houses as a team—a penetration element, an assault element, a security element. One or two troopers break down the door. Their mates burst through in armor, blades first, wheeling to cover both walls. Afghan houses are all the same: a court that branches to two hallways with rooms off each; sometimes a second story, with a stairway and a roof. The assault team pours through the initial breach, then clears the house room by room. If there are two doors, the team goes through both. But the foe is ready for this. He has rigged roof-beams to crash upon us and floors to give way beneath our tread. His women and children duel us from rooftops, slinging tiles and stones.

If we attack from the roof and a man gets wounded, it's hell to get him back out. Break in from the ground and you're fighting uphill in pitch black. Interior rooms are windowless. Bursting in is like plunging into a closet. Dust chokes everything; the foe lurks behind screens and crouches within trap-holes. In one house, Dice takes a spear square in the bollocks. Getting him out costs Little Red his ear and a *machate* dart—a cane arrow with a particularly wicked type of warhead—up under his jaw. We have to cut the head off with iron pliers and pull the thing out point-first, a whisker from his carotid. The foe is a master at playing dead. You pass a corpse in a dark hall and it suddenly springs to life, vaulting at you with daggers in both fists. The enemy slings naphtha in crocks with rag fuses; when they shatter against a wall they paint with flame any luckless scuff the juice splashes on.

There is only one answer to such resistance and that is to leave nothing living. Wounded are slain where they lie. Prisoners are herded into impounds, to be murdered later with their wrists bound behind them and their own *pettus* bagged over their heads. Mack troops cauterize a district the way a surgeon sears corrupted flesh. Entire quarters are left sterile, razed to ash. You know a position has been neutralized, our colonel Bullock declares, when nothing remains to support a flame.

In five days the army takes all seven cities. I hear fifteen thousand for numbers of enemy slain. Flag says a captain of the king's staff told him twenty. Alexander himself is gravely wounded, at dawn at Cyropolis, by a blow from a great stone. He recovers by noon, enough at least to show himself and signal the corps not to slacken its assault.

By the sixth day the entire region has been reduced to powder. I have not moved my bowels except in terror the whole time. My eyes are sockets. Dried blood cakes the cracks in my hands and lips. Every inch of flesh is lacerated, abraded, contused. We cannot sit; it's agony to stand. No one can eat, spit, or piss. We collapse like felled timber and sleep like blocks of stone.

Costas the chronicler finds us amid the rubble. We hate him. We hate everyone who has not burst through doors beside us. To his credit, the correspondent reckons this and treads with delicacy. His presence remains unendurable.

"Do you know what I hate about you wax-scratchers?" Lucas addresses the writer in a tone I have never heard from his gentle soul. "It's the phony phrases you use to make this shit sound like it makes sense."

My friend has changed in these six days. We all have. We have had to kill men in cold blood, unarmed men, bound and blindered. There is no option. The foe can't be held in custody. He can't be released. Besides, we hate and fear him. We line him up, in ranks twenty-across, and send him to hell as fast as a camp-cook goes through a brace of doves or thrushes. Lucas no longer resists this.

He takes part. Like me, he packs an Afghan *khofari* knife, curved for cutting throats, and wears his whetstone on a rawhide thong around his neck.

"What phrases?" Costas asks.

" 'Subdued the region,' " answers Lucas. "That's a beauty. I love that one."

We're all thinking of Dice and Little Red, and that no chronicler will put out a paragraph about either of them and, if they did, they'd fake it up to conform to some sham notion of honor or integrity. We're thinking of the sheepfold of Afghan prisoners, whose throats we slit yesterday. Or was it the day before? It's not fair taking this out on Costas, who's a decent fellow if the truth be told. We don't care. "Why can't you tell it straight?" Lucas demands.

Costas replies that the public only wants certain kinds of stories. There's no demand for the other kind.

"You mean the true kind," says Lucas.

"You know what I mean."

Flag appears in the doorway, or what had been a doorway but is now rubble. "Go easy on the man, Lucas. He's only trying to earn a living."

Costas defends himself. What does he, or any correspondent, want? "Just to acquire a modest name, sail home bearing tales of distant lands, and offer them for readings and recitals. What's wrong with that?"

"What's wrong, you fuck," answers Lucas, "is that *words have meanings*. People believe the bucketwash you put out. They think that's how it is, particularly young men, who are suckers for tales of glamour and glory. You have an obligation to *tell them the truth*."

The phrase Lucas hates most, he says, is "put to death."

"What the hell does that mean? That we tapped these sheep-stealers on the shoulder and they slipped off to slumber?"

I have never seen Lucas like this. I'm in awe of him. We all are. As each word spits from between his teeth, it's all we can do to keep from cheering. He feels it and lets it fly.

"Language matters, Costas. Words mean something. How dare you paint over with pretty phrases the acts of horror that turn us, who have to perform them, from soldiers into butchers and from men into beasts? Look at my feet. That black isn't dirt. I can scour my flesh with lye and caustic: That man-blood never comes out.

" 'Put to death?' Why don't you tell it plain? How we hood these luckless bastards in their own cawls, truss their limbs, and bend them over, asshole-to-navel alongside their fellows. Leave the throat bare, orders the sergeant. One stroke, mate. Mind your hand, you don't dice yourself. Where is that picture in all your 'chronicles'? Where is the line of living men, on their knees in the dirt with their hands bound behind them? Where are the smocks we wear, like butchers of the charnel house, and how when it's over we sling every garment into the fire, so deep goes the stink. You don't tell that, do you? Nor how the men we slaughter writhe on the earth, squirming away from the weapons' edge, how you have to pin their feet between your legs, or that it takes two of you. What shrift are these victims given? The less the better; none at all if possible. By the time we get to them, they're so bundled it's as if we're butchering packages. Soldiers call them 'bags.' Bags of blood. Bags of entrails. God, what a stench when a man's guts are opened to the air. That doesn't go into your dispatches, does it? We read nothing about the sound the 'follow-on' makes, going down the line of throat-slit men with a club, bashing skulls like walnuts, while the still-living men pray without voices or curse us in gurgling blood or plead for their lives. The silent ones are the scariest. Men with guts. Better men than we are."

Flag has stood still for Lucas's tirade, knowing how young soldiers can choke on horror and must be given the chance to spit it out. But he will not endure a word uttered in favor of the foe.

"Were they better men, Lucas, when they flayed our countrymen alive or spitted them over coals?"

"I hate the Afghan," Lucas replies. "He is a beast and a coward. But what I hate most is he has dragged us down to his level. Can you defend the massacres we enact, Flag? Is this Macedonian honor?"

Our sergeant's lips decline into a dark smile. "There is no honor in war, my friend. Only in poems of war."

"Then what *is* there?"

"Victory."

The circle falls silent.

"Victory," repeats Flag, addressing all of us. "Nothing else matters. Not decency, not chivalry. Look war in the face. See it for what it is. You'll go crazy if you don't."

He turns to Lucas.

"I admire you, Lucas. You're a good soldier and you showed guts to speak your mind. But with respect, my friend, your position is that of a woman. Your words are the words of women. You should be ashamed of yourself, even to think such thoughts, as I know your father and brothers would feel shame if they knew. It is a man's role to fight, to achieve, to conquer. In what era has it been otherwise? A man's call, if he *is* a man, is to exert his supremacy or die trying. As Sarpedon addressed his friend Glaucos, leading him into battle on the field of Troy,

Let us go on and win glory for ourselves, or yield it to others.

"Glory," replies Lucas, "is in short supply around here."

Flag rejects this. "Does a lion hesitate? Does an eagle hold back?

155

What is the call of a gallant heart, except to aspire to mighty deeds? Here is the standard Alexander holds before us. By Zeus, men a thousand years unborn will curse bitter fate that they have not strode here at our sides. They will envy us, who have labored in such a cause and wrought such feats as no corps-at-arms will ever achieve again."

"Like cutting unarmed men's throats?"

"Would you prefer them armed, Lucas?"

"I'm no coward, Flag. I'll fight anyone, including you. But I won't butcher you. I won't tie your hands and kill you like a pig and call it valor. And if you can perform such acts in good conscience, you're worse than a woman, you're a beast."

Flag comes out of his seat. I spring in front of him.

"Leave Lucas alone, Flag. He's a man and a Greek to think and ask questions, to question what is right."

In a moment Flag regains his self-command.

"And what *is* right, Matthias? Or do you take the enemy's side too?"

"When we were boys," I say, "we rode from dark to dark, training for the charge and the chase. We dreamed of standing before our king as knights and heroes. I still do." I turn to Lucas and the others. "There must be some way to be a good soldier in a rotten war."

Boxer laughs. "When you find it, Matthias, be sure and let us know."

23.

The brigades at Cyropolis are granted three days' rest. The men need it badly, but the break is even more critical for the horses and mules, who must get green forage or they'll break down. The siege train has caught up with the army now. With it comes mail. I get twelve letters from Danae, all in one packet. The most recent is seven months old. Flag gives me half an hour to savor this correspondence. "Then get back to camp and be ready to move."

I find a patch of shade beneath a mud-brick wall. In the square before me, our section and another are roping up women and children prisoners. As I said, Alexander has in this campaign for the first time permitted troopers to take captives and sell them for their own profit. Clearly our king's object is less to put money in the men's purses than to fire our zeal in rounding up every last dame and urchin, so that not so much as a runty whelp gets away to bear hope to his compatriots. We have thrown in together, our section and another, agreeing to divvy the proceeds of the day's take.

I flop in the dust with Danae's letters. Like every scuff, I arrange them first in order—most recent on top. That way I'll know early if my darling has sent me a "Sorry, Sweetheart."

Sure enough, she has.

Another man. Danae fears her youth passing. She loves me but . . .

Like all soldiers, I have dreaded this hour. I have rehearsed it and braced for it, expecting it to devastate me. Now in the event, I feel no distress. I feel nothing.

Across the square, the slavers are branding their catch. They're all Arabs, these villains; they know a poor crop when they see one, and these Afghan brats and bitches are certainly that. Insolent, illiterate, in love with freedom, they can be domesticated no more than a pack of jackals. On the trail they will bolt or die.

Danae's message is seven months old. It occurs to me that she has probably wed by now. Likely she is with child.

Some perverse impulse makes me open and read the other letters, the earlier ones when my betrothed is still mine. It is these that break my heart. The reality is apparent in lines unwritten that Danae has met and is growing attached to that man who now replaces me in her affections. Can I blame her?

I am with Shinar.

I have been for months.

I'm the one who has played false, not Danae.

The slavers appraise their inventory as they would horses or mules. They check teeth and feet. They take care when thrashing their stock (which they do with a cruelty exceeding even that of the Afghans themselves) not to inflict injury that will damage the goods.

I return to camp to find a blow-off going. Soldiers are not grim after massacres. They booze and crack wise. Have they taken prizes? Will there be a bonus or a step? If they have lost a friend, it enlarges their hatred of the foe. They feel no remorse. They have done a good day's work.

I grab chow with Knuckles and Lucas. I say nothing about Danae's letter. My mates are toting up the women and children in the day's bag. Boxer is off making a deal with the Arabs. Knuckles reminds Lucas and me of our first fighting debacle, long months ago, in the village with the sheep pens.

"You've come a long way."

"Rot in hell," Lucas tells him.

Flag appears with orders. We are to be ready to move two hours before dawn. We'll be part of the column heading south to pursue Spitamenes. Alexander will press north by forced marches to deal with the tribes beyond the Jaxartes. Knuckles stands and scratches. "How much did Boxer get?" He means for the slaves.

Flag makes no answer.

"What about those boys?" Knuckles cites three healthy youths we took captive in a quarry. Twelve or thirteen years old. Worth real money.

Flag squints away toward the mountains. "In the citadel," he says, "some of our fellows stumbled onto the site where the Afghans butchered our garrison."

He means all captives, in reprisal, will be put to the sword. There goes our slave money.

"What a war," says Knuckles.

24.

The Many Blessings is the river of Maracanda. Our relief column tracks along it, hurrying to catch Spitamenes, who's besieging the city. Where the river emerges from the heights northeast of the walls, it does so as a torrent, thundering down a gap called the Gorge of the Sisters (memorializing two Afghan virgins who, lore declares, leapt to their deaths in a gesture of defiance against some ancient invader); then it levels out and drops underground. When you ride over it, you can hear the waters rushing beneath the earth. Near the village of Zardossa the flow re-emerges, funneling down another defile, this time a sunken one, at a ford called Council Bluffs. By there, the river has spread to half a mile wide and become so shallow it can be waded by a child. Numerous bars and islands, called by the natives "travelers," stud the channel. From one bank you can barely see the other. The shore and islands stand thick with willow, broom, and cottonwood, the kind of stuff that flourishes near underground water. This day, in fall, the cottony seeds sail on the wind. The air is snowy with them.

Our column is twenty-three hundred, three-quarters infantry, all mercs, under Andromachus, called Whiskers for his great bushy red beard, and Menedemus, a dashing and brilliant cavalry commander, only twenty-seven years old, who at nineteen had taken the crown at Olympia in the pentathlon. Our half squadron under Flag and Stephanos is assigned flank security; we ride on the forward right wing, looking out for ambushes. It's a four-day chop, moving fast, through semidesert populated by scrub brush, camel thorn, and tamarisk. I trot, all the second day, with the poet.

Stephanos is one of the few Macks who does not carry, as the phrase goes, a camp woman. He has a wife and children back home, though no one has heard him speak of them; we know only that he pouches a letter to them every day. This reveals little, however, since the poet maintains simultaneous correspondence with scores of other colleagues, actors, philosophers, musicians, and heaven knows who else. When the army puts over at a foreign city, it is Stephanos's habit to take apartments in town, on his own, even if the corps has assigned him to camp or cantonments. He does this to write. It's easy to forget how famous he is. He is invited constantly to banquets and functions (which the army suffers in the interest of local relations), at which he appears in formal military dress, usually squiring one of the city's ladies of fashion, often poets themselves, or else patronesses of the arts. My fascination with the fellow has enlarged, if anything, as our acquaintance has grown. No one really knows him. Even drunk, he will not spill his guts. I find myself watching him when he doesn't know I'm looking. I study how he drinks and dines; the most minor detail of his conversation captivates me. Does he speak with approval of some author? I scour the camp for that fellow's book. Has he voiced distrust of a certain officer? I won't go near the man.

Since the mountains, the poet has become a champion for our Afghan women. On the march he will make occasion to fall in at their sides, conversing in Farsi or Dari or, with Shinar, in Greek. He takes their cause with the army. I have seen him teaching Shinar to read. He thinks I don't appreciate her, and he lets me know.

"What you must keep in mind, Matthias, is that this young woman who shares the hazards of your life—and all her sisters who do likewise with our fellows—has traversed seas of the soul such as you and I cannot begin to fathom. In her village, even to be glimpsed by a foreigner would cost her a beating. To speak to one would mean her life. Now here they are, with us. Do you think these women have put such disrepute behind them? It burns in their vitals every hour. Each scrap of pleasure they share with us, they pay for in the currency of secret shame. Yet they love us. This girl loves you. Have you heard her, ever, speak the name of God? She cannot, for in her eyes she and her sisters are heaven's outcasts, banished to an exile from which they can never return. 'May you see God's back' is the cruelest Afghan curse. Such is your girl's bitter bread, which she must choke down anew at every sunrise."

I ask, has he written verses of these girls? He will not answer.

"Soldiers and their women," declares the poet, "are not as crude as their betters imagine. To watch your brother Elias and his mistress, one could believe he was looking on a lord and lady, so solicitous is each of the other's weal. Even Flag, who prefers wantons, will not mistreat them. And what, while we're at it, of this corps of bawds and strumpets that tracks the army beneath all weathers? They have become sisters to us. No dame back home laughs as gaily as they, or so gives herself over to such simple pleasures as a bath in a river, a tussle in the snow. The army packs infants in thousands. Who cares for them? These wenches scorned by all. As whores they may have started; they have become mothers and sisters and wives. How excruciating must the torment be to them, who know that the man they call husband in this country will cast them aside when his discharge comes and return home to his real wife and children, never to speak again of this matron and her brats with whom he has shared the keenest joys and sorrows of his life. Do you remember on the Oxus when the told-off Thessalians were selling their horses? How poignant those partings! Yet next day those same men turned out mothers and children too. How did those abandoned feel? Have they endured less than we? Every league we tramp, they trek with us. They suffer casualties as we do. They perish of fatigue and want, of thirst and disease. They are kicked by mules; they spill down mountainsides; frost takes their limbs. Nor are they immune to enemy action, for the foe knows well how to raid our camps and in fact seeks them out, particularly these marauders of the Wild Lands—Daans and Sacae and Massagetae—for whom pillage and the taking of plunder is second nature. These maids know how to fight too. Every one packs a spike in her hair and reckons all the soft spots to sink it. These jades and doxies are the unhonored champions of our cause. Without them, we couldn't last a month."

The column relieves Maracanda without incident. Spitamenes, who has held the city briefly, takes to his heels at our approach. The natives claim that his flight is at their urging; they fear Alexander's vengeance if the king believes the city has harbored his foe. Or perhaps this is just their story. In any event, as soon as Andromachus and Menedemus learn this (before our fellows have even dismounted), the column puts about in pursuit. As always, no one tells us anything. Our half squadron, which had constituted one wing of the vanguard, receives no orders until a courier sent by Andromachus rides up, noontime of this breezy, cotton-aired day, and instructs us to hold in place while the column countermarches past, back the way it came, then reconfigure ourselves as the rear guard. In other words, no mooch for us or our horses.

"What genius came up with this stroke?"

I am with Rags, Boxer, and Knuckles where the highway turns beneath the city walls. When our mob hears we are not going in, a groan rises from all. The city means grain and sweet water for our animals, bunks for us, or at least a squat behind walls and the chance of half a night's sleep. Now instead we must make off, unfed, unrested, with night falling in a few hours, into country cut by hundreds of lateral defiles, any one of which could conceal a regiment, along a river which, with its dense brush and cottony air, will set us up blind as a fogbank, so that the foe may appear either from the brush of the desert, driving us into the soup, or from the shallow channel itself.

"Children," says Stephanos, "I don't like the look of this."

Back we trot, along the same route we came. There is a peril to serving under a commander as audacious as Alexander and the peril is this: When the king is not present in person but others command in his stead, those officers feel ashamed to act with less dash or boldness than they imagine he would. This can get you into trouble. Soldiers sense it. They can smell a shitstorm coming.

"Covers off!" bawls Flag, cantering along our front. He means strip the oxhide sleeves off our lanceheads. "Dust 'em up!" He bends for a handful of sand to abrade the shaft for a grip. I feel a brick descend in my bowels. I'd give ten days' wages to stop for a crap. Enemy hoofprints carve a highway east. The track is so fresh that horse turds are practically steaming. He is a liar, on a trail so hot, who claims his chestnuts have not retracted into his loins.

Our post is both wings, rear guard. We have passed Zardossa village; the river flows on our right, wide and shallow, choked with broom and willow. Left is all creosote and tamarisk. Bush country; you can't see a hundred feet into it. Each two hundred yards another ravine notches through, like a side road entering a thoroughfare. Dark lacks two hours. The horses snaffle at each tributary; they're thirsty, they want to get their noses down. Orders are to make speed. We quirt them across.

March discipline dictates that a column in country that so favors an ambusher should proceed with extreme circumspection. Wing cavalry should sweep the brush in fifty-yard relays. Each dry ravine should be secured before the column passes. But daylight works against us. And the brush is so dense, it would take forever to comb even a quarter-mile swath. Wing security should be out on the river side too. We should be two squadrons, not two halves, and they should search all islands, as far as the opposite bank (which we cannot see because of the intervening "travelers," the dense brush, and the snowing cotton).

An hour till nightfall.

Too far from Maracanda to summon help.

Suddenly riders appear behind us. Their numbers match our half squadron of the rear guard; like us, they advance at the trot, about a furlong back. They show themselves so boldly that at first, we think they must be ours.

Knuckles looses a piercing whistle, alerting Flag, who rides ahead on the wing. Beside him, on the bank road, march two companies of mercenary foot. Flag sends a rider to their captains. Already we can see the infantry deploy. Flag spurs back, signaling to us to form into wedges.

Our numbers are eighty. We break into twenties. My charge is the leftmost ten. I put Knuckles at the point (meaning the rear) and ride, myself, to the wing. Left, the nearest island is about a hundred yards. I've got a bad feeling about it.

Lucas spurs past, taking his slot in the wedge. "Are they ours?" he calls, meaning the riders behind us.

Flag laughs. "Ride back and find out!"

Already we can feel the column compressing. Men's voices are shouting ahead. Something is going on up front. Through the cottony air, we glimpse companies forming fronts left, facing the bush, and right, toward the shallows.

We enter a section of bluffs. High cut-banks ascend on the left. Horsemen appear atop them. Archers. Not ours. We have no archers. The riders behind have widened their front now. The tamarisk flat between river and bluffs is about an eighth mile. They fill it. Behind them more mounted men appear. Riding double—horseman and foot soldier. We have heard of this practice but never seen it. In action, the enemy drops off his second man at the gallop; this fellow joins the attack on foot.

Stephanos reins from his post at the tail. "Sons of whores!" he calls, indicating the foe. "They've set this up from the start."

He means Spitamenes' flight from Maracanda was fake all along. This ambush has been in place for days. The foe has had time to rehearse. Doubtless he has groomed the ground, carving deadfalls and leg-breakers, blocking escape routes with brush and felled timbers.

I call to Flag to let me check the island. Too late. Without a sound the treeline comes alive. Horse archers emerge in a front. They do not loose their missiles, nor do they charge; they simply advance to the water's edge and hold their position. That's enough. Our whole company is now fixed in place. We can't attack the riders to our rear or we imperil the foot troops we're posted to protect, and we can't charge the island or we leave our own rear exposed. Lucas is cursing our forward wings for not clearing this obvious blind. Perhaps they did, and found it vacant. The foe, concealed behind more distant islands, could easily have spurred forward unseen once our scouts had passed.

What other surprises has the Wolf laid for us? The island holds about two hundred men. When our infantry rushes, how many more will materialize?

Soldiers are drilled to respond without orders to certain situations. Facing an advancing front of horsemen, cavalry attacks in wedges. Ambushed from the flank, infantry assaults straight-on. Ours are crack troops; they can perform such evolutions in their sleep. But no amount of skill or valor can help us now. We are in the trap and the jaws are closing.

All glory to Spitamenes. The Desert Wolf has suckered us like bumpkins. He has used the terrain and the time of day, the length of the march and the dearth of water and fodder; he has used our arrogance and our ignorance. He has made us fight on his ground, by his rules.

Our force is equal in number to the enemy. We are better trained and disciplined, with superior armor and weaponry. But we are strung out like ducks on the water. The Wolf will "swarm" us. He will hurl his wings onto our column's head and tail, trapping and immobilizing our mates in the center. Then he'll cut the column into sections. His horse archers will ring each isolated element, galloping round and round, loosing their bolts point-blank upon us, then scampering out of range when we try to get to close quarters. We have no missile troops. If our infantry leave the shelter of the square, armed only with spear and sword, the mounted foe will cut them off and slaughter them in detail. If we on horseback try the same stunt, Spitamenes' men will back off till we don't dare pursue farther. Either way, we are finished.

It is clear what our rear guard must do, so obvious that our commanders don't rein in even to pass the word. They simply advance to their posts, knowing each man will move on the signal. It comes. Flag leads our two wedges straight at the horsemen closing from the rear. Simultaneously our adjacent merc infantry forms up, a hundred across and four deep, and advances into the river, seeking to come to grips with the horse archers of the island. Stephanos holds back our remaining troopers, about 40, while our foot commanders retain their own reserve, 150 or so. We all know that the foe will withdraw before our charge, then hit us from the flank with concealed elements when we've run out too far from our base. There is nothing we can do about it. We have to strike first or the Wolf will drive us even deeper into the snare.

Ahead, our column of infantry stretches along the river for more than a mile. From the rear we can see the foe already starting to swarm them. These are tactics ancient as hell itself. But they work. Run rings round the trapped enemy, shooting at him on the run; when he rushes you, pull back; when he wears out, attack again. Against infantry with no defendable flanks, like ours along this shallow river, victory is only a matter of patience and time. We can see Spitamenes' auxiliaries spurring up from the bluffs and the stream, leading mules and horses laden with additional arrows. The shafts are tied in bunches like sheaves, so the horse archers can grab them at the gallop and return to the fight with their saddle-quivers reloaded.

In the rear, the enemy does not wait to receive the charge of our wedges. His front parts while we're still two hundred feet off, scattering for the bluffs on one side and the river on the other. We have no tactic to counter this. We cannot break formation to chase these bastards man-on-man. But to maintain the assault past the foe's original front means being taken in the rear by them when they re-form, which they do as swiftly as swallows, and in flank by their fellows waiting in concealment, whom we now see, in hundreds, emerging from behind the shoulders of the washes descending from the cliffs. Our unit has been tasked as reconnaissance; we don't have the weight to take on such numbers. The Wolf knows this. He has outskulled us again. As Rags and I rein our tens, the foe's front reunites and gallops behind us, seeking to cut us off from the body of the column. We can do nothing except wheel and spur back as fast as we can.

We're dead and we know it. The sensation is like a game of Castle against a master, in which each move you make, no matter how right or valiant, only drives you deeper into the bag. Our minds race, seeking some ploy or stratagem that will return us to the initiative. But we are caught like thrushes in birdlime, and the more we struggle, the more furiously we are fixed. Events unravel so fast that our senses can conjure no scheme except to revert to basics: form up, face the foe, prepare to stand and die.

Meanwhile, the Wolf has sprung the same trap on our rearguard infantry assaulting the island. Our fellows advance, up to their calves in the river. Now the foe brings more horsemen from the flank. He cuts our troops off and swarms them. His mounts are massive Parthians, seventeen-handers, whose great hooves throw up spray in the shallows, dazzling in the late light. The sight would be beautiful if its import were not so calamitous. More horsemen swing round on our rear. Flag and Stephanos take their wedges straight at them.

The fight goes exactly as we have dreaded.

The foe falls upon our infantry in two columns—one inland, paralleling the bluffs, the other at the river's edge and in the river. In other words, he runs down both sides of our axis. At quarter-mile intervals he strikes across and severs the column. In the rear, we can't see this. But we hear. There is no sound in the world like armored cavalry clashing with heavy infantry. Spitamenes' Bactrians and Sogdians are disciplined troopers, main-force units recruited and trained under Persian officers. They are drilled to fight in columns and wedges; they can exploit gaps in infantry squares as efficiently as any horsemen in the world. The foe's Daans and Massagetae are simply savages. They have no tactics but to swarm. This is enough. The Massagetae pad their mounts' chests with thick felt-and-bronze plates called "bundlers" and armor their own legs, hip to ankle. Let such heavy horse get to close quarters with infantry and the men on the ground don't stand a chance. That said, our mercenaries under Andromachus are among the stubbornest and best-disciplined troops in the corps. They are Greeks—Arcadians, Achaeans, and Mantineans, with their own and Spartan officers—all veterans, many over fifty years old. They have fought on the side of the throne of Persia, first under the superb commanders Memnon of Rhodes and his son Thymondas, then under Glaucus and Patron, two extraordinary captains of infantry, who served Darius till the last—and have only come over to Alexander, accepting pay to take his service, when the Persian king's cause is utterly lost. These warriors have fought for five years across three thousand miles and endured every kind of action imaginable, in victory and defeat. Their weapon is the twelve-foot lance, a wicked anticavalry arm, and their prowess with it is without peer. The slaughter in the shallows that day surpasses any action of the Afghan war, outside of fixed battles and massacres, for neither side will yield. The Wolf's Daan, Sacae, and Massagetae tribesmen fight for plunder and glory, to destroy the hated invader, while the mercenaries struggle simply to survive.

Where our half squadron rides, in the rear, we can see none of this. We know nothing of the other battles playing out along the forward three-quarters of the column. We have been cut off. We are eighty horse and four hundred foot. That any get out alive at all must be credited to Flag and Stephanos, who, in the midst of the melee, divine that the Wolf's intention, structuring the ambush, is to drive our troops either in the direction of the rear or of the river (which routes seem to offer the only hope of breaking free) and that along these courses he, Spitamenes, has concealed further concentrations of horse and foot to massacre us. Our commanders drive us toward the bluffs instead. Here the enemy waits in place to pound us with javelins and hurled stones. But it's better than facing line after line in the other directions. If our mounts had been fresher, if we had gotten one rest of even an hour during the day, the main of the company might have broken through and, once up the bluffs, gotten clear.

But the foe is fresh and we are spent. Our limbs, and our horses', have no strength to mount the face. Hooves lose purchase in the sand; riders spill and tumble. Those who dismount are cut down where they fall; troopers who stay in the saddle wear their mounts out and crash beside them. Only handfuls get through. When our front gives way, the foe pours upon us from both flanks and begins to shove us, infantry and cavalry, in a great mass back into the river.

To fight and win is now out of the question. The only hope is to break away. I turn my ten, or what's left of them—Lucas, Little Red, Boxer, Rags, Knuckles, and two brothers called Torch and Turtle— to force a break on the river side. Lucas has the point. The foe are all horse archers, armed with powerful compound bows of horn and bone. They shoot for our mounts. I see Lucas's Intrepid take two shafts simultaneously, one in the chest and the other in the throat. The horse does not even slow but plunges onward; the arrow-shafts snap from the working of his great muscles, while his eyes roll white in terror. Lucas thrusts his lance into the throat of a Daan bowman. I am on his left and see the fellow's head snap back like a doll's and tear open at the gorge. Lucas's lance shivers, broken by the weight of the foe; he nearly spills from the sudden dislocation. My own half-pike has splintered long since; all I have is my saber, useless as a wand against the heavily armored foe. A Daan with great mustaches blocks my escape. I see his mace has lost its head; I go after him with my saber, but as I raise it to strike, something catches my arm and holds it. I have been shot. A bolt as long as a carpenter's rule and as thick as a thumb has entered my right shoulder from the rear and driven clean through. The arrowhead has broken off but the splintered shaft juts out half a foot before me. It binds my shoulder. My arm goes dead. My saber falls. The limb plunges like a puppet's whose strings have been cut. I am excruciatingly aware that whoever has shot the arrow is still right behind me, and very close, judging by the power with which the shaft has driven through. He will drill me again if I don't get clear. I spin Snow toward the river. Directly before me rises another Afghan archer, on foot. He fires. I can see both wings of his bow kick forward. Shaft and warhead hurtle straight at the center of my chest. Over my corselet I wear an ancient iron breastplate that had been my grandfather's and that I have cursed a thousand times for its weight and ungainliness. I have tried again and again to unload it on unsuspecting scuffs at bargain prices; no one has been dumb enough to take it off my hands. This piece of antique plate now saves my life. The bolt strikes me squarely in the solar plexus. The sound rings off the iron like a bell. But the warhead does not penetrate. The impact bowls me rearward over Snow's hindquarters.

All sounds ceases. Light goes queer. I can't move my limbs. Am I dead? Is this hell?

It's water.

I'm in the river.

Instinct makes me cling to my horse's reins. But as I go down, cleaving to this lifeline, Snow plants her hooves and rears; the leather snaps. I plunge under. The foe is everywhere. I'm going into the books for sure this time. The enemy is trampling us in the shallows. It's a tactic; they perform it with skill. A hoof steps on my back. I inhale a mouthful of mud. The weight of my armor is pulling me under. I can't tell up from down. I open my eyes underwater. Arrow-shafts are ripping through the gray-green silt. The Wolf's men are right above us, firing point-blank. Those with lances impale us like fish. I am seized by the mad notion that I must save my fellows. I grab hold of a merc I don't know and haul him surface-ward with my one good arm. I am furious that he makes no effort to help. It occurs to me that he is dead; this elevates the pitch of my rage. I heave to the surface. There, in the current, lurches my mate, Rags. Three arrow-shafts protrude from his belly. His eyes are the color of glass. He plunges in death; a Daan carves his scalp.

I am overcome with terror. I go under. A horse's knee wallops my skull; I hear as much as feel the bone crack. I vault upward, seeking air. A merc thrashes into the soup before me. A tribesman rides him down, impales him with a lance thrust through the dorsal spine. The savage dismounts into the current and scalps the Greek while he's still alive, then turns back, whooping, elevating his trophy. Impossibly, the merc emerges, blood sheeting from his torn and naked skull. With his last strength, he drives the severed shaft of his twelve-footer into his murderer's liver. At this, three more clansmen rush upon him; the merc inverts his weapon, plunging it into his own throat; while he's still alive the Daans hack off his head.

Scenes of matching horror are enacted all along the column. My last sight before unconsciousness closes over me is of my pretty little mare being led away by a dashing and handsomely accoutered Afghan. The warrior neither vaunts nor displays himself like his savage countrymen, but simply trots off, like a satisfied market-goer who has just made a canny purchase.

25.

Night has descended when I come to. Lucas supports me. We hunker in the river, the pair of us, concealed beneath a cut-bank, with only our eyes, noses, and mouths above the surface.

Lucas has been sabered across the forehead. He has lost an eye. The whole left side of his face, bound up, is a mass of matted blood, hair, and flesh. Several ribs are cracked, though I don't know this yet; his right knee is half-staved, stepped on by a horse. He holds me up from behind, arms round my chest to keep me from going under. My head lolls against his shoulder. Roots and branches screen our hideout. I struggle to speak, to thank him. He hisses me silent.

Out in the current, the enemy are pillaging corpses. They troll for survivors—their own to rescue, ours to murder and loot. They carry torches. When one of them spots movement, he elevates his brand; together he and his mates converge on the site.

I am freezing. A terrible thirst torments me. My skull is pierced with such agony as to nearly make me blind. The arrow shaft has been extracted from my shoulder. Lucas has saved my life. I feel bitter culpability. I plead with him to get away, save himself. He stills me with two fingers.

"You're out of your head, Matthias."

I pass out again. When I come to, the moon, which had been high over my left shoulder, now sinks below my right.

"Can you take your own weight?"

I find a root and sag against it. Lucas frees himself. God knows how long he has been holding me up.

The river sprawls thick with bodies. Corpses have piled up against deadfall and downed limbs. The Daans and Massagetae scalp a man, then strip everything of value. They leave the bodies naked. The dead Macks and mercs bump together in the current like a boom of logs. These are our fellows. Flag and Stephanos may be among them. Rags, I know has gone in the books. I saw Knuckles take a ticket. Flea, my last glimpse of him, had a lance through one hip and an arrow wedged through his windpipe.

River rats have found this banquet; they scamper across the boom of flesh, their wet fur glistening in the torchlight.

The foe has built bonfires along both banks. One would have thought of such savages that they would, by now, be given over to riot and licentiousness. But either they are possessed of strong native discipline or their officers are made of keener stuff than we have believed. Sentries have been posted. Mounts are being tended to. Even the parties plundering corpses in the river do so with the formality, even stateliness, of magistrates dividing an inheritance. A protocol governs the despoliation. We can hear the braves. "Did you kill this one? No, I think that one's yours." At least that's what we imagine they're saying—before the points of their scalping knives inscribe the half-circle ear to ear and then the trophy-taker's

fist, gathering the victim's hair into one hank, with a swift and prac-
ticed twist rips the crown free. The depth of horror one experiences
to witness this is impossible to convey by the medium of speech.
You're sick with it; your being, in every viscera, revolts. Most excruciating is to be disabled and weaponless. And of course you fear. You
loathe yourself for calling in your heart so shamelessly upon heaven,
in whose clemency you not only have never believed but have ac-
tively scorned and ridiculed. But you can't stop yourself. Your breast
pounds, setting up such a din, you are certain, that the enemy cannot fail to hear it and be led by its drumbeat to your hiding hole.
Yet you can't curb this, either, any more than you can quell the
throttled wheezing that passes for your breath.

Downstream, the foe has strung a barricade across the river.
Warriors on horseback and afoot form a picket line, bank to bank.
They inspect each drifting log and limb. A Mack who tries to ride
the current will fetch up against them.

Lucas shows me, by his mark scratched on a root, that the river
is dropping. By sunrise our nest will be exposed. We have to dig.

I said before that shame is mightier than terror. But even shame
has a master, and that is fatigue. We are too exhausted, Lucas and I,
to feel pride or fear. Numbness is all that's left. Search parties quarter the island above us. If they find our dugout, they will flay us
alive. We burrow into the muck, dumb as toads in a bog.

Spent as I am, I can still appreciate the brilliance of the ambush
and the massacre, which the Desert Wolf has orchestrated like a
master of war. It was boxes within boxes, wheels within wheels.
Each time he showed our captains elements of his design, they re-
sponded with the proper, even aggressive, counter. Yet each evolution only drove our fellows deeper into the snare. To participate was
like watching a tragedy on stage, where each scene reveals itself in
sequence, only the drama is death and we ourselves are its actors.

In Spitamenes, the enemy has found his genius—a commander of cunning, ruthlessness, and audacity, who understands not only Alexander's tactics but the heart behind them and is, in truth, ahead of our king both in conception and in execution.

The moon continues its descent; the foe winds down his search for survivors. At one point a man passes our hideout on horseback, in the current, at a walk, surrounded by a retinue of Bactrian and Sogdian knights. Can this be Spitamenes? The Wolf himself? If it is, he is younger than I imagined, not far over forty, with a hooked nose and hawk eyes, slender as a stalk. His mount is a chestnut Arabian, not big but with perfect conformation, a strong proud neck and a barrel like a racer.

For about the count of five, I get a look at the Wolf's face. If this is indeed he, and not some subordinate commander, he is, as we have heard, no savage, but a man of learning and cultivation. He looks more like a scholar than a warrior, and more like a priest than either. His dress is in the Bactrian style, except for the Persian *tarbousse*—the felt cap that covers ears, brow, and chin—with a dun-colored cavalry cloak over trousers and blouse. His boots are ox-hide troopers, not the calfskin skippers of the dandy. His lone emblem of command, if indeed it is one, is an ivory-handled dagger of the Damascene type, slung from a strap about his neck and shoulders. His aspect is grave, and his companions reflect this. Will you account me disloyal if I confess I felt attraction to the man? One could not help it. The fellow possessed that quality, innate to all born commanders, of focused and dominating intention. The champions about him were all of superlative comeliness, all mounted on spectacular stock. Yet I recall no aspect of any of them. My attention was held by this commander alone.

In later stages of the campaign, the myth surrounding Spitamenes evolved and enlarged. One heard again and again of his devout Zoroastrianism; the modesty of his bearing; his piety and austerity; devotion to scripture; that he employed no groom save his fourteen-year-old son, Derdas, but tended his own stock; that he slept on the ground alongside his warriors and would take no refreshment himself until every other's hunger had been sated. His hatred for the Macedonian invader was legendary, as was his valor in action. Though his tribal origins were of the Anah of Sogdiana, through his mother, he commanded the respect of all nations, even the Daans, Sacae, and Massagetae, for his dedication to the common cause; he was the only commander they would follow outside their own. We heard over and over of his reverence for the shrines of his ancestors, his eloquence in addressing his fellows, and his superiority to avarice. The Wolf was, men said, a yokemate for Alexander. Yet the sense that I took away from this brief glimpse by the river was that, if events had not dictated otherwise, he would have preferred the life of contemplation to that of action, and that he was at heart more of an ascetic than a warrior. In this he differed from our king, who was before all a fighter and a conqueror and who, deprived of the glory and exhilaration of war, would sooner abandon life than fashion some lesser mode of inhabiting it.

The moon sets. Dawn lacks two hours. We can hear servants in the foe's camp packing up. At sunrise Spitamenes will move out. Perhaps we will survive after all, Lucas and I.

But the lightening sky reveals a finish to our hopes.

Villagers.

Women and boys, a column approaching from Maracanda. They have marched out to pick the bones of the invader. They swarm in hundreds. It is a holiday to them.

Lucas and I have hollowed out an undermine in the bank. Into this we burrow like rats. But the villagers and their dogs are nosing all over. In minutes we are discovered.

Women and boys throng about our hiding place, cursing and hurling stones. We are hauled forth by lancers of Spitamenes' Sogdian brigades. The dames and youths pelt us with rocks and beat us with sticks. My good arm is nearly wrenched from its socket. We are stabbed with knives, our eyes and hair are clawed at by fingernails. Two words are shouted over and over, *utan* and *qoonan*, which later we learn mean shit-eaters and curs. We offer no resistance. If anything, we try to appear more feeble and beaten than we are. It doesn't work. Abuse redoubles. In the end the extravagance of the villagers' assault is what saves us, as the lancers, who are at least soldiers bound by discipline, shield us and spirit us apart, prisoners to be interrogated by their superiors.

Spitamenes has already ridden away with the lead elements. The rest of the column mounts up. No one knows what to do with us. A conference is held, of which Lucas and I can make out nothing except that no one wants the burden of our care and custody. It looks like they're going to dump us with the crones and urchins. The warriors' fever of trophy-taking has passed; they don't want our hair, there's no honor to it, and we have no weapons or armor to loot. "Ransom!" I call in as bold a voice as my bashed-in lungbox will offer, partly for the benefit of the Sogdians, hoping they'll seize upon the idea, but mostly for Lucas, to rally him and give him hope. For my efforts I am hammered across the crown with a stone mace. When I shield my face, more blows beat upon my back and arms. My skull feels like a spike has been driven through it. To my astonishment, I discover that captivity has reanimated me. A bubble of hate ascends. I welcome it. Men are born liars and so am I. Already I have resolved to give these blackguards nothing, to learn all I can about them and to use every scrap of it to work them harm, as rapidly and pitilessly as I can. No one of the foe savvies "ransom," of course. But the idea seems to have occurred to

them on its own. At least that's what we imagine the bucks are debating in such lively fashion. Meanwhile, the bitches and brats continue to spit on us through the cordon of our defenders; women
even piss into their cupped hands and hurl this at us. The parley
breaks up. We are handed over to two raw-looking braves, no older
than sixteen, who bind our wrists in front of us and lash the rawhide
thongs to the tails of two pack-ponies in the column. The animals
are beaten into motion and so are we. Off we go at the hot trot.
Stones and clods of dirt chase us half a mile down the road, with the
pack of dames and striplings howling for our blood. Throughout all
this Lucas and I offer not so much as a peep, nor even raise our eyes
from the dirt. Things have gotten bad and they are going to get
worse.

26.

Spitamenes' warriors derive from five nations. Bactrians and Sogdians make up his main force. These are legitimate Afghans, clansmen from the land between the Hindu Kush and the Jaxartes; they
fight as traditional cavalry, under civilized Persian and Persian-
trained officers. The Wolf also has as infantry tribesmen of the
south, from the Panjshir, Kabul, and Ghorband Valleys, from
Ghazni and Kandahar and from the flatlands as far east as Artacoana. These are his true Afghan units. The remainder of his fighting men are Scyths. These are out-and-out savages. The first nation,
the Sacae, are a mountain and desert people who subsist off their
flocks and herds and follow the seasonal grass. The second, the
Daans ("robbers") make their living as brigands. The Daans are not
as numerous as the Sacae but are far more warlike. Both are nomads
of the steppes north of the Jaxartes, the so-called Wild Lands, who
for centuries have chased out every imperial monarch who tried to

make them knuckle under. Third and most fearsome of the Scythian nations are the Massagetae. These are a true warrior race, who scorn physical labor and who live by raiding and looting alone. The braves of the Massagetae dismount only to sleep. They are the most spectacular riders in the world. To them goes the glory of having slain in battle Cyrus the Great, two hundred years ago, defending their native steppe.

It is to these devils that Lucas and I are handed over. They already hold half a dozen other Mack prisoners. The force splits up. Spitamenes and his Bactrians have spurred off toward Maracanda. The Sacae and Daans scatter for their villages, or more accurately to the migrant bivouacs where their women and children wait with the enclosed wagons that constitute their homes. The Massagetae, our captors, drive north for the Jaxartes. This movement comes by no means in one bunch. Rather the various clans and bands break up, each bolting in its own direction. Lucas and I have been hooded, with the other captives, but in such rags that we can steal a glance between the weave. Even blindfolded, one can estimate numbers of cavalry from their sound, and bearing can be guessed at by the sun. I gauge two thousand in this drove of Massagetae (the nation, we have been told, numbers well over 100,000), which breaks up now into no fewer than a hundred bands. Our group is about forty. A buck has been placed in charge of us, who speaks good Dari and a smattering of Greek. We can communicate. His method of interrogation is straightforward. He shouts questions through the sacks over our heads; if we answer unsatisfactorily or with insufficient promptitude, he bashes our ribs, knees, and kidneys with a cudgel that we haven't seen but that feels like a field club.

I am suffering terribly with my skull and arm. It is worse for Lucas, whose wound of the face weeps blood and will not stop; with the heat and the infernal Afghan insects, the hood over his head becomes an oven in which he roasts. His ribs and hobbled knee torture him further. And, for both of us, the terror of death. "If I die," he tells me when we stop the first night, "don't let the army cook up some phony story. Tell my people what really happened."

As for my own end, I make no such scruple. "Tell 'em the biggest-balled lie you can think of."

On the move the Massagetae subsist on curds and blood. The latter they tap from the veins of their stock by means of a sharpened reed; they close the wound with spit and mud. No one makes a fuss over this, least of all the animals. The warriors supplement this dish with a species of rice or millet meal, not unlike our own "scratch," which they eat cold with dried grapes, lentils, or walnuts. For spirits they pack *khoumiss*, fermented mare's milk. Like us they hunt on the tramp, so that meat from the odd bustard or wild goat finds its way into the pot. The Massagetae kindle fires only in daytime, when they break on the march. They move again at night. Days are blistering in this season, nights bone-rattling cold. No halt lasts longer than a few hours, except at certain defensible eminences and cave complexes. There, the troop snoozes the day round—men and ponies.

On the trek the Massagetae sing. A chantey will drone for hours, led first by one brave, then another, till every desperado in the column has taken his turn. Excepting the most precipitous pitches, no man dismounts. The Massagetae do everything from horseback, including heed nature's call. In their lexicon, to walk is the province of women and dogs. Lucas and I and the others are driven until we can no longer stagger; then we are dragged. Care is reserved only for the ponies that haul us. When our weight becomes too much to pull, we are lashed upright onto our *yaboos'* backs, with staves wedged beneath our elbows and our wrists bound before us, ankles tied together beneath the animal's bellies. When we lose our balance and topple, which we do again and again, we are left to hang upside down. Our skulls pound into rocks along the trail. We bleed from ankles, wrists, mouths, and ears. Crossing streams our heads plunge underwater, that is, when they're not being bludgeoned by whatever logs and boulders our beasts hump us over. Amazingly we manage, inverted, to get enough of a slosh to keep from perishing of thirst. When the party makes camp, our hoods are removed; we are allowed a feed, then spread-eagled on our backs and staked to the ground. The first night, one not-unintelligent-looking fellow appears and stands over me, saying nothing. Clearly he is assessing me as an example of the European invader. He studies my face with grave concentration, then bends and picks up a weighty stone. I brace to have my brains bashed, but the buck only lifts my neck and slips the pillow gently beneath.

On the tramp I hold the image of Shinar before me. This gives me strength. What would she think if she knew? Would it gratify her? Has word of the massacre reached her? Does she fear for my life?

Resolutions present themselves. I make deals with heaven. If I get out of this alive, I vow to . . . what? Take better care of Shinar? Discover some means to bridge the gulf between us?

For six days the band presses north. At intervals, other war parties intersect our course; parleys are held, news exchanged. Clearly something is afoot to the north and east. The tribesmen confer with eager animation. Then the bands go their ways.

The Afghan wasteland, which appears barren and featureless to European eyes, holds to these tribesmen trunk roads and thoroughfares as unmistakable as the Athens-Corinth highway or the Persian Royal Road. The desert contains for them inns and serais, places of worship, public squares, and marketplaces. They know every twist of it, where the sweet springs are, and green grazing, and every over-night out of the wind. The band beats from one buried cache to the next. Night descends; the company dismounts and digs. Our chief (whom Lucas and I, between ourselves, call "Hook" for his nose) oversees. Up from a bunker come *bichees* and jerked gazelle, *ghalla* (dried bean curd), weapons, clothing, and wine. Packing out next dawn, the clan buries all spare gear and grub—*kishar*, ground cloths, an extra bridle—for whatever group comes along next. *"To dal Iskandera chounessi,"* says our guard. "Alexander doesn't have this."

Interrogations have evolved beyond the routine nightly wallop-ings. We have picked up a few words, Lucas and I. And our guard-ian, Ham, has revealed himself to know a good deal more Greek than he originally let on. We are propped against boulders in groups of four with our hands free but our ankles staked to the dirt. The chieftain Hook grills us now. He wants to know why we follow Alexander. Are we of the same tribe? Related by blood or marriage? When we answer no, his mystification deepens. Why have we come here? What do we seek? He gestures to the wasteland. "Have you trekked a thousand leagues to rob us of our poverty?"

Hook's name is Baropamisiates, Man of the Hills.

He wants to know of our country, Macedon. Can horses be raised there? How many wives may a man own? West of our borders, do the heavens truly plunge to the sea?

Beyond all, Hook is curious about Alexander. That our lord is of less-than-average height confounds and infuriates the Afghan.

"If the gods had willed that your king's bodily stature should be equal to his greed, the earth itself could not contain him, but with one hand he would touch the rising sun, and with the other the set-ting. What kind of man desires that which he can never attain? From Europe he passes to Asia, and from Asia to Europe. Mountains and deserts cannot stop him, nor mighty seas check his advance."

Hook lectures us on the folly of monarchs past, who brought war to the free peoples of the plains—Semiramis, doughty Sargon, Cyrus the Great.

"This prideful tyrant, styling himself Chosen of God, whose servants carried before him an image in gold of the sun . . . his bones lie mingled now with our dust and his entrails have been scattered, a feast for dogs and crows."

The Afghans, Hook declares, possess two invincible confederates: the scale of their land and its desolation. "Your king may defeat us, but he can never overcome such allies."

It is a misconception to think of the desert as level plain, flat as a tabletop, over which travel is simply a matter of direction and speed. On the contrary, the waste is a maze of natural snares and pitfalls, bluffs and blind canyons. Rivers of quicksand appear amid rocky scarp; salt marshes materialize in the midst of sand barrens. Rifts a quarter mile deep pop up out of nowhere and cannot be gotten round. An enemy who knows his way through such country possesses an insurmountable advantage. In flight he can lure his pursuers onto spurs or dead-end promontories, from which the only way out is back the way you came, or bait you into labyrinths of gorges and ravines, from which he can escape but you can't. He can get you lost, run you in circles. And always there is water, or the lack of it. Navigating such wilderness without precise knowledge of its springs and wells is suicidal. A unit can work no more than two days in any direction; men and horses simply can't carry enough water to get out and back. Native guides are useless. They all work for the enemy. An Afghan who aids the invader returns to his village to find his wife and children butchered, or waiting themselves to butcher him. The foe bested in a fight makes his getaway with ease while you in the chase must negotiate a tangle of defiles and dry courses, knowing always that the enemy is a master of the feigned flight and the double-back ambush.

In all this, our captors take pains to instruct us. Hoods and blindfolds have been dispensed with now. Our jailers want us to see what we and our king are up against. By the time the band crosses the Jaxartes (at night on *bhoosa* bags with the horses swimming alongside), we are no longer even guarded. Where can we run?

North of the river, a succession of jagged spurs intersects the plain. We are in the Wild Lands now. The band mounts into the hills, working up a track so precarious that even these peerless riders must dismount and walk. I am thinking, not even scorpions can live in this hell. Then we round a shoulder and there appears the prettiest little camp one could imagine. Lasses and dames of striking comeliness dash into the arms of fathers and husbands; proud-looking youths relieve the warriors of their horses and of those captured at the river massacre. Lucas and I are shoved, arms pinioned, into a dead end between high rocks. Savage matrons and urchins surround us.

Will we be dismembered now?

Our interrogator leaves us. All the bucks do. The women and boys begin probing at us. They pull our hair and stick their fingers into our ears. Some poke our bellies with sticks, others pinch our skin. Our eyelids are prized open. One crone thrusts her claw into my mouth; when I recoil, she picks up a stone and bashes me between the eyes. Another squaw gropes for my testicles. I scream. Our interrogator's name, as I said, is Ham. I bawl this in terror.

In moments the youth appears, trailed by half a dozen of his countrymen. They convulse with laughter. Ham makes us understand that the dames and brats have been told that all Macks are not men but devils; they are just checking to see.

All next day the matrons troop at our shoulders. They batter us with flung stones and bash our backs and legs with clubs. Our wrists have been bound behind us. Descending rocky defiles, the women kick our feet out from under; they hoot with glee when we crack our skulls in the falls. Lucas suffers terribly with his eye and ribs; the dames discover this and torment him without letup. They don't hate us, that's not the impetus behind their cruelty. We are indeed devils to them. Our straw-colored hair and hazel eyes are the signs to these tribeswomen, not of a race of fellow humans, but of the spawn of hell. When Lucas's eye begins to weep dark fluid, the females poke at it and lick the discharge from their fingertips, confounded to discover that we Macedonians bleed blood just like them. Finally around dusk they get bored and leave us. "By Zeus," croaks Lucas, "I could not have survived another hour."

Only one maid of the band has refrained from participation in this savaging—a lass of fifteen, with eyes like obsidian and hair black as a raven's wing. Now, when we prisoners are staked down for the night, she slips to us through shadow, kneeling beside Lucas to swab his eye with the bunched-up weave of her *pettu*, which she has soaked with cold springwater. I am staked three feet away, beside another captive named Medon; I feel my chest heave with emotion, to witness such an act of mercy in this terrible place.

Suddenly a man appears from the darkness. He wrenches the girl to her feet and begins cuffing her violently. His curses accuse her of some felony we can't decipher; the maid puts up no defense. In moments, half the war party has assembled. The clansmen are howling; Lucas and I and the other prisoners shout back. The girl did nothing! Let her loose, you sons of whores! The man clutches the child before him by the hair; the tribesmen roar approval. The brute turns toward us captives. A curved *khofari* knife flashes in his hand. He shows it to us, slowly and deliberately, then draws the blade across the girl's throat, slicing so hard and so deep he almost severs her spine. I am screaming. We all are. The man dumps the maid into the dirt at his feet. He does not linger, even for the count of twenty it takes for the poor girl's blood to form a lake on the stone. He simply turns and strides off, surrounded by tribesmen trumpeting their approval. "God Almighty!" cries Medon. "Who is that man? Why did he do that?"

Ham and his mates stare down at the butchered child. "He is her father."

Women drag the lass's body into the darkness. She has violated, Ham tells us, the code of A'shaara. The crime is not us Macks' for being aided, but the girl's for aiding us. The suddenness and monstrousness of the act have stricken us mute. How can such a thing be possible? Can a father slaughter his own daughter?

Sleep is out of the question. We huddle, shivering in our rags. Our captors kick us to our feet sometime in the second watch. We expect, all of us, to be slaughtered like the raven-haired girl. But our jailers have forgotten her completely. Ham and an older brave haul Lucas and me to a crest with a thirty-mile vantage. The rest of the band has already collected. Ham points to a line of fires in the far distance—as many, it seems, as stars in the heavens.

"Iskander," he says.

Alexander's camp on the south bank of the Jaxartes. I glance to Lucas. What do our captors want of us now? To confirm that the watch-blazes are indeed Alexander's? To speculate on our king's intentions or direction of march? But no, the Afghans want nothing. Only to show us the massing of our countrymen. It is what these devils want. What they've been waiting for.

In minutes Hook's camp is packed and on the move. All night the band chops at flying speed. Wives and children are shed without ceremony; the dependents melt away, up dry watercourses and into stony vales. Past midnight, twenty new warriors reinforce the band; in the morning two more groups, of sixty and ninety, swell the total still further. My skull is on fire, seeking the significance of Alexander's presence on the Jaxartes. If the tally of watch fires is genuine and not a ruse to deceive the enemy as to his numbers, then our king has massed the bulk of his army along the river, including even the siege train. This can mean only one thing: that Spitamenes has come north from Maracanda and crossed into the Wild Lands. Otherwise Alexander would have made straight for the city, to avenge the massacre of the Many Blessings, which without doubt will have been reported to him by now.

By the second night the forces trekking with Hook's band have grown to nearly a thousand, with riders shuttling continually between it and other divisions. Clearly a battle is coming. The foe is massing to face Alexander.

Now more prisoners are brought in—other survivors of the Many Blessings, who have escaped the river only to be taken in the hills and desert. The bands drag them in in ragged lots. They are about thirty in all. They look worse than we do. Senior officer is Aeropus Neoptolemus, a captain of Companion cavalry. I know the man by reputation; he was my brother Elias's commanding officer at Kandahar. He is young, not yet thirty. He had been one of Alexander's *syntrophoi*, schoolmates, tutored by the philosopher Aristotle alongside our king and his other mates when they were boys. The Afghans have put out both of Aeropus's eyes. He is led about by another prisoner.

We are herded into an impound near the center of the camp. Despite his sightlessness, Aeropus leads. He takes all our names, committing them to memory, and organizes us into a unit with an object—resistance in unity—and a chain of command. To my surprise, the foe permits this.

"They're going to kill him," Lucas says.

Night is falling; clansmen in scores and hundreds continue to swell the camp.

"They'll make a spectacle of him first," my friend says, "then butcher him before our eyes." Lucas crosses at once to Aeropus and, with respect, informs him of this fear.

The captain shows no surprise. He remarks only that barbarians traditionally nerve themselves before a fight by abusing the weakest among them. "Tonight," he says, "that will be me." He counsels Lucas and me to pray to whatever gods we believe will most capably assist us in containing our bowels. "Personally," he says, "my favorite is Hate."

Midnight, Aeropus is hauled before the assembly, whose senior war chief (superseding Hook and the other petty *maliks*) is named Sadites, in the open beneath basalt bluffs. The night is bright as noon. The conjoined bands number well into the thousands now, with more and more riding in each hour. The camp laps the base of an entire mountain.

Aeropus serves as surrogate for Alexander. His role this night is to be harangued and brutalized. At the base of the bluffs stands Sadites. A commotion beyond our sight distracts his attention. More riders appear. Around Sadites, the front of barbarians swells outward and begins to part. The chief comes forward toward Aeropus, who waits, held by two braves, in the center of the torchlit flat.

"God has spared you this night," declares Sadites. He indicates the shoulder of the mountain. From there, mounted on his pretty Arabian, surrounded by his honor guard of knights, advances into view our nemesis and now savior, Spitamenes.

27.

"Tell me, Macedonians and hirelings, who have crossed deserts and seas to bring war to our impoverished peoples: What harm have we worked to your king? Have our armies set foot within his dominions? Have we made away with his livestock? Outraged his women? Are not even we, who dwell in the wilderness, permitted to be ignorant of his glory?"

The Desert Wolf addresses us prisoners, but his oration is for the ears of his fellows. The mob packs every square foot of the lower mountain. Their clamorous citations break in on Spitamenes' speech again and again. The throng beats spear-shafts against shields and pounds the earth with the butts of its cudgels and skull-busters.

"Your lord Alexander," Spitamenes continues to us captives, "has vanquished Lydia and Syria; Egypt and Mesopotamia bow before him; Persia he possesses; the Afghans of Bactria have been taken into his power. Now he stretches his insatiable hands for our flocks and herds. Is the world not wide enough to contain his greed?"

Thunderous acclamation again compels the Wolf to break off. He holds up his arms for silence. Lucas and I can see him clearly. He is indeed the man we glimpsed at the Many Blessings. Up close, he looks older and thinner. But his eyes in the torchlight shoot sparks of fierce intelligence and his voice carries easily with power and command. The hair stands up on my neck. Here is an adversary. Here is an enemy to freeze the blood.

"Macedonians, can your king not see that while he subdues the Bactrians, the Sogdians revolt, and when he turns, seeking to bring these to heel, the Daans and Sacae leap at his throat? All other tyrants grow sated with conquest. For yours only, victory is the spring of further avarice! He cannot go on winning forever. See how our tribes unite to face him? Hatred of him has made brothers of the wolf and the lion and causes raven and eagle to soar as comrades in the sky."

For days, Spitamenes informs the assembly, Alexander has been massing his army, preparing to cross the Jaxartes. He poises now to invade even the Wild Lands.

"Soon this supposititious bantam will learn how far the races of the Scythians extend, yet he will never overtake them. Our poverty will be swifter than his army, which bears the plunder of so many nations. How can he get to grips with us? When he believes us far off, he will see us in his camp. When his eyes say we stand before him, he will find us at his back. We are the cloud and the ghosts of night. He cannot bear us down with fire nor fix us in place with stone. For we pursue and flee with the same swiftness. I hear that the solitudes of the Scythians are made fun of in Greek proverbs, but we seek after places that are desert rather than cities and rich fields. Why? For freedom! Rather would we dine on coarse meal at liberty than feast on honeyed cakes in chains."

At this the whole mountain seems to levitate off its base. The host bawls for our blood and the blood of our king.

Spitamenes prowls beneath the torchlight. He has stripped his *tarbousse*; he paces bareheaded. Gray streaks his hair, which is thick and falls below his shoulders. His gait hitches; his flesh appears sallow. Is he unwell? Only in his voice and eyes does he seem to command unbroken strength. He speaks of Alexander's presumption to strike across the Jaxartes.

"As our warriors, only days past, have slaughtered the foe in the shallows of the Many Blessings, so shall we now butcher Alexander and his paid murderers when they attempt to force the Jaxartes. God will not permit this blasphemer to set foot upon holy soil. By the sword of the Almighty shall our river run red, stained with the blood of the invader!"

Like Hook in prior harangues, Spitamenes rattles off the catalog of would-be conquerors whom Afghan and Scythian valor has in the glorious past brought to grief. Let Alexander not trust in his celebrated good fortune, for that wind which commences in the north comes about and blows from the south. The Wolf turns again to address us prisoners.

"Your king believes us savages and ignorant, but we have learned a thing that he has not: the proper measure of man's portion under heaven.

"Great trees are long in growing but fall in a single hour. Even the lion has been made food for the smallest of birds, and rust consumes iron. Therefore tell your king to hold his fortune with tight hands; she is slippery and cannot be confined against her will.

"Finally, if your lord Alexander is a god, he ought to confer benefits on mankind, not strip them of those few they have. But if he is a mortal man, let him remember his place in the scheme of the Almighty. For what indeed is madness, save to recall those things that make one forget himself?"

Two dawns later, Alexander strikes across the Jaxartes. Our knot of captives, held by Ham and others, observes from a peak overlooking the vast, treeless plain.

The river is three hundred yards wide. On the near bank mass thirty thousand Bactrians and Sogdians, Daans, Sacae, and Massagetae. The host blackens the shore for two miles, dense as a mound of ants. I can't make myself even glance at Lucas. What chance do our fellows have, forcing a hostile shore against such numbers?

Alexander's rafts and floats launch into the crossing. We can see riders, dispatched by Spitamenes, gallop to the troops on their right and left wings, calling them in. The foe's front contracts. His depth and density concentrate within that section of the bank, a thousand yards across, toward which Alexander's armada advances. The Wolf stations his bowmen up front, at the very brink of the shore. Numbers of archers thrash forward on their own, thigh-deep into the river, so eager are they to hurl their bolts upon our men. The massive Scythian bow is wielded with one foot bracing it against the earth; it launches shafts half the size of javelins. Such missiles can fly a hundred yards with enough power to pierce armor.

How will Alexander cross the final stretch into the teeth of such volleys?

Among our first rank of captives watching from the peak is Aeropus. We can hear his mates narrating the action to him. Have our troops, he asks, made any kind of flanking move? Is this crossing point only a ruse? Has our king sent cavalry upstream or down, to get over and take the foe from the flank and rear?

Every eye strains.

Nothing.

What about our watercraft? Aeropus curses his blindness. Are they barges or rafts? How many are they?

The Mack assault advances in waves. Rafts built up into bunkers. Floats carrying twenty, thirty, fifty men, rigged with side-screens and prow mantlets. The fleet numbers at least five thousand. They cross in ranks, dense as hornets. Scores of pontoon spans have been prerigged. These extend from the Macedonian shore two-thirds of the way across the river—as far as they dare, without getting in range of Scythian bows. From these fixed platforms, anchored in the channel, hundreds of cables run back to the embarkation bank. From our peak we can barely make these threads out, so great is the distance, but clearly our fellows are not propelling their craft by oar (or we would see the current deflecting their course). Instead, they are warping the vessels across by tackle strung from the pontoon stations fixed in the channel.

"Our fellows must be hauling hand-over-hand," Aeropus says when this is described to him. "How much of the channel have they crossed?"

Halfway, he is told. Another fifty yards will bring them in range of the Scythian bows.

"What of the horses?"

They are being swum across. They trail the rafts and barges. Light infantry in tens of thousands swim behind the horses, floating their arms and armor on *bhoosa* bags of goatskin filled with straw.

"Where is Alexander? Can you see?"

Up front of course. Even at our extreme distance, we can make out the flash of his armor and the dazzle off his double-plumed helmet, of iron burnished to silver.

The first Mack barges have reached the two-thirds mark. At the pontoons. Archers of the Scyths begin loosing their volleys from shore. We can see the broadsides arcing across the open space, to splash within yards of our foremost craft. Great shouts ascend from the enemy. We can see the tribesmen surging forward. Thousands jam up at the water's edge. Hundreds press into the current in their zeal to get to grips with the advancing Macks.

On our peak, Ham and the guards have come forward. They want to see the show too. Captors and prisoners take up posts side by side, transfixed by the drama mounting to a pitch below. I can see Ham's jaw work, and his feet beat a dance upon the earth. "Now," says he to Lucas and me, "we will see your king strangle on his own blood."

"Don't bet on it," Lucas tells him.

The first wave of Macedonian assault craft has come to a stand-still. The second moves up behind, then a third and fourth. United, they form a solid mass, a thousand yards end-to-end and seventy-five deep. A hundred-odd yards across from them, the Scythian hordes jig on the shoreline, bawling curses and taunts. We all hold our breath.

Suddenly a pennant ascends on Alexander's craft. Along the Macedonian shore stand a thousand tented squares, what we (and the foe) have assumed are quarters for the army. Now at our king's signal, the hides and fabric are flung back. Crews and machines appear beneath.

"What is it?" cries Aeropus.

"Catapults!" one of our fellows cries. "Bolt- and fire-throwers!"

A thousand-bolt volley hurtles skyward from the Macedonian shore. Streaks of smoke smudge the sky. Trajectories light up like parabolas of fire.

Every eye strains. We can barely see the machines, the range is too far. But there's no mistaking the salvos of smoke and flame slinging from the Macedonian shore.

Incendiary jars.

Flaming naphtha.

"Stones and bolts! The barges are hurling them too!"

Now the assault craft surge forward. They have catapults too. Each craft is a naval bunker armed with a hurling engine; the thousand-yard front is one great platform for artillery.

So densely have the barbarians packed themselves at the water's edge that it's impossible for our gunners to miss. A second volley arcs over. Before these missiles strike, our catapults launch a third. Stones, shafts, and fire rain upon the foe. Chaos seizes the enemy shore. Every Mack bolt impales a man or horse of the Scyths, every fire-jar explodes among a jam-up of warriors and beasts.

The Afghan has no experience of modern artillery. Ham certainly hasn't. He goggles in horror at the spectacle unspooling below. That sound which is like no other—the clamor of men and beasts giving over to panic—ascends with such amplitude that we hear it plain, far away as we are. The foe's archers up front have turned and stampeded, throwing the horse warriors behind them into disorder. Great rifts open in the enemy's fore ranks. We can see his wings bolting right and left and his rear guard taking to flight. In the melee, riders trample foot troops, infantry inflicts chaos on horse cohorts.

Alexander's first wave presses forward, fifty yards from shore. Bolt- and stone-throwers fire point-blank. Where is Spitamenes? The condition of the enemy can only be described as pandemonium. Mack assault waves make for the bank at full speed. Over their heads stream volley after volley of fire and iron. The enemy's thousand-yard front, which had been carpeted so densely with troops, now scatters and breaks apart like smoke in the wind.

We captives whoop in elation. Ham and his mates hold stricken. And now the oddest thing happens. Though our captors are as numerous as we and are armed, while we stand before them with empty hands, it is *they* who are gripped by terror and we to whom initiative flows.

First to strike the shore is Alexander. We won't learn this till later. But we can see the swarms of our countrymen surging from the shallows, while the enemy slings away his shields and weapons and flees in disorder.

On the peak, we rush our captors. Before we've taken three strides, Ham and his confederates are in full flight down the mountain.

By nightfall the plain below has emptied entirely, as the foe flies north into the Wild Lands, pursued by the horse and foot brigades of Alexander.

28.

Twenty-one days later the army of Macedon returns to the Many Blessings, this time in force and with Alexander in command. Our king has chased Spitamenes a hundred miles into the steppe before bad water poisons him and compels the king to break off pursuit. The Wolf gets away. Autumn approaches. Alexander returns to Jaxartes town. We prisoners have been incorporated there into the hospital camp. Inside of a month we are well enough to travel. The corps returns to the site of the original massacre.

Both margins of the Many Blessings have been secured, days past, by the brigades of Antigenes and White Cleitus and by the Horse Command of Hephaestion. Stewards of Graves Registry have collected what remains they can recover of our fallen comrades. The official number of dead is 1,723. The army is given a day to inspect the site at leisure and to learn from us survivors, who have been held apart under Alexander's orders for this purpose, what out-rages have been visited upon the living flesh of their countrymen, not only by those Afghans and Scyths serving under Spitamenes but by the matrons and brats of Maracanda and the downvalley villages.

A funeral mound is raised. At dawn the army assembles. Full military honors are rendered to the fallen. By regiments the army parades past the barrow, upon whose summit the colors of her en-tombed battalions flutter on the air.

Alexander conducts the obsequies in person. The rite is per-formed entirely in silence. In that interval where the Hymn for the Fallen would customarily be given by the corps, a solitary flame is lit, by Alexander's own hand, again without speech. This mute en-actment produces a keen and excruciating grief and a terrible hard-ening of resolve.

When at last the king speaks, it is to offer only five lines, not from the funerary canon but from Euripides' *Prometheus*. In this scene, which closes the tragedy, Odysseus in his wanderings has reached the Rock upon which the titan lies fettered, by judgment of Zeus, in chains of adamant. Odysseus inquires of Prometheus if there is anything he can do to ease his suffering. The captive de-clines with gratitude so much as a mouthful of water to slake his thirst. Then he offers the wanderer such wisdom as he has gleaned from his revolt against heaven.

> *Even at earth's extremity,*
> *Almighty Zeus reigns.*
> *Men fly in vain from his justice,*
> *from which no crag stands too distant*
> *and no fastness too remote.*

This is the sum of Alexander's oration. He turns and retires.

That night passes like no other. There is no drinking and no gambling. Men wait only for orders. They apprehend what their king means by "justice." Here at earth's end, they will exact it. Each time a messenger appears, the soldiers rise, eager to receive their assignments.

Lucas and I are still too infirm to participate. Still we must, or never face our comrades again. Orders are passed next morning. With them comes mail from home. This from my sister Eleni's husband Agathon, a decorated captain of infantry, who lost his right hand at Issus in Alexander's earlier, more honorable wars.

> Matthias from Agathon, greetings,
>   I feel I can talk to you, now that you've been out there a while and know what it's like. I sit now, watching my infant son, who is your sister's child and your nephew, playing in the sunlight of the yard. Do you know, dear brother, that my own disfigurement had impressed itself so powerfully upon my imagination that when this child was born I expected that he, like me, would possess a stump instead of a limb. When I saw him whole and perfect, I wept. Through this babe I feel the whole world has been made new.
>   Come home, brother! Well I know the seduction of war and of anger and fear! When your term expires, let no folly hold you. Come home to us before it is too late!

Tears drizzle into the brush of my beard as I read these lines. Come home? How can I?

Am I blind to the madness of vengeance? Can I not imagine armies and armies, stretching back across centuries, each crying the same meritless anthem of payback and revenge?

I roll Agathon's letter into my pack. There it remains, wedged beneath my sack of lentils and parched barley, when the corps moves downvalley, village to village, exacting God's justice, until nothing remains living in all the region except old women and crows.

BOOK
FIVE

Winter Quarters

29.

The army winters at Bactra City.

Alexander has retaken Maracanda; the Desert Wolf has fled north to the Wild Lands. Spitamenes' purpose is still not served by facing Macedonians straight-up. The foe disperses, waiting for spring.

Afghanistan—once the passes close—becomes six different nations, each isolated from the others. Susia and Artacoana in the west are cut off from Bamian in the center, itself separated by impassable peaks from Phrada (now called Prophthasia, "Anticipation") and Kandahar in the south, and from Kabul in the central Paropamisus. From the Areian Plateau, a hardy force can take the caravan road south via the Desert of Death and work back up the Helmand and Arghandab Valleys to Ghazni and Kapisa and Bagram, but from there there's no mounting out via the Panjshir, Khawak, or any other pass north into Bactria. In Bactra City you're

cut off from the south by the Hindu Kush and from the northeast
by the Scythian Caucasus. South of the Oxus, the tribal Sogdians
scatter to their strongholds. As for the steppe beyond the Jaxartes,
the place in winter becomes so inhospitable that the Daans, Sacae,
and Massagetae themselves retire to balmier quarters.

Lucas and I are confined to hospital at Bactra City. We hate it.
No one who has not been a soldier can understand the imperative
to get back to one's unit. When Flag or Boxer and Little Red visit,
our torment redoubles. Our mates joke with us about "tickets
home." Hell itself cannot make us take one. "Are you crazy?" our
mate Pollard tells Lucas. "You lost an eye!"

"An eye isn't enough."

The hospital is not a tent affair, but the converted estate of some
Bactrian grandee. We have rope beds and fountains and black plums
in the court. Mail comes, and chow shows up hot and on-time.

We are far from recovered, Lucas and I. "You don't feel it so
much while it's happening," my friend observes. "It catches up
later." Lucas watches me sometimes. I watch him too. We laugh
when we catch each other. "You all right?" he asks. We laugh again,
but it's not funny. The equation has altered between us. Before, Lucas and I shared all secrets; no one came between us. Now he puts
Ghilla before me. He tells her things he won't tell me. This is as it
should be; I am happy for him. God knows I can't do the same with
Shinar. But it's an estrangement. I am closer to Flag now. I worry
about Lucas. He was never a brooder; he has always spoken up. He
still does, but it's different. You can't put a name to it. He's just . . .
not who he was. Of one thing I'm certain: I will die before I'll let
harm come to him. The shaft that impales him must pass first
through my flesh. I feel the same toward the others in my litter, including the new ones fresh from home, whom I haven't even seen
yet. I sound Flag out about this.

"You're becoming a soldier," he says.

Lucas and I can't talk about the Many Blessings. It's too painful. I speak to Flag instead. I lost my squad there, and my horse and my weapons. Only luck and Lucas's heroism kept me from losing my life.

I can't put Macks serving under me in such a position again. I won't. I will not let officers, however well intentioned, lead me and my men into danger without speaking my mind. I will balk if I have to. I have buried Rags and Flea and Knuckles, and the brothers Torch and Turtle. They were boys, all of them, but they were men too. Good men. Now at a table beneath plum trees, I write letters to their fathers and mothers. It is the hardest thing I have ever done.

"Things change you in war," Flag says. "Not always the things you expect."

For Lucas, I can tell, it's not the loss of an eye or the ordeal of captivity. He takes both remarkably in stride. It's the buildup, he says. The accumulation. We've been gone from Macedon now twenty-five months. It feels like twenty-five years.

"A soldier keeps hold of himself by dreaming of going home," says Flag. "That's how Lucas has done it, counting the days. Now he realizes the days go on without end."

In hospital I appreciate Flag more than ever. Every time I think I've caught up with him a little, I realize he's still leagues beyond me. I tell him what it felt like, being at the mercy of the Massagetae. "I always imagined that hard experience would make you stronger and less afraid. But it's the opposite. It undermines you because you know how vulnerable you are and how bad things can get." When I remember being a prisoner now, I wake with my bones rattling. Ten times a day my knees go queer. I have never put much freight in the gods. Now I'm starting to think about it.

A soldier should never think. Flag doesn't have to say it; I hear his voice in my head. "That's why God made pank and nazz."

We drink. I understand thirst now. We get varnished. Numbness is good. It helps you heal.

My right shoulder still will not unseize. I hoist the bumper with my left. The surgeons say my skull has been fractured; I should have joined the majority three months ago. How long till it heals? They don't know. I know I can feel every tread on the plank floor of our sick ward. When I hang my cloak on a peg, I aim to one side, then slide it over. Otherwise I'll miss completely. My skull feels like an onion someone dropped on the floor.

Lucas has been awarded a Bronze Lion for his wounds. I get my second. Lucas is decorated with a King's Garland for gallantry. He is promoted to corporal. Our bonuses are a year's pay and forgiveness of all debts to the army. This is less of a windfall than it sounds, as we'll both have to buy new horses and replace our kit from scratch.

Our women have caught up with us. They have trekked from Bactra City to Maracanda and back again. Ghilla is pregnant by Lucas, from before, early summer. You can see it even under her clothes. She tells everyone she and Lucas will marry. Should any of her male kin learn her state, no force beneath heaven will stop them from splitting her belly. She doesn't care. She has put her tribe and its cruel codes behind her. This is at once a brilliant and a terrifying thing to witness.

The other girls have abandoned Ghilla. Her revolt appalls them. Only Shinar remains her friend. Shinar has found employment in the infirmary. The job suits her. Her Greek has become fluent, and she is squeamish of nothing. "Your girl," the chief surgeon tells me, "has capacity." He promotes her from the laundry to the ward, putting her on at an obol a day, one-fourth of an infantryman's pay—a fortune alongside anything she has known. He outfits her in proper hospital kit and will permit no man, officer or enlisted, to address her except with respect.

Shinar thrives. She is changing too.

Throughout autumn and early winter Alexander dispatches divisions to distant quadrants of the country. He will not give Spitamenes the season to rest. More to the point, Bactra City cannot support the numbers of troops flooding in. Seventeen thousand reinforcements have arrived from Macedon and Greece. Dependents of the army, sutlers, contractors, and the general crowd, make above sixty thousand. The camp has become the fourth-largest city in the world, behind only Babylon, Susia, and Athens.

On the day the army disperses to its winter positions, Alexander calls the force together and addresses it in what may be the most extraordinary oration ever offered by a king of Macedon. He takes the unprecedented step of transcribing the speech and having it distributed to every unit in every post across the country.

Citing the massacre on the Many Blessings, he places responsibility not with his troops or subordinate commanders but himself.

"All fault resides with me, my friends. I have committed the cardinal sin of the commander: underestimation of the foe. The Desert Wolf has not beaten you who rode in that column; he has beaten me. By Zeus, I believed we would thrash these devils in a matter of months. I deemed them ignorant savages, unlettered in modern warfare, and no match for our force, which has vanquished the mightiest empire on earth. I was wrong. Clearly the enemy understands us, while we do not understand him. He has made us dance to his tune. He possesses answers for every tactic we throw at him. He is shrewder than we are. He has outfought us and he has out-generaled me."

All winter, Alexander declares, the corps will train in new tactics. The Afghan campaign now enters its second phase. Detailed orders will follow, but for now it is enough that all troops understand that operations-as-usual are over.

As part of this new program, officers of Alexander's intelligence interview all survivors of the Many Blessings. They quiz Lucas and me in the hospital. Everything we can remember of the massacre and afterward is recorded for examination by our king. We write down names and descriptions of our captors, sketch approximations of their routes, attempt to site their springs and supply dumps.

On Solstice Day, my brother Elias arrives at Bactra City. His woman Daria travels with him; they take up cantonments by the river in Anahita town, with two other officers of Forward Operations. I spend evenings with them when Shinar is on duty in the infirmary.

"Have you apprised Mother of this development?" Elias teases me. "She will not stand losing another son to the wiles of foreign wenches!"

And he squeezes his mistress.

Elias, through his role in Forward Operations, participates in briefings at the highest level. He knows everything. His interest regarding me is to keep me out of danger. His influence continues to scuttle all my applications to Reconnaissance. He worries, too, about Lucas. "What's the matter with your friend?" he asks. And he doesn't approve of my drinking. "You'll wind up like me if you're not careful." He means this to scare me. I take it as a compliment.

Every evening they'll let me, I linger with Elias and his comrades. They are the finest fellows I have ever known, equals to Flag and Stephanos in courage, prowess, and soldierly sense, and beyond them in dash and color. It sobers me to see how seriously they take the enemy.

"This place is worse than Persia," declares Elias's mate, Demetrius.

"It will test every man," agrees Arimmas, a captain, "but our king most of all."

The Companions fear that Alexander still does not appreciate what he's up against. In their view, we should clear out the entire region. Deport the population, man and boy, like Cyrus did in Ionia and Nebuchadnezzar in Palestine. "Nothing less," says Demetrius, "will subdue this country."

The bane of the Afghan war is getting the foe to stand and fight. Only one measure will compel him to do so, believes Alexander, and that is to chase him with one force and block him with another. Thus our king's second step: reconfiguring the corps into autonomous divisions. To each of his brigade commanders Alexander now cedes an army in miniature, possessed of all combat and support elements—light and heavy cavalry and infantry, artillery and siege train, reconnaissance, intelligence, medical, supply, and logistical organizations. Achieving contact with the foe, Ptolemy or Perdiccas or Coenus will no longer pursue him on his own, hoping to grab all the glory. From now on, one division will drive the enemy toward another. Then both will finish him off.

These steps are solid innovations. Far more controversial is the third: the integration into the corps of massive numbers of Afghan troops. This, the Companions believe, is rank folly. "We've been riding with Afghan *shikaris* for two years," declares Arimmas. "There's not one who wouldn't eat us raw if he thought he could get away with it."

But Alexander's mind is made up. In camp we're already seeing hillmen of the Panjshir, infantry of Ghazni and Bagram, Sogdian and Bactrian tribal horse as well as newly hired contingents of Daan, Sacae, and Massagetae raiders. Can we trust them? Our king doesn't care. By hiring these bandits for pay, Alexander reasons, at least he has kept them from going over to Spitamenes.

Our lord intends to make the country over by all means, civil as well as military. His boldest innovation is the *oikos* ("household") system. By decree he establishes "site incentives." What this means is that soldiers of the army, who in the past have received wages only as individuals, will from now on get their pay and allowances as households. In other words, your girlfriend is included. A man makes extra for the woman he is packing.

Further, Alexander directs, the sons of lawful unions between Macks and foreign wives are now considered Macedonian citizens. They may collect their fathers' pensions and be educated at state expense. This is unprecedented. It is revolutionary. At one stroke it overturns a thousand years of custom and *nomos*.

The decree outrages the troopers of the Old Corps. One cannot overstate the depth of conservatism among soldiers. Change is abhorrent to them. They revere the old and despise the new. And they refuse to see shades of gray. The issue to them is of right and wrong. What Alexander proposes by the introduction of pay-by-household is a slap in the face to all decent matrons of Macedon, our wives and mothers who have held the nation together by their devotion and fidelity. (Of course, these same Macks have themselves taken every foreign strumpet they can lay two fists on.)

But the soldiers feel threatened for a far more personal reason. They perceive the *oikos* system as a device to sever them from home emotionally. Clearly it is. Payment by household spurs new men like Lucas and me to take a bride "out here." And worse, from the Old Corps' point of view, to conceive of our future out here.

What the old soldiers dread most is this: that Alexander will never go home. Never lead *them* home. Clearly our lord hates this Afghan war. But not the way the troops do. They want to wrap it up and turn for Macedon; he wants to finish and keep going east.

In the end the veterans cannot stay angry with Alexander. He is sun and moon to them. They are pained by this revolution of their commander, but being the simple fellows they are, they know only to strive harder, fight more bravely, show that they remain in-dispensable. They crave above all to win back his love. Alexander, of course, is exquisitely attuned to this and knows how to exploit it for all it is worth. Now he adds a further element to set the country on its ear.

Money.

The wealth that has poured into Afghanistan with the army of Macedon has deformed the economy of the entire region. In the city market, a pear costs five times what it used to. The locals can't pay. Meanwhile, a second economy has sprung up—the camp econ-omy, the economy inside the Macedonian gates, where the pear may still cost five times its original price, but at least a man can af-ford it. The natives face the choice of starvation or submission to this new economy, either as suppliers or servants, both of which oc-cupations are abhorrent to Afghan pride. Worse still, the *oikos* sys-tem lures their young women. Soldiers reckon every currency of seduction that can nail them dish, fig, cooch. Now they have a new plum to dangle: marriage. The native patriarchs seek to lock up their daughters. But the draw of the Mack camp is irresistible, for money, adventure, novelty, romance, and now even the prospect of acquiring a husband. For by no means are these invaders unappeal-ing. Mack regiments parade, awash with youthful captains and Flag Sergeants, horseback and afoot, made swashbucking by the brass of their tunics and the dazzle of their glittering arms. Maids slip from midnight windows to consummate trysts in the arms of their ardent, hazel-eyed lovers. When delegations of city fathers appeal to Alexander for assistance in curbing this traffic, he makes all the right noises but takes care to do nothing. He wants the girls infil-trating. His object is to weaken, even sever, the bonds of family, clan, and tribe. He prosecutes this deliberately. It is his policy.

As for Lucas and me, even our own women begin acting

strange. Ghilla, pregnant, waddles in Lucas's train like a duckling. If I venture from the hospital, Shinar's eyes shoot daggers as I go.

This, too, is as Alexander wants it. What iron and gold will not accomplish, he will work by flesh. He will stand this country on its head and shake it till it quits.

The month is Afghan Saur, late winter. Shinar has stopped talking to me. She will not sleep in our tent.

"What is it now?"

"Nothing."

She remains day and night within the hospital grounds. She wears a veil when she works or, more accurately, binds her headdress up to her eyes. So do Ghilla and the other women. Not one of them will give me a true answer.

I go to Jenin, the girl who supplies our section with pank and nazz. "By Zeus, what is going on?"

The woman indicates the new Afghan troops passing in the camp. "Brothers," she says, "and cousins."

I don't understand.

"Brothers who recognize sisters. Male cousins who recognize female cousins."

There was a boy in camp, Jenin says, from our women's native village. He saw them. He spoke to them. "He told us that my own father and Shinar's brother are here in Bactra City."

"You mean as part of Alexander's army?"

"They will slice our throats if they find us."

So the veils. So the remaining within walls.

"What can we do?"

"Kill them," says Jenin.

30.

By the last month of winter Lucas and I are well enough to ride. We rejoin our company, training with new Afghan units. Coenus's brigade has been assigned two hundred "volunteers," Daans mostly, with some tribal Ghazals and Pactyans. Our colonel Bullock's orders are to render them fit to operate in conjunction with Macedonian forces—solve the language problem, pay, maintenance, feed, quarters, and so forth. And to train them and their ponies to fight like we do.

I like these young Afghan bravos. I make friends. Through them I put out feelers, trying to find Shinar's brother, whose name I still do not know. Surely he and I can talk. How can he fault his sister for taking up with Macks when he has done the same thing?

But I can't get these fellows to talk. Do they trust me? Yes. Like me? Indeed. The Afghan tree of tribes, clans, and *khels* can be traced like a directory to find anyone. But they won't do it. Two brothers I knew at Bagram have signed up here with Meleager's brigade—the Panjshiris, Kakuk and Hazar.

The pair volunteer to murder Shinar's brother for me. Their tribe is at war with his; it will redound to their glory to slash his throat. I thank them but decline.

"What if I pay an indemnity?" I ask. A blood-price, like for murder. "Will the brother take his sister back?"

He will, says Kakuk. "Then he'll kill her."

The Afghan mind, I am beginning to understand, has not altered one jot in a thousand years. These clansmen are more lodged in the past than our own Macedonians. Outside Bactra City stand three training grounds, the Crescent, the Widow's Veil, and the Panhandle. Upon these, Bullock, Stephanos, and our other officers form up our Daan companies, trying to teach them to ride in wedge formation and to charge boot-to-boot. The exercise is sketched out; a walk-through is performed; all hands attest to their understanding of the design. Then the trumpet sounds and the Afghans revert as one man to the swarming tactics they have always used—galloping in circles round the foe while whooping and loosing arrows and darts. Our commanders employ every incentive to make them ride like modern cavalry. We hold their pay. We cut off their chow. I have never seen Stephanos lose self-possession. Yet these fellows drive him to apoplexy. The concept of unit cohesion remains alien to them. They fight as individual braves, each seeking glory in the eyes of his chief. Most infuriating of all is the blandness with which they endure our captains' tirades. You cannot make them mad. They keep smiling. Those who speak a little Greek play back our orders word-for-word. No matter. The trumpet blares and they spur off again, thundering in circles.

Kakuk and Hazar explain the problem to me. It's not that the tribesmen don't want to learn Mack tactics. It's their horses. Their horses won't let them.

I am learning the Afghan mind and the tribal manner of expressing a thought. The brothers don't mean their horses won't let them. They mean their hearts won't. Fighting Macedonian-style, as a unit, is unmanly to Afghan eyes. It lacks honor. It is effeminate. For the tribesman of the steppe the object of battle is to count coup, to distinguish himself in the eyes of his fellows. The Daans have a phrase, "to kiss the mouth of death." This is their warrior ideal. You cannot kiss the mouth of death except as an individual. So they won't fight in wedges. They won't charge boot-to-boot.

When I confer with Stephanos over this, he understands. It's a turning point. We stop trying to change our Afghans. The implications are not lost on the poet or on me. "What *are* you going to do," he asks, "about Shinar's brother?"

My mates, too, volunteer to put the fellow out of the way. There doesn't have to be bloodshed, says Stephanos. Just find him and get him out of camp. He's working for the Wolf anyway; they all are.

No, I don't want it that way. I can work something out.

I have become close with Stephanos over the winter. He is compiling for the king's intelligence a roster of Daan tribes, clans, and *khels*. I assist him. I'm the only one who can half-savvy the language.

Daan means "robber" in Persian. To the Afghan of Bactra City or Kabul, who can quote Zoroaster, these northern tribes are the offal of the earth. But Stephanos and I find them brave and decent and honorable. The Massagetae (my former captors under the war chief, Hook) are a pure raiding culture, arrogant and proud, who whip their women and practice torture. The Daans are as savage but not as cruel. Habituated to the direst poverty, they lark on payday like sailors on a spree. Cash flows through their hands. They are in-capable of niggardliness. The concept of lending does not exist for them. Ask and they give, with never a thought of payback. The no-tion of tomorrow lies beyond them. The hour is everything. I never saw anyone get as blind as these fellows. And they are merry drunks. Heat and cold are the same to them, as are pain and pleasure, penury or opulence; they will brag but not complain, take revenge but never hold grudges. On watch, a Daan sentry will man his post till the sky cracks or, dispatched alone across a hundred miles of waste, run himself and his mount to death before giving in. Though they hate us for our incursion upon sacred soil, they will ride at our sides into battle and never betray us. Such is their word. They are loyal and gay and kind and so corrupt that you cannot even get an-gry at them. To them a bribe is simply good manners, and paying someone off no more than friendship and consideration. One may be terrified of them or appalled by them, but it is impossible not to respect them.

I am well enough to participate fully in winter's final exercise. The corps in its entirety takes part; Alexander himself commands. The simulation of combat is so real that scores of men and horses are injured and a half dozen wounded mortally. Our own mate Dice gets the neck-guard of his helmet shot clean through by a bolt from a catapult. I have to escort him to Bactra City in a field ambulance.

Shinar is absent from the hospital when I get there. No one will tell me where she has gone. Fearing that her brother has found her, I gallop to our quarters. She's not there, either. I find her past mid-night at Elias's house, on the floor of Daria's cooking room. Ghilla and Jenin hunker over her. Shinar lies on her side, shivering in a blanket, with her blood saturating the carpet.

Her brother has not caught up with her.

She has had an abortion.

Jenin is the girl in our section who performs this service.

I understand what has happened.

I am heartbroken. For the unborn child, for Shinar, but most of all for the fact that my woman has acted with stealth to keep this from me, to get it done while I was away, and, now, for the wall of silence and evasion that I know she and her sisters will throw up the instant I try to help.

"Are you all right, Shinar? Why did you do this? Why didn't you tell me?"

Because, she says, she feared I was getting ready to put her aside. She weeps. I kneel beside her. "Shinar," I hear my voice saying with tenderness that surprises me. "Shinar."

Ghilla supports her. Jenin presses a linen compress where the blood still seeps.

"Tell me truly. Are you all right?"

"No," she says.

My mind is racing. What to use for a litter. How to get her to the hospital. I stroke her soaking brow. I recall other absences of hers. "Have you done this before?"

She won't answer.

I confront Ghilla and Jenin.

They all go mum. Whose worlds can be farther apart than mine and Shinar's? "I don't want you to do this ever again." I glare at both other women, then back to mine. "Do you understand, Shinar? If you do, I *will* leave you."

She has lost quantities of blood. We have to get her to help. Why has she let herself get pregnant? Army women all have ways to prevent this. Why carry the child at all? In the teeth of threats from her clan and countrymen and secured by no pledge or surety from me. The opposite in fact; for clearly she believes I am ready to discard her.

Can it be that this woman feels love for me?

I dismiss the possibility out of hand, not because it seems so remote (she has been in my bed, after all, for more than a year), but because it makes so much sense—and every time I think something makes sense with her, her response confounds me.

What of my own heart? I have thought myself in control of my feelings about her. Yet I discover myself holding her with exquisite gentleness. Tears start. I tense, seeking to drive them back. But Shinar feels them.

"Will you leave me now?" she asks.

I hold her closer.

"You will," she says.

"No." I surprise myself by the certainty with which I state this. "But you must do something for me."

"What?"

"You must let me help you."

The hospital will take her. The chief surgeon is her patron; the other physicians all know and care for her. They can't put her in the soldiers' ward but the town wing, which is just as good. The surgeons have seen ten thousand induced miscarriages. I tell her this, which she well knows. I kiss her. All the resistance goes out of her body.

She says, "I don't think I can walk."

"I won't leave you, Shinar. I'm not angry with you. Only concerned for you, and for this poor child"—I cannot make myself say of *ours*—"that we have lost because others hate us."

She holds me and tries to stand.

"Help me," she says.

BOOK
SIX

The Big Push

31.

How do you know when a region has been subdued? When its villages have food for you.

All winter, Forward Operations units have been parleying with Afghan villages along the army's projected routes north, arranging for dumps of provisions to be stockpiled for the advance.

Now when we get there, not one has them.

Entering a village before the main advance, we plead with the elders for their own sake to scrounge up something, anything, for the army. That or flee. The young men of the villages have already made off with every item of value; they have gone to fight for Spitamenes. Only the old remain. They refuse to abandon their homes. What will happen to them?

"Nothing," says Stephanos, "that hasn't happened to them before."

Afghanistan south of the Oxus is ribbed with rugged, ocher-colored mountains, separated by dusty barren ravine country. Each valley contains scores of forts—old clan strongholds, employed by the natives in tribal wars. Mack engineers take these over. Sites that will serve are reconfigured, garrisons installed. Those that won't are leveled. Our bunch spends two days with an engineer company in one of the high valleys. Their captain shows us how they do it. I have never given much thought to forts. A good one, we learn, is linked by lines of sight to sister strongholds, so its garrison can go to their assistance and be aided in turn by theirs. The blockhouse's siting must dominate the area, commanding all approaches. The captain shows us how his men lay out linked bastions, above and behind one another, so that if the foe overruns a lower post, he finds himself vulnerable to bombardment and counterattack from its mates above. The science is quite clever and needs nothing more than a few mules, a mason's plumb, and a stonejack.

Our columns press north, subduing their sectors. There are no roads in this country; trails snake along dry wadis and channels carved in sandstone by the wind. Upon these trek refugees fleeing south. We pass women in columns, muffled to the eyes, balancing their belongings in bundles atop their heads. Their urchins and hounds trail in the dust; they cart their ancients in barrows or drag them on pole-litters behind emaciated asses. Last year the army would have rounded them up and sold them as slaves. This year we don't even try. Who will buy them? Packed off five hundred miles, the Afghan returns. He is either stupid or stubborn. *Narik ta?* What difference does it make?

Cresting a ridge, we rein and look back. Smoke ascends from a score of razed settlements. We'll try to talk the villagers ahead into saving themselves. They won't listen, either. Their eyes tell you.

Shinar's eyes are like the eyes of these villagers. When I held her on the floor in Daria's kitchen, I saw the same look. You see it in the faces of Afghan matrons when we Macks roust them out at midnight, to bind their sons and drag them into the dark—a look of rage but mostly of resignation, of submission to that unknowable power that we call Necessity and they call God. It is a look more fitting to a beast than to a human being, and more proper to a stone than to either. To feel pity for these brutes is folly, for they loathe us in their bones. To seek to remedy their state is arrogance, for in their hearts they are, if not happy in the sense that we of the West understand, then at least at one with their fate. Who are we to instruct them otherwise?

Flag trots alongside me. "You're thinking again."

I laugh.

"About your girl, eh?" He has heard about Shinar's abortion. Everyone has. "Why don't you marry her?"

"Yes, we'll make a fine pair."

"Get yourself a 'ticket home,'" Flag says. Meaning a crippling wound. "Pack her back to Macedon."

We trot across a pan so devoid of all that sustains life that neither we nor our horses permit ourselves the luxury of hunger or thirst.

"I did ask her, you know?" I gesture across the waste. "Promised to take her away from all this. I meant it."

Flag grins. "I always mean it too."

"No," I say. "I'm serious."

He laughs. "I'm serious too."

32.

The army pushes north in five columns spread across 280 miles. Commanders are Hephaestion, Ptolemy, Perdiccas, Coenus and Artabazus jointly, and Alexander himself. Areas in-between are "wolf country," enemy territory, across which the foe moves with impunity. Brigade commanders dispatch patrols into these deserts. These operations are of three types—probes, penetrations, and reconnaissances-in-force. The first may be comprised of as few as two or three men, the second and third of up to hundreds. All aims are the same—to find and track the enemy, take prisoners, bring back intelligence of any kind that will permit our columns to hedge off and close with the foe.

Before the Big Push, Alexander calls the army together. The force assembles at Bactra City beneath the great fortress of Bal Teghrib, "Stone Mountain," whose slopes hold a hundred thousand.

"Brothers, are you tired of this war?"

The corps erupts.

"I am!" Alexander cries. "By the rivers of hell, I am!"

Our lord likens Afghanistan to a great dusty floor. He intends to sweep it clean. We start here where we stand, in Bactra City, and drive north, subduing every village and camp, however remote, and reducing every stronghold as we go. Indeed, Alexander acknowledges, we will be bringing into submission the same country we vanquished in last year's campaign. This time we will make it stick.

"Note this, you officers who will be dictating dispatches and situation reports. There is a phrase I wish never to read: *pockets of resistance.*"

Again the army roars.

"We shall leave no pockets of resistance. The unsubdued foe—man, woman, or child—shall be driven before us, north toward the Oxus, and beyond across the Jaxartes. Along the way we shall found a mighty string of forts. We will cut off the foe's lines of retreat. Where he shelters, we will rout him out. We will make all Afghanistan between here and the Wild Lands hostile to him. He shall find no patch of green to graze his stock and no shade to get his men out of the sun. This will be our summer's work, my friends. And when it is done we will not go into winter quarters. We will pursue the enemy into his sanctuaries. We will hunt him down and kill him. I do not intend to spend another winter in this sphere of hell, do you?"

The corps answers with a tumult of spearshafts clashing on shields.

"Spitamenes! He is the head of the hydra. Slay him and the serpent dies. Every act we take must have this object: Bring the Wolf to battle!"

Alexander underscores one final point: that in this campaign, columns and individual units will of necessity be dispersed across hundreds of miles and thus out of communication with higher command. Junior officers, and even sergeants and corporals must act on their own.

"Act for this then, men, and I shall never fault you: Find the Wolf! Attack him! Drive him toward our allied columns! Brothers, I pledge this night his weight in gold to that man who brings me Spitamenes—the living man or his head!"

Thunder breaks across the plain, as it does in that season. The army's ovation joins the storm in riotous uproar.

I am sitting between Flag and Stephanos as Alexander finishes.

"Sounds easy, doesn't it?" observes the poet.

Flag rises, scratching his buttocks. "Nothing to it."

The columns roll out of Bactra City next morning. The king's division takes the rightmost track, the ancient camel trace across the spurs of Paraetacae toward Cyropolis. Our column under Coenus parallels his advance, sixty miles west. West of ours comes Ptolemy's brigade, then Perdiccas's, and Hephaestion's. It takes all day for the full force to get clear of the city and another five for each division to reach its assigned axis. The blank spaces between columns are so vast—two days' ride at some points—that existing reconnaissance elements can't cover them all. New companies must be formed.

Our section under Stephanos becomes one of these. This is good news. It means bonuses and hazard pay, and it gets us out from under column discipline. It's also, by far, the most dangerous duty we've ever undertaken.

It is no small thing to set out into such country with five men or ten, guided by *shikaris* who are almost certainly working for the foe and, if they're not, stand ready to go over at a moment's notice. When contact is made with the enemy, riders must be sent back to column. The Afghan knows this. He lets you spot him, then picks off the lone courier or the pair galloping in tandem. If his party is numerous enough, he takes on your whole patrol. He gets behind you, cuts you off from the way you came. The enemy loves to attack out of the rising or setting sun. In the mountains, vales and even shadows can conceal battalions. In prairie country, dust storms building late in the day provide cover behind which the foe maneuvers and strikes. The tribesman appears along your track, where you think only your own men are coming from. He knows how to use glare to blind you and grit and rain to obscure his numbers. Suddenly he's on top of you.

The foe has other tricks. One is to lure a lesser detachment into trouble, then ambush the more numerous column dispatched to its aid. Another ruse is the counterfeit convoy. The enemy baits our patrols with a slow caravan or a herd of sheep or horses. When our greed overcomes caution, the foe strikes from hiding. He fattens himself on our convoys. Every strongpoint that Mack troops fortify must be garrisoned and supplied. The train bringing their mooch is a duck on the water. In this desert you come upon "write-ups"— massacres for which nothing can be done except file the report.

In the forty-three days the column takes to advance from Bactra City to Nautaca, our section runs twenty-one probes and penetrations. Nine times we make contact and set up blocking positions, observation posts, ambushes. But always the enemy uncovers our intentions and either slips away or turns the tables. East and west, no one can find Spitamenes. One thinks of such wilderness as being uninhabited; in truth the waste supports a surprising density of population—nomads and herdsmen, "shy camps," pocket villages. Here every goatherd is a lookout and every caravanner a sentry. Wherever Spitamenes is, he learns of our approach days in advance. Can our forces track him? We never even come on his trail. The desert is so vast, it swallows armies like stones in the sea.

Under such conditions, morale takes a beating. Not so much for us in scout detachments, who can keep on the move and thus fend off boredom, as for the foot troops of the central columns, whose experience of campaign is nine-tenths tedium, in which they endure the tramp, the heat and dust, the constant wind, frigid nights and baking days, and one-tenth pandemonium, in which they are rousted out of a dead sleep to arm and form up double-quick, then chop at flying speed into the wasteland, with no mooch, no bonze, evil water, where they must prepare an assault or take up a blocking position, only to watch the crisis fizzle for cause of arriving too soon, too late, upon the wrong site, or because the foe has fucked off under their very noses and they're too beat or parched to give him chase.

Candor compels me to cite another factor adding to the troops' frustration and exasperation. I mean liquor and dope. In conventional warfare, commanders knew when a battle was coming; the quartermasters had days if not months of buildup, throughout which they could lay in stocks of spirits to ease the men's anxiety. In Afghanistan there's no such luxury. Here, action can break out any moment. The result is men get varnished every chance they get. We learn from the natives. Our allied Afghans live on black nazz and *juto*, a desert plant the juice of whose spiny leaves will keep you awake day and night. This stuff catches on among the Macks. I myself use it. We all do. You can buy "jute" from the Daans and Sacae or harvest it from the desert yourself. You get thin on it. Your cheeks get hollow, you lose muscle. But you can stay up forever and never get hungry. In these badlands, where a man must pack every ounce of mooch he cooks for his dinner, such advantages are hard to resist.

ON THE FIFTY-FIRST day out of Bactra City, two of our scouts spot an enemy convoy threading its way across the badlands. The foe's train is forty mules, traveling by night and lying up by day, escorted by an equal number of tribal cavalry. We are thirty-two, counting two *shikaris* and four Afghan muleteers. Stephanos decides not to attack the convoy but to send back to the column for help. He picks two Macks—our comrades Tower, so called for his height, and Pollard for his doughy complexion—and a guide named Hakun. Their orders are to track the foe from concealment while our main body continues parallel on the far flank of a ten-mile spur. In that country, dust will betray an outfit as small as three or four.

Our company emerges next morning beyond the ten-mile spur. No sign of Tower or Pollard. Instead, where the enemy convoy should have appeared, we mark a swath of earth gouged in a great livid X. Hoofstrikes. Our *shikaris* refuse to ride in. Stephanos sends riders onto all wings, anticipating an ambush, while he and Flag spur forward. Their search turns up nothing except the violently hoof-scarred earth.

Several ravens are observed pecking at a patch of dark dirt.

Stephanos and Flag dismount. They discover, planted upright in the earth, the headless corpses of Tower and Pollard. The scout Hakun is missing. Murdered by the foe? Or welcomed, betraying the men he was supposed to protect?

The enemy has buried our comrades alive, with only their heads sticking from the dirt, then either trampled them or used them for some grisly manner of horseback sport.

"These are the savages," says Stephanos, "that our king proposes to hire for pay, to fight at our sides."

Despite such tragedies and misfortunes, the Big Push is working. On the highway south of Nautaca, our company runs into Costas the chronicler. Give this fellow credit; he has crossed the waste on his own from Bactra City, supported only by two servants and a Daan guide. He tells us of battles east and west. Hephaestion's column has killed eight hundred in one clash, and Alexander has cut off a number of powerful bands trying to slip around his eastern wing. Soon we are in the action too.

Along the caravan trace to Maracanda lies a broad grass valley called To'shoma, "the Lakes," because it becomes that in the winter rains. Here, in the second month of the advance, wings of Coenus's brigade and Ptolemy's pin elements of the foe and rout them with great slaughter.

In desert war, pursuit is everything. This is how you make kills. The chase from the Lakes goes on two months. Our sections under Stephanos are reintegrated into the battalion commanded by Bullock; we become an element, now, of a line unit.

Our charge is to pursue the foe wherever he flees. "Come back with kills," Bullock tells us, "or don't come back at all." A terrible competition arises between companies of the same battalions. Sooner than return empty-handed, we bag any luckless bastard we see. Every village that aids the foe is obliterated. We take no prisoners. Every man we catch, we kill. Driving a band into the mountains, we pursue till not one soul remains. Nothing stops us. Fugitive contingents are chased across the steppe for hundreds of miles.

The instrument of counterguerrilla warfare is the massacre. Its object is terror, to make oneself an object of such dread that the foe fears to face you ever. This practice has worked for the army of Macedon across all Asia. It does not work here. The Afghan is so proud, so inured to privation, and so in love with liberty that he prefers death to capitulation. The more terror we apply, the more stubborn his resolution becomes. His dames and urchins are worse than he is. They hate our guts. For all the blood we have drained into Afghan soil, we have succeeded neither in breaking the foe's will to resist nor severing him tribe from tribe, but have instead ignited in his breast a fierce and unquenchable defiance and united him against us in a front of a thousand once-warring tribes, clans, and *khels*.

When the chases at the Lakes are over, our company is in a state beyond exhaustion. The hair beneath our desert caps is so matted with dust, grease, and sweat that we can't shear it even with a razor. The nails of our toes and fingers are busted to nubs. Our kit can't be peeled off. We have to cut it away. We reek. We're so dirty, rivers can't get us clean.

Our horses are skin and bones. So are we. We can't eat. We've forgotten how to sleep. We've been living on nazz and jute for so long, we can't keep down so much as a turnip. Wine when we get it runs through us like water. Speech has become superfluous. Who needs it? Flag knows what I'm thinking. At the gallop I glance to Lucas across a hundred feet of steppe. He knows. Even our horses know.

We have kept Tower's and Pollard's ashes. One night, on an eminence north of the Lakes, a likely spot presents itself. Our urns are leather sacks. We inter them not within cairns, which the foe will sniff out and desecrate, but beneath stones marked underside with our names and unit. We offer the Hymn for the Fallen. Stephanos composes these lines:

Hunting for Baz
The boys need their nazz.
Lacking soap, dope, and hope; coochless, moochless,
We achieve the unachievable, sustained by belief
in the unbelievable.

Lucas has been keeping a notebook. He won't tell anyone what's in it. Finally this night he breaks it out.

He calls it *Letters I Never Sent Home.*

The document tells what we do in a day. No story. Just a list.

"When we first marched out from Macedon," says Lucas, "trekking was our life. It was all we did. We thought nothing of it. You remember.

"Now we get up in the morning and we kill people. We kill them all day, and the next day we kill some more. That's our life. It's so ordinary to us, we think nothing of it."

He rattles off the chases we've run in the last two days. Already the others call him to quit.

He won't.

"How do you know how far-gone you are? When you write letters home. Try to tell your people what you've been doing. You can't. Not even your old man, a decorated vet himself. He can't understand; no words can make him. So you write in this crazy prose that says less than nothing."

Dark laughter now. Lucas doesn't smile.

"You look in the faces of your mates, boys of twenty who look fifty, and you know that's how you look too. But you're not fifty. You're twenty. You're twenty *and* fifty. Things you thought you'd never do, you've done, and you can never tell anyone . . ."

Dice lobs a fist of pebbles. "Sack it, Lucas."

". . . never tell anyone except your mates. Only you don't need to tell them. They know. They know *you*. Better than a man knows his wife, better than he knows himself. They're bound to you and you to them, like wolves in a pack. It's not you and them. You *are* them. The unit is indivisible. One dies, we all die. Individual mind? It doesn't exist anymore. We've become incapable of independent thought or any thought at all except when is the next mooch, the next bonze, the next chop. Where is the foe? One day we chase him into the mountains, next day over the plains. That's all we know. That's all we do. That's all—"

This *is* enough. Even I tell Lucas to stop.

He looks up. "Why doesn't some correspondent write about *this*? Stephanos, you're a literary fellow. Why don't you set some of this to stanzas?"

Our leader stands above the circle. He tells Lucas his harangue has gone on long enough. "You're tired, my friend."

Lucas's eye glitters in the firelight.

"You have no idea," he says, "how tired I am."

33.

The army reaches Maracanda on Daesius 28, midsummer. A letter is waiting for me from my brother Philip at Bactra City.

Elias has died.

> *His woman Daria poisoned him. I know, I can't believe it either. She was caught introducing aconite into the rations of others in the hospital. Apparently she'd been dosing Elias in small quantities all winter. I have his ashes. I shall send them home to Mother. I won't leave him out here.*

I am struck dumb to read this. It can't be true! I strain at the letter, to make certain the handwriting is Philip's. How can Elias be dead? He was well! I saw him just ninety days ago!

> *Forgive me, brother, for communicating this unhappy report by post. But you must know at once. Army*

regulations permit a brother to escort his brother's
remains home. You must do this, Matthias. I have set
the process in motion through Headquarters Bactra City.
I am certain that approval will not be withheld.

Home? I know at once that this is out of the question. I cannot leave Lucas and Flag and Stephanos. I cannot leave my mates.

I have to sit. The letter has been delivered by pouch rider, along with everyone else's mail, in camp on the Many Blessings. I pass the letter to Flag. He scans it in silence and hands it on. Everyone reads it.

My mates are as shaken as I. Not just by Elias's death (he was a favorite of all), but by its manner. Suddenly the war seems more unwinnable than ever.

Worse news comes by verbal report. There's a reason our patrols have not encountered Spitamenes all summer. The Desert Wolf has been raiding in our rear. He crossed the Oxus two months ago, heading south with six thousand Daan, Sacae, and Massagetae horse, despite our saturation coverage of the region. He has captured Bani Mis and both Bactra-region freight compounds, constructed last winter. More massacres. Our general Craterus is defending central Afghanistan with four brigades; he has chased the Wolf but lost him, as usual, north in the steppe country.

I respond at once to Philip, declining his offer with respect.

Elias.

Must I speak of my brother now in the past tense? Must I say "was"?

Elias was Mother's darling; how will she endure his loss? How will our sister Eleni? Will Philip inform them of Daria?

The next ten days pass like a hundred. Grief has overhauled me. I have ducked it for so long. Since Father. Tollo. Rags, Flea, Knuckles, Torch and Turtle, Tower and Pollard.

Now Elias.

It all catches up to me.

I saw my brother last just before the Big Push stepped off. He was in the officers infirmary at Bactra City. A wound of the foot, got not in action but from stepping on a nail on his way to the latrine. This is a grand joke to him. The surgeons bled him to defend against lockjaw. It works. I visit him twice. He seems in fine spirits. I spend six weeks in the field, training. When I get back, a note tells me Elias has been moved from the hospital to a private home. I go straight over.

When I enter, I see his right leg elevated. The foot has been amputated. The stump starts twelve inches below the knee.

"Don't go green on me, brother," pronounces Elias gaily. "I've got what every soldier dreams of—a ticket home!"

Daria is with him. She sleeps on a fleece at his bedside. We talk of everything except what's in front of us. Each time I look at my brother, tears well.

"Will you control that please, Matthias? It's unsoldierly."

Daria brings *chai* and sesame cakes. To witness the tenderness with which she cares for Elias makes my eyes burn.

My brother counsels me. He wants me out of a line company. The army owes him, he says. He can get me a headquarters job. We argue. I assure him I am with a crack outfit; I'm safer than in my own bed at home.

"This is no game, Matthias. . . ."

I assure him I'm aware of that.

". . . nor shall we best this foe, as we have all others."

My brother has lost his first love, the army. His grief endows him with a kind of clarity.

"Listen to me, Matthias. I'm going to tell you how to fight

this war. You will do as I instruct you, as I am your elder and I so command."

He makes me promise. His eyes hold me like our mother's, the color of iron.

"Show the foe no mercy. What he tells you will be a lie. Fear his women more than his men and act toward them with greater implacability. You will be told to take prisoners to sell as slaves. Do not. Kill them. That is the only way you will get out of here alive."

My brother regards me gravely.

"I know you, Matthias. The more you come to know this country, the more sympathy you will feel for the foe. You will admire his fighting qualities and respect his love of freedom. You will see him as a human being, not unlike our own highlanders, and thus worthy of respect.

"Forget this. Howsoever legitimate such sentiments may be, if you indulge them they will bring you to grief. We are here and we must win. The sooner we bring the foe to his senses, the better for us and the better for him.

"Now listen to me carefully, for what I tell you now is most critical of all.

"We are wrong to be here. The enemy are better men than we are, and their cause, which is liberty, is just. Never tell yourself otherwise. If you do, you will go mad. Fight the foe as you would fight hell itself. Seek nowhere for honor. You will not find it. Get yourself a 'ticket home' if you can. And if you can't, kill the enemy to the last man."

34.

Two packets arrive from Shinar while I am at Maracanda. She doesn't know how to write, so she sends stuff. Candy, beadwork, a pony carved of oryx horn. My emotion upon receiving these little gift boxes surprises me. I have registered Shinar under my *oikos*. She gets half my pay. In her second packet is a note scratched on beaten leather, with the sign of a scribe from the marketplace. The broken Greek is his, not hers.

> *I come to Maracanda. Ghilla's son is born. The soldiers*
> *kill Daria for your brother. I bring your pay. If you find*
> *a new woman, I make my own way.*

So Lucas is a father now. Ghilla has not yet sent a letter. He's happy to learn, any way he can. We roast a goose to celebrate.

"Do you know," Lucas confesses, "I'm still writing to my fiancée back home? I am a loathsome cur."

His betrothed is my cousin Teli, a darling girl who worships him.

"Forgive me, Matthias. I keep waiting to get killed. Then I can avoid giving her the bad news."

He *is* a dog for this dereliction. Still we laugh. We're all waiting to get killed.

Lucas acknowledges his happiness with Ghilla. The fact astonishes him. "Who could have foreseen it? But look at her. She's beautiful, she cares for me tenderly. I can talk to her, she understands. I don't have to pretend the world is different than it is or that I'm a better man than I am. Yet she stays. Why? Would any of our girls back home do the same?"

I think: Would they poison us? But I bite my tongue.

"This woman," says Lucas with truth, "makes no demands for herself, yet she is willing to die at my side. Just being with me puts her at risk of her life, from her family and tribe and even from strangers. Still she remains." He shakes his head. To me he promises to write to Teli, come clean.

Dice asks, "Will you ever go home, Lucas?"

Our festive hall is the ruins of a farmhouse.

"I am home," he says.

35.

Maracanda is the principal city of Sogdiana. This is the same place Alexander has chased the Wolf from twice. The same place that he, Spitamenes, has captured as many times. The same place our column of mercs was relieving when the Wolf and his Scyths and Sogdians made hash of us.

It's a pretty spot just the same. A spur of the Ocher Range juts from the west, not lofty enough to catch clouds and bring rain, but possessed of a rugged, almost sculptural quality that sets the city off like a jewel. Approaching from the south you feel like you're entering, if not an enchanted realm, then at least a civilized and agreeable oasis. The city incorporates two satellite districts, Ban Agar and Balimiotores, which flank the river half a mile below the upper town. Ban Agar is the horse market. Balimiotores, which the troops call Little Maracanda, is the shantytown.

The upper city is sited on the summit of a jagged scarp, whose approaches have been built up and fortified over centuries. It would be no small chore to storm the place. The district contains a governor's palace with royal residences, erected by the Persians, within a parklike enclave that remains surprisingly cool even beneath the blistering Afghan sun. Alexander and his entourage occupy this. The army itself spreads out across the plain and along both banks of the meandering, sludge-colored river, whose breadth in summer varies from a hundred yards to a quarter mile. A small dog could cross at the trot and not wet its haunches. It goes without saying, you can't drink it.

Why are we here, other than to rally midsummer as operational orders prescribe? The place cannot support us. It can't support a force one-quarter our size. But the corps must get in out of the wind. The men need twenty days to wash the desert off and to get blind, and the mounts must get into their bellies more than bush grass and camel thorn. The heavy baggage can come up now from the Oxus. And our wages.

Mule trains carrying gold make their way up the secure zone that the five columns have cleared by their sweep north. This at least has been accomplished. The frustration is that no element of Alexander's forces, or all collectively, has been able to force the foe to a main-force showdown. All we've done is drive the tribes north.

This is progress as far as it goes. But since Spitamenes has shown that he can slip major formations past us to raid unchecked in our rear the feeling throughout the Maracanda camp is vexation, exasperation, even alarm that the vaunted Big Push has accomplished nothing at all.

Boozing, never moderate among Macks in the field, has escalated here to heroic proportions. The king convenes his council atop the citadel. Every drunken outburst finds its way down to the troops. Alexander rips his officers. Forward Operations is singled out for censure. Where is Spitamenes? How did he get past us? The object of this push north, the king declares, is to deprive the foe of the initiative. Instead, the Wolf has seized it and hurls it back in our face.

It is not our king's style to blame others. Always he takes the weight himself. The men love him for this. But frustration, now, gnaws at his guts. "This place," says Flag, "is getting to him too."

Another stone digs beneath Alexander's heel. This is the person of Black Cleitus, former commander of the Royal Squadron of Companion cavalry, now sharing with Hephaestion charge of all of Alexander's elite mounted brigades. Cleitus is fifty-three and Old Corps to the bone. He has come late to the Afghan theater (summoned by Alexander, who will appoint him governor of Bactria), having been hospitalized for a year, eleven hundred miles east at Ecbatana. There, the war still "feels Persian"—meaning conventional, the kind a soldier of the Old Guard can understand. There the army is all Greek and Macedonian. Cleitus is unprepared for the miscegenated cavalcade that comprises the divisions at Kandahar and Bactra City, and now at Maracanda.

He sees Persians and Medes in stations of power. Cavalry formations, once all-Mack scarlet, now glitter with the leopard-skin mantles of Hyrcania and the serpent pennants of Syria and Cappadocia. Alexander has begun to integrate Bactrian and Sogdian cohorts— the very Afghans we're fighting—and worse, to Cleitus's eyes, savage Daans, Sacae, and Massagetae, also our enemies, and at rates of pay beyond what our own countrymen earn in garrison in Greece.

In his youth Cleitus served as a page under King Philip. It was his honor to bear the infant Alexander to his naming bath. Cleitus's right arm saved Alexander's life at the battle of the Granicus River.

Cleitus will not hold his tongue. He hates what he sees and he lets the army hear it. He lets Alexander hear.

You who are familiar with the history know of the midnight drinking bout in which Cleitus insulted our lord; how the offender's comrades dragged him, drunken, from the banquet tent; how he returned a second time to slander his sovereign even more viciously, calling him a petty prince and a knave, who would have achieved nothing without commanders like himself and others—Parmenio, Philotas, Antipater, Antigonus One-Eye—whom he, Alexander, has now put out of the way for no cause other than to gratify his vanity.

You have heard how Alexander, driven past endurance by this abuse, seized a pike from one of the attendants and drove it into his antagonist's belly, then, recoiling in horror at this homicide committed by his own hand, flung himself upon Cleitus's corpse, first beseeching heaven for its reanimation, then seeking with the same blood-defamed lance to end his own life. You know how Hephaestion, Ptolemy, and the king's other mates overpowered him and bore him, only with extreme exertions, to his quarters, within which he retired, refusing all food and drink for three days, until his friends and attendants, desperate at the army's state while deprived of his presence and leadership, succeeded at last in drawing him forth from his retreat.

It is my object here neither to reprieve Alexander's actions (who can exonerate murder?), nor to extenuate Cleitus's part in his own drunken demise. I address only the effect on the army.

Let me speak plain. Not a man in the corps gave a damn about Cleitus. He deserved his end. He got what was coming to him.

When Alexander at last emerges from his quarters, he looks like a ghost of himself. He neither addresses the men nor permits a surrogate to do so in his name. He sacrifices. He inters Cleitus's corpse with honor. He takes exercise.

This is enough. Sergeants, even colonels weep. Men kneel on the earth in thanksgiving.

The king lives!

We are preserved!

At once Maracanda, our garden and oasis, has become hateful to us. We can't get out soon enough. Where has the Wolf flown? Find him. Kill him. The army must get back to what it was.

But can it?

"This country," says Flag. "This god-abandoned country."

BOOK
SEVEN

Wolf Country

36.

South of the Jaxartes, where the peaks of the Scythian Caucasus mount back from the plain of the river, stand three impregnable natural fastnesses called Tora Giraya, the Black Beards. Each is a mountain unto itself. All have summits broad as prairies, year-round springs, and unscaleable flanks. Among these strongholds Spitamenes, our spies report, has taken refuge. He has with him seven thousand Bactrian and Sogdian cavalry and all their goods and women.

Alexander names the operation Summer Thunder. He leads in person, calling in from their own deployments the brigades of Ptolemy, Polyperchon, and Coenus, and half the siege train under Craterus's deputy Bias Arimmas. This combined force numbers over twenty-four thousand. Everything, we are instructed, depends on speed. We must get to the Black Beards before the Wolf has time to flee or prepare a trap.

Among the units hastening north from Bactra City are the Silver Shields, the elite heavy infantry of Alexander's Royal Guard. With them, accompanying their cavalry escort, rides my brother Philip.

He finds me in camp along the Little Polytimetus, an alkaline trickle amid creosote and tamarisk, midway between Maracanda and the Black Beards.

I have not seen Philip since I was fifteen. "I must tell you," he says after our initial emotional embrace, "I am very angry with you."

Philip is fourteen years my senior. His cloak of Companion cavalry bears the silver eagle of a lieutenant colonel. He is taller, even, than I remember. I am daunted by him. I find myself calling him "sir," nor is he prompt to tell me to stop.

Philip is upset at my evading his call to escort Elias's ashes home. His anger has nothing to do with Elias. Its object is to protect *me*, to get me out of Afghanistan. When I repeat what I said in my letter, that I can't leave my mates, Philip groans in frustration.

I see that he loves me. My eyes sting.

"Forgive me, Philip. But Elias himself would have dodged that duty."

For the first time, my brother smiles. His beard, I see, has gone gray. His hair, once raven, is the color of iron. I note from his gait that both knees have gone stony (from wounds perhaps, or falls, as is not uncommon among horsemen). I have brought wine for him as a present, and a duck in a sack. For me, Philip carries Elias's regimental sash, of wool dyed black and tan.

He tells me how Elias died and what happened to Daria.

"In custody, the woman tried to make away with herself, chuffing down some poison she had smuggled past the guards. The surgeons flushed her gut, so she could be properly executed. She was the first Afghan woman to be charged before a military tribunal.

She offered no defense and refused to make a statement of any kind. They crucified her."

My brother has seen Shinar too. "She sought me out at my quarters at Bactra City. I thought she was some shepherdess. When she opened her mouth and good Greek came out, I nearly keeled over. Then she showed me her *oikos* papers with your name on them." He laughs. "I said to myself, 'My baby brother is all grown up.' "

It is through Philip's intercession that Shinar (and Ghilla and Lucas's baby) have been documented through to Maracanda. They will arrive with the heavy baggage, probably in ten days. Too late for me; I'll be a hundred miles east, up in the Black Beards, by then.

"How much time," my brother asks, "do you have left on your enlistment?"

I tell him. "Why?"

"We'll tear it up. I want you out of harm's way." He's serious. Strings can be pulled. "What makes you stay in this pit of hell?" Philip demands. "Duty? Love of country? Please spare me any oraculations on the subject of Macedonian honor. Money? Let me guess: You owe the army more now than you've earned in your entire enlistment." He faces me in vexation. "I don't understand you, Matthias. Is your aim to cast your life away?"

I ask why this is so important to him.

"I will not," he says, "lose another brother."

We have to get out of the public way. We're making a scene. Along the riverbank stands a slope where the muleteers unkink their new ropes; for hundreds of yards there's nothing but wet lines stretching in the sun. "Philip," I say when we have walked down, "you know I can't leave my mates. Not when there's still fighting to do."

My brother regards me with infinite weariness. "Let me tell you something you may not know. This war will soon be over. For all our frustrations, Alexander's scheme is bearing fruit. The new forts have cut Spitamenes off from the north; our devastation of villages has stripped him of supplies; our hiring of native troops has drained his source of recruits. Oxyartes and the other warlords—everyone except the Wolf himself—see the end approaching. They've all sent undertakings in secret to Alexander. Deals are being worked out right now. We could have peace as soon as fall. And let me disabuse you of another fancy that may be fueling your hopes of a future in the army: the riches of India. I've been there. There's nothing in India but monsoon rains, poisonous snakes, and half-naked fakirs."

Go home, Philip tells me. If you serve out your enlistment, you'll wind up crippled or dead. "I've heard what happened with your sweetheart Danae. You're free. What's stopping you? Take your Afghan girl. Farm Father's land."

"That's your land, Philip."

He faces me in exasperation. Two teamsters pass, checking their ropes; we wait till they've moved on out of earshot. My brother draws up.

"Forgive me, Matthias. When I hear your voice, which sounds so much like . . ."

He cannot say Elias's name.

". . . then to see you as a soldier." Philip's long hair has fallen across his face; he sweeps it back with dark, sunburnt fingers. "You were just a child."

And he weeps.

We walk by the river. The sun plunges; the sky turns the color of pearl.

"You know," Philip says, "Elias and I used to talk about you. More than you may realize." He smiles at some remembrance. "Our own lives meant little to us. But yours always seemed impossibly precious. Perhaps because you were the baby."

My brother bends and scoops a fistful of flat stones, the kind you skim across a surface of water.

"They say a man becomes old," he says, "when more of his friends reside beneath the earth than above it."

"Is that how you feel, Philip?"

He doesn't answer. Only hands me half the stones. We send trails skipping.

"Don't end up like Elias and me."

My brother turns away, eyes across the dark water.

"To be a soldier," he says, "is no lofty calling. Who acts as a brute *is* a brute."

37.

The column moves out the next day, pushing hard to gain the Black Beards. Philip rides ahead with the Silver Shields.

Let me here address the army's state of mind in the aftermath of the Cleitus debacle and make plain, if I can, by the following minor but extremely significant incident, the undiminished love the corps bore for its king.

Dispatching Ptolemy's and Polyperchon's brigades round the western shoulder of the Scythian range, Alexander struck straight across with his own divisions, Coenus's, and that portion of the siege train that had come up from Maracanda. This force made good speed for two days. But mounting a pass called An Ghojar, "the Barber," on the third morning, the column was brought up in its tracks. A torrent in spate with late-summer snowmelt had washed out half the valley. I chanced to ride up, delivering dispatches, just as all progress ground to a halt.

The gorge down which the cataract thundered stretched, bank to bank, broader than a bowshot. Where the downshoot plunged against boulders in midchannel, each the size of a two-story house, the impact sent geysers of mud-colored spume fifty feet into the air. The din was so deafening that troopers, even hundreds of feet up the slope, could make themselves heard only by shouting directly into their fellows' ears. How to get across? The alternative, back-tracking the way we came, would have cost days and wiped out every advantage of speed and surprise Alexander had worked so hard to attain. Any lesser commander would have elected this op-tion. And even our lord, drawn up before the torrent, seemed to consider it. His presence on-site alone, however, drove the divisions into action.

Without waiting for orders, combat engineers began surveying the ascending slope, seeking spots where rockfalls could be started. Rigging teams of mules and setting great timbers as levers, the sap-pers and bucket-men succeeded in dislodging several critical boul-ders. Half the mountainside came down, straight into the river. The fall didn't span the flood, but at least it brought the banks closer together. From a perch atop one newly formed promontory, archers launched scores of light lines across, of which the looped ends of two, after infinite pains, were at last coaxed into holds around outcrops on the far bank. Upon these filaments, which looked in the scale of the scene no stouter than threads, two young and athletic volunteers, stripped naked to make themselves as light as possible, worked their way across hand-over-hand. By now the column had massed like spectators at the games at Olympia. The youths swung perilously above the torrent (and even slipped once or twice into it), while their onlooking countrymen's emotions al-ternated between ecstatic citation and excruciating suspense. Alexander had pledged a talent of gold to the man whose sole first touched the far shore and a talent of silver to the second. When the champion at last found footing and turned back, raising his arms in triumph, the roar could be heard even above the cataract. Heavier lines were warped across. By midafternoon a rope bridge had been rigged. By the following dawn a span of timbers stood in place, stout enough that laden mules—hoodwinked and shielded by side-screens from sight of the plunge below—could be coaxed across.

This was what Alexander's presence alone meant.

The result was that two of our four columns appeared in the enemy's rear days before even the Wolf could have anticipated. Coenus's division assaulted the least-well-defended of the Black Beards, driving its occupants into refuge on the other two. Beard number two was separated by a cavernous rift from the only spot upon which sufficient siege elements could be assembled. Under Alexander's direction, however, the soldiers working in shifts succeeded in dumping into the chasm such tonnage of boulders and cartloads of soil and brush that by the fourth dawn the interval had been built up enough for a crude mole to be laid across its spine. By this time the engineers, assisted by hundreds of carpenters and mechanics drafted from the ranks to assist, had put together a rolling siege tower, seventy feet high, shielded by hide-faced mantlets, and had rigged a system of tackle and cables by which it could be warped across the gap and thrown against the face of the cliff.

That the Wolf got his forces safely away, even his women and wagons, must be accounted a feat of tactical brilliance equal to any in this campaign. He made his escape by back trails unknown to the besiegers, concealing his withdrawal by darkness and by the ruse of hundreds of watch fires, which boys and youths kept blazing nightlong, to simulate the appearance of a camp on customary alert.

Still, the foe had been dealt a tremendous moral defeat. Our chronicler friend, Costas, evaluated it in the following account, which made its way in under three months, I am told, via Sidon and Damascus to Athens:

> The enemy's tribal troops cannot appreciate the utility of such a tactical withdrawal, engineered here with such brilliance by their commander Spitamenes. To them it is an ashan, or "runaway," a term of shame. Who is the enemy? His types run in hundreds. He is a Sogdian soldier; he is a sheepherder; he is a savage, a shopkeeper. He has fought under Darius, trained by Persian officers; he is a boy armed with a sling and a stone. The Wolf's rolls contain thugs and bandits, patriots in it for glory and opportunists out only for gold. The foe is someone whose son we have killed, whose village we have burned, whose sister we have outraged. He enrolls with the spring and vanishes in the fall. Sometimes brothers take turns serving, employing by rounds the one pony and one set of arms the family possesses. Is this weakness in an army? Not the way Spitamenes manages it. For what all own in common is hatred of the invader. The native is not going anywhere, but we are—and he knows it.
>
> The Afghan fights neither as we do, nor for what we do. He lives to distinguish himself as an individual champion. By nature he is a raider, restless, avaricious, constantly craving excitement and opportunity for plunder. The Bactrians and Sogdians, and especially their allies of the savage Daans, Sacae, and Massagetae, are not soldiers in the Greek or Macedonian sense, that is, disciplined men possessed of patience, order, and cohesion. They are more

like wild children; impatient, hot-blooded, easily bored. Spitamenes, who understands their hearts better than they do themselves, knows he must produce a redeeming strike soon against his nemesis, Alexander, or forfeit a portion of the faith his dashing and piratical cohorts have placed in him.

Summer ends with more Mack victories, no one conclusive but all collectively diminishing the Wolf's freedom of maneuver. Hephaestion's division has constructed and garrisoned no fewer than forty-seven forts and strongpoints, forming a chain south of the Jaxartes. Many of these are no grander than a dozen meres roosting on a stone summit, but all are in communication by courier and by fire and smoke. Wherever Spitamenes sticks his head up, one of these outposts will sound the alarm.

Meanwhile, construction nears completion on a new garrison city—the bastion of Alexandria-on-the-Jaxartes. Palisades and ditches stand ready; the armed force will be in place by fall. Oxyartes and the other Afghan warlords have retired south for the winter to fastnesses in the Scythian Caucasus, unassailable after the first snows. Alexander takes his elite brigades, with Perdiccas's, Ptolemy's, and Polyperchon's, and establishes a ready base at Nautaca. From here he can ride quickly to the aid of Craterus in the south or us in the north. That is his plan.

The initiative has gone over to the Macedonians. Alexander tasks our brigade with flushing Spitamenes from his sanctuaries beyond the Jaxartes. He reinforces Coenus by placing under his command Meleager and his regiment of mobile infantry, stiffened with four hundred Companion cavalry under Alcetas Arridhaeus; all the mounted javelineers of Hyrcania; and the allied Bactrians and Sogdians who had been attached to the brigade of Amyntas Nicolaus

(Amyntas himself being named governor of Bactria, the post that would have belonged to Black Cleitus). Alexander's instructions to Coenus are to hunt and harass Spitamenes.

"Drive the Wolf from his lair," are our king's orders posted throughout the Maracanda camp. "And I will finish him in the open."

38.

In this operation I encounter Shinar's brother for the first time. It happens like this:

The brigade has pushed north to Alexandria-on-the-Jaxartes, preparing to cross into the Wild Lands on the hunt for Spitamenes. Several days earlier, however, the foe has made an attack on the pontoon bridges that here span the river. Striking from upstream, using fire-rafts and booms of pitch-soaked logs, the enemy has succeeded in cutting both spans. Mack engineers on-site are overtaxed, racing winter to complete construction of the garrison town. The upshot is it's up to us. We have to rebuild the bridges.

Every able-bodied scuff in camp is drafted into the labor gangs, including three companies of southern Afghan irregulars who happen to be on hand, awaiting orders to rejoin Ptolemy's brigade down south.

Except the Afghans refuse to work. In their eyes, such labor is for women. They won't do it.

The Afghans are under Macedonian captains, but these officers' orders must be passed via the *maliks* beneath them, who alone command obedience of the actual troops. You may imagine with what patience our commander Coenus regards this practice.

He summons the two ranking Afghan chiefs and, when they again defy his orders, has them hauled up in chains. The brigade is assembled to witness punishment. There is no doubt that Coenus intends to flog these fellows, if not to death, then to within an inch of it. The catastrophe is averted at the last instant by the intercession of Agathocles, the captain of Intelligence who originally debriefed Lucas and me after our captivity. Or perhaps the whole spectacle has been staged for the Afghans' benefit. In any event, it concludes with a tribal council, or *jurga*, to which the call is put out for a Mack who can speak the southern dialect.

That's me.

I know it from Shinar.

My Afghan counterpart in the parley tells me he knows who I am. He is Shinar's cousin. His male cousin—Shinar's brother— serves in this company as well.

In the rush of events, I pay little attention to this. It is only days later, when the bridge repairs are near completion, that it occurs to me that here is an opportunity I must seize—to sit down with the brother and make peace.

You don't just ride into an Afghan camp. They'll kill you if you do. You must first send your *dashar* (a sort of calling card), announcing your presence and requesting permission to be escorted in.

I go with Flag and Lucas. The day is bright and bone-rattling cold. All of us are armed to the teeth. Dice, Boxer, and three other mates back us up from the perimeter.

The brother meets us in a field of winter clover. He is accompanied by the cousin I met and another cousin. All are muffled to the
eyeballs and packing gut-cutters and iron lances, whose use they
have learned from us. A dozen armed Afghans keep the conclave in
sight from the margins.

The brother is not at all what I expected. He's young, only a few
years older than Shinar, but with eyes stony as an ancient. He is
dressed entirely in black. Though his *khetal* cloak is threadbare, his
belt and sling are studded with silver spits—trophies of enemy slain.
I tell him my name and hold out my hand. Afghans do not share
our European admiration for a firm grip. They touch your palm as if
they think you are carrying something contagious. Nor does the
Asiatic believe in looking you in the eye and speaking plain and
strong. They mutter and look away. They don't introduce themselves. The brother does not tell me his name.

I feel Flag stiffen at my shoulder. He hates these bastards.
Lucas, on my other side, takes everything in with a ready, open
receptivity.

The interview is over as soon as it begins. The brother plainly
wants no part of it. He keeps glancing to the caucus of elders looking on, whose presence, it is clear, compels him against his will to
this appointment.

I tell him that Shinar is well and that I hope to return her to
him and her family. He grimaces as if I have just plunged a spike
into his guts.

"Can you understand," he says in perfect Dari, "that I have no
wish for this obligation?"

I don't get it. "You mean to take her back?"

"You should have killed her."

He means it. I think of our former guide Elihu. My crime in
Afghan eyes, I understand, is not that I have slept with Shinar, or

impregnated her, or taken her away among foreigners. What I can never be forgiven for is that I have taken that action—preserving her life on the trail in the mountains—that by the code of *nangwali* should have been taken only by her own kin.

The cousins hate me. Their eyes speak plain.

The brother is different. His expression looks . . . condemned.

"Do you imagine, Macedonian," he says, "that I wish to bring grief to my sister? I am twenty-two years old and responsible for forty-one people, most of whom are women and children." He means, apparently, his immediate family, whose protection must have fallen to him by reason of elders' deaths or other misfortunes. "I have had to take service in the cause of my enemy, only to fill the bellies of those for whom I must provide."

To my surprise, I find myself respecting the fellow. I study his intelligent, fine-featured face.

"The blood that will be shed over this matter," he says, "is your doing, not mine. For though you and your countrymen call us barbarians, it is you who are brutish and meanly bred—and blind to all concept of pride and honor. You should have killed her," the brother repeats, turning on his heel. In a moment he has stalked away across the brown clover.

Flag turns to me and Lucas. "What was that all about?"

The cousins remain. Hate radiates from their postures.

"What," I ask, "is your cousin's name?"

The elder faces me.

"Baz."

39.

Coenus's division crosses the Jaxartes on the morning setting of the Pleiades, the first day of winter. It's cold. A dusting of snow howls across the frozen steppe. Our orders, as I said, are to hunt Spitamenes. The sense is of climax approaching.

The Wolf has been sighted eighty miles east on the frontier, near a village called Gabae. This is a trading outpost frequented by tribesmen of the Massagetae. They rally there in spring before raiding to the south. Will Spitamenes bring them forth in winter?

Indeed, something must be up: Costas the correspondent rides with us. So does Agathocles, the intelligence captain. "By Hades," says Flag, "the mice have all come out of their burrows."

Patrols push north and east into the wasteland. Our company is split into three to make the broadest possible sweep. Scores of penetrations are being run by other outfits. Day on day we discover sign of the passage of great numbers of horses, not fanned wide as tribesmen customarily ride but in column to conceal their numbers. Winter has come down hard. We have just made camp along some iced-over creek when a courier gallops in from Coenus with orders to break off our patrol and follow him at speed.

West of the region we've been searching lies a gale-scoured grassland called Tol Nelan, "the Nothing." There, a probe of one of our sister companies has stumbled onto a camp of several hundred of the foe, on the move without wagons and women. The patrol has gotten under cover without being spotted and sent back to the column for help. Our section is among the units called in to reinforce.

We ride for a night and day, linking with another recalled patrol and two companies of mounted infantry dispatched from Coenus. Scouts from the original patrol pick us up ten miles out and lead us in by a wide circuit. We take up concealed positions.

Our force consists of three patrols, about sixty men, and the two companies sent from column. Coenus has stiffened it with artillery, two furlongers—stone-throwers—and a half battery of light bolt catapults, the kind that can be broken down and carried, one on two mules. Our commander is Leander Arimmas, a Companion captain sent with the two companies. Costas the chronicler has come with him. So has Agathocles. Apparently they're expecting a show. Leander orders a base camp set up in a frozen watercourse two miles from the enemy camp, then divides our force into strike elements and a blocking force.

For once a scheme actually works. Two hours before dawn, our companies get two wings of thirty horses each into position on the steppe side of the enemy camp. Lucas and I ride with the southern arm. The troop shows itself at first light, striking out of the pale sun. At the same time a company of infantry, which had got into position that night on the adjacent heights, rushes down on the foe.

The enemy flees into the iced-over courses. Their horses carry two, even three fugitives. When the foe strikes the riverbed, Mack artillery opens up. A furlonger can sling a ten-pound stone two hundred yards, downhill three hundred. As these missiles crash among the rocks and the ice-shards of the frozen river, panic undoes the enemy. Our captain Leander falls, struck by one of our own stones. The fight is sharp and violent. When it's over, the bag is sixty ponies and forty men. And an unexpected bonus:

Derdas, the fourteen-year-old son of Spitamenes.

40.

A melee erupts over this prize. Our Daans scrap with each other like barn cats (they recognize the lad from their days fighting on his father's side), believing the boy's head will bring a bucket of gold. Stephanos and other Mack officers order the lad impounded apart. Meanwhile, despite desperate efforts to save him, our captain Leander bleeds to death. Three other Macks have received fatal wounds; a dozen more have been cut up badly by the fiercely defending foe. The boy looks on with cool, intelligent eyes.

Spitamenes' son is dressed Massagetae style, in boots and bloused trousers, long *khetal* cloak, and earflap cap. Nothing distinguishes him from his less illustrious companions, save an onyx-handled dagger, which two of our Daans have produced from the youth's undervest when he and the others are disarmed. A fracas breaks out over ownership of this trophy. In the confusion a handful of the foe make getaways, on horseback, before our fellows can throw a cordon around the capture scene.

These runaways will fly on wings to Spitamenes, whose forces may be as close as beyond the next range of hills. Wherever he is, the Wolf will not spare the whip, racing to pay us out—and rescue his boy.

Stephanos and two lieutenants struggle to establish order. A council is called. As corporals, Lucas and I take part. Stephanos declares that the mixed composition of the enemy party—Daans and Massagetae with main-force Bactrians and Sogdians—can mean only that the foe is assembling. "When these bastards scatter, they break up into tribal bands. They only ride in one pack when they're massing."

Lucas and I confirm this. We saw it with our own eyes when we were captives.

Costas backs up Stephanos's supposition. "Persian-trained officers"—meaning Spitamenes—"bring their sons when they believe they're entering a fight to the death. The youth must be on hand to witness his father's heroism in victory—or to secure from violation his remains in defeat."

In other words, something big is coming.

A rider must be dispatched back to column. A row breaks out over this. Agathocles, the intelligence officer, demands custody of Spitamenes' son. Whatever the meaning of the lad's presence, his physical person must be delivered at once—to Coenus and then to Alexander. The boy represents a significant counter in the game of war and peace. Agathocles will bring the prize in himself. He commands Stephanos to detail an escort.

Stephanos refuses.

Agathocles, the poet declares, will be run down by the foe in hours, alone on the steppe with only a few men. "You must stay with the main body, sir." Both lieutenants defer to Stephanos, though they outrank him, in favor of his experience in war and his fame as a soldier. The poet orders the column organized, prisoners bound, and our wounded tended to. We will move out as a body, as soon as we're able.

Agathocles insists on starting off with Spitamenes' son at once. Time, he says, is of the essence. He demands a guide and eight men on fast horses.

Stephanos laughs in his face. It goes without saying that our commander despises the intelligence officer's unspoken motive: to claim for himself the glory of this capture.

"I'm not going to argue with you, Color Sergeant," says Agathocles.

"Nor I with you," answers Stephanos. He will not risk the loss of so valuable a prisoner, nor any Mack sent onto the steppe to protect him.

Costas steps up. "I'll go."

The parley cracks up. Flag points into the badlands. "They bleed blood out there, correspondent, not ink."

To his credit, the chronicler stands fast. "Then I'll write my story in it."

Agathocles' patience has run out. "If you refuse to give me men, poet, then come yourself. Protect me. Or do you lack the belly?"

I have rarely seen Stephanos parted from his self-command. But Agathocles, now, drives him to it. Flag and Lucas have to step in, restraining Stephanos.

Agathocles calls for horses. His aide picks out men to form an escort. Several are Daans, never to be trusted; the Macks who come forward can charitably be called opportunists. I glance to Lucas. Something has to be done. "I'll go," I say.

My mate blocks me.

"You went with Tollo."

He means it's his turn to risk his neck for no good reason.

Stephanos bars everyone. "No one's going!"

But Agathocles is already in the saddle. His rank is full captain; Stephanos is only a color sergeant. The other riders bring their prize captive. Lucas takes up his arms and kit; he mounts; Agathocles again orders Stephanos to remember his station.

I catch Lucas's bridle. Into his saddle-pouch I press my woolen overcloak and a sack of *kishar* and lentils. He takes my hand.

"Whatever happens to me, brother," he says, "tell the truth."

41.

It takes six days, pushing our animals and prisoners, to relink with the main column. This is at Gabae, the trading camp on the frontier between Sogdiana and the Wild Lands. We catch up with the siege train; the fighting elements have already pushed north. The Wolf's tribesmen, a scout tells us, are massing above the border. "Looks like an all-in skull-buster."

No one has seen Lucas or Costas or Agathocles. The capture of Spitamenes' son is news to them. They have heard nothing and know nothing.

We drop our prisoners and press north along the military highway, or what has become the military highway. Mule trains of hundreds bring up rations and heavy gear. How far ahead is Coenus? No one knows. Where is Spitamenes? The rear-boggers give us the blank stare.

Our animals are too fagged to keep pace. They need a day. We carve a camp alongside the trudging supply column, in an ice-crusted wash in the middle of nothing. Gales howl. We chop sod for a windbreak. Plunging my pike into the turf, I pull up a skull. Flag digs up a hip joint. The site is a barrow. An ancient burial mound.

Soldiers are superstitious. "I ain't bonzing here," says Dice.

We bed down with the muleteers. Breakfast is wine and millet scratch, both frozen. We share it with a squad of Paeonian lancers—Alexander's elite scouts—who have ridden three days without rest from Nautaca.

"Where's the king?"

"Coming fast, mates. And bringing every bat and bumper!"

The lancers wolf their gruel, then spur north, putting the supply column behind them.

By postnoon Alexander's merc cavalry are passing. Rumor says his Royal Squadron of Companions—and he himself—have already pushed past Gabae by the eastern caravan trace. They're ahead of us.

We slog on. The supply train has plenty of dry fodder, but their sergeants won't let us have it. Every bale is tagged for a line unit. We have nothing for our ponies. The steppe sprawls gray and frozen; grass is frost-stiff straw. Our horses' turds gush like soup.

Still no one has word of Lucas.

My mind searches for reasons. "You're thinking again," says Flag.

In this multitude, he reasons, what's the chance of getting news of one man? Besides, it's almost certain Lucas got through. "They're heroes, him and that captain. It was their report that set off this whole show."

I want to believe it. It makes sense; the timing of it rings right. Lucas is probably in camp with forward elements right now. He's with Coenus and Alexander, soaking up the glory.

We press on. A thaw hits. The steppe becomes a bog. Laden mules sink halfway to their hocks; wagons are mired by scores. The lane of the column's passage looks like a field plowed by oxen. It's so miserable, death itself sounds like a vacation. Better than another night's kip in this slop.

It rains all day, the tenth and eleventh. Our horses are skeletons. We look like ghosts. Then on the twelfth, the temperature plummets. The heavens dump sleet, then snow. We come over a rise. Ahead: an assembly area. Quartermasters route us off the highway behind a range of hills.

We have caught up with the front. Tents and field kitchens. Mack infantry in thousands, all arming for battle. No half-pikes. Full-length *sarissas*. Stephanos sends me to find someone from Coenus's brigade to report to. It's impossible. The site spreads for miles. We're among elements of Alexander's elite merc cav. Their horses make ours look like dogs. Before I can spot a familiar face or a standard I recognize, a colonel's aide calls us to mount and ride. The fight isn't tomorrow, it's now.

Still no one has seen Lucas.

42.

I have never seen men so eager for battle. Twenty-seven months of frustration have driven our Macks more than a little mad. They want to crack skulls. They burn to make widows.

Our companies form up under Bullock in a vale alongside a line of catapults being fixed to their limbers. Unit strength is supposed to be 256. Count tops out at 91. Nobody cares. Wherever a man finds himself, let him pick a crew and slot in.

Stephanos canters the line, forming us into wedges. We'll be backing up the merc cav. "I don't suppose," Flag says, "anyone has anything like actual orders."

Stephanos indicates the mercs. "Just do what they do."

The hired cav are Phrygians and Cappadocians. You can tell by their pointy caps. We don't even speak the same language. Dice reins alongside Boxer and Little Red. "Welcome to gang-fuck!" He's laughing.

The mercs pull out in column of wedges. They seem to know what they're doing. They're all lancers, with earflap cawls and pennants snapping on the ends of their twelve-footers. We're trotting down a swale between tall barrows. It's like passing between burial mounds. The battlefield, or what will become the battlefield, is just over the left-hand rise. We turn a corner and there it is.

Snow is dumping in sheaves now. Clear of the vale, the cold hits like a wall of ice. Where is the foe? The weather is deteriorating so fast we can't see more than one wedge in front of us. With the wind and snow, we can't hear a thing.

Where is Alexander?

Where's Spitamenes?

In every other scrape I've been in, the dominant element has been confusion, succeeded by doubt and terror. Here it's only confusion. I feel no fear at all. I keep scanning round for Lucas. Let him be all right and I'll croak without a second thought.

Our wedges follow the mercs. The column swings right. The barrows are at our right shoulder now; we're at the canter, paralleling them. To our left and down a long gale-scoured slope stretches a vast bowl filling up with snow. We pass company after company of light infantry advancing into this. They make no haste. They're jabbering to each other, careless as fishwives in the market. Curtains of snow descend; you can see the troops but can't hear them. The footing beneath my pony's hooves is hard as stone and slick as marble.

Historians will demonstrate later that Spitamenes had no choice but to come, on this site at this hour, into the open. Alexander's forts have compassed the Wolf, leaving him no safe patch to set down upon. The foe's supplies have been cut off. Doubtless his hot-blood tribesmen provoke him in council. The Massagetae won't stay the winter without some adventure after plunder. He'll lose them and the Daans and Sacae if he doesn't act with audacity. They'll scatter and never rally round him as a leader again.

The Wolf has no choice but to attack. He knows Alexander wants him to. He knows our king has contrived events to give him no other option. And he knows that as soon as he does attack, Alexander will race north from his ready camp at Nautaca with every man and horse he's got.

So be it.

A straight-up brawl at last.

Our merc cav come left in column. We follow. The mercenaries transit directly behind the light infantry, forming a second front rearward of the foot troops; then their leaders come about in that evolution called the Laconian countermarch, like racehorses round a turning pole or a team of oxen plowing a field. Dice hails me as we skipper through the blowing snow. "What the hell's going on?"

"Just follow these bastards!" I'm as lost as he is.

Our mounted force draws up on the rim of the snow bowl, behind the broad front of infantry. We're in the middle now, in column with our long axis flank-on to the fight; the merc cav rein on our right wing in the same formation. We can hear but not yet see the clash taking place half a mile downslope.

Alexander has sent forward in a hollow square eight hundred Lydian and Median cavalry with twelve hundred merc infantry (the same troops, we'll learn later, that Lucas and I marched out from home with). These are the bait. Against them, Spitamenes has flung a crescent of Massagetae and Daan horsemen. The horns of the enemy's charge have enveloped our fellows. The foe assaults the square of infantry by swarms, barbarian-style, ringing it with a great whooping mass of horsemen, who circle at the canter, keeping just out of spear and javelin range, while making rushes in groups upon our men, pulsing in and out, slinging volley after volley of arrows and darts.

Right and left, we can hear Mack trumpets. The infantry down-slope of us step out now. They drop down the flank of the snow bowl at the double, their boots lifting great eddies of white. The foot troops' front extends right and left out of sight. They make straight for the swarming circle of enemy horsemen. Stephanos wheels his gelding Parataxis, "Pitched Battle," out front. He holds us back till the infantry has advanced about a hundred yards down the hill. Now we go. Behind the dirt-eaters, at the walk. On our right, the merc cav advance in the same manner. I still have no idea what the hell we're supposed to do. Neither does Dice; neither does Boxer. We all strain toward Stephanos. He doesn't know either.

This is my first real stand-up battle. Like everyone, I've heard a thousand accounts of such clashes, of trumpets and pennants and great thundering charges of massed troops and horses. But nothing prepares me for the scale or the sound or the mad irresistible sweep of the thing. The emotion of the animals is overwhelming. Like us, horses evacuate their innards when seized by fear and excitement. Everywhere you look, mounts are shitting and pissing; the stink cuts our nostrils; the frozen air steams with it. The ponies stamp and whinny; you can feel them slipping from their riders' control. They are reverting to the law of the herd. So are we. Hooves fling divots of frozen sod. The earth bucks and shudders beneath us. The field puts up an inhuman, throbbing thrum.

I am a corporal; I command a litter of eight. Every sense screams to me, Grasp your orders! Take charge! This is impossible. We are caught, all of us, in the tide and current of the hour. When our horses go, we'll go with them. Orders? Zeus himself could not make himself heard above this din, and even if he could, the momentum of the instant would overwhelm his mightiest cries. I understand more with my seat than with my senses. The infantry's job, I see, is to screen the merc cav, to prevent the foe from discovering our advance. Out front the enemy pours squadron after squadron of tribal horsemen into his great galloping ring. He thinks to finish off our initial divisions, then turn on the advancing foot troops and pull the same stunt on them.

We're halfway down the slope now. Battle sounds ascend from the bowl in a deafening cacophony. I see Stephanos gallop before our front; an officer of the merc cav rides beside him. This fellow trails a pennant rider, a youth no older than fourteen, at his shoulder. The boy bears aloft a great snaky "serpent" of crimson. Without a word every man understands.

Follow him.

Follow his flag.

The merc cav on our right are turning rightward now, by the flank. Into column again. The way we entered. They go from the walk to the trot. Our horses understand before we do. They want to canter. At once I get it. We all do.

"Understand, Dice?" I bawl into the sheeting snow.

He laughs, pointing his lance toward the merc cav. "Do what they do!"

Here we go. The last glimpse I get before our column spurs rightward is of the corps of pages galloping onto the slope above us, bearing the banner of the *agema* of the Companions, the former Royal Squadron, and the Lion Standard of Macedon. Alexander and the Companions. A thrill shoots from my pony's hooves through the crown of my skull and right out the top.

This is the day.

The only way to counter Scythian tactics, the great wheeling circle of horse archers, is to block it from the side. Make it break down. Drive it against a river or a mountain or a precipice. Then infantry and cavalry can bring their weapons to bear. But here on the steppes of the Wild Lands, there are no rivers or mountains or precipices. That's why Scythian tactics work so well.

What you must do—and what Alexander does now—is to use men and horses to make a river, a mountain, a precipice. That is our role now. Ours and the merc cav. At the gallop, the elite hired troopers of Phrygia and Cappadocia emerge from behind the horns of the screen of advancing infantry. One wing goes right, one goes left. In a great sweep they swing out and back. They hit the wheeling enemy on both extremities of his ring.

Now the foe is pinned between infantry front and back and cavalry right and left. His circle shatters like a wheel against four stones. Our litter trails the columns of merc cav as they thunder onto the foe.

It would give me supreme pleasure to relate how the shock of our company's rush broke the enemy and drove him before us in flight, not to mention how my lance personally dispatched this hero and that champion. In fact, the merc cav does everything before we even get there. Ours is probably the twentieth column to strike the foe. He is already reeling. We are just a wall. A hedge of pikes and horseflesh to pin Spitamenes' hordes and crack his wheel into spokes and splinters.

Now Alexander and his Companions charge.

Our king leads eighteen hundred heavy cavalry in squadron column of wedges, two hundred men each. At the gallop, this force can cross a hundred yards in seven seconds. When it rips into the belly of the last of the circling foe, it shatters his momentum and turns his multitude into a milling, disordered mass.

The fight is over so fast it's almost disappointing. By now the tribesmen's bolts have been shot. His mounts are blown, the fever of his assault is exhausted. Now the *sarissas* of our light and heavy infantry and the lances of the merc cav turn upon him. In moments, twelve hundred of the foe are slain. Thousands fling down their arms. Spitamenes himself bolts the field.

Our company ranges about the belly of the bowl, snatching every loose horse we can lay hands on. The field is soup. The frozen turf has been punched through in every quarter. It's all muck now. Everywhere the foe holds up empty hands. Their spent animals floundering in the slop, Bactrians and Sogdians drop their arms by the hundreds. Their erstwhile allies, the Sacae and Massagetae, seize the chance to raid their own mates' baggage, lingering long enough to grab all the ponies and women they can before using the snow to screen their getaway into the Wild Lands.

With victory, the field has become a churning mill of horseflesh. War mounts in hundreds stamp the mud to lather. Our lads whoop and whistle, on fire to snatch a prize mount, or at least a plug *yaboo* they can turn over for a quick purse of silver. Where is Lucas? I spur through the roundup. Suddenly a flash of white strikes my eye.

Snow!

My pretty little mare that I lost on the Many Blessings!

Only a rider will believe it, that out of such a seething stampede of livestock, one's glance can pick out an individual beast. But there she is. I whistle. Her ears turn. In an instant I have dismounted and crossed to her; I fling my arms round her neck. When she smells me, she knows me.

Emotion overwhelms me. I stroke my darling's muzzle. I understand, even as my heart overflows with it, that my elation at her recovery is a surrogate for other losses, far keener and not yet made good. Beloved comrades for whom my heart cannot yet mourn; missing brothers for whom even now I seek. They all become one for me in the form of this dear animal, whom I believed I would never see again and who now, one horse out of five thousand, has miraculously been delivered into my arms.

I can hear men talking roundabout. Spitamenes, they're saying, has gotten away. Our fastest riders pursue him. Where is Alexander? Seeing to the surrender of the Bactrians and Sogdians.

A Mack sergeant says he saw Spitamenes' son. I come alert in the instant. "Where? When?"

"What, mate?"

"You said you saw him. Where?"

The sergeant is busy with his own captured horses. He and his mates turn away. I chase them, demanding to know if they saw or didn't. The sergeant faces back, hot and chapped. "Take it easy, brother. I'm just telling what I heard . . ."

"Then you didn't see him?"

"No, but many did."

I'm furious. I demand to know how he dares pass such tales without substantiation. He repeats: Spitamenes and his son have fled. "They fucked off, the pair of them! Is that enough for you, mate?"

The sergeant's comrades shove me back. Boxer and Little Red collar me. I feel like the top of my skull is coming off. If Spitamenes' son is alive, then . . .

"Matthias!"

Dice's voice booms above the din.

"Matthias, here!"

I turn to see him and two other mates rein in, coming from the battlefield. Despite the cold, they're sweating. They've been looking all over for me, Dice declares. Their expressions are grave. Then I see the Headquarters lieutenant with them. I salute.

"You're Matthias, son of Matthias, of Apollonia?"

I tell him I am.

His face looks grimmer, even, than the others'.

"You will come with me now," he says.

43.

In the staff tent stand an iron brazier, three trunks serving as chairs, and a campaign table. The lieutenant sets Lucas's notebook on top. "Do you recognize this?"

It's a worn leather roll with two rawhide ties. Into the grain of the flap is carved the device of an elk being slain by a griffin.

"Did you hear me, Corporal? Do you recognize it?"

Soldiers know how to make their hearts go dead. You drop out of yourself. Light changes; sound goes queer. It's like you're looking down a tunnel. You see nothing but what's right in front of you and even that appears as if it's being observed not by you but by some surrogate, some counterform of yourself that has been denatured and hollowed out, leaving only a shell numb as stone.

I am aware of the lieutenant placing onto the table Lucas's helmet and dagger. He even produces the overcloak I gave Lucas as he rode off with Agathocles—and the sack of *kishar* and lentils.

"I'm sorry," he says. And turning to his aide: "Get him something to drink."

When the lieutenant leaves, Dice spits out the story.

The party of Agathocles, Lucas, and Costas, escorting Spitamenes' son, was fallen upon by Bactrian tribesmen only two days after striking out from the capture site. The foe had carried the Macks, bound and blindfolded, to a camp called Chalk Bluffs, where a multitude of their kinsmen had assembled. The clansmen nailed our countrymen to boards, painted them with pitch, and set them alight. Further outrages were performed upon them while they still lived. Then they were beheaded. Their remains were dragged behind the foe's ponies until they broke apart and fell away.

I ask Dice how he knows this.

"The villains made boast of it. In a post to Alexander."

Our troops, Dice says, found the skulls in the enemy camp immediately after the battle, in captured wagons of the Bactrians, along with our fellows' weapons and kit, which the foe had taken as trophies.

Night falls. Mack patrols fan across the steppe, seeking Spitamenes, who has become now, in the snow, one set of tracks among thousands. Alexander prepares the brigades to give chase as soon as the Wolf is discovered. Our section under Stephanos has been pulled out of the line. No one tells us why. I do not sleep. I will not eat. Only one object animates my purpose: to return to action as soon as possible and pay these fiends out for the abominations they have visited upon my friend.

44.

But Headquarters has quarantined us. Our section has been segregated to a compound on the margins of the camp. Intelligence has set up two tents. That night they bring in our officers and chief sergeants—Stephanos, Flag, the two young lieutenants who were present when Spitamenes' son was captured. What they're asking, no one knows. When they're finished, they direct our commanders to the opposite wing of the compound, so they can't talk to us who haven't been called yet.

My turn comes around midnight. A hailstorm has got up; pellets of ice rip through the camp, tearing up tents and windbreaks. The cold and din are indescribable.

The Headquarters lieutenant interviews me. This is in the same tent where he showed me Lucas's notebook. He congratulates me and our company on our part in this glorious victory. I am to be decorated and promoted sergeant. Bonuses for all. Then he sets a document on the table before me. I am to read and sign it.

"You do read, Corporal?"

I regard him. "Barely."

The scroll is a report of the action against Spitamenes. It is accurate within reason. Except at the finish, where it recounts the deaths of Lucas, Agathocles, and the journalist Costas. All are given heroic demises, in combat on the field.

"That isn't how it happened," I say.

The ice storm booms against the sailcloth of the tent. Coals in the brazier flare with the gale.

The lieutenant dismisses my statement. "All your mates have signed it."

He shows me Flag's mark, and Stephanos's and the two lieutenants, and our officers all the way up to Bullock.

"Lucas and the others were killed," I say, "days earlier, on the prairie. Run down by Afghan cavalry and butchered."

"Please," says the lieutenant. "Make your mark."

Why, I ask, is it even necessary for me to sign? I'm only a corporal. Who cares what I say?

"Headquarters wants marks from all."

If it hadn't been so bitter cold, if I hadn't been so exhausted, I might have scrawled my sign. *Narik ta?* What difference does it make? But the lieutenant's manner puts my back up. With emotion I recount the capture of Spitamenes' son on the steppe. I describe Agathocles' insistence on delivering the prisoner to the column at once, and how Costas the correspondent and my friend Lucas volunteered to join the party that set off alone into the void. "The enemy caught them and massacred them. That's what happened."

"Will you sign, Corporal?"

"No."

The lieutenant excuses himself. When he comes back, a captain accompanies him. This time they bring a secretary.

The captain is more affable than the lieutenant. Wine is brought, and bread and salt. We chat. It is discovered that we have friends in common. The captain, it seems, knew my brother Elias; he praises Elias's valor and expresses grief at his untimely end.

"Look," he says, "you and I know what happened to your friend Lucas. By Heracles, the brutes who did it deserve crucifixion!"

"Then let's find them and give it to them."

The captain's concern, he says, is for the kin of the bereaved.

"What good will the truth do your friend's mother and sister? Will it ease their suffering? How will they remember their beloved boy?"

"As he was," I say.

"No. They'll see him butchered. Is that what you want?"

He slides the paper across.

"Your friend was a hero, Corporal. Let his loved ones remember him that way."

Now I'm getting really chapped. I slide the chair back and start to rise.

"Sit down," commands the captain.

I stand up.

"Put your ass in that chair, damn you!"

I obey.

But I won't sign.

Two Hyrcanian lancers man the portal. They escort me outside, to an unused supply tent. I am to wait there, speaking to no one. Dice and Boxer are called in to the captain's tent. They finish and are sent off to the good part of the camp. It's now the middle of the night. The ice storm lets up, succeeded by hyperborean cold.

At dawn I'm called back. It's the same captain, alone this time. "All right," he says. "It's a cover story."

He meets my eyes, as if to communicate that I'm special; he's going to clue me in on the true noise.

"Headquarters believes it vital that no word of these atrocities reach the army's ears."

"Why not?"

"Twelve hundred Bactrians and Sogdians surrendered to us yesterday. Alexander wants to integrate them into the corps. These hundreds will bring in hundreds more. But if our fellows learn of what happened . . ."

I get it.

"This is about peace," says the captain. "It's about ending this bung-fucked war!"

I ask him about the post the Bactrians sent to our king. "Don't the troops know from that?"

"That message was buried the instant it showed up. The only ones who know about it are the officers in this compound and a couple of your mates whom we told when we brought them in."

On a side table sits a steaming pot of lentils and chicken. There's wine and barley mooch. The captain asks if I've eaten. I'm not hungry, I say.

"What line are you defending, Corporal? By Zeus, why won't you sign?"

I know I'm being mulish. What difference does one lousy inkscratch make in the scheme of things?

"Listen to me, son. This order comes straight from Alexander. Don't you love your king?"

I do.

But I won't sign.

"Do you understand how important this is? We're talking about men's lives! If peace can be made this winter, we save an entire spring campaign."

I understand.

"Do you imagine," the captain asks, "that Command will let one pigheaded corporal stand in the way of shortening this war?"

"Are you threatening me, sir?"

"I'm begging you, man."

45.

I spend the morning frozen in the supply tent.

I understand Command's predicament. I understand its solution. The phony report will be sent home to Macedon; it will be accepted without hesitation. Headquarters will publish it here throughout the army. No one who has signed it can then call it false. The Bactrians and Sogdians will be enrolled in the corps; they will bring in their cousins and brothers. It's sound strategy. If I were a staff officer, I'd contrive it too.

But I still won't sign.

One of the guards set over me is an Arcadian mercenary. Polemon is his name, a good fellow; I know him from the city-building at Kandahar. He sneaks me some stew and half a jar of wine. "What's the bone?" he asks. Why am I being so stubborn?

I tell him about Lucas, how the truth meant everything to him.

"Mate, you don't know how deep you're in it. These fuckers aren't dogging around."

Yes, I say. "I'm sure they've got a story made up about *me* too."

"Damn right they have. And I'll sign it. We all will."

Exhaustion has shattered me, but I can't sleep. In my mind I see Lucas's eyes. I can't let him down. I steel myself for the worst that can be thrown at me. I will not prove false to my friend.

By midmorning the camp is boiling with action. Spitamenes' trail has been picked up. Orders are being issued. Alexander's brigades will push off by noon. Our company will rejoin its division. Everyone but me.

This is the keenest torture yet. I cannot be left behind!

I am kicked out of the supply tent, so its contents can be broken down into mule-loads for the march out. Back in the first tent, I can hear my mates outside, rigging up. I can't stand it. New guards are posted over me. I'm supposed to sit and say nothing, but my jailers let up when Flag and Stephanos, mounted to move out, rein outside.

"Sign," says Flag, with a look that communicates, "It's all rubbish anyway." Stephanos taps his skull, meaning don't be such a hardhead.

I am taken away again. This time to the king's precinct. Another tent, bigger, with compartments. I stew through midday. Where is my horse? Has she been taken care of? The portal opens; the captain from yesterday enters. This time he has a staff colonel with him. The colonel says he's through pissing around. He slaps the document down and commands me to sign it.

I will not.

"Hell take you!" The colonel pounds the table. "Do you want to make me a murderer?"

I hold at attention.

"You are a disgrace! You discredit the Corps!" And he stalks out.

The captain still hasn't spoken. He motions me to sit. He does too. He pours a cup for me from a pitcher. "It's only water."

I take it. The captain smiles. "Your brother Philip is somewhere out on the steppe. Otherwise we'd have him here, too, to reason with you." He regards me. "But you wouldn't listen to him either, would you?"

He takes a different document from a case and slides it toward me. "This is your rag sheet." The record of my debts. The captain gives me a moment to scan it. It's every tick I owe the army, for my horse, advances, allowances. The roll must run forty lines. "We'll tear it up." Next: my enlistment contract. "I'll knock twelve months off."

The captain meets my eye with a look that says, "Let's cut through the crap."

"You're promoted to sergeant. You've earned a Bronze Lion; I see no reason not to make it a Silver. The award comes with two years' pay. Bonuses on top, plus your *oikos* allowance. We'll get your girl up to Nautaca. Make the winter a little warmer."

He indicates the original report.

"You don't have to sign. Just give me your word you won't contradict its contents, verbally or in written communication."

He's very good. But each word renders me more furious. In my mind I see Lucas's charred remains, being dragged in the dirt behind some Bactrian *yaboo*.

"You might as well kill me, sir, and get it over with."

The colonel sighs. "By Zeus, you're a hard knot."

He stands. I'm waiting for the guards to come in and seize me. The portal rustles. I hear a step from the adjacent chamber. Light enters. A man follows.

It is Alexander.

46.

The captain springs to his feet. I brace at rigid attention. The king comes all the way in. He entreats our pardon for entering unannounced. He has overheard our words from outside; he could not help himself. "Stand easy, Corporal."

Alexander comes round front, where I can see him.

Our lord wears a plain winter cloak with no breastplate and no insignia save a single Gold Lion as a shoulder clasp. "The brigades move out in an hour. Forgive me if I don't have much time."

I am struck by how worn he looks. The contrast to his youthfulness, when we replacements first saw him two years ago, is overwhelming. He is only twenty-eight. Up close he looks forty. His skin is abraded to leather by sun and wind. His honey-colored hair holds streaks of silver. He dismisses the captain but does not sit himself, nor indicate that I may.

"I know what it means to lose a friend," he says, "and in such a ghastly manner. I respect your courage in defying an order that seems to you unjust, and I understand that promise of reward offends your sense of honor."

The chamber is close, no bigger than an eight-man tent, with nothing in it but a table, three chairs, and a stand for maps and charts.

"But you must understand what is at stake. We have a chance now to end this war, a chance that will not endure. Hours count. Amnesty must be extended to our Bactrian and Sogdian captives as quickly as possible, so it looks like a gesture of spirit and generosity, not a calculated act of politics."

I am pierced to the heart by this token of our lord to address, as he would a commander of stature, a soldier of such mean rank.

"This is what war is," says Alexander. "Glory has fled. One searches in vain for honor. We've all done things we're ashamed of. Even victory, as Aeschylus says,

in whose august glow all felonies are effaced,

is not the same in this war. What remains? To prevent the needless waste of lives. Too many good men have perished without cause. More will join them if we don't make this peace now."

He straightens and meets my eye.

"I rescind the captain's offer of promotion and reward. It's an insult to your honor. Nor will I coerce you, Matthias, to take an action that runs counter to your code. Proceed as your conscience dictates. I shall take no measures against you, now or ever, nor will I permit any to be taken by others. Nothing is nobler than the love of friend for friend. Let it go at that."

And he turns and exits.

Ten days later, near a scarp called by the Scythians Mana Karq,

"Salt Bluffs," a detachment of Massagetae appear under a banner of truce and present themselves to a forward unit attached to Hephaestion's brigade, which comprises the right wing of the Macedonian northward thrust.

Their chiefs, the Massagetae claim, have Spitamenes' head.

They will deliver this trophy to Alexander, they declare, if he will call off his advance and accept their undertakings of friendship.

BOOK
EIGHT

An End to Hostilities

47.

Shinar has conceived.

She is pregnant. This time I won't let her terminate it. She doesn't want to, anyway. She's happy. So am I.

Our division has gone into winter quarters at Nautaca. It's the best place we've been. The city is sited atop an impregnable eminence, so there's no work fortifying it, and what there is was completed by the engineers before they moved on to finish construction on Alexandria-on-the-Jaxartes.

At Frost Festival all line troopers receive their back wages. Mine is seven months', with two years' on top as a king's premium. My third Bronze Lion has come through. A year's pay goes with it and, better yet, the option to elect discharge at the end of my next bump. Three Lions equals a skip. Am I stupid? I'll grab it with both hands! I'm flush. We all are.

The best part of Nautaca is Digger Town, the compound that

the Corps of Engineers has put up for its own quarters and that we scuffs have now moved into. No tents for the engineers. They've built themselves real stone-and-timber barracks with a bathhouse, wood floors, and enclosed walkways to the latrines. When they move on at winter's start to the Jaxartes, the compound is converted to a hospital. By midwinter the wounded have either recovered and rejoined their units or been moved back south to Bactra City.

Our fellows take over. Shinar and I get a room to ourselves with a window and a clay *khef* oven. An armload of kindling keeps the place toasty all night. Ghilla shares the space with us, along with her infant son, whom she has named Lucas. I have never been around a child. I adore the little fellow. We take naps together. He loves to sleep back-to-back. At first I am terrified I will roll over on him, but his squalling soon eases that fear. He has lungs like a flag sergeant. If Shinar's child is a boy, we will name him Elias. The women have carpeted the floors for warmth and snugged down the roof. Our mates Boxer and Little Red have the next two rooms, with their women; Flag and Stephanos are in the cottages built for officers just down the lane.

We're almost embarrassed to be so comfortable.

Winter's chore is to prepare an offensive for spring. I'm a line sergeant now. I command a file of sixteen. I'm included in all platoon-level briefings and some even up to battalion.

I have written to my mother, telling her about Shinar. For once I can speak the truth in a letter.

When the Massagetae campaign ended, three months ago, our section was two hundred miles into the Wild Lands. Not a man was unwounded. The horses were hide-and-bones. Three storms struck in succession. I lost two toes and part of four fingers, including the top of my left thumb. Many suffered far worse. When at last the column staggered back into Nautaca, Shinar was waiting for me. She had come north alone, first to Maracanda, then to Alexandria-on-the-Jaxartes, finally to here.

When I saw her, bundled sole-to-crown among the crowd of wives and lovers at the intake gate, I knew I would look no farther for my life's companion. No barracks had been built at that time, but the engineers had put up stables, still under construction but at least out of the wind.

There Shinar takes me. I fall into the straw in a stupor. When I awake, as I do for days in fits of terror and dislocation, I see her tending to Snow. She rubs the mare down, dries and wraps her feet, gets good grain and sweet water into her belly. "What about me?" I groan.

"I'll get to you in good time," she says.

I sleep for a month, it seems, enveloped by her scent. The warmth of her flesh restores me.

It seems she has become a different person, warmer and kinder and less crippled within. Have I altered too? Or just never known her?

Ghilla is sweet about vacating our chamber. She senses the moment and takes up little Lucas. "Time for a walk, Tiny Bundle."

Like all army women, Shinar knows the corps' plans before we soldiers do. The spring offensive will be full-scale. Four Afghan warlords remain—Oxyartes, Chorienes, Catanes, and Austanes—commanding a total of about forty thousand men. They have repaired to various fastnesses in the Scythian Caucasus. In spring we will besiege them. Advance elements have already taken station, investing the foe and cutting off all escape.

I cannot think of Lucas. When his memory enters my thoughts, I banish it. It's too soon. I will break down otherwise.

His child is a blessing. What would we do without him? Ghilla and I tread gently around each other. Nothing she can ask is too much. And she acts the same toward me. We never speak Lucas's name. Next year maybe. I will not be first to do it.

Winter stays dark this far north. How these tribes survive, or even wish to, is past my comprehension. Even Alexander must respect this remoteness. He has come to call Jaxartes City "Alexandria Eschate"—Alexandria-the-Furthermost. He renounces all claim to the Wild Lands. Let the Massagetae keep them. Our lord will mark here the northern extremity of his empire and call the free Scyths beyond it his allies and friends.

It's as good a plan as any.

On a day when the west wind brings the first scent of spring, my brother Philip arrives from Maracanda. He has been south in the mountains, treating with tribal chiefs of Chorienes and Oxyartes. We spend a long, happy night—Shinar and Ghilla and I, with Flag and his woman and Stephanos (who still will have none but his wife back home).

"What's holding up the peace?" the poet asks my brother.

"Same thing that always holds it up. Pride."

A way must be found, Philip says, that will let both sides claim victory. For the warlords this is a matter of life and death; they will not survive their own tribesmen's fury if they are seen as having presided over defeat. Intertribal suspicion further impedes the process. Each chieftain fears that he will lose power in postwar Afghanistan; he will not set his name to any accommodation until he knows where he—and his rivals—stand in its scheme. No one wants to keep fighting. War has devastated the country. Philip reckons we've wiped out half the men of military age, in a society where that means every male from twelve to eighty.

"Where is your woman?" Shinar asks him.

He laughs. "Can't afford one."

Shinar schemes of putting Philip together with Ghilla. Even

one night would do them both good. But when the moment presents itself at evening's close, Philip with grace declines.

"Stay at least and talk," says Shinar. "The night is cold and we may not see you again for many months."

We stay up—my brother, Shinar, and I—into the deep hours.

"Don't say you heard this from me," Philip says, "but more bonuses are coming." Alexander will rain gold this spring upon the troops who have suffered with him through this campaign. It only wants peace for the treasury doors to open. "Will you marry?" he asks Shinar and me.

"If she'll say yes."

It makes Philip happy to see us together.

"Whatever you do, don't stay out here. The army will tempt you with cash incentives and grants of land larger than counties back home. Don't fall for it. This place will revert to tribal ways as soon as Alexander moves on. Take your pay home, Matthias. You're rich. You can buy any place you fancy, or farm Mother's with Agathon and Eleni. They'd like nothing better. It will not be as bad as you think, Shinar. We Macks are not all devils. You'll be a citizen, and so will your child."

Shinar absorbs this impassively, like some dream she believes can never come true. Philip regards her with tenderness.

"May the gods bless you, dear child, and your infant on the way. I know you have suffered more than Matthias and I can imagine. It's good to see you happy. And I can never thank you enough for the change you have wrought in my brother."

His voice cracks. Shinar crosses to the carpet beside him. She takes his hand. "What about you, Philip? Will you go home now?"

"The corps is my home, Shinar."

Lamplight shows the gray in Philip's hair. Fever, I know, has carried off his wife back home; his son in a few years will be out east with the army. Heaven alone knows how many mates he has lost in action. He smiles at Shinar's hope for his remarriage.

"What wife could I take, dear child? What woman could I bring happiness to? I have gone to army whores too long. I like them. I don't have to explain myself to them. Do you understand? Can I really dandle some infant on my knee?" He laughs darkly. "I have been at war now, man and boy, for two-thirds of my life. What other trade do I know? My home resides in hell, if anywhere, where those I love wait for me." He smiles. "I think I shall not keep them long."

"Don't talk like that," Shinar scolds him. "I've done it myself. It serves no purpose."

She's right of course, Philip acknowledges.

"Can I return to Macedon?" he asks. "Before Elias died, perhaps. Now never. The only thing that keeps me above the earth is you two and your child on the way. So I say to you both, as I have before: Don't be like me. Get out of here. Seize your happiness while you still can."

Dawn lacks an hour when Philip takes his leave. We walk outside under stars bright as embers. Philip's bad leg locks up in the cold.

"What about Shinar's brother?" he asks.

He knows of the brother's obligation under *nangwali* to efface the shame she brings to her family by being with me—and of her two cousins', who stand with him, wanting only the chance.

"They're all bluff," I say. "In any event, the lot of 'em are three hundred miles south with the mountain brigades."

"We'll all be down south in the spring."

Philip wants the brother's and cousins' complete names—given, patronymic, clan, and tribe.

"Look," I say, "I don't want you doing anything to them."

Philip regards me soberly.

"Why not?"

48.

Spring comes. Coenus's brigade deploys south to the mountains. Alexander and the heavy divisions are already there.

For efficiency and mastery of combat arms, the world has seen nothing like this force. The king has been modernizing all winter, upgrading and expanding the corps' capacities for mountain warfare. Siege gear that formerly needed transport by freight wagons and oxen has been simplified and stripped down so that it can be packed on the backs of mules. We have mountain catapults now that can sling a stone or a pot of flaming naphtha a fifth of a mile. Trains pack thin sheets of bronze to face mantlets of timber, rendering them flame- and fireproof. Tortoise-type carapaces have been fashioned, beneath which men can mount scaling ladders and not fear scalding oil or superheated sand. Carpentry shops have labored all winter producing block and tackle; rope-makers have laid in miles of cable. Ingenious mechanisms have been fashioned, like the mountain windlass that uses torsion bands instead of heavy iron ratchet teeth. Two of these, braced to boulders, can raise a siege tower forty feet high. In the past, mountain warfare has been limited to clashes between skirmishers, who sling missiles and scamper away, while siege warfare has been confined to the plains. No more. To take down these summit citadels, Alexander's engineers have advanced siege technology to a whole new sphere and scale. The supply corps has half a thousand mules packing nothing but oil of terebinth—turpentine—for making incendiary bombs and as solvent to clean the blades of the axes, hewing mountain pines to be made into cat arms and tower timbers.

Mountain fortresses are assaulted by stages. A base camp is first established on the plain. Now come the provisions. Rations and fodder in hundreds of tons are rafted in by river or trucked overland via caravan or mule train. Now the first forward camp is raised in the foothills. Up come the convoys of supplies and matériel. The foe in this case has retired to four monumental strongholds. Imagine Mount Olympus. That's what they're like, mountain systems covering scores of square miles, with hundreds of approaches.

First to be invested, before winter has ended, is that fastness called by the troops the Sogdian Rock. The warlord Oxyartes is up there with eleven thousand troops and all their goods. The defenders are sitting on year-round springs, with enough provisions to hold out for years. When Alexander's emissaries call for the Afghan's surrender, Oxyartes taunts them, asking if our men have wings, for by no other means will we scale this stronghold.

Up trails and switchbacks come our supplies, on trains fifteen miles long, to the higher camps. For us scuffs, all hopes hang on negotiations. Oxyartes' envoys shuttle in supposed secrecy in and out of camp. We know them all. We pave a highway for them. "What is wanting," says Stephanos, "is for Alexander to pick one horse."

One warlord to hand Afghanistan over to.

One chieftain to rule all others.

Supplies are in place by late winter. The summit is the size of a small county. Bare piney slopes approach, of loose scree and shingle, too steep even for mules. An assault is possible from the west, where the incline is least severe, but here Oxyartes has fortified the approaches with stone ramparts and great deadfalls of timber. South and north the faces loom impregnable. East is worse—raw stone for the approach march and sheer cliffs for the final four hundred feet.

Alexander calls the youth of the army together. He pledges twelve talents of gold to the first man to mount by this route to the summit and extravagant premiums to every trooper who joins him. Six hundred men set out by night, clawing their way up the face by means of iron tent pegs, which they wedge into fissures in the rock, and from which they belay one another by rope. Thirty-seven valiant souls plummet to their deaths. But three hundred reach the summit. When they show themselves in armor next dawn, the foe, believing Alexander must indeed possess winged warriors—or be, himself, a god—sues for peace.

Oxyartes and a handful of chiefs get away down a back track. But our rangers capture his suite in its entirety—horses, wagons, wife, and three daughters. The youngest, Roxane, is a proud beauty, said to be the darling of her father's eye.

Will Alexander crucify her? Hold her as hostage? Will he ransom her? Exploit her father's fears for her safety, to bring him to heel?

Not for nothing is our king acclaimed a genius of politics and war.

He appears before the army with the princess at his side.

He will marry her.

49.

Alexander has picked his horse.

By taking to wife the daughter of the warlord Oxyartes, our king transforms his most formidable foe into his father-in-law. War is all in the family now. Envoys shuttle between the Afghan camps and our own, my brother Philip among them. The army buzzes with details of the prospective peace.

If Oxyartes will come in amity to Bactra City and there give his daughter in marriage, Alexander will honor him with such treasures and esteem as to effectively render him lord of all Afghanistan and peer to Amyntas Nicolaus, who will govern Bactria and Sogdiana in Alexander's name. This can be sold to the tribes as a mighty coup for the sons of Afghana, since, under Darius' rule, none but Persian nationals had stood so tall. Now, by the blood of her patriots and the grace of heaven, the land has been restored to its rightful rulers.

At least that's the story.

Who's quibbling?

Then he, Alexander, will take his army and depart Afghanistan.

In return for these pledges of peace, Oxyartes will use his influence to bring his confederates to the table of peace. Affairs will be so arranged, Alexander warrants, that no chieftain's portion will suffer, and each, secure in his lands and station, will discover no cause for complaint.

"What we must accept about this theater of war," Philip explains one night to me, Flag, Stephanos, and our fellows, "is that military victory is impossible. So long as even one man or woman of these Afghans draws breath, they will resist us. But what we *have* achieved, by the ungodly suffering we have inflicted upon them, is to drive them to the point where they'll accept an accommodation, an alliance if you will, that they can call victory, or at least not defeat, and that we can live with.

"Then, between paying them off, severing them from their northern allies and sanctuaries, and keeping enough forces in garrison here, we may be able to stabilize the situation sufficiently so that we can move on to India without leaving our lines of supply and communication vulnerable to assault. That's the best we can do. That's enough. It will suffice.

"In the end," Philip says, "the issue comes down to this: What is the minimum acceptable dispensation? Short of victory, what can we live with? We cannot slaughter every man, woman, and child in Afghanistan, however gratifying such an enterprise might be."

Peace at last. The corps of Macedon exhales with relief. For me, only one impediment remains:

Shinar will not marry me. She refuses.

To celebrate his wedding to Roxane and the end of the war, Alexander has pledged rich dowries to every Mack who joins him in taking to wife his own Asiatic consort. The couples will take their vows at the same hour as Alexander and his princess and on the same site, the palace of Chorienes in Bactra City.

But Shinar won't do it.

It is the old story of *A'shaara*.

"Don't ask me! If you care for me, you will never mention this again."

Will I ever understand this woman? My child grows in her belly. I can't let her refusal stand. "What will you do then? Go away?"

I see she will. Her expression is despair. "Will you make me speak of this?"

"Yes! You must explain it to me now, once and for all, and make me understand."

She has to sit. Her back groans under the weight she carries. "Can I have some water please?"

I get it for her. Cool, with a sliver of apricot, the way she likes it.

"*A'shaara* means shame, this much you know, Matthias. But it means soul as well, and family or tribe. I have forfeited mine by permitting you, an alien and an invader, to rescue me. For this, I stand *ad benghis*, 'outside,' and can never be brought back in."

I reject this. "You're not 'outside,' with me. Your god cannot touch me, and when you join with me in marriage, he can't touch you either."

She smiles darkly. "God cannot, perhaps. But others." She means her kin. Her brother.

My Afghan bride. She and this country are one and the same. I love and fear her and can grasp her secrets no more than I can these ocher mountains or this storm-riven sky.

In the end it is my brother who wins her over. The peace deal done, Philip's unit is among the first to pack out for Bactra City, to make political preparations for Alexander's wedding. He visits Shinar and me on his last evening, bringing *baghee*, a dish of lamb and lentils roasted in the beast's own intestines, and a jar of plum wine.

Shinar's belly has become taut as a drum. You can thump it with a finger; it rings like a melon. Philip dotes upon her like a bachelor uncle. She makes him set his ear and listen for the child's kick. When it comes, they both giggle like innocents.

Later, Philip addresses Shinar in earnest. She will listen to him when she won't to me. For the sake of the child, he says, she must make me her husband. For love of this infant, she must become my wife.

"You are no longer responsible only for yourself, Shinar. You have another life to consider. Your child cannot grow to adulthood in this land, with only you to protect it, and no Afghan male will accept you in wedlock, when you bring into his household the issue of the invader. But the babe *can* live in Macedon. It can flourish, embraced as the offspring of heroes, growing to man- or woman-hood among numerous others just like him or her."

He reads the woe on Shinar's face.

"I know, dear child, that you believe heaven has turned its back on you. Perhaps that was so, once. But all things turn in their sea-son. Not even as cruel a deity as that of this pitiless land can remain unmoved forever by his people's affliction. The proof grows now in your belly. Your suffering has redeemed you, Shinar. God holds out his hand. Take it, I beg you. Can any act be more impious than to spurn the clemency of heaven?"

50.

The wedding of Alexander and Roxane will be held at Bactra City, atop the great fortress, Bal Teghrib. The rites will be celebrated out-doors, in the Persian fashion. The captains of the corps—and half the princes of Afghanistan, it seems—will assemble in their finery at Koh-i-Waz, the palace of the warlord Chorienes.

Flag will take his discharge from the army. Going home. His salary and bonuses, counting premiums from five Silver Lions and a Gold, come to twenty-two years' wages. He's rich.

I'm filing my papers too. I've got the equivalent of six years' pay coming.

Fourteen hundred couples—Macks and their foreign brides—will take their vows along with our king and his princess on this happy day. Half, we hear, have elected Afghan postings. They'll settle with their brides in the various garrison Alexandrias—Artacoana, Kanda-har, Ghazni, Kabul, even Alexandria-the-Furthermost. Every trooper will receive at least a handsome farm; officers will be awarded estates. "They'll never see Macedon again," says Flag. "The witless bastards."

No such folly for him or me. We'll take our skip and never look back. Flag himself will not farm at home, he says. "The life of a country huntsman for me. I'll sire a pack of brats and train them up in the hill chase. We'll raise horses. You and Shinar will visit every summer. You'll try to get me to put in a crop but, by Zeus, I won't do it!"

I ask him seriously: Can he really put the army behind him?

"Fuck the army," says he. "Who needs it?"

51.

Shinar gives birth on the nineteenth of Artemisius. A healthy boy. We name him Elias. He weighs exactly the same as my *pelta* shield (about eight pounds) and fits handily inside its leather-and-bronze bowl. When I bathe him, he bawls like a trooper. He has ten fingers and ten toes and a tiny pink penis, with which, prone on his back, he spouts a stream like a marble fountain. I could not be more delighted. His birth has humbled me. Shinar, too, has changed. The boy has black hair like hers and hazel eyes like mine. A regular amalgam.

With the arrival of this little bundle, our life is altered forever. Vanished is my *Narik ta?* attitude toward death. To stay alive and be of use to this child has overnight become everything to me.

Flag and Stephanos visit to inspect this newest campaigner. He salutes their entrance with a stupendous defecation. My friends acclaim its volume and its manly stink. I could not be prouder if the child had produced a second *Iliad*.

I don't want my boy to be a soldier. Let him teach music or practice the physician's art. May he raise horses and cultivate the earth.

I am changed, yes. But Shinar is transformed. She is a mother now. I'm in awe of her. I fasten upon this aspiration: to see her in feminine converse with my mother. I want to watch them laughing together in our kitchen at Apollonia, or walking with little Elias in the hills above our home.

It occurs to me that my child has two cousins. The son and daughter of my sister Eleni and her husband Agathon. How I long to see these three toddlers at play! The night of our son's birth, while mother and child slumber, I dig out my brother-in-law's letter, which I have preserved among my kit these many months.

> *I sit now, watching my infant son . . . playing in the sunlight of the yard. Do you know, dear brother, that my own disfigurement had impressed itself so powerfully upon my imagination that when this child was born I expected that he, like me, would possess a stump instead of a limb. When I saw him whole and perfect, I wept. Through this babe I feel the whole world has been made new. . . .*

Six days after the birth, a bridal festival called Mazar Dar, "New Life," is celebrated throughout the city. Its protagonist is the princess Roxane. The day is in her honor. The rites are for women only.

Something happens to Shinar during these rituals. She will not say what. But she is changed unmistakably on her return. Perhaps the cause is the warmth of being enveloped by scores of her countrywomen, cooing over her new son. Perhaps meeting and speaking with the many Afghan brides, who in days will take husbands of Greece and Macedon. I can't say. But when she settles beside me in our bed that evening, she declares that she has changed her mind.

"Is it too late for us to get our names on the wedding list?"

"You mean get married?"

My sweetheart smiles. "If you will have me."

52.

I have a friend, Theodorus, in the logistical corps. This wedding, he says, will tax the supply arm like no operation of the entire war. Oxyartes, to honor his daughter, has brought every clan chief and *malik* from between Bactra City and the Oxus and all their retainers from six to eighty. The other warlords, not to be outdone (or left out in the new order) have summoned all their minions. Preceding the wedding will be Antar Greb, the Ten Days of Forgiveness. During this period prisoners will be pardoned, debts forgiven, feuds patched up. Tribal councils will be in session night and day, adjudicating disputes. Where will this multitude sleep? How will it be fed? Tents alone, to house the throngs, will need a thousand camels just for transportation. The tally of mules is past calculation, as are the invoices already being sent in by their wranglers. How will we water all these beasts? The River Bactrus is home to hundreds of sacred otters. "By Heracles, these boogers will be paddling for their furry lives!"

The town cannot support such a host, so unofficial camps spring up. Tent bivouacs carpet the riverbanks, mount the foothills, sprawl across the Plain of Sorrows, which seems, at last, to have overthrown its name. Every tailor and bootmaker east of Artacoana has trekked in for the celebration, hoping to earn ten years' wages in twenty days. Barbers shave men's skulls for luck. Charcoalers hawk fuel in ribbon-cinched bundles from the backs of their two-wheeled carts; swordmakers set up *bichees;* stalls in hundreds squat chockablock with fullers, haberdashers, cloth benders, tin- and iron- and bronzesmiths. Alms-beseeching amputees share shops with tattoo artists; snake-handlers split their quarters with peddlers of jute, nazz, and *bhang.* Boys work the lanes, packing bronze vessels of hot *chai* on their backs, dispensing cupfuls from spouts set about their waists. One thing Afghanistan does not lack is fish. Speckled and brown trout in tons are towed down from mountain streams by *dhuttie* pole-boatmen in ingenious wicker floats, the fish still alive in the water. No accommodations remain in the city, so camel trains set up shop at the edge of the desert. A tent bazaar sprawls over hundreds of acres, offering Median vests and shoes, Damascene daggers, quilted *aghee* caps, and Parthian tunics. Fortune-tellers read the future in cast stones; astrologers scribe it down from the skies. Peddlers of gimcracks and geegaws work in pairs, one bearing before him a great jingling gibbet from which dangle in hundreds finger and toe rings, bracelets, anklets, necklaces, fetishes, amulets, and charms, while his confederate jigs at his side, flogging their common wares. Souvenir images of the bride and groom are painted onto cups and dishes, woven into carpets, lacquered upon trays, and stitched into pennants, prayer bells, and skullcaps; you can buy likenesses of Alexander and Roxane upon beads and coins, cowrie shells, scarves, and undergarments. Troupes of actors and acrobats, jugglers, contortionists, mountebanks, and professional fools put up impromptu shows; poets recite; rhapsodes sing; philosophers edify. I never saw so many amateur orators. One crackpot after another declaims his deranged doctrine atop a stone in the marketplace; within one tented kennel I count half a score, haranguing crowds whose expressions range from zeal to stupefaction. A stroll across the city discovers yogis from India, ascetics from Cos, self-mutilators from Khumar. I watch one *sadhu* pierce both cheeks with a dozen iron kebab sticks, grinning all the while. His basket brims with coppers from the Macks; apricots and black plums from the Afghans. A girl swallows swords, another contorts her body to set her soles atop her skull. Brazier-men sell sheep brains, poached in the skull; swine's hooves; bull's testicles on beds of steaming rice. You can buy eyeballs and knuckles, shrunken skulls, rawhide strings of tusks and teeth, ears and fingers, charms against death and disfigurement, poems to bring love, fortune, happiness; lubricants and asphyxiants, emollients and aphrodisiacs, potion and lotions, emetics and panaceas. I see the same halt fellow chuck his crutches three times in one day. From Babylon have come kite-masters; their paper carp soar aloft on the Afghan gale. Long life, Alexander and Roxane! The union of king and princess will constitute the country's most glorious day since the birth of Zoroaster—Macks jubilant to be getting out, Afghans ecstatic to see them go.

Meanwhile, hundreds of *jurgas* and tribal councils are being held. Clemency is the order of the season. The theme of a fresh start animates all.

The weddings, as I said, will be celebrated in the Persian manner. Preliminary events will take place over five days, culminating with the actual marriage on the fifth. Five is the number of love in Persian numerology. Everything in the ceremony must be divisible by five. Five hundred prisoners will be pardoned, five thousand slaves set free. The same number of kites will soar over the palace on the wedding day, and twice five thousand white doves be released at the nuptials' height.

The ceremony uniting Alexander and the princess Roxane will take place at sunset, the start of the day in the Persian convention. A military tattoo will precede the wedding; it will take place on the plain and be viewed by the dignitaries, Mack and Afghan, who will then mount to the citadel, where the actual ceremony will be performed. When the rites are concluded and the kites and doves have flown, the festivities will begin; they'll last all night, even after the bride and groom retire at dawn, and into the next day, when the various clemency rites will take place. As for our company, we will rehearse one last time at midmorning, then dine and prepare our uniforms, weapons, and armor. We'll bathe and have a final barbering, beards trimmed, teeth waxed.

Several days before this, a memorial column is dedicated to the fallen of Greece and Macedon. The ceremony takes place at dawn. Elias's name and Lucas's and Tollo's, with sixty-nine hundred others, have been carved into the stone. Our own Stephanos has composed the valedictory ode:

IN THE COMPANY OF SOLDIERS

In the company of soldiers
I have no need to explain myself.
In the company of soldiers,
everybody understands.

In the company of soldiers,
I don't have to pretend to be a person I'm not
Or strike that pose, however well-intended, that is expected
by those who have not known me under arms.

In the company of soldiers all my crimes are forgiven
I am safe
I am known
I am home
In the company of soldiers.

Funeral games accompany these rites. Hundreds come out. The mood is solemn but gay. The Corps of Engineers has built a hippodrome, four *stades* down and back, round a turning post. The horse races are meant to be all-Greek and Macedonian, so as not to affront the natives, whose participation might be seen by their fellows as honoring the outlanders' dead. But in the event, so many Bactrian and Sogdian camps ring the racetrack, since there's no place else to sleep, and these fellows are such keen horsemen, that they are invited too. I myself enter, riding Snow. We win one heat and come third in the next, but in the end campaign fatigue has worn my poor mare to tatters. We finish dead last in the next and join the throng of spectators. I am standing in line with Flag outside the wagering tent when I spy a familiar *spin gar*, "white beard," the Afghan term for old man.

Ash, our muleteer of Kandahar, who hired out to me the female porters for the crossing of the Hindu Kush.

I cross to the villain and clap him on the back. "By Zeus, I thought the constables had rounded up all criminals!"

He turns with a gap-toothed grin. "Then how," he says, "can you remain at large?"

We embrace like brothers. The proverb holds true, that even mortal foes find amity with enough passage of time. "What brings you here, Ash?"

"Mules. What else?"

We find a place out of the crush and catch each other up on the news. "No women this time?" I ask. He elevates both palms to heaven.

Flag tells Ash about me and Shinar.

The old man roars at this jest.

"No, it's true!"

It takes an oath to heaven to make Ash believe. He twists his beard, trying to remember. "Which one was she?"

"The one you beat. The one I bought from you."

"God preserve us!" Again the palms to heaven. "This country has made you madder than I thought."

Flag tells him of Lucas and Ghilla, of their child, and of Lucas's end. Ash goes sober. "He was a good fellow. May his soul find peace."

Ash shares a tent, he says, about a mile up the river in the great camp of the Panjshiri. "Dine with me, my friends."

We can't. We have to rehearse for the military parade that precedes the wedding. We make plans with Ash, though, to meet again the day of the horse races. As he takes his leave, the old brigand catches my arm.

"Her brother is here, you know."

He means Shinar's. I have dreaded this. With so many allied Afghans gathered for the wedding, Baz could be anywhere. He could be in our own camp.

"Where?" Flag demands.

"He serves with the Sogdian lancers attached to the brigade of Hephaestion—he and two of his cousins." Ash describes a bivouac several miles out on the plain. "Brother and kin seek to put right the shame brought on their family by your deliverance of his sister. I have heard him speak of it. I did not know *you* were his object."

I ask Ash how seriously he takes this.

"One must fear these violent young bucks," he says, "and fear their wenches more, for *A'shaara* binds them as pitilessly as an eagle's claw holds a dove."

I know what Flag is thinking. Pay the old man, find the brother. Kill him. Part of me favors this. But our own Mack code of *philoxenia*, "love for the stranger," forbids shedding the blood of my bride's clan—and the kinsmen of my infant son.

Besides, I see a chance sent by heaven.

"Now is the Ten Days of Forgiveness, isn't it, Ash?"

Indeed, he says, such a time may not come again for years. I turn to Flag. "We met with Shinar's brother before, remember? He never wanted this feud. His heart isn't in it. He'd leap at the chance to set it aside."

I feel hopeful for another reason. My son's birth date is Artemisius 19. This is Annexation Day back home, the anniversary of Apollonia's incorporation into Greater Macedonia. In my town on that day, every dwelling will be flying the lion standard; the lanes will be filled with dancing. There, too, debts will be forgiven. A good omen.

I ask Ash what we need to do.

"Leave it to me," he says.

A tribal council must be convened. The clansmen will embrace this prospect. It will be great entertainment; they'll jabber about it for years. I must appear in person, Ash says, and beseech forgiveness for my crimes.

"Forgiveness, my scarlet ass!" says Flag.

But Ash knows what he's talking about. "These *dussars*," he says, using the term for rubes or bumpkins, "will take great joy in debating your appeal, Matthias. You must play the part. It may cost you money." He means reparations. Blood lucre, like to absolve a murder. "Do you have it?" he asks.

"Enough," says Flag, "for a villain like you to skim his cut."

But I am heartened.

"You're welcome to whatever you can claim, Ash. And so is Baz, the brother."

What is money for anyway? Only to get what you need—or keep away what you dread.

"How soon," I ask, "can we set this thing up?"

53.

The *jurga* takes place the night before the wedding. A quorum, it seems, cannot be convened earlier because so many of the tribal participants, who are hired troops serving under Alexander, must rehearse during the daylight hours for their companies' parts in the military review that will precede the morrow's nuptials. This is fine with Flag and me. Our outfit has to prepare too.

Stephanos lets me out of final rehearsal, so I can get my papers in to the Corps Quartermaster, permitting Shinar and me to be married with the fourteen hundred in the collective ceremony. This rite will take place at the same sunset hour as Alexander and Roxane's wedding, but outside the fortress gates in the new Greek-style amphitheater that has been carved into the slope of Bal Teghrib, the site where our king first addressed the corps after its crossing of the Hindu Kush.

Flag and I ride out to the Afghan camp. The time is an hour before sunset. Ash is supposed to meet us, to serve as escort and guarantor. He's nowhere to be found. We grab one of our *shikaris* instead, a grizzled mountaineer named Jerezrah, to present our *dashar,* our request for admittance. Alas, the fellow turns out to be of the Agheila, one of the Panjshiri tribes with whom our hosts, who are Pactyans as well but of another order, are at war. They won't let him in. Now Ash appears. He has been waiting all along, it seems, wondering what is keeping Flag and me. He takes over. Appealing to the spirit of the Days of Forgiveness, he convinces our hosts to permit entry to Jerezrah. Only now Jerezrah's chapped at the insult and won't go in. "I have known these bandits all my life," he says, turning on his heel. "They are as dirty and disreputable as ever."

Flag, Ash, and I enter the camp. It seems that every rock-hopper for a hundred miles has got noise of the event, and they have congregated eagerly to attend it. They're a savage-looking pack, armed to the eyeballs, unbarbered for months. Every man carries an elaborately fringed and feathered quirt, whose whip-end he sets before him on the earth when he sits, holding the butt lightly between his fingers, so that when the whole assembly has taken up positions in a circle, the riding-crops all point to the center and all jiggle rhythmically, tapping on the dirt. The spectacle is colorful and, in its way, quite charming.

The mob has now formed up before the chief's pavilion, a goatskin structure supported by multiple timber columns and fronted by an enormous tent portico, whose entry is carpeted with rugs laid on the earth. We are shown our place. We sit. The sun slips behind the mountains; at once the night air stings with cold. Ash folds his knees on my right. Chiefs and elders sit directly across from us, with Shinar's brother and cousins standing behind them. No greetings are exchanged, nor is the least notice taken of our arrival. This is customary, says Ash. It is called the "settling in," when the parties acquaint themselves in stages, by their mutual presence, without direct speech.

The circle buzzes with social jabber. Everyone chatters except Flag and me. Now great brass bowls of water are brought, not to drink but to wash our right hands in. An excited yipping ascends. At once a mound of rice, mutton, and peas appears, trucked in on a four-handled barrow. Everyone digs in. Flag and I do, too, fearing to offer offense if we demur, even though we've just bolted a gut-busting supper back at camp. The brother and cousins do not sit. They don't eat. They maintain their posts immediately behind the headman. I have no idea what this means. Their demeanor is sullen and combative; they stand with arms folded. When the mountain of rice has been devoured, which takes no more than ten minutes, the men begin debating, in Pactyan, the issue of Shinar and her violation of the code of *A'shaara*. No one invites me or Flag to speak, nor even glances in our direction. The chief and elders keep up a dialogue of their own of abundant mirth, apparently having nothing to do with our case. Passion animates the debate; at one point several clansmen have to be separated, nearly coming to blows. All hands are having a wonderful time.

Suddenly, as if by some signal that everyone can hear except Flag and me, all palaver ceases. Brother and cousins are called forward. They sit, facing me. *"Toumah!"* bawls an interpreter. "Speak."

I do. I address the brother and cousin.

"Nah! Nah!"

The master of ceremonies corrects me. I'm supposed to plead my brief to the elders.

I make my case in Greek, with Ash translating. When I finish, a second round of debate begins. Again the headmen pay no attention. Several actually get up and leave, to relieve themselves I assume, returning to resume their animated converse. The period ends. Now Shinar's brother Baz gets up to speak.

I would feel better if he were more angry. Instead, his manner is flinty and dour. He addresses the elders and the tribe, not me. When he gestures in my direction, which he does infrequently, his voice rises in register. I understand enough Pactyan to reckon that he hates me less as an individual, or for any injury I have personally inflicted upon him, than as a representative of the corps of Macedon, the detested invader. I am to him *all* aliens, *all* Macks. He hates us with a crimson passion.

Ash speaks into my ear. "Don't take this too seriously. The man is good."

Baz finishes his harangue to the elders and the tribe. Now he turns to me. In terms of cold and stony truculence, he reads out an indictment that would blanch the mane of Zeus. I make out three words from their repetition: "honor," "insult," and "justice."

The brother finishes.

"Now," prompts Ash, "offer money."

Start low, he advises. I do. It's not working. I ante nearly half my total bonus, three years' pay. I'm getting nowhere.

"I add," I say, "my horse."

The congress erupts. Quirts jiggle exuberantly. Tribesmen rap each other with the backs of their right hands (to use the palm, or the left, would constitute a mortal insult). By magic my mare materializes, led by Afghan grooms. The throng surrounds her, five deep. Give these bandits their due; they know horses. From their animated jabbering, it is clear that Snow meets with their approval. I glance to Baz and the cousins. Clansmen are swatting them merrily. It looks good, Flag says. "These sheep-stealers are showing your boy respect."

He's right. Men continue congratulating Baz. Certainly no stain of dishonor remains in their eyes.

Offering my horse proves a brilliant stroke. Greedy as the Afghan is, gold holds less appeal for him (since he has so few opportunities to spend it) than articles of honor, such as the armor or weapons of an enemy, and more so his warhorse, particularly if that animal is a superb specimen like Snow in the prime of her fighting years. To acquire such a prize is almost as satisfying as murdering the foe himself.

"Have we got a deal?" I ask Ash.

Indeed, says he. Except for another hour of haggling over bridle and tack. Ash has taken over; he negotiates for me. "Give them everything," I say. "Who cares?"

"Never! They will despise you and the animal if we don't fight for this."

In the end, Ash preserves my armor and weapons.

Now comes a second meal.

"Ash," says Flag. "Get us the fuck out of here."

The deal is struck. Shinar's brother will give up his claim to vengeance under the laws of *tor* and *A'shaara*. I will recompense him with my horse and the agreed-upon indemnity.

I want to get this over with. But the amount I've pledged is too big to deliver in gold (I don't have a tenth of it anyway). It will have to be an army draft, and acquiring that will take all night and most of tomorrow, if I'm lucky, to procure through the Quartermaster.

We'll meet, the brother and I agree, tomorrow at the gate of the Pactyan camp, an hour before the military parade forms up.

Baz does not give me his hand on our understanding; that office is performed by the chief, according to custom. "Good deal!" says the old man in Greek.

I meet the brother's eye. "Will this stand with you?"

"Bring the money and the horse."

"If our nations can make peace, surely you and I can."

Still Baz will not acknowledge.

"Leave my country," says he. "Never come back."

54.

Ash adds one caution as we ride out: I must make absolutely certain, when I deliver them, that the brother takes the money and the horse into his hands. "Once he accepts the bridle, he cannot go back on his oath. Until then, you have nothing but air."

I report everything to Shinar as soon as I return. She has known, from the day of the Women's Festival, of her brother's presence in camp. Two girls of her village spoke to her there. "They said nothing of him. But I could read their eyes."

Ghilla is staying with us. Both women are uneasy. They want to move to a new camp. Now, tonight. They fear that Baz and the cousins, despite their pledges, will come after them here.

But where can we move? The city is overrun. There's not a slave's closet left.

Stephanos saves us. Through a friend he gets us into the bachelor officers' compound, the most secure part of the military camp.

Macks only. We get a tent with the grooms. It's not bad. Because of the horses, there's day-and-night security. Among the scores of camps sprawling over thousands of acres, it's impossible that Baz could locate us here.

Dawn lacks only an hour by the time I get the women and infants settled. I'm too frayed to sleep, and besides, I have to present myself early at the Quartermaster's to apply for the army monetary draft.

I'm changing into a clean tunic when Stephanos appears with his friend, the captain who got us in to the secure compound. He vows to watch over Shinar and Ghilla. He'll put three men on the tent, so two will always be awake.

I should stay myself. I should get Flag and Boxer and squat on the threshold all day, till it's time for the wedding.

But I have to get the money.

I have to seal the contract.

By noon I have crossed and recrossed the city half a dozen times. Every clerk hands me a different story. The Quartermaster's office is closed for the wedding. The office is open but it's been moved across town. The office wants to help me, but the secretary can't find my service scrolls. The office is closing in twenty minutes.

Alexander's wedding has sent the town into hysteria. Every lane is jammed with tailors and laundry-runners. Shoeless urchins dash along army-camp byways, delivering freshly shined boots and just-burnished helmets. I have never seen so many military cloaks so pressed and dazzling. Bronze grommets flash like diadems. At the river's edge, horses line up flank-to-flank, being lathered and scrubbed by their grooms. The plain must hold a thousand camps. At the margins of each squat natives by the hundred, saddle-soaping tack and wax-buffing bridles and brightwork. To keep the city spotless, our host, the warlord Chorienes, has pledged one copper coin for every gallon of horse droppings scooped from the public way and delivered to his stable stewards. Urchins brawl over turds at every street corner. The city sparkles.

The third quartermaster shunts me to the Honor Registry. The clerk can't find my service documents, but does succeed in locating those of my brother Elias. Did I know I have a disbursement coming? Half of Elias's death benefit (the other half goes to Philip).

This will save me.

Can I collect it?

Indeed. At home in Apollonia, in six months.

The clerk has to shutter his office. He's a decent sort, though, and as I turn away, muttering, he hails me. "What about your dowry, Sergeant?"

The king's treasury, he reminds me, will today present each wedded couple with a golden cup—easily worth the amount I need.

The problem is, the gift comes *after* the wedding.

"Find an Egyptian," says the clerk. A payday lender. Someone who'll advance me cash against my pledge of the dowry.

I try for two more hours. The bankers' quarter has been sealed off by security forces. Its lane offers access to the Citadel; no one gets by except with a pass stamped with the royal seal. Someone tells me the usurers have decamped to temporary quarters; their tables are set up behind the Lane of the Armorers. I get within twenty feet before a procession of priests walls off the way. Zoroastrians, shuffling at a pace that makes a slug look speedy. Ceremonial mace-bearers shield the holy men's flanks; you can't cut through or the whole mob will fall on you. I can see the bankers' tables, though. Each has a line before it, twenty men deep. Every other tapped-out scuff has the same idea I do. By the time I get round the parade, the tables are being taken away. No more shine. The crows have lent it all at double-and-a-half.

I get back to the bachelor officers' compound an hour past noon. Ghilla and two other girls are preparing the ritual bath for Shinar. They won't let me in the tent; it's bad luck. My pressed cloak hangs on the post. I'm matted in dust. I have failed completely. I don't have the cash for Baz and there's no chance of getting it. As I sink onto a bench outside the tent, Flag rides up. He leads his own horse and my Snow, both curried and gleaming, and a third animal for me to ride back.

"Get the money?"

I shake my head.

Flag tosses a leather pouch. It strikes the ground, heavy and jingling.

"Shut up," he says, "and take it."

He won't let me thank him.

"I'll be back in an hour with Boxer and Little Red." He means we four will ride out to meet with Baz. "Pack extra iron. In case they disarm us."

I nod. "Where's Ash?"

"At the Pactyan camp. Or he said he'd be."

The site where we are to meet Shinar's brother and the cousins is about twenty minutes out on the plain. It will take twice that long to get there today, with the throngs packing the roads.

I dress in five minutes. The remainder of the hour I spend prowling the perimeter of our lane. The captain's guards stand in place. All our women are accounted for except Jenin, the abortion girl, who is off fetching laundry.

I repeat Ash's warning to myself: Get Snow's bridle into the brother's hands. That will seal the compact.

So close now.

One last turn and we're in the clear.

Flag comes back with Boxer and Little Red. He has changed

into full formal uniform, for the wedding, including his military cloak, under which he has stashed a Spartan-style gut-cutter (in case Baz and the cousins try to pull something shady) with a *khofari* knife strapped to his thigh and a pair of throwing daggers tucked in his boots. Boxer and Red wait outside on their horses. I part from Shinar. It takes my mates and me an hour to reach the Pactyan camp. Three thoroughfares converge there; the approach lanes swarm with companies of cavalry, allies, and irregulars, and thousands of festival-goers on foot. The postnoon sun is blistering. Grit kicks up from a hundred heat dusters. "There it is," says Flag.

We can see the entry, where our *shikari* was turned back yesterday. A cluster of tribesmen awaits. Ash paces out front.

No Baz.

No cousins.

I rein before him.

"Where's the brother?"

Ash looks distraught.

"Where are they?"

"I knew they'd pull this," says Flag.

"Ash . . ."

"I don't know," he says.

". . . what's going on?"

"I don't know!"

Flag's glance scans the onlookers' faces. *They* know. They have come to watch us. To enjoy our discomfiture.

Two Afghans make a grab for my mare. I jerk her clear. "Where is Baz?" I shout in Dari.

The men lunge to steal Snow. Flag looses his saber; Boxer's and Red's lances freeze the pack where they stand. "Ash," I bawl, "what the fuck is going on?!"

"Matthias!" Flag points into the crowd looking on.

Jenin.

The abortion girl.

She sees us pointing and takes off like a hare. My spurs dig. In a heartbeat Flag and I are at the gallop. The girl dodges between tents. A crowd blocks our pursuit.

"The fuckers have skulled us," Flag calls. Lured us away from our compound. From protecting Shinar and the baby.

I see Jenin bolt away down a lane of the camp. Ash's warning from yesterday screams in my ears.

Fear these wenches, for A'shaara binds them as pitilessly as an eagle's claw holds a dove.

55.

My whip tears discs of flesh from my poor mare's flanks; my heels
pound the cage of her ribs. We have been suckered. Baz has played
us false.

Flag and I tear along the riverfront road, racing back for Shinar
and our camp. Three bridges span the stream below Bal Teghrib. All
are jammed with pilgrims and wedding-goers. Across the river
sprawls the great flat of the parade field and beyond it the stone massif of the citadel. Already we see regiments entering in formation.
How can we get round? We'll never make it over the bridges, and the
river is too deep to ford. Our horses will burst their hearts if we swim
them and, besides, the far bank is end-to-end with security barri-
cades; the King's Guards will intercept us in our frenzied state and
may even shoot us down. We have no choice but to gallop the mile
and a half to the first upstream ford. When our animals finally mount
out on the far bank, we can feel their knees coming unstrung.

The road approaching Bactra City from the west forks at a great copse of tamarisk that houses the shantytowns of the city's poorest. The south branch becomes the River Road, yokes to the terminus of the southern highway, and enters the town through the Drapsaca Gate. This bottleneck will be crammed with people. We spur left, up the rising slope toward the fortress. My mare is fatiguing but she's still ten lengths ahead of Flag. I can see the approaches to the western gate; they're backed up a mile. I rein, letting Flag catch up. "Through there!" We leap the wall at a low point.

We enter a maze of city lanes. Every artery is choked with revelers. We swim against a tide of thousands, all decked in their plumage. They are so happy. I hate them all. We pound into their mass like riot troops into a front of rebels. Where is our camp? We're lost. Not even urchins who've lived in this labyrinth all their lives can tell us. We keep pounding. Uphill is all I know. The camp is on high ground.

I know I'm going combat-stupid. When I wipe the sweat from my face, my hand comes away bloody. I have bitten through my lip and don't even know it.

Checkpoints seal off street after street. "Don't stop!" bawls Flag. Can we imagine explaining our haste to some barricade-manning corporal?

In my mind I conjure our camp's captain—Stephanos's friend who swore to shield Shinar and Ghilla. If by screaming I could make him hear, I would bellow such that the city walls would topple. If by desperation alone I could make him know the peril in which our women stand, my skull would explode with the force of my extremity.

I whip Snow uphill with furious violence, then realize I'm beating my own right leg. I have flayed the flesh to hash.

Somehow we find the camp. I see it ahead. Deserted, save a

skeleton watch. Everyone has vacated for the nuptials. Blood is coming from my mare's nostrils. She is moments from caving beneath me. Behind, Flag has already loosed his exhausted mount; he trundles on foot.

Into the camp. No one's on guard. They're all gone. Only women remain. My mare stumbles. I leap clear. With my weight off her back, she recovers. I drag her by the reins.

"Flag . . ."

"I'm all right." He huffs beside me, chest working like a bellows.

We hear screams ahead. Already I know the worst has happened. We plunge on like the doomed. I recognize the horse pens and the lane of our tent. At its head, women cluster, shrieking in woe. They tear their cheeks; blood sheets down their faces. There's our captain. He cries something but I can't hear. His expression is one of abjection. He holds his hands out before him. I see two corporals, our guards. One clutches a half-pike, dirty with blood. The other gapes at me in a state of consternation.

I tear round the corner into the lane. The bodies of Baz and the two cousins sprawl in the dust. A mob of gawkers surrounds them. The crowd sees us. Their eyes dart toward the tent.

I cling to hope. Maybe the corporals have cut the murderers off. Maybe they intercepted them before they got to Shinar and the baby. I see Ghilla, clutching her own infant. I plunge into the tent with Flag one step behind. Soldiers and grooms pack the interior.

Overturned is the army chest that had served as a dressing table. A woman's body lies where the carpet has been thrown back, as if by a struggle. The earth is painted with blood.

56.

One look at Shinar tells me she no longer breathes. There is nothing I can do for her. The sensation is like combat. I turn at once to the infant Elias. A corporal whose name I don't know holds the child. Everyone backs away. A path opens from me to the baby. I take him. His swaddling wrapper is soaked like a sponge. The corporal has tugged a shade-flap over the child's face. The package is so small. Like a parcel you get in the post. I take my tiny son in both hands.

Men tell me later that I appear to be out of my head. On the contrary. I am vividly, preternaturally lucid. I know with absolute certainty that more enemy are coming. This is how the Afghan fights. He hits you once, and when you think you're safe he hits you again.

I am bawling orders. We have to move, get clear. The grooms stare at me as if I have gone mad.

Outside, a boy holds my mare. The beast is spent. If I make her take my weight, she'll cave underneath me. I start off afoot, carrying my little son in the crook of my left arm, beneath the square of my cavalry shield. I can hear the captain behind me. "Someone stick with him."

Flag.

My mate overhauls me. His face drips sweat. Dust coats his dress uniform, from our dash from the Afghan camp. The wedding. I realize that I, too, wear formal kit. It seems ridiculous. "Where are we going?" Flag bawls.

He thinks I've gone stupid. He'll stay with me. Protect me. But he thinks I've gone combat-stupid.

I set off up the hill. The camp squats at the base of Bal Teghrib's western shoulder. Above it twines a dry watercourse, drainage for the slope, and beyond that, a shantytown. Lanes twist in a labyrinth whose course is dictated by how floodwater sluices off the hill. Every street is deeply rutted. Deserted. The whole town has emptied for the wedding of Alexander and Roxane.

I labor up the slope. Flag pants at my shoulder. He wants to know where we're going.

"I'll know," I say, "when I see it."

What happens when you get combat-stupid is the simplest tasks become excruciatingly difficult. Sense deserts you. Limbs turn to lead. You have to summon all your resources simply to remain in the present. Hearing changes; you go deaf and dumb. Your mate can be shouting from two feet away, but you can't hear him. In action sometimes, a man will become possessed with accomplishing some pointless, even deranged task, like evacuating to safety a mate already dead, instead of continuing to support the mission in progress. Such individuals must be taken in hand by their mates or squad leaders. Flag should punch me now, I know it. But he hasn't the heart.

I know Shinar is dead. I know the child in my arms has been butchered. But I can't stop myself from seeking desperately to protect them. A part of me believes, or wishes to, that if I can only exert myself vigorously enough, beseech heaven fervently enough, offer my own life in place of this infant's, that the gods will hear me and restore animation to this poor bundle in my arms.

I lead Flag up lanes toward the citadel. The way is a warren of wattle-and-daub shanties and mud-brick hovels. Over my left shoulder rides my cavalry *pelta*. Beneath this, I shelter my baby. The Macedonian cavalry plate is not a full shield but a smallish wedge of oak and oxhide, faced with bronze. It's handy. With a rearward toss, you can sling it across your back or, shrugging forward, propel it atop your shoulder and upper arm. In this position, the block protects against lance thrusts and saber blows of right-handed opponents while leaving your left arm free to handle the reins.

Beneath this, defended by this, I bear my lifeless infant.

How long do we labor through the shanty quarter? I don't know. We pass lane after lane, sealed off by security details. We traverse the shoulder of the entire mountain, each forced deflection carrying us farther from the summit. Why do I seek these heights? I have no idea. The instinct for high-lining perhaps.

Suddenly everything drops into shadow. Behind the fortress, the sun plunges. Great cheers ascend. We can hear drums and cymbals, bells and tambours, celebrating the wedding. The five hundred kites have been loosed; I glimpse their soaring shapes in the gaps above the twisting lanes. Flag hangs on at my shoulder, spent from this lunatic chase upon which I have led him.

We collapse against a mud-brick wall. Our knees give out. Flag drops across from me. The lane is so narrow that our splayed legs flop atop one another. We are too exhausted to disentangle them.

I have not lost my senses.

I understand what has happened.

I apprehend the fatal inevitability of this hour. Events, it is clear to me, as it has been all along to Shinar, have unfolded as if preordained, from the Macedonian army's initial invasion of Afghanistan to this moment. We who enacted it—from Baz and Ash and Jenin to me and Flag and Shinar—owned no more freedom of will than planets in their passage or days in a month.

Wedding kites sail above. They soar in sun; we hunker in shadow. I meet Flag's eye. Behind him ascends a ragged slat-fence, screening a tributary alley. A puppy and a naked little boy, no more than twelve months old, squat together in the powdery earth. A young mother steps from a door. She sees Flag and me and snatches up her child; in an instant she has vanished. I hear the sound of beating wings.

Doves.

White doves.

Across a shaft of sunlight the brilliant flock streaks, celebrating the union of Alexander and the princess Roxane.

The war is over.

EPILOGUE

God of the Afghans

57.

Among the more dolorous rites any soldier must perform is the inventorying of the unclaimed personal effects of a fallen comrade. When the property is that of a woman and a child, for whom he has come to care more than he imagined possible, the chore becomes even more heartbreaking.

In the end I keep only two tokens of Shinar: her shoes (the ragged *pashin* in which she crossed the Hindu Kush) and the letter she sent me from Bactra City, written out by a scribe in the marketplace, in Greek that was far inferior to her own.

> *I come to Maracanda. Ghilla's son is born. The soldiers*
> *kill Daria for your brother. I bring your pay. If you find*
> *a new woman, I make my own way.*

I will have other women if I live. Perhaps memory of Shinar will fade with time. But I doubt it. She was braver than I, stronger and wiser. It was my folly that brought about her end, which she foresaw so clearly, while I, blind and unheeding, hauled her forward to our doom.

As for Shinar's brother, I cannot hate him. I can't condemn even the code under whose compulsion he took her life. We were three. The empire holds thirty million. Show me one whose heart has not been riven by the pitiless harrow of war.

When the divisions march out for India in the spring, it chances that our company parades alongside that Afghan contingent of which Shinar's brother and cousins had been part. I see faces from the *jurga*. These men will form, now, one element of the garrison force under Alexander's banner, to hold Afghanistan in his name. What monument shall we erect to this achievement, that these men serve the same warlord they served before, in the same place, to the same profit, only salaried now in Macedonian tender?

I have sold my mare, Snow. She was not lucky for me.

I decided not to take my discharge. I re-upped instead. To the infantry. Signed for two more bumps. The corps gave me a promotion. I hold Flag's old rank now.

He did indeed go home, my mate and mentor. It is I, now, who instruct the raw scuffs who trek in with the latest train of replacements. They are dumb as puppies. I ride them hard. You have to, to keep them alive.

Stephanos and I remain together. We "bumped over" in the same patch. He wants to see India. He's a captain now; princes of Old Macedon are not as rich as he. He sends it all home, keeping only enough to replace weapons and armor. "The soldier," he says, "needs no more than that."

We part that final morning, Flag and I, on the Plain of Sorrows.

He digs into my pack, comes up with Tollo's boars'-tusk cap. He works it onto my skull.

"There," he says. "That's better."

Ghilla stands at my shoulder. I have taken her and her son, little Lucas, under my protection. I will raise the child as my own.

"As a soldier?" asks Flag.

We laugh. The lad will grow into that, no doubt, no matter what I say.

Earlier this morning, as the mule trains were forming in the dark, my brother had cantered along the column on his way to his march post. Philip will ride out to India too. He is all-business still, or pretends to be. He dismounts. Inspects my kit. "You break my heart, Matthias."

He weeps.

"Finding you here," he says, "all my worst fears have been realized."

The column groans into motion up ahead. When the army of Macedon deploys to a new theater of war, it does so by divisions in order of seniority. Mine, the *taxis* of Coenus, is number two behind Alexander's elite brigades.

Philip remounts, stretches down his hand. I take it. "Keep off the high line," he says.

"Don't outgallop your cover."

He tugs his reins over; his spurs dig. With a start, his mount bolts away down the line.

The plain over which the camp sprawls is a welter of dismantled field kitchens and struck sixteen-man tents. These will not accompany the marching army. They'll follow with the heavy baggage. On the trek, the troops will bonze under goatskin *bichees* and dine on mooch and hurry bread. The trail will be the same one we descended from the Khawak Pass three springs ago. This time the column will take lower, easier passes. We'll lay over for training in the Kabul Valley until the worst of the summer heat has passed, then descend with autumn to the Punjab.

My mother writes:

Have I lost you, child? Will my arms never hold you again?

It would comfort this dear lady to understand why I can't come home. How can I explain it? What would I become there except another sad old man, a fractured veteran good neither to my family, my country, or myself?

I wished once to become a soldier. I have become that. Just not the way I thought I would.

The motion of the column at last reaches our station. The first day's trek is never far. In case you forget something important, you need to be able to send a man back.

Passing down the camps of the trailing divisions, I spy a familiar white beard.

Ash wrangles a train of two dozen. The mules' loads are roped up and balanced, but sit now on the ground, so their weight won't wear out the beasts prematurely. Ash has taught me that—and how to shave a pack animal's back so the hairs of his coat don't get twisted into burrs that chafe beneath his load.

"I told you, Meckie, that we would drive you out."

Indeed he did.

I stop and take the old bandit's hand.

"I'm sorry for your girl, Matthias."

I quote his proverb:

Though blind, God sees; though deaf, He hears.

I rejoin the column. "See you in India."

"May I starve first!"

The beauty of Afghanistan lies in its distances and its light. The massif of the Hindu Kush, a hundred miles off, looks close enough to touch. But before we get there, hailstones big as sling bullets will ring off our bronze and iron; floods will carry off men and horses we love; the sun will bake us like the bricks of this country's ten thousand villages. We are as overjoyed to be quit of this place as it is to see us go.

I scoffed, once, at Ash's god. But he has beaten us. Mute, pitiless, remote, Afghanistan's deity gives up nothing. One appeals to him in vain. Yet he sustains those who call themselves his children, who wring a living from this stony and sterile land.

I have come to fear this god of the Afghans. And that has made me a fighting man, as they are.

GLOSSARY OF SLANG

BAZ = *any Afghan male*

BHANG = *opium*

BLINKERED = *pregnant*

BLOW-OUT/BLOW-OFF = *party, celebration*

BONE = *complaint, problem*

BONZE = *sleep*

BOOGER = *walk, shuffle*

BOZZLE = *alcoholic spirits*

BRISKETS-DOWN = *dead*

BUMP = *eighteen-month term of enlistment for the Macedonian army*

BUMP OVER = *to re-up; reenlist*

CAULK = *kill*

CHAPPED = *irritated, angry; pissed off*

CHOP = *march, trek*

COOCH = *women; sex in general*

CURE = *kill*

DUST = *discard, throw away; also kill*

FIG = *female genitalia; women in general*

IN THE BOOKS = *dead*

JUTE = *Afghan narcotic*

MACK = *Macedonian*

MOOCH = *barley meal; or, in broader usage, any type of food*

NAZZ = naswar, *cheap Afghan opiate*

NOISE = *rumor, news*

PANK (AND JACK) = *cheap rotgut booze*

SCUFF = *soldier*

SEND HOME = *kill*

SHINE = *gold, money, cash of any kind*

SKIP = *a discharge from the army*

SPIKE = *noun: involuntarily extended enlistment;*

> *verb: to extend troops' enlistment without their permission; "We got spiked."*

STEAM = *women*

STITCH = *kill*

STUNT = *an allowance, above and beyond wages, given to cavalry and mounted infantry to cover expenses for grooms and feed*

WAX SCRATCHER = *writer, war correspondent*

SPECIAL THANKS

To Richard Silverman and Jody Hotchkiss for their astute reading of the text and their many helpful suggestions. To Captain David J. Danelo, for the invaluable perspective he provided as a writer, a combat Marine, and a veteran of the Iraq war. And to Dr. Charles Salas and Dr. Thomas Crow of the Getty Research Institute in Los Angeles, for including me among their company of Resident Scholars.

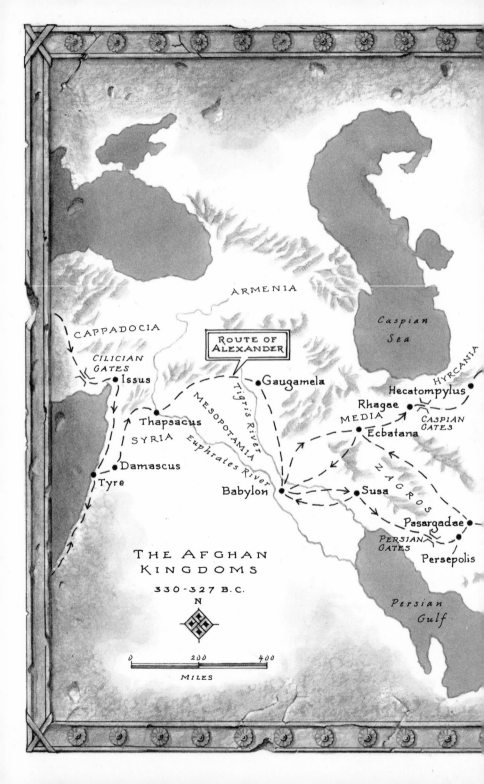